From B
to Bedroom

Taken – by the tycoon!

Three passionate novels!

*In February 2008 Mills & Boon bring
back two of their classic collections,
each featuring three favourite
romances by our bestselling authors…*

FROM BOARDROOM
TO BEDROOM

His Boardroom Mistress
by Emma Darcy
Luca's Secretary Bride
by Kim Lawrence
Hired by Mr Right by Nicola Marsh

THE ROYAL HOUSE
OF CACCIATORE

by Sharon Kendrick
featuring
The Mediterranean Prince's Passion
The Prince's Love-Child
The Future King's Bride

From Boardroom to Bedroom

HIS BOARDROOM MISTRESS
by
Emma Darcy

LUCA'S SECRETARY BRIDE
by
Kim Lawrence

HIRED BY MR RIGHT
by
Nicola Marsh

MILLS & BOON®
Pure reading pleasure

*Harlequin Mills & Boon Limited,
Eton House, 18-24 Paradise Road, Richmond, Surrey TW9 1SR*

FROM BOARDROOM TO BEDROOM
© by Harlequin Enterprises II B.V./S.à.r.l 2007

His Boardroom Mistress, Luca's Secretary Bride and *Hired by
Mr Right* were first published in Great Britain by Harlequin
Mills & Boon Limited in separate, single volumes.

His Boardroom Mistress © Emma Darcy 2003
Luca's Secretary Bride © Kim Lawrence 2004
Hired by Mr Right © Nicola Marsh 2004

ISBN: 978 0 263 86119 8

05-0208

*Printed and bound in Spain
by Litografia Rosés S.A., Barcelona*

HIS BOARDROOM MISTRESS

by

Emma Darcy

MILLS & BOON

100

YEARS

of pure reading pleasure

100 Reasons to Celebrate

We invite you to join us in celebrating
Mills & Boon's centenary. Gerald Mills and
Charles Boon founded Mills & Boon Limited
in 1908 and opened offices in London's Covent
Garden. Since then, Mills & Boon has become
a hallmark for romantic fiction, recognised
around the world.

We're proud of our 100 years of publishing
excellence, which wouldn't have been achieved
without the loyalty and enthusiasm of our
authors and readers.

Thank you!

Each month throughout the year there will
be something new and exciting to mark the
centenary, so watch for your favourite authors,
captivating new stories, special limited
edition collections…and more!

Initially a French/English teacher, **Emma Darcy** changed careers to computer programming before the happy demands of marriage and motherhood. Very much a people person, and always interested in relationships, she finds the world of romance fiction a thrilling one and the challenge of creating her own cast of characters very addictive.

Many thanks to Phil Asker and his wonderful team for providing me with so many wonderful experiences on The Captain's Choice Tour of South-East Asia – all in such a safe and friendly atmosphere. Great memories!

CHAPTER ONE

'THE kind of man you want, Liz, is the marrying kind.'

The quiet authority of her mother's voice cut through the buzz of suggestions being tossed around by her three sisters, all of whom had succeeded in marrying the men of their choice. This achievement made them feel qualified to hand out advice which Liz should take, now that she had been forced to confess her failure to get a commitment from the man who'd been her choice.

Brendan had told her he felt their relationship was stifling him. He needed space. So much space he was now in Nepal, half a world away from Sydney, planning to find himself or lose himself in the Himalayas, meditate in a Buddhist monastery, anything but make a life with a too managing woman.

It was shaming, humiliating to have to admit his defection to her family, but there was no excuse for not attending her father's sixtieth birthday luncheon today and no avoiding having to explain Brendan's absence.

The five of them—her mother, her sisters and herself—were in the kitchen, cleaning up after the long barbecue lunch which had been cooked by the male members of the family, now relaxing out on the patio of her parents' home, minding the children playing in the backyard.

Liz knew she had to face up to her situation and try to move on from it, but right now she felt engulfed by a sense of emptiness—three years of togetherness all drained away—and her mother's statement hit a very raw place.

'How can you know if they're the marrying kind or not?' she tossed back derisively.

Mistake!

Naturally, her wonderfully successful siblings had the answers and leapt in to hit Liz over the head with them.

'First, you look for a man with a good steady job,' her oldest sister, Jayne, declared, pausing in her task of storing leftovers in the refrigerator to deliver her opinion. 'You want someone to support you when the kids come along.'

Jayne was thirty-four, the mother of two daughters, and married to an accountant who'd never deviated from forging a successful career in accountancy.

'Someone with a functional family background,' Sue contributed with a wise look. 'They value what they've had and want it for themselves.'

Sue was thirty-two, married to a solicitor from a big family, now the besotted father of twin sons, loving his wife all the more for having produced them.

Liz silently and bitterly conceded two black marks against Brendan who'd never held a steady job—preferring to pick up casual work in the tourist industry—and had no personal experience of a functional family background since he'd been brought up by a series of foster parents.

There was no longer any point in arguing that she earned enough money to support them both. A small family, as well, if Brendan would have been content to be a house husband, as quite a few men were these days. The traditional way was not necessarily the *only* way, but Jayne and Sue weren't about to appreciate any other view but theirs, especially with the current inescapable proof that Liz's way hadn't worked.

'What about your boss?'

The speculative remark from her younger sister, Diana, jolted Liz out of maundering over her failures. 'What about him?' she retorted tersely, reminded that Diana, at only twenty-eight, was rather smug at having scooped the marriage pool by snagging her own boss, the owner of a chain of fashion boutiques for which she was still a buyer since they had no immediate plans to start a family.

'Everyone knows Cole Pierson is rolling in money, probably a billionaire by now. Isn't his divorce due to go through? He's been separated from his wife for ages and she's been gallivanting around, always in the social pages, linked to one guy or another. I'd certainly count Cole Pierson available and very eligible,' Diana declared, looking at Liz as though she'd been lax at not figuring that out for herself.

'Get real! That doesn't mean *available* to me,' Liz threw back at her, knowing full well she didn't have the female equipment to attract a man of his top-line attributes.

'Of course it does,' Diana persisted. 'He's only

thirty-six to your thirty, Liz, and right on the spot for you to snaffle. You could get him if you tried. After all, being his P.A. is halfway there. He depends on you…'

'Cole Pierson is not the least bit interested in me as a woman,' Liz snapped, recoiling absolutely from the idea of man-hunting where no love or desire was likely to be kindled.

Besides, she'd long ago killed any thought of her boss *that way* and she didn't want to do anything that might unsettle what had become a comfortable and satisfying business relationship. At least she could depend on *its* continuing into the foreseeable future.

'Why would he be interested?' Diana countered, apparently deciding she'd done her share of the cleaning up, propping herself on a stool at the island bench and examining her fingernails for any chipped varnish. 'You've been stuck with Brendan all the time you've been working for Cole Pierson, not giving out any availability signals,' she ran on.

'He is quite a hunk in the tall, dark and handsome mould,' Jayne chimed in, her interest sparked by the possibility of Liz linking up with the financial wizard who managed the money of several of her accountant husband's very wealthy clients. As she brought emptied salad bowls to the sink where their mother was washing up and Liz drying, she made a more direct remark. 'You must feel attracted to him, Liz.'

'No, I don't,' she swiftly denied, though she certainly had been initially, when he'd still been human and happily married. He'd been very distractingly attractive *then*, but being the remarkable man he was and having a beautiful wife in the background, Liz had listed him in the no hope category.

Besides, she'd just found Brendan—a far more realistic and reachable choice for her—so she'd quelled any wayward feelings towards her boss.

'How couldn't you be?' Sue queried critically, frowning over what she assumed was totally unnatural. 'The few times I've dropped in on you at your office and he's appeared…the guy is not only a stunner but very charming. Fantastic blue eyes.'

Cold blue eyes, Liz corrected.

Cold and detached.

Ever since he'd lost his baby son eighteen months ago—a tragic cot death—Cole had retreated inside himself. The separation from his wife six months later had not come as a surprise to Liz. The marriage had to be in trouble. Her boss had moved beyond *connecting* to anyone.

He switched on a superficial charm for clients and visitors but there was no real warmth in it. He had a brilliant brain that never lost track of the money markets, that leapt on any profitable deal for his clients' investments, that paid meticulous attention to every critical detail of his business. But it was also a brain that blocked any intrusion to whatever he thought and felt on a personal level. Around him was an impenetrable wall, silently but strongly emitting the message—*keep out*.

'There's just no spark between us,' she told Sue, wanting to dampen this futile line of conversation. 'Cole is totally focused on business.'

Which made *him* appreciate her management skills,

she thought with black irony. He certainly didn't feel *stifled* by her being efficient at keeping track of everything. He expected it of her and it always gave her a kick when she surprised him by covering even more than he expected. He was a hard taskmaster.

'You need to shake him out of that one-track mindset,' Diana advised, persisting with her get-the-boss idea.

'You can't change what drives a person's life,' Liz flashed back at her, realising she'd been foolish to think she could change any of Brendan's ingrained attitudes.

Diana ignored this truism. 'I bet he takes you for granted,' she rattled on, eyeing Liz assessingly. 'Treats you as part of the office furniture because you don't do anything to stand out from it. Look at you! When was the last time you spent money on yourself?'

Liz gritted her teeth at the criticism. It was all very well for Diana, who had a rich husband to pay for everything she wanted. *She* didn't need to siphon off most of her income to make the payments on a city apartment. Liz had figured the only way she'd ever have a home to call her own was to buy it herself. Besides which, real estate was a good solid investment.

'I keep up a classic wardrobe for work,' she argued, not bothering to add she had no use for fancy clothes anyway. She and Brendan had never gone anywhere fancy, preferring a much more casual lifestyle, using whatever spare money they had to travel where they could. Jeans, T-shirts and jackets took them to most places.

'Dullsville,' Diana said witheringly. 'All black suits and sensible shoes. In fact, you've let yourself get positively drab. What you need is a complete makeover.'

Having finished putting everything away, her two older sisters joined Diana on stools around the island bench and jumped on this bandwagon. 'I've never thought long hair suits you,' Jayne remarked critically. 'It swamps your small face. And when you wear it pulled back like that, it does nothing for you at all. Makes your facial bones appear sharper. No softening effect. You really should get it cut and styled, Liz.'

'And coloured,' Sue said, nodding agreement. 'If you must wear black suits, mouse brown hair doesn't exactly give you a lift.'

'There's no *must* about it,' Diana declared, glaring a knowing challenge as she added, 'I bet you simply took the cheap route of having a minimal work wardrobe. Am I right or not, Liz?'

She couldn't deny it. Not making regular visits to a hairdresser saved her time and money and it was easy enough to slick back her long hair into a tidy clip at the back of her neck for work. Besides, Brendan had said he liked long hair. And the all-purpose suits she wore meant she didn't have to think about putting something smarter together—a sensible investment that actually cost less than a more varied range of clothes.

'What does it matter?' she countered with a vexed

sigh at being put under the microscope like this. 'I get by on it,' she added defiantly. 'Nobody criticises me at work.'

'The invisible handmaiden,' Diana scoffed. 'That's what you've let yourself become, and you could be a knockout if you made the effort.'

'Oh, come off it!' she protested, losing patience with the argument. 'I've always been the plain one in this family. And the shortest.'

She glared at tall, willowy Jayne with her gorgeous mane of dark wavy hair framing a perfectly oval face and a long graceful neck. Her eldest sister had thickly fringed chocolate brown eyes, a classical straight nose, a wide sensuous mouth, and a model-like figure that made everything she wore look right.

Her gaze moved mockingly to Sue who was almost as tall but more lushly feminine, round curves everywhere topped by a pretty face, sparkling amber eyes and soft, honey-coloured curls that rippled down to her shoulders.

Lastly she looked derisively at Diana, a beautiful blue-eyed blonde who turned heads everywhere she went, her long hair straight and smooth like a curtain of silk, her lovely face always perfectly made up, her tall slim figure invariably enhanced by fabulous designer clothes. Easy for her to catch the eye of *her* boss. He'd have to be blind not to appreciate what an asset she was to him.

Next to her sisters Liz felt small, and not just because she was only average height and had what could be called a petite figure. She felt small in every sense. Her hair was a mousy colour and far too thick to manage easily. It did swamp her. Not only that, her eyes were a murky hazel, no clear colour at all, there was a slight bump in her nose, and her cheekbones and chinline *were* sharply angular. In fact, her only saving grace was good straight teeth.

At least, people said she had a nice smile. But she didn't feel like smiling right now. She felt utterly miserable. 'It's ridiculous to pretend I could be a knockout,' she stated bitingly. 'The only thing I've got going for me is a smart brain that keeps me in a good job, and it's been my experience that most men don't like too much smart in their women when it comes to personal relationships.'

'A smart man does, Liz,' her mother said quietly.

'And Cole Pierson is incredibly smart,' Diana quickly tagged on. 'He'd definitely value you on that score.'

'Would you please leave my boss out of this?' Liz almost stamped her foot in frustration at her younger sister's one-track mind. Any intimate connection with Cole was an impossible dream, for dozens of reasons.

'Regardless of your boss, Liz,' Jayne said in a serious vein. 'I truly think a makeover is a good idea. You're not plain. You've just never made the most of yourself. With some jazzy clothes and a new hairdo…'

'A lovely rich shade of red would do wonders for your hair,' Sue came in decisively. 'If you had it cut and layered to shape in just below your ears, it could look fantastic. Your skin is pale enough for red to look great with it and such a positive contrast would bring out the green in your eyes.'

'They're not green!' Liz cried in exasperation. 'They're...'

'More green than amber,' Sue judged. 'Red would definitely do the trick. Let me make an appointment with my hairdresser for you and I'll come along to advise.'

'And I can take you shopping. Outfit you in some smashing clothes,' Diana eagerly tagged on.

'At a discount price,' Jayne leapt in. 'Right, Diana? Not making it too frightfully expensive?'

'Right!'

'Hair first, clothes second,' Sue ordered.

'A visit to a beautician, too. Get the make-up right to match the new hair.'

'And accentuate the green in her eyes.'

'Don't forget shoes. Liz has got to get out of those matronly shoes.'

'Absolutely. Shapely legs should be shown off.'

'Not to mention a finely turned ankle.'

They all laughed, happy at the thought of getting their hands on their little sister and waving some magic wand that would turn her into one of them. Except it couldn't really happen, and as her sisters continued to rave on with their makeover plan, bouncing off each other, meaning well...she knew they *meant well*...Liz found herself on the verge of tears.

'Stop! Please stop!' she burst out, slamming her hands onto the island bench to gain their undivided attention. 'I'm me, okay? Not a doll for you to dress up. I'm okay as me. And I'll live my life my own way.'

The shaking vehemence in her voice shocked them

into silence. They stared at her, hurt showing on their faces at the blanket rejection of their ideas. They didn't understand where she was coming from, had never understood what it was like to be *her,* the odd one out amongst them. The tears pricked her eyes, threatening to start spilling.

'I'd like some time alone with Liz.'

Her mother's quiet demand floated over Liz's shoulder. She was still at the sink, wiping it back to its usual pristine state. Without a word of protest, her other three daughters got to their feet and trooped out to the patio. Liz turned to her mother, who slowly set the dishcloth aside, waiting for the absolute privacy she'd asked for, not turning until the others were gone.

Having screwed herself up for more talking, Liz was totally undone when her mother looked at her with sad, sympathetic understanding. Impossible to blink back the tears. Then her mother's arms were around her in a comforting hug and her head was being gently pressed onto a shoulder that had always been there for her to lean on in times of strife and grief.

'Let it out, Liz,' her mother softly advised. 'You've held in too much for too long.'

Control collapsed. She wept, releasing the bank of bad feelings that had been building up ever since Brendan had rejected all she'd offered him, preferring to be somewhere else.

'He wasn't right for you,' her mother murmured when the storm of tears eased. 'I know you tried to make him right for you, but he was never going to be, Liz. He's footloose and rootless and you like to be grounded.'

'But I did enjoy the travelling with him, Mum,' she protested.

'I'm sure you did, but it was also a way of going off independently, not competing with your sisters. You may not think of it like that, but being different for the sake of being different is not the answer. By attaching yourself to Brendan, you virtually shut them out of your life. They want back in, Liz. They want to help you. They're your sisters and they love you.'

She lifted her head, looking her mother in the eye. 'But I'm not like them.'

'No, you have your own unique individuality.' Her mouth curved into a tender, loving smile. 'My one brilliant daughter.'

Liz grimaced. 'Not so brilliant. Though I am good at my job.'

Her mother nodded. 'That's not the problem, is it? You're not feeling good about yourself as a woman. I don't think you have for a long time, Liz. It's easy to sweep away your sisters' makeover plan as some kind of false facade, but you could treat it as fun. A new look. A new style. It might very well give you a lift. Don't see it as competing with them. See it as something new for you.'

'You're urging me to be their guinea pig?'

This drew a chiding shake of the head. 'They're proud of your career in high finance, Liz. They ad-mire your success there. How about conceding that they have expertise in fields you've ignored?'

She winced at the pointed reminder that in the feminine stakes, her sisters certainly shone and undoubtedly had an eye for things she hadn't bothered with. 'I guess they do know what they're talking about.'

'And then some,' her mother said dryly.

Liz sighed, giving in more because she was bereft of any plans for herself than in any belief that her life could be instantly brightened, along with her hair. 'Well, I don't suppose it will hurt.'

'You could be very pleasantly surprised. Jayne is right. You're not plain, Liz. You're just different.' Her mother patted her cheek encouragingly. 'Now go and make peace with them. Letting them have their way could be a very positive experience for all of you.'

'Okay. But if Diana thinks a new me will make any difference to Cole Pierson, she's dreaming.'

Her boss occupied a different planet.

A chilly one.

Even fiery red hair wasn't about to melt the ice in that man's veins. Or make him suddenly see her as a desirable woman. Why would he anyway, when he'd had Tara Summerville—a top-line international model—as his wife? Even Diana wasn't in that class.

A totally impossible dream.

CHAPTER TWO

His mother was upset.

Cole didn't like his mother being upset. It had taken her quite a while to get over his father's death and establish a life on her own. For the past few years she'd been happy, planning overseas trips and going on them with her bridge partner, Joyce Hancock, a retired school principal who was a natural organiser, a person he could trust to look after his mother on their travels. As misfortune would have it, Joyce had fallen and broken her hip so the tour they'd booked to South-East Asia had to be cancelled.

He'd spent the whole weekend trying to distract his mother with his company, cheer her up, but she'd remained down in the dumps, heaving miserable sighs, looking forlorn. Now, driving her back to her Palm Beach home after visiting Joyce in Mona Vale Hospital, Cole saw she was fighting tears. He reached across and squeezed her hand, trying to give sympathetic comfort.

'Don't worry about Joyce. Hip replacement is not a dangerous procedure,' he assured her. 'She'll be up and about soon enough.'

'She's annoyed with me for not going ahead with the trip by myself. But I don't want to go on my own.'

Unthinkable to Cole's mind. His mother would undoubtedly get flustered over the tour schedule, leave

18

things in the hotel rooms, be at the wrong place at the wrong time. She'd become quite fluffy-headed in her widowhood, not having to account to anyone anymore, just floating along while Cole took care of any problems that were troublesome. He saw to the maintenance of her far too large but beloved home and looked after her finances. It was easier than trying to train her into being more responsible for herself.

'It's your choice, Mum. Joyce probably feels guilty about disappointing you,' he soothed.

She shook her head dejectedly. 'I'm disappointing her. She's right about *The Captain's Choice Tour Company*. Their people do look after everything for you. They even take a doctor along in case anyone gets sick or injured. Joyce wants me to go so I can tell her all about it. She says I'll meet people I can talk to. Make new friends…'

'That's easy for her to say,' Cole said dryly, knowing Joyce was the kind of person who'd bulldose her way into any company and feel right at home with it. His mother was made of more fragile stuff.

Her hands twisted fretfully. 'Maybe I should go. Nothing's been cancelled yet. I was going to do it tomorrow.'

Clearly she was torn and would feel miserable either way. 'You need a companion, Mum,' Cole stated categorically. 'You'll feel lost on your own.'

'But there's no one in our social circle who's free to take up Joyce's booking.'

He frowned at this evidence of her actively trying to find someone congenial to travel with. 'You really want to go?'

'I've been looking forward to it for so long. Though without Joyce…' Her voice wavered uncertainly.

Cole made a decision. It meant a sacrifice on his part. Liz Hart had been on vacation for the past two weeks and her fill-in had tested his tolerance level to the limit. He hated doing without his efficient personal assistant. Nevertheless, when it came to entrusting the management of his mother to someone else, he couldn't think of anyone better. No hitches with Liz Hart.

'I'll arrange for my P.A. to take up Joyce's booking and accompany you on the tour,' he said, satisfied that he'd come up with the perfect solution, both for his mother's pleasure and his peace of mind.

It jolted her out of her gloom. 'You can't do that, Cole.'

'Yes, I can,' he asserted. 'I'll put it to Liz first thing in the morning. I'm sure she'll agree.'

'I don't even know the girl!' his mother cried in shocked protest.

'You can come into the city tomorrow and I'll set up a lunch meeting. If you approve of her…fine. If you don't, I'm afraid the trip will be off.'

The lure of the tour clearly held a lot of weight. After a few moments, his mother gave in to curiosity. 'What's she like…this personal assistant of yours?'

'She's the kind of person who can handle anything I throw at her,' he replied, smiling confidently.

'Well, she'd have to be, wouldn't she, to keep up with you, Cole,' came the dryly knowing comment. 'I meant…what is she like as a person?'

He frowned, not quite sure how to answer. 'She fits in,' was the most appropriate description he could come up with.

This earned an exasperated roll of the eyes. 'What does she look like?'

'Always neat and tidy. Professional.'

'How old is she?'

'Not sure. Late twenties, I guess. Maybe early thirties.'

'What colour are her eyes?'

He didn't know, couldn't recall ever noticing. 'What does eye colour have to do with anything?'

His mother sighed. 'You just don't look, do you? Not interested. You've closed off all involvement with anyone. You've got to get past this, Cole. You're still a young man.'

He gritted his teeth, hating any reference to all he'd put behind him. 'Her eyes are bright.' he answered tersely. 'They shine with intelligence. That's more important to me than colour.'

The blank look her temporary fill-in had given him too many times over the past fortnight had filled him with frustration. He'd have to second someone else to take Liz Hart's place while she was off with his mother.

'Is she attractive…pretty…big…slight…tall… short…?'

Cole sighed over his mother's persistence on irrelevant detail. 'She's ordinary average,' he said impatiently. 'And always obliging, which is the main point here. Liz will ensure you have a trouble-free tour, Mum. No worries.'

His mother sighed. 'Do try to tell me more about her, Cole.'

She should be satisfied with what he'd already told her but he stretched his mind to find some pertinent point. 'She likes travel. Spends most of her time off travelling somewhere or other. I expect she'll jump at the chance of accompanying you to South-East Asia.'

'Then it won't be a completely burdensome chore for her, escorting me around?'

'Of course not. I wouldn't load you with a sour-puss. I'm sure you'll find Liz Hart a delight to be with.'

'Do you?'

'Do I what?'

'Find her a delight to be with.'

'Well, I'll certainly miss her,' he said with feeling.

'Ah!'

He glanced sharply at his mother. Her 'Ah!' had carried a surprising depth of satisfaction, making him wonder what she was thinking.

She smiled at him. 'Thank you, Cole. You're quite wonderful at fixing things for me. I'll look forward to meeting your Liz tomorrow.'

'Good!'

Problem solved.

His mother wasn't upset anymore.

Monday morning...

Cole heard Liz Hart arrive in the office which adjoined his—promptly at eight-thirty as she did every workday. Totally reliable, he thought with satisfaction.

He had not qualms whatsoever about entrusting his mother's well-being and pleasure in this upcoming South-East Asia tour to his punctual and efficient personal assistant.

It didn't occur to him that the request he was about to make was tantamount to inviting Liz Hart into his personal and private life. To his mind it was simply a matter of moving people into position to achieve what had to be achieved. He could manage another two weeks more or less by himself, asking the absolute minimum of another temporary P.A., while his mother enjoyed a stress-free trip. Once the fortnight was over, everything would shift back to normal.

He rose from his desk and strode to the connecting door, intent on handing the tour folder to Liz so she could get straight to work on doing what had to be done to become Joyce Hancock's replacement. In his business, time was money and his time was too valuable to waste on extraneous matters. Liz would undoubtedly see to everything required of her—passport, visas, whatever.

He opened the door to find some stranger hanging her bag and coat on Liz's hatstand, taking up personal space that didn't belong to her. Cole frowned at the unexpected vision of a startling redhead, dressed in a clingy green sweater and a figure-hugging navy skirt with a split up the back—quite a distracting split, leading his gaze down a pair of finely shaped legs encased in sheer navy stockings, to pointedly female high-heeled shoes.

Who was this woman? And what did she think she was doing, taking up Liz's office? He hadn't been informed that his P.A. had called in, delaying her scheduled return to work. Unexplained change was not acceptable, especially when it entailed having someone foisted on him without his prior approval.

His gaze had travelled back up the curve of thigh and hip to the indentation of a very small waist before the unwelcome intruder turned around. Then he found himself fixated on very nicely rounded breasts, emphatically outlined by the soft, sexy sweater, with more attention being drawn to them by a V-neckline ending in a looped tie that hung down the valley of her cleavage.

'Good morning, Cole.'

The brisk, cool greeting stunned him with its familiarity. His gaze jerked up to an unfamiliar mouth, painted as brightly red as the thick cropped hair that flared out in waves and curls on either side of her face. The eyes hit a chord with him—very bright eyes—but even they looked different, bigger than they normally were and more sparkly. This wasn't the Liz Hart he was used to. Only her voice was instantly recognisable.

'What the devil have you done to yourself?' The words shot out, driven by a sense of aggrievement at the shock she'd given him.

A firmly chiseled chin which he'd previously thought of as strong, steady and determined, now tilted up in provocative challenge. 'I beg your pardon?'

He was distracted by the gold gypsy hoops dangling from her earlobes. 'This is not you, dammit!' he grated, his normal equilibrium thrown completely out of kilter by these changes in the person who worked most closely with him, a person he counted on not to rock his boats in any sense whatsoever.

Her eyes flashed a glittery warning. 'Are you objecting to my appearance?'

Red alert signals went off in his brain...sexual discrimination...harrassment...Liz was calling him on something dangerous here and he'd better watch his step. However disturbingly different she looked today, he knew she had a core of steel and would stand up for herself against anything she considered unreasonable or unjust.

'No,' he said decisively, taking firm control over the runaway reactions to an image he didn't associate with her. 'Your appearance is fine. It's good to have you back, Liz.'

'Thank you.' Her chin levelled off again, fighting mode discarded. She smiled. 'It's good to be back.'

This should have put them on the correct footing but Cole couldn't help staring at her face, which somehow lit up quite strikingly with the smile. Maybe it was the short fluffy red hair that made her smile look even whiter and her eyes brighter. Or the bright red lipstick. Whatever it was, she sure didn't look average ordinary anymore.

He wanted to ask...why the change? What had happened to her? But that was personal stuff he knew he shouldn't get into. He liked the parameters of their business relationship the way they were. Right now they felt threatened, without inviting further infringements on them.

He had to stop staring. Her cheeks were glowing pink, highlighting bones that now seemed to have an exotic, angular tilt. They must have always been like that. It made him feel stupid not to have noticed before. Had she been deliberately playing herself down during business hours, hiding her surprisingly feminine figure in unisex suits, keeping her hair plain and quiet, wearing only insignificant make-up?

'Is that something for me to deal with?' she asked, gesturing to the folder he was holding.

Conscious that his awkward silence had driven her to take some initiative, he didn't stop to reconsider the proposition he'd prepared. 'Yes,' he said, gratefully seizing on the business in hand. 'I need you to go to South-East Asia with my mother,' he blurted out.

She stared at him, shocked disbelief in her eyes.

Good to serve it right back to her, Cole thought, stepping forward and slapping the folder down on her desk, a buzz of adrenalin shooting through him at regaining control of the situation.

'It's all in here. The Captain's Choice Tour. Borneo, Burma, Nepal, Laos, Vietnam, Cambodia— all in fifteen days by chartered Qantas jet, leaving on Saturday week. You'll require extra passport photos for visas and innoculation shots for typhoid, hepatitis, and other diseases. You'll see the medical check list. I take it you have a usable passport?'

'Yes,' she answered weakly.

'Good! No problem then.'

She seemed frozen on the spot, still staring at him, not moving to open the folder. He tapped it to draw her attention to it.

'All the tickets are in here. Everything's been paid

for. You'll find them issued in the name of Joyce Hancock and first thing to do is notify the tour company that you'll be travelling in her place.'

'Joyce Hancock,' she repeated dazedly.

'My mother's usual travelling companion. Broke her hip. Can't go. None of her other friends can take the trip at such short notice,' he explained.

Liz Hart shook her head, the red hair rippling with the movement like a live thing that wasn't under any control. Very distracting. Cole frowned, realising she was indicating a negative response. Which was unacceptable. He was about to argue the position when she drew in a deep breath and spoke.

'Your mother…Mrs. Pierson…she doesn't even know me.'

'*I* know you. I've told her she'll be safe with you.'

'But…' She gestured uncertainly.

'Primarily my mother needs a manager on this trip. I have absolute faith in your management skills, not to mention your acute sense of diplomacy, tact, understanding, and generally sharp intelligence. Plus you're an experienced traveller.' He raised a challenging eyebrow. 'Correct?'

Another deep breath, causing a definite swell in the mounds under the clingy sweater which was a striking jewel green, somewhere between jade and emerald, a rich kind of medieval colour. The fanciful thought jolted Cole. He had to get his mind off her changed appearance.

'Thank you. It's nice to have my…attributes… appreciated,' she said in a somewhat ironic tone that sounded unsure of his end purpose. 'However, I do think I should meet with your mother…'

'Lunch today. Book a table for the three of us at Level 21. Twelve-thirty. My mother will join us there. She is looking forward to meeting you.'

'Is Mrs. Pierson…unwell?'

'Not at all. A bit woolly-headed about directions in strange places and not apt at dealing with time changes and demanding schedules, but perfectly sane and sound. She'll lean on you to get things right for her. That's your brief. Okay?'

'She's…happy…about this arrangement?'

'Impossible for her to go otherwise and she wants to go.'

'I see. You want me to be her minder.'

'Yes. I have every confidence in your ability to provide the support she needs to fully enjoy this trip.'

'What if she doesn't like me?'

'What's *not* to like?' he threw back at her more snappishly than he'd meant to, irritatingly aware that his mother would think this new version of Liz Hart was just lovely. And she would undoubtedly mock his judgment at having called his P.A. ordinary average.

No answer from Liz. Of course, it would be against her steely grain to verbally put herself down. Which increased the mystery of why she had *played* herself down physically these past three years. Had it been a feminist thing, a negation of her sexuality because she wanted her intellect valued?

Why had she suddenly decided to flaunt femininity now?

Dammit! He didn't have time to waste on such vagaries.

He tapped the folder again. 'I can leave this with you? No problems about dealing with it?' His eyes locked onto hers with the sharp demand of getting what he expected.

'No problems I can see,' she returned with flinty pride.

Her eyes were green.

With gold speckles around the rim.

'Fine! Let me know if you run into any.'

He stalked off into his own office, annoyed at how he was suddenly noticing every detail about a woman who'd been little more than a mind complementing his up until this morning. It was upsetting his comfort zone.

Why did she have to change?

It didn't feel right.

Just as well she was going off with his mother for two weeks. It would give him time to adjust to the idea of having his P.A. looking like a fiery sexpot. Meanwhile, he had work to do and he was not about to be distracted from it. Bad enough that he had to take time off for the lunch with his mother, which was bound to be another irritation because of Liz Hart's dramatic transformation.

Bad start to the morning.

Bad, bad, bad.

At least the food at Level 21 was good.

Though he'd probably choke on it, watching his mother being dazzled by her new travelling companion. No way was *she* going to be upset by a *colourful* Liz Hart, which was some consolation, but since he was decidedly upset himself, Cole wasn't sure that balanced the scales.

CHAPTER THREE

LIZ took a deep, deep breath, let it out slowly, then forced her feet to walk steadily to her desk, no teetering in the high-heels, shoulders back, correct carriage, just as Diana had drilled her. It was good to sit down. She was still quaking inside from the reaction her new image had drawn from Cole Pierson.

Diana had confidently predicted it would knock his socks off but Liz had believed he would probably look at her blankly for a few seconds, dismiss the whole thing as frivolous female foibles, then get straight down to business. Never, in a million years, would she have anticipated being *attacked* on it. Nor looked at so...so *intensely*.

It had been awful, turning around from the hatstand and finding those piercing blue eyes riveted on her breasts. Her heart had started galloping. Even worse, she'd felt her nipples hardening into prominent nubs, possibly becoming visible underneath the snug fit of the cashmere sweater.

She'd clipped out a quick greeting to get his focus off her body, only to have him stare at her mouth as though alien words had come out of it. Even when he had finally lifted his gaze to hers, she'd been totally rattled by the force of his concentration on how she looked. Which, she readily conceded, was vastly different to what he was used to, but certainly not warranting the outburst that came. Nor the criticism it implied.

Her own fierce response to it echoed through her mind now—*I will not let him make me feel wrong. Not on any grounds.*

There was no workplace law to say a woman couldn't change the colour of her hair, couldn't change the style of her clothes, couldn't touch up her make-up. It wasn't as if she'd turned up with hair tortured into red or blue or purple spikes or dreadlocks. Red was a natural hair colour and the short layered style was what she'd call conservative modern, not the least bit outlandish. Her clothes were perfectly respectable and her make-up appropriate—certainly not overdone—to match the new colouring.

In fact, no impartial judge would say her appearance did not fit the position she held. All her sisters had declared she was now perfectly put together and Liz herself had ended up approving the result of their combined efforts. Her mother was right. It did make her feel good to look brighter and more stylish. She'd even started smiling at herself in the mirror.

And she wasn't about to let Cole Pierson wipe *that* smile off her face, just because he'd feel more comfortable if she merged into the office furniture again so he could regard her as another one of his computers. Though he had attributed her with management skills, diplomacy, tact, understanding, and sharp intelligence, which did put her a few points above a computer. And amazingly, he trusted her enough to put his mother into her keeping!

Having burned off her resentment at her boss's totally intemperate remarks on what was none of his business, Liz focused on the folder he'd put on her desk. Surprises had come thick and fast this morning. Apart from Cole's taking far too much *physical* notice of her, she had been summarily appointed guardian to a woman she'd never met, and handed a free trip to South-East Asia, no doubt travelling first-class all the way on The Captain's Choice Tour.

Right in the middle of this, Cole had listed Nepal amongst the various destinations.

Brendan was in Nepal.

Not that there was any likelihood of meeting up with him, and she didn't really want to…did she? What was finished was finished. But there was a somewhat black irony in her going there, too. Especially in not doing everything on the cheap, as Brendan would have to.

You can do better than Brendan Wheeler, her mother had said with a conviction that had made Liz feel she had settled for less than she should in considering a life partner.

Maybe her mother was right.

In any event, this trip promised many better things than bunking down in backpacker hostels.

On the front of The Captain's Choice folder was printed 'The leader in luxury travel to remote and exotic destinations.' Excitement was instantly ignited. She opened the folder and read all about the itinerary, delighted anticipation zooming at the places she would be visiting, and all in a deluxe fashion.

The accommodation was fantastic—The Hyatt Regency Hotel in Kathmandu, The Opera Hilton in

Hanoi, a 'Raffles' hotel in Phnom Penh. No expense spared anywhere…a chartered flight over Mount Everest, and a chartered helicopter to Halong Bay in Vietnam, another chartered flight to the ancient architectural wonder of Angkor Wat in Cambodia, even a specially chartered steam train to show them some of the countryside in Burma.

She could definitely take a lot of this kind of travel. No juggling finances, no concern over how to get where, no worry about making connections, no trying to find a decent meal…it was all laid out and paid for.

Even if Cole's mother was a grumpy battleaxe, Liz figured it couldn't be too hard to win her over by being determinedly cheerful. After all, Mrs. Pierson had to want this trip very much to agree to her son's plan, so mutual enjoyment should be reached without too much trouble.

Tact, diplomacy, understanding…Liz grinned to herself as she reached for the telephone, ready now to get moving on sealing her place for this wonderful new adventure. Her changed appearance had probably knocked Cole's socks off this morning, though in a more negative way than Diana had plotted, but he had still paid her a huge compliment by giving her this extra job with his mother. Better than a bonus.

It made her feel good.

Really good.

She zinged through the morning, booking the table at Level 21—no problem to fit Cole Pierson's party in at short notice since he regularly used the restaurant for business lunches—then lining up everything necessary for her to take Joyce Hancock's place on the tour.

Cole did not reappear. He did not call her, either. He remained secluded in his own office, no doubt tending meticulously to his own business. At twelve-fifteen, Liz went to the Ladies' Room to freshen up, smiled at herself in the mirror, determined that nothing her boss said or did would unsettle her again, then proceeded to beard the lion in his den, hoping he wouldn't bite this time.

She gave a warning knock on the door, entered his office, waited for him to look up from the paperwork on his desk, ignored the frown, and matter-of-factly stated, 'It's time to leave if we're to meet your mother at twelve-thirty.'

Since Cole's financial services company occupied a floor of the Chifley Tower, one of the most prestigious buildings in the city centre, all they had to do was catch an elevator up to Level 21, which, of course, was also one of Sydney's most prestigious restaurants. This arrangement naturally suited Cole's convenience, as well as establishing in his clients' minds that big money was made here and this location amply displayed that fact.

Cold blue eyes bored into hers for several nerve-jangling moments. He certainly knew how to put a chill in a room. Liz wondered if she should have put her suitcoat on, but they weren't going outside where there was a wintery bite in the air. This was just her boss, being his usual self, and it was good that he had returned to being his usual self.

Though as he rolled his big executive chair back

from his work station and rose to his full impressive height, Liz did objectively note that Sue was not wrong in calling him tall, dark and handsome, what with his thick black hair, black eyebrows, darkly toned skin, a strong male face, squarish jaw, firm mouth, straight nose, neat ears. And those piercing eyes gave him a commanding authority that accentuated his *presence*.

The Armani suits he invariably wore added to his presence, too. Cole Pierson had dominant class written all over him. Sometimes, it really piqued Liz. It didn't seem fair that anyone should have so much going for him. But then she told herself he wasn't totally human.

Although the robotic facade *had* cracked this morning.

Scary stuff.

Better not to think about it.

Move on, move on, move on, she recited, holding her breath as Cole moved towards her, mouth grim, eyes raking over her again, clearly not yet having come to terms with her brighter presence.

'Did you call up to see if my mother had arrived?' he rapped out.

'No. I considered it a courtesy that we be there on time.'

'My mother is not the greatest time-keeper in the world.' He paused beside Liz near the door. 'Which is why she needs you,' he rammed home with quite unnecessary force.

'All the more reason to show her I'm reliable on that point,' she retorted, and could have sworn he breathed steam through his nostrils as he abruptly waved her to precede him out of both of their offices.

It made Liz extremely conscious of walking with straight-backed dignity. It was ridiculous, given his icy eyes, that she felt the bare nape of her neck burning. He had to be watching her, which was highly disconcerting because usually his whole attention was claimed by whatever was working through his mind. She didn't want his kind of intense focus trained on her. It was like being under a microscope, making her insides squirmish.

She breathed a sigh of relief when they finally entered the elevator and stood side by side in the compartment as it zoomed up to Level 21. Cole held his hands loosely linked in front of them and watched the numbers flashing over the door. It looked like a relaxed pose, but he emanated a tension that erased Liz's initial relief.

Maybe he was human, after all.

Was it *her* causing this rift in his iron-like composure, or the prospect of this meeting with his mother?

This thought reminded Liz that *she* should be thinking about his mother, preparing herself to answer any questions put to her in a positive and reassuring manner. Of course, her response depended largely on the kind of person Cole's mother was. Liz hoped she wasn't frosty. Cole had said fluffy, but that might only mean her mind wasn't as razor-sharp as his.

Liz was fast sharpening her own mind as they were met at the entrance to the restaurant by the maitre d' and informed that Mrs. Pierson had arrived and was enjoying a drink in the bar lounge.

'Must be anxious,' Cole muttered as they were led to where a woman sat on a grey leather sofa, her attention drawn to the fantastic view over the city of Sydney, dramatically displayed by the wall of windows.

Her hair was pure white, waving softly around a slightly chubby face which was relatively unlined and still showing how pretty she must have been in her youth. About seventy, Liz judged, taking heart at the gentle, ladylike look of the woman. Definitely not a battleaxe. Not frosty, either. She wore a pink Chanel style suit with an ivory silk blouse, pearl brooch, pearl studs in her ears, and many rings on her fingers.

'Mum!'

Her son's curt tone whipped her head around, her whole body jerking slightly at being startled. Bright blue eyes looked up at him, then made an instant curious leap to Liz. Her mouth dropped open in sheer surprise.

'Mum!' Cole said again, the curt tone edged with vexation now.

Her mouth shut into a line of total exasperation and she gave him a look that seemed to accuse him of being absolutely impossible and in urgent need of having his head examined.

Liz thought she heard Cole grind his teeth. However, he managed to unclench them long enough to say, 'This is my P.A., Liz Hart...my mother, Nancy Pierson.'

Nancy rose to her feet, her blue eyes glittering with

a frustration that spilled into speech as she held out her hand to Liz. 'My dear, how *do* you put up with him?'

Tact and diplomacy were right on the line here!

'Cole is the best boss I've ever had,' Liz declared with loyal fervour. 'I very much enjoy working with him.'

'Work!' Nancy repeated in a tone of disgust. 'Tunnel vision…that's what he's got. Sees nothing but work.'

'Mum!' Thunder rolled through Cole's warning protest.

Liz leapt in to avert the storm. 'Cole did cover your trip to South-East Asia this morning, Mrs. Pierson.' She beamed her best smile and poured warmth into her voice as she added, 'Which I think is wonderful.'

It did the trick, drawing Nancy out of her grumps and earning a smile back. She squeezed Liz's hand in a rush of pleasure. 'Oh, I think so, too. Far too wonderful to miss.'

Liz squeezed back. 'I'm simply over the moon that Cole thought of me as a companion for you. Such marvellous places to see…'

'Well…' She gave her son an arch look that still had a chastening gleam. 'Occasionally he gets some things right.'

'A drink,' Cole bit out. 'Liz, something for you? Mum, a refill?'

'Just water, thank you,' Liz quickly answered.

'Champagne,' Nancy commanded, and suddenly there was a wickedly mocking twinkle in her eyes.

'I'm beginning to feel quite bubbly again, now that I've met your Liz, Cole.'

His Liz? Exactly what terms had Cole used to describe her to his mother? Nothing with a possessive sense, surely.

'I'm glad you're happy,' he said on an acid note and headed for the bar.

Nancy squeezed Liz's hand again before letting go and gesturing to the lounge. 'Come and sit down with me and let us get better acquainted.'

'What would you like to know about me?' Liz openly invited as she sank onto the soft leather sofa.

'Not about work,' came the decisive dismissal. 'Tell me about your family.'

'Well, my parents live at Neutral bay...'

'Nice suburb.'

'Dad's a doctor. Mum was a nurse but...'

'She gave it up when the family came along.'

'Yes. Four daughters. I'm the third.'

'My goodness! That must have been a very female household.'

Liz laughed. 'Yes. Dad always grumbled about being outvoted. But he now has three sons-in-law to stand shoulder to shoulder with him.'

'So your three sisters are married. How lovely! Nice husbands?'

Under Nancy's eager encouragement, Liz went on to describe her sisters' lives and had just finished a general rundown on them when Cole returned, setting the drinks down on the low table in front of them and dropping onto the opposite sofa. Into the lull follow-

ing their 'thankyous,' Nancy dropped the one question Liz didn't want to answer.

'So what about your social life, Liz? Or are you
like Cole...' a derisive glance at her son. '...not having one.'

It instantly conjured up the hole left by Brendan's
defection. She delayed a reply, picking up the glass
of water, fiercely wishing the question hadn't been
asked, especially put as it had been, linking her to her
boss who was listening.

Unexpectedly he came to her rescue. 'You're getting too personal, Mum,' he said brusquely. 'Leave it
alone.'

Nancy aimed a sigh at him. 'Has it occurred to you,
Cole, that such a bright, striking young woman could
have a boyfriend who might not take kindly to her
leaving him behind while she travels with me?'

He beetled an accusing frown at Liz as though this
was all her fault, then sliced an impatient look at his
mother. 'What objection could a boyfriend have? It's
only for two weeks and you can hardly be seen as a
rival.'

'It's short notice. The trip takes up three weekends.
They might have prior engagements,' came the ready
arguments. 'Did you even ask this morning, or did
you simply go into command mode, expecting Liz to
carry through your plan, regardless?'

A long breath hissed through his teeth.

Liz felt driven to break in. 'Mrs. Pierson...'

'Call me Nancy, dear.'

'Nancy...' She tried an appeasing smile to cover
the angst of her current single state. '...I don't have

a boyfriend at the moment. I'm completely free to take up the amazingly generous opportunity Cole handed me this morning. I would have told him so if I wasn't.'

Tact, diplomacy...never mind that the hole was humiliatingly bared.

'Satisfied?' Cole shot at his mother.

She smiled back at him. 'Completely.' It was a surprisingly smug pronouncement, as though she had won the point.

Liz was lost in whatever byplay was going on between mother and son, but she was beginning to feel very much like the meat in the sandwich. Anxious to get the conversation focused back on the trip, she offered more relevant information about herself.

'I haven't been to Kuching but I have travelled to Malaysia before.'

Thankfully, Nancy seized on that prior experience and Liz managed to keep feeding their mutual interest in travel over lunch, skilfully smoothing over the earlier tension in their small party. Cole ate his food, contributing little to the table talk, though he did flash Liz a look of wry appreciation now and then, well aware she was working hard at winning over his mother.

Not that it was really hard. Nancy seemed disposed to like her, the blue eyes twinkling pleasure and approval in practically everything Liz said. Oddly enough, Liz was more conscious of her boss watching and listening, and whenever their eyes met, the understanding that flashed between them gave her heart a little jolt.

This had never happened before and she tried to analyse why now? Because his mother made this more personal than business? Because he was looking at her from a different angle, seeing the woman behind the P.A.? Because she was doing the same thing, seeing him as Nancy's son instead of the boss?

It was confusing and unsettling.

She didn't want to feel...*touched*...by this man, or close to him in any emotional sense. No doubt he'd freeze her out again the moment this meeting with his mother was over.

'Now, are you free this Saturday, my dear?' Nancy inquired once coffee was served.

'Yes?' Liz half queried, wondering what else was required of her.

'Good! You must come over to my home at Palm Beach and check my packing. Joyce always does that for me. It eliminates doubling up on things, taking too much. Do you have a car? It's difficult to get to by public transport. If you don't have a car...'

Liz quickly cut in. 'Truly, it won't be a problem. I'll manage.'

She'd never owned a car. No need when public transport was not only faster into the city, but much, much cheaper than running a car. Palm Beach was, however, a fair distance out, right at the end of the northern peninsula, but she'd get there somehow.

'I was going to say Cole could bring you.' She smiled at her son. 'You could, dear, couldn't you? Don't forget you're meeting with the tradesman who's going to quote for the new paving around the pool on Saturday.' She frowned. 'I think he said eleven o'clock. Or was it one o'clock?'

Cole sighed. 'I'll be there, Mum. And I'll collect and deliver Liz to you,' he said in a tone of sorely tried patience.

Oh, great! Liz thought, preferring the cost of a taxi to being a forced burden loaded onto her boss's shoulders. But clearly she wasn't going to get any say in this so she might as well grin and bear it. Though she doubted Cole would find a grin appropriate. He was indulging his mother but the indulgence was wearing very, very thin.

'You'd better come early. Before eleven,' Nancy instructed, then smiled at Liz. 'We'll have a nice lunch together. I've so enjoyed this one. And, of course, we have to be sure we've got all the right clothes for our trip.'

Liz had been thinking cargo pants and T-shirts for daywear and a few more stylish though still casual outfits for dinner at night, but she held her tongue, not knowing what Nancy expected of her. She would see on Saturday.

A great pity Cole had to be there.

He was probably thinking the same thing about her.

In fact, Liz wondered if Nancy Pierson was deliberately putting the two of them together to somehow score more points off her son. She might be fluffy-headed about time, but Liz suspected she was as sharp as a tack when it came to people. And she was looking smug again.

'Everything settled to your satisfaction, Mum?' Cole dryly inquired.

'Yes.' She smiled sweetly at him. 'Thank you, dear. I'm sure I'll have a lovely time with your Liz. So good of you to give her to me. I imagine you'll be quite lost without her.'

'No one is indispensable.'

A chill ran down Liz's spine. She threw an alarmed look at Cole, frightened that she'd somehow put her job on the line by courting his mother. The last thing she wanted at this uncertain point in her life was to lose the position that gave her the means to move on.

Cole caught the look and frowned at the flash of vulnerability. 'Though I must admit it's very difficult to find anyone who can remotely fill Liz's shoes as my P.A.,' he stated, glowering at her as though she should know that. 'In fact, I may very well take some time off work while she's away to save myself the aggravation.'

Both Liz and Nancy stared at him in stunned disbelief.

Cole taking time off work was unheard of. He ate, drank, and slept work.

Surprises were definitely coming thick and fast today!

The best one, Liz decided with a surge of tingling pleasure, was the accumulating evidence that Cole Pierson really valued her. That made her feel better than good. It made her feel...*extra special*.

CHAPTER FOUR

COLE had expected Liz Hart to manage his mother brilliantly. That had never been in doubt. However, while the meeting had achieved his purpose—his mother happily accepting his P.A. as her companion for the trip—there were other outcomes that continued to niggle at his mind, making the rest of Monday afternoon a dead loss as far as any productive work was concerned.

Firstly, his mother considered him a blind idiot.

That was Liz's fault.

Secondly, his mother had neatly trapped him into some ridiculous matchmaking scheme, forcibly coupling him with Liz on Saturday.

While he couldn't entirely lay the blame for that at his P.A.'s door, if she hadn't completely changed how she looked, his mother wouldn't have been inspired to plot this extraneous togetherness.

Thirdly, what had happened to the boyfriend? While Cole had never met the man in Liz Hart's life and not given him a thought this morning, he had been under the impression there was a long-running relationship. The name, Brendan, came to mind. Certainly on the few occasions Liz had spoken of personal travel plans, she'd used the plural pronoun. 'We...'

Had she lied to put a swift end to the fuss his

mother had made? Surely insisting her boyfriend wouldn't object could have achieved the same end.

Cole wanted that point cleared up.

Maybe the departure of the boyfriend had triggered the distracting metamorphosis from brown moth to bright butterfly.

Lastly, why would Liz feel insecure about her job? She had every reason to feel confident about holding her position. He'd never criticised her work. She had to know how competent she was. It was absurd of her to look afraid when he'd said no one was indispensable.

The whole situation with her today had been exasperating and continued to exasperate even after she left to go home. Cole resolved to shut it all out of his mind tomorrow. And for the rest of the working week. Perhaps on the drive to his mother's house on Saturday he'd get these questions answered, clear up what was going on in Liz's head. Then he'd feel comfortable around her again.

On Tuesday morning she turned up in a slinky leopard print outfit that totally wrecked his comfort zone, giving him the sense of a jungle cat prowling around him with quiet, purposeful manoeuvres. She also wore sexy bronze sandals with straps that crisscrossed up over her ankles, making him notice how fine-boned they were.

Wednesday she gave the tight navy skirt with the slit up the back a second wearing, but this time topped with a snug cropped jacket in vibrant violet, an unbelievably stunning combination with the red hair. Cole found his gaze drawn to it far too many times.

Thursday came the leopard print skirt with a black sweater, and the gold hoop earrings that dangled so distractingly. *Striking,* his mother had said, and it was a disturbingly apt description. Cole was struck by thoughts he hadn't entertained for a long time. If Liz Hart was free of any attachment…but mixing business with pleasure was always a mistake. Stupid to even be tempted.

Friday fueled the temptation. She wore a bronze button-through dress which wasn't completely buttoned through, showing provocative flashes of leg. A wide belt accentuated her tiny waist, the stand-up collar framed her vivid hair and face, and the strappy bronze sandals got to him again. The overall effect was very sexy. In fact, the more he thought about Liz Hart, the more he thought she comprised a very desirable package.

But best to leave well enough alone.

He wasn't ready for a serious relationship and an office affair would inevitably undermine the smooth teamwork they'd established at work. Besides which, he reflected with considerable irony, Liz had not given any sign of seeing *him* in a sexual light. No ripple of disturbance in her usual efficiency.

She did seem to be smiling at him more often but he couldn't be sure that wasn't simply a case of the smile being more noticeable, along with her mouth, her eyes, and everything else about her. Nevertheless, the smile was getting to be insidious. More times than not he found himself smiling back, feeling a lingering pleasure in the little passage of warmth between them.

No harm in being friendly, he told himself, as long

as it didn't diminish his authority. After all, Liz had worked in relative harmony with him for three years. Though getting too friendly wouldn't do, either. A line had to be drawn. Business was business. A certain distance had to be kept.

That distance was clearly on Liz's mind when she entered his office at the end of their working week, and with an air of nervous tension, broached the subject—'About tomorrow…going to your mother's home at Palm Beach…'

'Ah, yes! Where and when to pick you up.'

Her hands picked fretfully at each other. 'You really don't have to.'

'Easier if I do.' Cole leaned back in his chair to show that he was relaxed about it.

'I've worked out the most efficient route by public transport. It's not a problem,' she assured him.

'It will be a problem for me if I arrive without you,' he drawled pointedly.

'Oh!' She grimaced, recalling the acrimony between mother and son. Her eyes flashed an anxious plea. 'I don't want to put you out, Cole.'

'It's my mother putting me out, not you. I don't mind obliging her tomorrow, Liz.' He reached for a notepad. 'Give me your address.'

More hand-picking. 'I could meet you somewhere on the way…'

'Your address,' he repeated, impatient with quibbling.

'It will be less hassle if…'

'Do you have a problem with giving me your address, Liz?' he cut in.

She winced. 'I live at Bondi Junction. It would mean your backtracking to pick me up...'

'Ten minutes at most from where I live at Benelong Point.'

'Then ten minutes back again before heading off in the right direction,' she reminded him.

'I think I can spare you twenty minutes.'

She sighed. 'I'd feel better about accepting a lift from you if we could meet on the way. I can catch a train to...'

'Are you worried that your boyfriend might object if I pick you up from your home?' The thought had slid into his mind and spilled into words before Cole realised it was openly probing her private life and casting himself in the role of a rival.

She stared at him, shocked at the implications of the question.

Cole was somewhat shocked at the indiscretion himself, but some belligerent instinct inside him refused to back down from it. The urge to know the truth of her situation had been building all week. He stared back, waiting for her answer, mentally commanding it.

A tide of heat flowed up her neck and burned across her cheekbones, making their slant more prominent and her eyes intensely bright. Cole was conscious of a fine tension running between them, a silent challenge emanating from her, striking an edge of excitement in him...the excitement of contest he always felt with a clash of wills, spurring on his need to win.

'I told you on Monday I don't have a boyfriend,' she bit out.

'No. You told my mother that, neatly ending her blast at me.'

'It's the truth.'

'Since when? The last I heard, just before you left on vacation, you had plans to travel with...is it Brendan?'

Her mouth compressed into a thin line of resistance.

'Who's been floating around in your background for as long as you've been working with me,' Cole pushed relentlessly. 'Probably before that, as well.'

'He's gone. I'm by myself now,' she said in defiant pride.

'Send him packing, did you?'

'He packed himself off,' she flashed back derisively.

'You're telling me he left you?'

'He didn't like my style of management.'

'Man's a fool.'

Her mouth tilted into a wry little smile. 'Thank you.'

No smile in her eyes, Cole noted. They looked bleak. She'd been hurt by the rejection of what she was, possibly hurt enough to worry about how rightly or wrongly she managed her job, hence the concern about losing it, too.

Satisfied that he now understood her position, Cole restated his. 'I shall pick you up at your home. Your address?'

She gave it without further argument, though her tone had a flat, beaten quality he didn't like. 'I was only trying to save you trouble,' she muttered, excusing her attempt to manage him.

'I appreciate the value you place on my time, Liz.' He finished writing down her address and looked up, wanting to make her feel valued. 'You're obliging my mother. The least I can do is save *you* some of your leisure time. Does ten o'clock suit?'

'Yes. Thank you.' Her cheeks were still burning but her hands had forgotten their agitation.

He smiled to ease the last of her tension. 'You're welcome. Just don't feel you have to indulge all my mother's whims tomorrow. Do only what's reasonable to you. Okay?'

She nodded.

He glanced at his watch. 'Time for you to leave to get those injections for the trip.' He smiled again. 'Off you go. I'll see you in the morning.'

'Thank you,' she repeated, looking confused by his good humour.

Cole questioned it himself once she left. He decided it had nothing to do with the fact she was free of any attachment. That was irrelevant to him. No, it was purely the satisfaction of having the mysteries surrounding her this week resolved. Even the change of image made sense. Given that Brendan was stupidly critical, no doubt she'd been suppressing her true colours for the sake of falling in with what he wanted.

Liz was well rid of that guy.

He'd obviously been dragging her down.

Cole ruefully reflected that was what his ex-wife had accused him of doing, though he'd come to recognise it had been easier to blame him than take any responsibility herself for the breakdown of their marriage. At the time he hadn't cared. All that had been good in their relationship had died...with their baby son.

For several moments the grief and guilt he'd locked away swelled out of the sealed compartment in his mind. He pushed them back. Futile feelings, achieving nothing. The past was past. It couldn't be changed. And there was work to be done.

He brought his concentration to bear on the figures listed on his computer monitor screen. He liked their logical patterns, always a reason for everything. Figures didn't lie or deceive or distort things. There were statiticians who used them to do precisely that, but figures by themselves had a pure truth. Cole was comfortable with figures.

He told himself he'd now be comfortable again with Liz Hart. It was all a matter of fitting everything into place—a straightforward pattern built on truth and logic. It wouldn't matter what she wore or how she looked tomorrow, he wouldn't find it distracting. It was all perfectly understandable.

As for the sexual attraction...a brief aberration.

No doubt it would wear off very quickly.

His desk telephone rang, evoking a frown of annoyance. No Liz to intercept and monitor his calls. He didn't talk to clients off the cuff, but it could be an in-house matter being referred to him. Hard to ignore the buzzing. He snatched up the receiver.

'Pierson.'

'Cole…finally,' came the distinctive voice of his almost ex-wife.

'Tara…' It was the barest of acknowledgments. He had nothing to say to her. An aggressive tension seized his entire body, an instinctive reaction to anything she might say to him.

'I tried to get hold of you all last weekend. You weren't at the penthouse…'

'I was with my mother at Palm Beach,' he cut in, resenting the tone that suggested he should still be at Tara's beck and call. She'd been *enjoying* the company of several other men since their separation, clearing him of any lingering sense of obligation to answer any of her needs.

'Your mother…' A hint of mockery in her voice.

It had been one bone of contention in their marriage that Cole spent too much time looking after his mother instead of devoting his entire attention to what Tara wanted, which was continual social activity in the limelight. Not even her pregnancy and the birth of their baby son had slowed her merry-go-round of engagements. If they hadn't been out at a party, leaving David in the care of his nanny…

'Get to the point, Tara,' he demanded, mentally blocking the well-worn and totally futile *if only* track in his mind.

She heaved a sigh at his bluntness, then in a sweetly cajoling tone, said, 'You do remember that our divorce becomes final next week…'

'The date is in my diary.'

'I thought we should get together and…'

'I believe our respective solicitors have covered

every piece of that ground,' he broke in tersely, angry at the thought that Tara was thinking of demanding even more than he had conceded to her in the divorce settlement.

'Darling, you've been more than generous, but…do we really want this?'

The hair on the back of his neck bristled. 'What do you mean?' he snapped.

She took a deep breath. 'You know I've been out and about with a few men since our separation, but the truth is…none of them match up to you, Cole. And I know you haven't formed a relationship with anyone else. I keep thinking if David hadn't died…'

His jaw clenched.

'It just affected everything between us. We both felt so bad…' Another deep breath. 'But time helps us get over these things. We had such a good life going for us, Cole. I was thinking we should give it another shot, at least try it for a while…'

'No!' The word exploded from him, driven by a huge force of negative feelings that were impossible to contain.

'Cole…we could try for another child,' she rolled on, ignoring his response, dropping her voice to a soft throaty purr that promised more than a child. 'Let's get together tomorrow and talk about it. We could have lunch at…'

'Forget it!' he bit out, hating what could only be a self-serving offer. Tara had never *really* wanted a child, hadn't cared enough about David to spend loving time with him. The nanny had done everything

Cole hadn't done himself for his son—the nanny who'd been more distraught than Tara when…

'I'll be lunching with Mum tomorrow,' he stated coldly, emphasising the fact he was not about to change any plans at this point. 'I won't be doing anything to stop the divorce going through. We reached the end of our relationship a long time ago, Tara, and I have no inclination whatsoever to revive it.'

'Surely a little reunion wouldn't hurt. If we could just talk…'

'I said forget it. I mean precisely that.'

He put the receiver down, switched off his computer, got up and strode out of the office, the urge for some intense, mind-numbing activity driving him to head for the private gymnasium where he worked out a couple of times a week.

He didn't want sex with his almost ex-wife.

It was sex that had drawn him into marrying Tara Summerville in the first place. Sex on legs. That was Tara. It had blinded him to everything else about her until well after the wedding. And there he'd been, trapped by a passionate obsession which had gradually waned under one disillusionment after another.

He might have held the marriage together for David's sake, but he certainly didn't want back in. No way. Never. If he ever married again it would be to someone like…he smiled ironically as Liz Hart popped into his mind.

Liz, who was valiantly trying to rise above being dumped by her long-term lover, revamping herself so effectively she'd stirred up feelings that Cole now recognised as totally inappropriate to both time and circumstance.

No doubt Liz was currently very vulnerable to being desired. It was probably the best antidote for the poison of rejection. But he was the wrong man in the wrong place to take advantage of the situation. She needed to count on him as her boss, not suddenly be presented with a side of him that had nothing to do with work.

Still the thought persisted that Liz Hart could be the perfect antidote to the long poisonous hangover from Tara.

Crazy idea.

Better work that out of his mind, too.

CHAPTER FIVE

FORTUNATELY, Liz wasn't kept waiting long at the medical centre. The doctor checked off the innoculations on the yellow card which went straight into the passport folder, along with the reissued tickets and all the other paperwork now acquired for the trip to South-East Asia. *Done,* Liz thought, and wished she was flying off tomorrow instead of having to accompany Cole Pierson to his mother's home.

It was quite scary how conscious she'd become of him as a man. All this time she'd kept him slotted under the heading of her boss—an undeniably male boss but the male part had only been a gender thing, not a sexual thing. This past week she'd found herself looking at him differently, reacting to him differently, even letting her mind dwell on how very attractive he was, especially when he smiled.

As she pushed through the evening peak hour commuter horde and boarded the train for Bondi Junction, she decided it had to be her sisters' fault, prompting her into reassessing Cole through their eyes. Though it was still a huge reach to consider him a possible marriage prospect. First would have to come…no, don't think about steps towards intimacy.

If her mind started wandering along those lines while she was riding with him in his car tomorrow, it could lead her into some dubious response or glance that Cole might interpret as trouble where he didn't want trouble. As it was, he was probably putting two and two together and coming up with a readily predictable answer—boyfriend gone plus new image equals man-hunting.

She would die if he thought for one moment she was hunting him. Because she wasn't. No way would she put her job at risk, which would certainly be the case if anything personal between them didn't work out. Bad enough that this trip with his mother had bared private matters that were changing the parameters of how they dealt with each other.

It didn't feel *safe* anymore.

It felt even less safe to have Cole Pierson coming to her home tomorrow, picking her up and bringing her back. Liz brooded over how he'd torpedoed her alternative plan, making the whole thing terribly personal by questioning her about Brendan and commenting on the aborted relationship.

She must have alighted from the train at Bondi Junction and walked to her apartment on automatic pilot, because nothing impinged on her occupied mind until she heard her telephone ringing in the kitchen.

It was Diana on the line. 'How did it go today?' Eager to hear some exciting result that would make all her efforts worthwhile.

'My arm is sore from the injections,' Liz replied, instinctively shying from revealing anything else.

'Oh, come on, Liz. That bronze dress was the pièce de résistance. It had to get a rise from him.'

'Well, he did notice it…' making her feel very self-conscious a number of times '...but he didn't *say* anything.'

Diana laughed. 'It's working. It's definitely working.'

'It might be angry notice, you know,' Liz argued. 'I told you how he reacted on Monday.'

'Pure shock. Which was what he needed to start seeing you in a different light. And don't worry about anger. Anger's good. Shows you've got to him.'

'But I'm not sure I want to get to him, Diana. It's been a very...uneasy...week.'

'No pain, no gain.'

Liz rolled her eyes at this flippant dictum. 'Look!' she cried in exasperation. 'It was different for you. A fashion buyer operates largely on her own, not under her boss's nose on a daily basis. There was room for you to pursue the attraction without causing any threat to your work situation.'

'You're getting yourself into a totally unnecessary twist, Liz. Cole Pierson is the kind of man who'll do the running. All you have to do is look great, say *yes,* and let things happen.'

'But what if...'

'Give that managing mind of yours a rest for once,' Diana broke in with a huff of impatience. 'Spontaneity is the key. Go with the flow and see where it takes you.'

To not being able to pay the mortgage if I lose my job, Liz thought. Yet there was something insidiously tempting about Diana's advice. She'd been *managing* everything for so long—*stifling* Brendan—and where had it got her?

On the discard shelf.

And Diana was right about Cole. He'd rolled right over the arrangements she'd tried to manage for tomorrow. If there was any running to be done, he'd certainly do it his way. Of course the choice to say yes or no was hers, but where either answer might lead was still very tricky.

'Maybe nothing will happen,' she said in her confusion over whether she wanted it to or not.

'He's taking you to a meeting with his mother tomorrow, isn't he?'

Liz wished she hadn't blabbed quite so much to Diana on Monday night. 'It's just about the trip,' she muttered.

'Wear the camel pants-suit with the funky tan hip belt and leave the top two buttons of the safari jacket undone,' came the marching orders.

'That's too obvious.' The three buttons left undone on her skirt today had played havoc with her nerves every time Cole had glanced down.

'No, it's not. It simply telegraphs the fact you're not buttoned up anymore. And use that *Red* perfume by Giorgio. It smells great on you.'

'I'm not good at this, Diana.'

'Just do as I say. Got to go now. Ward's arrived home. Good luck tomorrow and don't forget to smile a lot.'

Liz released a long, heavy sigh as she put the receiver down. This linking her up with Cole Pierson was turning into a personal crusade for her younger sister. Liz had tried to dampen it down, to no avail. She had the helter-skelter feeling that wheels had been set in motion on Monday and she had no control over where they were going.

At least she'd had little time to feel depressed over her single state. This weekend could have looked bleak and empty without Brendan. Instead of fretting over how to act with Cole, she should be grateful that the Piersons—mother and son—had filled up tomorrow for her.

Besides, she had Diana's instructions to follow and she carried them out to the letter the next morning, telling herself the outfit would undoubtedly please Nancy Pierson's sense of rightness. Classy casual. Perfect for a visit to a Palm Beach residence, which was definitely in millionaire territory. After all, she did want to assure Cole's mother she was a suitable companion for her in every way.

Her doorbell rang at five minutes to ten. Cole had either given himself more time than he needed to get here, or was keen to get going. Liz grabbed her handbag on the way to the door, intent on presenting herself as ready to leave immediately. She wasn't expecting to have her breathing momentarily paralysed at sight of him, but then she'd never seen him dressed in anything other than an impeccably tailored suit.

Blatant macho virility hit her right in the face. He wore a black polo sweater, black leather jacket, black leather gloves, black jeans, his thick black hair was slightly mussed, adding an air of wild vitality, and his eyes were an electric blue, shooting a bolt of shock straight through Liz's heart.

'Hi!' he said, actually grinning at her. 'You might

need a scarf for your hair. It's a glorious morning so I've put the hood of my car down.'

Scarf...the tiger print scarf for this outfit, she could hear Diana saying. 'Won't be a moment,' she managed to get out and wheeled away, heading for her bedroom to the beat of a suddenly drumming heart, leaving him standing outside her apartment, not even thinking to invite him in. Her mind was stuck on the word, scarf, probably because it served to block out everything else.

Despite the speedy collection of this accessory, Cole had stepped into her living room and was glancing around when she emerged from the bedroom. 'Good space. Nice high ceilings,' he commented appreciatively.

'Built in the nineteen thirties,' she explained on her way to the door, feeling his intrusion too keenly to let him linger in her home.

'Do you own or rent?' he asked curiously.

'It's partly mine. I'm paying off the bank.'

'Fine investment,' he approved.

'I think so. Though primarily I wanted a place of my own.'

'Most women acquire a home through marriage,' he said with a slightly cynical edge.

Or through divorce, Liz thought, wondering how much his almost ex-wife had taken him for and whether that experience had contributed to his detachment from the human race.

'Well, I wasn't counting on that happening,' she said dryly, holding the door and waving him out—a pointed gesture which was ignored.

'You like your independence?' he asked, cocking a quizzical eyebrow at her.

She shrugged. 'Not particularly. I've just found it's better to only count on what I know I can count on.'

'Hard lesson to learn,' he remarked sympathetically.

Had he learnt it, too?

Liz held her tongue. He was finally moving out, waiting for her to lock the door behind them. She didn't know what to think of the probing nature of his conversation. Or was it just casual chat? Maybe she was too used to Cole's habit of never saying anything without purpose.

Still, the sense of being targeted on a personal level persisted and it was some relief that he didn't speak at all as they descended the flight of stairs to street level. Perversely the silence made her more physically aware of him as he walked beside her. She was glad when they emerged into the open air.

It was, indeed, a glorious morning. There was something marvellous about winter sunshine—the warmth and brightness it delivered, the crisp blue of a cloudless sky banishing all thought of cold grey. It lifted one's spirits with its promise of a great day.

'Lucky we don't have to be shut up in the office,' Liz said impulsively, the words accompanied by a smile she couldn't repress.

'An unexpected pleasure,' Cole replied, his smile raising tingles of warmth the sun hadn't yet bestowed.

Liz was piqued into remarking, 'I thought work was the be-all and end-all for you.'

His laser-like eyes actually twinkled at her. 'My life does extend a little further than that.'

Her heart started fluttering. Was he *flirting?* 'Well, obviously, you do care about your mother.'

'Mmmh…a few other things rate my attention, too.'

His slanted look at her caused a skip in her pulse beat and provoked Liz into open confrontation. 'Like what?'

He laughed. He actually laughed. Liz was shocked into staring at him, never having seen or heard Cole Pierson laugh before. It was earth-shaking stuff. He suddenly appeared much younger, happily carefree, and terribly, terribly attractive. The blue eyes danced at her with wicked amusement, causing her to flush in confusion.

'What's so funny?' she demanded.

'Me…you…and here we are.' Still grinning, he gestured to the kerb, redirecting her gaze to the car parked beside it.

Hood down, he'd said, alerting her to the fact that he had to be driving some kind of convertible. If anything, Liz would have assumed a BMW roadster or a Mercedes sports, maybe even a Rolls-Royce Corniche—very expensive, of course, but in a classy conventional style, like his Armani suits.

It was simply impossible to relate the car she was seeing to the boss she knew. She stared at the low-slung, glamorous, silver speed machine in shocked disbelief, her feet rooted on the sidewalk as Cole moved forward and opened the passenger door for her.

'You drive...a Maserati?' Her voice emerged like a half-strangled squawk.

'Uh-huh. The Spyder Cambio Corsa,' he elaborated, naming the model for her.

'A Maserati,' she repeated, looking her astonishment at him.

'Something wrong with it?'

She shook her head, belatedly connecting his current sexy clothes to the sexy car and blurting out, 'This is such a change of image...'

'Welcome to the club,' he said sardonically.

'I beg your pardon?'

She was totally lost with this Cole Pierson, as though he'd changed all the dimensions of his previous persona, emerging as a completely different force to be reckoned with. To top off her sense of everything shifting dangerously between them, he gave her a sizzling head-to-toe appraisal that had her entire skin surface prickling with heat.

'You can hardly deny you've subjected me to a change of image this week, Liz,' he drawled, 'And that was at work, not at play.'

Was he admitting the same kind of disturbance she was feeling now? Whatever...the old boat was being severely rocked on many levels.

'So this is you...at play,' she said in a weak attempt to set things right again.

'One part of me.' There was a challenging glint in his eyes as he waved an invitation to the slinky low black leather passenger seat. 'Shall we go?'

Diana's voice echoed through her head... *Go with the flow.*

Liz forced her feet forward and dropped herself onto the seat as gracefully as she could, swinging her legs in afterwards. 'Thanks,' she murmured as the door was closed for her, then trying for a light note, she smiled and added, 'Nothing like a new experience.'

'You've never ridden in a high-performance car?' he queried as he swung around to the driver's side.

'First time,' she admitted.

'Seems like we're clocking up a few first times between us.'

How many more, Liz thought wildly, acutely aware of him settling in the seat next to her, strong thigh muscles stretching the fabric of his jeans.

'Seat belt,' he reminded her as he fastened his own.

'Right!'

He watched her pull it across her body and click it into place. It made Liz extremely conscious of the belt bisecting her breasts, emphasising their curves.

'Scarf.' Another reminder.

She flushed, quickly spreading the long filmy tiger-print fabric over her hair, winding it around her neck and tying the floating ends at the back.

'Sunglasses.'

It was like a countdown to take-off.

Luckily she always carried sunglasses in her handbag. Having whipped them out and slipped them on, she dared a look at him through the tinted lenses.

He gave her a devil-may-care grin as he slid his own onto his nose. 'You want to watch those jungle prints, Liz. Makes me wonder if you're yearning for a ride on the wild side.'

Without waiting for a reply—which was just as well because she was too flummoxed to think of one—he switched on the engine, put the car into gear, and they were off, the sun in their faces, a wind whipping past, and all sorts of wild things zipping through Liz's mind.

CHAPTER SIX

LIZ couldn't help feeling it was fantastic, riding around in a Maserati. The powerful acceleration of the car meant they could zip into spaces in the traffic that would have closed for less manoeuvrable vehicles. Pedestrians stared enviously at it when they were stopped at traffic lights. They looked at her and Cole, too, probably speculating about who they were, mentally matching them up to the luxurious lifestyle that had to go with such a dream car. After one such stop, Liz was so amused by this she burst out laughing.

'What's tickling your sense of humour?' Cole inquired.

'I feel like the Queen of Sheba and a fraud at the same time,' she answered, grinning at the madness of her being seen as belonging to a Maserati, which couldn't be further than the truth.

'Explain.'

The typical economical command put her on familiar ground again with Cole. 'It's the car,' she answered happily. 'Because I'm your passenger, people are seeing me as someone who has to be special.'

'And you think that's funny?'

'Well, it is, isn't it? I mean you are who you are...but I'm just your employee.'

'Oh, I don't know.' His mouth quirked as he

glanced at her. 'You do have a touch of the Queen of Sheba about you today.'

This comment wasn't boss-like at all. Liz tried to laugh it off but wasn't sure the laughter sounded natural. She was glad he was wearing sunglasses, dimming the expression in the piercing blue eyes. As it was, the soft drawl of his voice had curled around her stomach, making it flutter.

'And why shouldn't they think you're special?' he continued with a longer glance at her. 'I do.'

Liz took a deep breath, desperate to regather her scattered wits. 'That's not the point, Cole. I mean…this car…your wealth…I'm sure you take it all for granted, but it's not me.'

'Do you categorise anyone born to wealth as *special?*' he demanded critically.

'Well…they're at least privileged.'

'Privileged, yes. Which, more times than not, means spoiled, not special.' He shook his head. 'I bought a Maserati because I like high performance. You've remained my P.A. because you give me high performance, too. In my view, you match this car more than any other woman who has ridden in that passenger seat.'

More than the fabulous Tara Summerville?

Liz couldn't believe it.

Unless Cole had acquired the Maserati *after* the separation with his wife.

On second thoughts, he'd been talking performance, not appearance, which reduced the compliment to a work-related thing, puncturing Liz's bubble of pleasure.

'You know, being compared favourably to how well an engine runs doesn't exactly make a woman feel special, Cole,' she dryly informed him.

He laughed. 'So how do I answer you? Hmm...' His brow furrowed in concentration. 'I think you were being a fraud to yourself all the time you were with Brendan, but now you're free of him, the real you has emerged in a blaze of glory and everyone is seeing the shine and recognising how special you are, so you're not a fraud today.' He grinned at her. 'How's that?'

She had to laugh. It was over the top stuff but it did make her feel good, as though she really had shed the miserable cloak of feeling less—deserving less— than her beautiful sisters. 'It wasn't so much Brendan's influence,' she felt obliged to confess. 'I guess I've had a problem with self-esteem for a long time.'

'What on earth for?' he demanded, obviously seeing no cause for it.

She shook her head, not wanting to get into analysing her life. 'Let me relish *blaze of glory*. I can smile over that for the rest of the trip.' Suiting action to words, she gave him her best smile.

He shook his head, still puzzled. 'Would it help for you to know I hold you in the highest esteem?'

'Thank you. It's very kind of you to say so.'

'I can hear a *but* in there.'

Her smile turned rueful. 'I guess what you're giving me is respect for what I can carry out for you. And I'm glad to have your respect. Please don't think I'm not. But I've never felt...incompetent...in that area, Cole. Though I have wondered if being too damned smart is more a curse than a blessing.'

'It's a gift. And it's stupid not to use it. You won't be happy within yourself if you try denying it. You know perfectly well it pleases you to get things right, Liz.'

'Mmmh…but I'm not happy living in a world of my own. I want…' She stopped, realising just how personal this conversation had become, and how embarrassing it might be in retrospect, especially on Monday when she had to face Cole at work again.

'Go on,' he pressed.

She tried shrugging it off. 'Oh, all the usual things a woman wants.'

'Fair enough.'

To Liz's immense relief, he let it go at that. She'd been running off at the mouth, drawn into speaking from her heart instead of her head, all because Cole had somehow invaded her private life and was involving himself in it.

Her gaze drifted to the leather gloved hands on the steering wheel. Power controlling power. A convulsive little shiver of excitement warned her she should get her mind right off tempting fantasies. But it was very difficult with Cole looking as he did, driving this car, and dabbling in highly personal conversation.

She did her best to focus on the passing scenery, a relatively easy task once they hit the road along the northern beaches, passing through Dee Why, Collaroy, Narrabeen, then further on, Bilgola, Avalon, Whale Beach. Apart from the attraction of sand and sea, there were some fabulous homes along the way, making the most of million dollar views. Liz had never actually visited this part of Sydney, knew it only by repute, so it was quite fascinating to see it firsthand.

Finally they came to Palm Beach, right at the end of the peninsula, where large mansions overlooked the ocean on one side and Pittwater the other. Cole turned the Maserati into a semicircular driveway for what looked like a palatial Mediterranean villa with many colonnaded verandahs. It was painted a creamy pink and positively glowed in the sunshine. A fountain of dolphins was centred on the front lawn and a hedge of glorious pink and cream Hawaiian hibiscus lined the driveway.

'Wow!' Liz breathed.

'It is far too large for my mother, requires mountainous maintenance, but she won't leave it,' Cole said in a tone of weary resignation.

'Neither would I,' Liz replied feelingly, turned chiding eyes to Nancy's son. 'She must love it. Leaving would be a terrible wrench.'

Cole sighed. 'She's alone. She's getting old. And she's a long way out from the city.'

Liz understood his point. 'You worry about her.'

He brought the Maserati to a halt, switched off the engine. 'She is my mother,' he stated in the sudden quiet.

And he loved her, thereby passing the functional family background test, unlike Brendan. Liz clamped down on the wayward thought and pushed her mind back onto track.

'I *will* look after her on this trip, Cole.'

He smiled. 'I know I can count on you. And while your ex-boyfriend may not have appreciated your responsible streak, I do. And I don't count on many people for anything.'

Over the past year she had considered him totally self-sufficient. Coldly self-sufficient. It gave Liz a rush of warm pleasure to hear him express some dependence on her, even if it was only peripheral.

No man is an island, she thought.

No woman is, either.

Liz was very conscious of needs that remained unanswered. They'd just been highlighted by Cole's comparing himself to Brendan.

Deliberately highlighted?

For what purpose?

He took off his sunglasses and tucked them into the top pocket of his leather jacket. Liz was prompted into taking hers off, too. She was about to meet his mother again and she didn't need any defensive barrier with Nancy Pierson.

'Want to remove your scarf before we go inside?'

She'd forgotten the scarf, forgotten her hair. Cole sat watching as she quickly unwound the protective cover and tucked it under the collar of her jacket, letting the ends fall loose down the front. Having whipped out a brush from her handbag, she fluffed up her flattened hair and trusted that she hadn't eaten off her lipstick because painting her mouth under Cole's gaze was not on. As it was, she was super conscious of him observing her actions and their effect.

'Okay?' she asked, turning to show herself for his approval.

His eyes weren't their usual ice blue. They seemed to simmer over her face and hair, evoking a flush as he drawled, 'All things bright and beautiful.'

Then he was out of the car and at the passenger door before Liz found the presence of mind to release her seat belt. As she freed herself and swung her feet to the ground, he offered his hand for the long haul upright. It was an automatic response to take it, yet his grip shot an electric charge up her arm and when she rose to her full height, they were standing so close and he seemed so big, she stared at the centre of his throat rather than risk looking up and sparking any realisation of her acute physical awareness of him.

She could even smell the leather, and a hint of male cologne. His broad shoulders dwarfed hers, stirring a sense of sexual vulnerability that quite stunned her because she'd never felt overwhelmed by the close presence of any other man. And this was her boss, who should have been familiar, not striking these weird chords that threatened to change everything between them.

'I didn't realise you were so small,' he murmured in a bemused tone.

Her head jerked up as a sense of belittlement shot through her. The gold sparks in her green eyes blazed at him. 'I hate being *small.*'

His brows drew together in mock concern. 'Correction. Dainty and delicate.'

'Oh, great! Now I sound breakable.'

'Woman of steel?'

His eyes were twinkling.

She took a deep breath and summoned up a wry smile. 'Sorry. You hit a sore point. Unlike you, I was behind the door when God gave out height.'

He openly grinned. 'But you weren't behind the door when God gave out quick wit. Which you'll undoubtedly have to use to keep my mother in line.'

With that comment he led off towards the front door of the pink mansion and Liz fell into step beside him, still fiercely wishing she was as tall as her sisters, which would make her a much better physical match for him. Somehow that 'small' comment felt as though she'd been marked down in the attraction stakes.

On the other hand, she was probably suffering from an overactive imagination to think Cole was attracted at all, and she'd do well to concentrate her mind on exercising the quick wit he credited her with, because the real purpose of this trip was about to get under way.

The front door was opened just as they were stepping up onto the ground floor verandah. 'At last!' Nancy Pierson cried in a tone of pained relief.

Cole checked his watch. 'It's only just eleven, Mum.'

'I know, dear, but I've been counting the minutes since Tara arrived. You could have warned me...'

'Tara?' Cole's face instantly tightened. 'What the devil is she doing here?'

Nancy looked confused. 'She said...'

'You shouldn't have let her in.'

The confusion deepened, hands fluttering a helpless appeal. 'She *is* still your wife.'

'A technicality. One that will end next week.'

This evoked a huff of exasperation from his mother. 'Tara gave me the impression it was arranged for her to meet you here.'

'There's no such arrangement. You've been manipulated, Mum.'

'Well, I'm glad you recognise Tara's skill at doing that, Cole,' came the swift and telling retort. Clearly Nancy held no warm feelings for the woman her son had married. 'I set out morning tea in the conservatory. She's there waiting for you, making herself at home as though she had every right to.'

'Makes for one hell of a scene,' Cole ground out.

'Well, it's not my place to shut her out of your life. It's you who has to make that good. If you have a mind to.'

'Tara's made you doubt it?'

Another huff of exasperation. 'How am I supposed to know what you feel, Cole? You never talk about it. For all I know, you've been pining over that woman…'

'No way!'

'Then you'd better go and convince her of that because she's acting as though she only has to crook her little finger at you and…'

'An act is what it is, Mum.' He flashed a steely glance at Liz. 'As you've just heard, we have some unexpected company for morning tea.'

'I'll take Liz upstairs with me,' Nancy rushed out,

shooting an anguished look at her. 'I'm sorry, dear. This isn't what I planned.'

'Which is precisely why you won't scurry off with Liz,' Cole broke in tersely. 'I will not have her treated like some backroom nonentity because my almost ex-wife decides to barge in on us.'

Nancy looked shocked. 'I didn't mean…'

'It's an issue of discretion, Cole,' Liz quickly supplied. 'I don't mind giving you privacy.'

'Which plays right into Tara's scheme. We're not changing *anything* for her.' Angry pride shifted into icy command. 'Mum, you will lead back to the conservatory. Liz, you will accompany my mother as you normally would. We are going to have the morning tea which has been prepared for *us.*'

He gestured her forward, unshakable determination etched on his face. Liz glanced hesitantly at his mother whom she was supposed to be pleasing today. The anguish was gone from Nancy's expression. In fact, there seemed to be a look of smug delight in her eyes as she, too, waved Liz into the house.

'Please forgive me for not greeting you properly, dear,' she said with an apologetic smile. 'These problems in communication do throw one out.'

'Perfectly understandable,' Liz assured her. Then taking her cue from Cole's command to act normally, she smiled and said, 'I love the look of your home, Nancy. It's very welcoming.'

'How nice of you to say so!' Nancy beamed her pleasure as she hooked her arm around Liz's and drew her into a very spacious foyer, its tiled floor laid out in a fascinating mosaic pattern depicting coral and seashells. 'I picked everything myself for this house. Even these tiles on the floor.'

'They're beautiful,' Liz said in sincere admiration, trying not to be too conscious of Cole closing the door behind them, locking them into a scene that was bound to be fraught with tension and considerable unpleasantness, since Tara Summerville had obviously come expecting to gain something and Cole was intent on denying her.

Nancy continued to point out features of the house as she showed Liz through it, feeding off the interest expressed and enjoying telling little stories about various acquisitions, quite happy not to hurry back to her uninvited guest. Liz suspected Nancy was taking satisfaction in keeping Tara waiting.

Cole didn't push his mother to hurry, either, seemingly content to move at her pace, yet Liz sensed his seething impatience with the situation that had been inflicted on all of them by the woman he'd married.

He must have loved her once, Liz reasoned.

Had the love died, or had husband and wife been pulled apart by grief over the loss of their child?

She had never speculated over her boss's marriage—none of her business—but the exchange between mother and son at the door had ignited a curiosity Liz couldn't deny now. She wanted to see how Cole and Tara Summerville reacted to each other, wanted to know the cause of the ruction between them, wanted to feel Cole was now truly free of his wife...*which may not be the case.*

Surely a private meeting would have served his purpose for ending it more effectively.

Was his angry pride hiding a vulnerability to his wife's power to manipulate his feelings?

Was he using Liz and his mother as a shield, not trusting himself in a one-on-one situation?

As they approached the conservatory, Nancy's prattling began to sound nervous and the tension emanating from Cole seemed to thicken the air, causing Liz to hold her breath. She sensed something bad was about to happen.

Very bad.

And she found herself suddenly wishing she wasn't in the middle of it.

CHAPTER SEVEN

LIZ caught a quick impression of abundant ferns, exotic plants, many pots of gorgeous cyclamens in bloom, all forming a glorious backdrop to settings of cane furniture cushioned in tropical prints. However, even as she entered the conservatory her gaze was drawn to the woman seated at the far end of a long rectangular table.

'Cole, darling...' she drawled, perfect red lips pursing to blow a kiss at him as she rose from her chair, giving them all the full benefit of what the media still termed 'the body' whenever referring to Tara Summerville.

She wore a black leather jacket that moulded every curve underneath it, with enough buttons undone to promise a spillage of lush feminine flesh if one more button was popped. This was teamed with a tight little miniskirt, also in black leather, and with a front split that pointed up the apex of possibly the most photographed legs in history—long, long legs that led down to sexy little ankle high boots. A belt in black and white cowhide was slung jauntily around her hips and a black and white handkerchief scarf was tied at the base of her very long throat.

Her thick mane of tawny hair tumbled down to her shoulder-blades in highly touchable disarray and her artfully made-up amber eyes gleamed a provocative challenge at the man she was intent on targeting. Not so much as a glance at Liz. Nor at Nancy Pierson. This was full power tunnel vision at Cole and Liz suspected the whole beam of it was sizzling with sexual invitation.

'I'm glad you're on your feet, Tara,' Cole said in icy disdain of this approach. 'Just pick up your bag and keep on walking, right out of this house.'

'Very uncivil of you, darling, especially when *your mother* invited me in,' she returned with a cat-like smile, halting by a side chair and gripping the back of it, making a stand against being evicted.

'You lied to her,' came the blunt rebuttal.

'Only to get past your pride, Cole. Now that I'm here for you, why not admit that pride is…' She rolled her hips and moved her mouth into a sensual pout. '…a very cold bedfellow.'

'Waste of time and effort, Tara. Might as well move on. I have,' he stated emphatically.

'Then why haven't I heard a whisper of it?' she mocked, still exuding confidence in her ability to get to him.

'I no longer care to mix in your social circle.'

'You're *news,* Cole. There would have been tattle somewhere if you'd…*moved on.*'

'I prefer to guard my privacy these days.'

He was stonewalling, Liz thought. If there'd been any woman in his life since Tara, some evidence of the relationship would have shown up, at least to her as his personal assistant—telephone calls, bookings to be made, various arrangements. Was it pride, resisting the offer Tara was blatantly making? Or did he truly not want her anymore?

'Don't tell me you've taken to slumming it,' Tara tossed at him derisively.

'Not every woman has your need for the limelight,' Cole returned, icy disdain back in his voice. 'And since I'll never be a party to it again, I strongly recommend you go and find yourself a fellow game player to shine with. You're not about to win anything here.'

Her eyes narrowed, not caring to look defeat in the face. For the first time, her gaze slid to Liz. A quick up and down appraisal left her feeling she'd been raked to the bone. The fact that Nancy was still hugging her arm didn't go unnoticed, either. Without any warning, Tara flashed a bolt of venom at Cole's mother.

'You never did like me, did you, Nancy?'

Liz felt the older woman stiffen under the direct attack, but she was not lacking in firepower herself. 'It's difficult to like such a totally self-centred person as yourself, Tara,' she said with crisp dignity.

A savagely mocking smile was aimed right back at her. 'No doubt you've been producing sweet little protégées for Cole ever since I left.' Her glittering gaze moved to Liz. 'So who and what is this one?'

'*I* brought Liz with me,' Cole stated tersely. 'Her presence here has nothing to do with you and your exit is long overdue.'

'*Your* choice, Cole?' One finely arched eyebrow rose in amused query. 'In place of *me?*'

The comparison was meant to humiliate, but on

seeing his wife in the flesh again, Liz had already conceded she'd never be able to compete in the looks department. She just didn't have the female equipment Tara Summerville had. Not even close to it. But since it could be argued there was something positive to be said for an admirable character and an appealing personality—neither of which was overly evident in Cole's wife—the nasty barb didn't hit too deeply. What actually hurt more was Cole's response to it.

'Oh, for God's sake! Liz has been my personal assistant for the past three years. You used to waltz past her on your way to my office in times gone by, though typically, you probably didn't bother noticing her.'

It was a curt dismissal of the *his choice* tag, implying there was no chance of her ever being anything more than his personal assistant. It shouldn't have felt like a stab to her heart, but it did.

'The little brown mouse!' Tara cried incredulously, then tossed her head back as laughter trilled from her throat.

Liz's stomach knotted. She knew intuitively that Tara Summerville hadn't finished with her. The nerve-jangling laughter was bound to have a nasty point to it. The amber eyes glinted maliciously at her as the remarks rolled.

'How handy, being Cole's P.A.! Saw your chance and took it, jazzing yourself up, making yourself *available,* and here you are, getting your hooks into Mummy, as well, playing Miss All-Round-Perfect.'

The rush of blood to Liz's head was so severe she didn't hear what Cole said, only the angry bark of his voice. She saw the response to it though, Tara swinging back to pick up her bag, slinging the strap of it over her shoulder, strutting towards Cole, pausing to deliver one last broadside.

'You've been *had,* Cole. No doubt she's hitting all the right chords for you...but I bet she can't match me in bed. Think about it, darling. It's not too late to change your mind.'

Both of them left the conservatory, Tara leading off like a victor who'd done maximum damage, Cole squeezing Liz's shoulder first in a silent gesture of appreciation for her forebearance, then following Tara out to enforce her departure and possibly have the last word before she left.

Liz was so sick with embarrassment, she didn't know what to do or say. The worst of it was, Tara had literally been echoing Diana's calculated plan to *get the boss.* While that had not been part of Liz's motivation for going along with her sisters' makeover plan, Tara's accusations had her squirming with guilt over the feelings that had emerged this past week, the growing desire for Cole to find her attractive.

Fortunately, Nancy moved straight into hostess mode, drawing Liz over to the table and filling the awkward silence with a torrent of words. 'Tara always did make an ugly scene when she wasn't getting her own way. You mustn't take anything she said to heart, dear. Pure spite. You just sit yourself down and relax and I'll make us a fresh pot of tea. Help yourself to a pastry or a scone with strawberry jam and cream. That's Cole's favourite. I always make him Devonshire tea.'

Liz sat. Her gaze skated distractedly over a selection of small Danish pastries with fillings of glazed fruit—apricot, apple, peach—the plate of scones beside dishes of cream and strawberry jam. Nothing prompted an appetite. She thought she would choke on food.

Nancy moved to what was obviously a drinks bar, easily accessible to the swimming pool beyond the conservatory. She busied herself behind it, apparently unaffected by the suggestion that Liz and Cole were having an affair, though she must be suspecting it now, adding in the fact that Cole had arranged for his P.A. to accompany her on a pleasure trip. It was, after all, an extraordinary thing to do, given there was no closer connection between them than boss and employee.

Liz couldn't bear Nancy thinking she was Cole's mistress on the side. It made her seem underhand, sleazy, hiding the intimacy from his mother, pretending everything was straight and aboveboard.

'I'm not having a secret affair with Cole. I've never slept with him…or…or anything like that,' she blurted out, compelled to clear any murkiness from their relationship.

Nancy looked up from her tea-making, startled by the emphatic claim. Her blue eyes were very direct, projecting absolute certainty as she replied, 'I have no doubt whatsoever about that, dear. I questioned Cole about you before we met on Monday. His answers revealed…' She heaved a deep sigh. '…he only thought of you as very capable.'

The flush in Liz's cheeks still burned. Although she'd known Cole had not been aware of her as a woman, certainly not before this past week, that truth was not quite so absolute now. He *was* seeing her differently, and even though it might not *mean* what Diana wanted it to mean, Liz couldn't let Tara's interpretation of her changed appearance go unanswered.

'I'm not out to *get* him, either.'

Nancy heaved another deep sigh, then gave her a sad little smile. 'I almost wish you were, dear, but I don't think it's in your nature.'

It startled Liz out of her wretched angst. 'You wish…?'

'I probably shouldn't say this…' Nancy's grimace revealed her own inner angst. '…but I'm very afraid Cole is still stuck on Tara. What she said is all too true. And I'm sure you must know it, as well. There hasn't been any other woman in his life since she left him. It's like he's sealed himself off from every normal social connection.'

Liz nodded. She was well acquainted with *the untouchable ice man.*

Nancy rattled on, voicing her main concern. 'But if Tara is now determined on getting her hooks into him again…' A shake of the head. 'I can only hope Cole has the good sense to go through with the divorce and have done with her.'

Liz kept her mouth shut. It wasn't appropriate for her to comment on Cole's personal life when it had nothing to do with her. The stress of Tara's visit had wrung this confidence from Nancy, just as it had driven Liz to defend herself. Where the truth lay about Cole's feelings for his wife, she had no idea.

Though now that Nancy had spelled out her viewpoint, it did seem he had to be carrying a lot of emotional baggage from his marriage—baggage he'd systematically buried under intensive work.

Was the physical confrontation with his wife stirring it all up? He hadn't come back from seeing her out of the house. Maybe they were still talking, arguing as couples do when neither of them really wanted to let go. Any foothold—even a bitter one—was better than none. And Cole was unhampered by witnesses now. What if Tara had thrown her arms around him, physically pressing for a resumption of intimacy? Was it possible for him to be totally immune to what 'the body' was offering?

A sick depression rolled through Liz. Cole had only noticed her this past week because *the little brown mouse* didn't fit that label anymore. Which was probably still an annoyance to him. Or a curiosity, given his questioning about Brendan. Nothing to do with a sudden attraction which she'd probably fabricated out of her own secret wanting it to be so.

A foolish fantasy.

Why on earth would a man like him—a handsome billionaire—be attracted to her when he could snap his fingers and have the Tara Summervilles of this world? She must have been mad to let Diana influence her thinking. Or desperate to feel something excitingly positive after being dumped by Brendan.

'Oh! There's Cole with the tradesman!' Nancy cried in relief.

The remark halted Liz's miserable reverie and directed her gaze out to the pool area where Nancy was looking. Cole was, indeed, with another man, pointing out a section of paving and leading him towards it.

'He must have arrived while Cole was seeing Tara out. They've come down the side path,' Nancy prattled on, her spirits perking up at this evidence that her son's delayed return did not mean he was being vamped by his almost ex-wife. 'The appointment was at eleven o'clock, after all. So fortuitous.'

It didn't guarantee that Cole had maintained his rejection of any reunion, but it certainly minimised the opportunity for persuasion on his wife's part. Liz found herself hoping that Tara had not *won* anything from him, and not just because of being interrupted by the arrival of the tradesman. Nancy didn't like the woman and Liz certainly had no reason to. But no doubt the power of sex could turn some men blind to everything else.

'Now we can enjoy our morning tea,' Nancy declared, carrying an elegant china teapot to the table and setting it down with an air of happy satisfaction. Clearly danger had been averted in her mind. She settled on the chair opposite to Liz's and eyed her with bright curiosity.

'Pardon me for asking, dear, but was it just this week that you...uh...jazzed yourself up?'

'During my vacation,' Liz answered, not minding the question from Nancy, knowing she could find out from Cole anyway. 'My sisters ganged up on me, saying I'd let myself become drab, and hauled me off to do their Cinderella trick.'

'Well, whatever they did, you do look lovely.'

'Thank you.'

'Tea?'

'Yes, please.'

Nancy poured. 'So you came back to work on Monday with a new image,' she said, smiling encouragement.

'Yes.'

'Did Cole notice any difference?'

Liz grimaced. 'He didn't like it.'

'Didn't like how you looked?'

'Didn't like me looking different, I think.' Liz shrugged. 'No doubt he'll get used to it.'

'Milk and sugar?'

Liz shook her head. 'Just as it is, thank you.'

'Do have a scone, dear.'

Liz took one out of politeness, though she did feel calmer now and thought there'd be no problem with swallowing. It was a relief to have Nancy understanding her situation. It would have been extremely uncomfortable accompanying Cole's mother on the trip, with her still thinking all sorts of horribly false things.

Having cut the scone in half, Liz was conscientiously spooning strawberry jam and cream onto her plate when her ragged nerves received another jolt.

'Oh, good! Cole is coming in for his tea,' Nancy announced, causing Liz to jerk around in her chair to see her boss skirting the pool and heading for the conservatory, having left the tradesman to measure the paving area and calculate the cost of the work to be done.

Totally mortified by the tide of heat that rushed up her neck again, Liz focused hard on transferring the jam and cream to the halved scone. If she shoved the food into her mouth and appeared to be eating, she reasoned that Cole might only speak to his mother. It might be a cowardly tactic but she didn't feel up to coping with his penetrating gaze and probing questions. She didn't even want to look at him. He might have lipstick smudged on his mouth.

Which was none of her business!

Why she felt so violent about that she didn't know and didn't want to know. She just wanted to be left out of anything to do with Tara Summerville.

She heard a glass door slide open behind her and it felt as though a whoosh of electric energy suddenly permeated the air. Her hands started trembling. It stopped her from lifting the scone to her mouth. She glared at her plate, hating being affected like this. It wasn't fair. She'd done nothing wrong.

'Liz…'

She gritted her teeth.

He had no right to put her on the spot, commanding her attention when they weren't even at work. She was here in her spare time, as a favour to his mother, not as *his* personal assistant.

'Are you okay?' he asked, amazingly in a tone of concern.

Pride whipped her head around to face him. There was no trace of red lipstick on his mouth. His expression was one of taut determination, the piercing blue eyes intensely concentrated, aimed at searching her mind for any trouble.

Her chin tilted in direct challenge as she stated, 'I have no reason not to be okay.'

He gave a slow nod. 'I didn't anticipate a collateral hit from Tara. I regret you were subjected to it.'

'A hit only works if there's damage done. I've assured your mother there's no truth in what was assumed about me...and you.' *And don't you dare think otherwise,* she fiercely telegraphed to him.

His gaze flicked sharply to Nancy. 'You didn't believe that rank bitchiness, did you, Mum?'

'No, dear. And I told Liz so.'

'Right! No harm done then,' he said, apparently satisfied. 'Got to get back to check that this guy knows what's he's quoting on.'

'What about your tea?' Nancy asked.

'I'll have it later.'

He stepped outside, closed the door, and to all intents and purposes, the nasty incident with Tara Summerville was also closed. Liz certainly wasn't about to bring the subject up again. She realised her hands were clenched in her lap and consciously relaxed them. The scone was waiting to be eaten. She'd eat it if it killed her. It proved she was okay.

'Well, isn't that nice?' Nancy remarked, beaming pleasure at her as Liz lifted one half of the scone from her plate.

She looked blankly at Cole's mother, completely lost on whatever had struck her as *nice.*

'He cares about you, dear.' This said with a benevolent smile that thoroughly approved of the supposed caring.

Liz felt too frazzled to argue the point.

She only hoped that Cole had completely dismissed the idea—planted by Tara—that his personal assistant was focused far more on climbing into bed with him than doing the work she was employed to do.

CHAPTER EIGHT

MAKE another baby…

Cole seethed over Tara's last toss at him and all the memories it aroused. He ended up accepting the quotation for the paving work around the pool without even questioning it. He didn't care if the guy was overcharging. As long as the job was done by a reputable tradesman, the cost was irrelevant. All the money in the world could not buy back the life of the baby son he'd lost. Though it could obviously buy back a wife who was prepared to pay lip-service to being a mother again.

A mother…

What a black joke that was!

And the gross insensitivity of Tara's even thinking he'd consider her proposition was typical of her total lack of empathy to how he felt. God! He wouldn't want her in the same house as any child of his, let alone being the biological mother to it, having the power to affect its upbringing in so many negative ways.

David had only ever been a show-off baby to her— trotting him out in designer clothes when it suited her, ignoring him when he needed her. *Their son* hadn't even left a hole in her life when he died, and she'd resented the huge hole he'd left in Cole's—impatient with his grief, ranting about how cold he was to her, seeking more cheerful company because he was such *a drag*.

Did Tara imagine he could forget all that just because they'd started out having great sex and she still had 'the body' to excite him again if she put her mind to it?

He hadn't even felt a tingle in his groin when she'd tried her come-on this morning.

Not a tingle.

Though he had felt a blaze of fury when she'd painted Liz in her own manipulative colours, casting her as a calculating seductress, mocking her efforts to look more attractive. Which she certainly did, though Cole had no doubt the change had been motivated by a need to lift herself out of the doldrums caused by Brendan's defection. Nothing to do with him.

If Liz withered back into a little brown mouse now…because of Tara's bitchiness…Cole seethed over that, too, as he made his way back to the conservatory after seeing the tradesman off. Liz had insisted she was okay, but she hadn't wanted to look at him when he'd asked. When she had turned to answer, her eyes had been all glittery, her cheeks red hot. She'd denied any damage done but Cole suspected her newly grown confidence in herself as a woman had been badly undermined. He wanted to fix that but how…?

Liz and his mother were gone from the conservatory by the time he returned to it, Just as well, since he had no ready antidote for Tara's poison. At least he could trust his mother to be kind to Liz, involve her in the business of packing for their trip. Probably overkind, trying to make up for the nasty taste left behind by her uninvited guest.

He'd made one hell of a mistake marrying that woman. Five more days and the divorce would become final. Thursday. It couldn't come fast enough for Cole.

He made himself a fresh pot of tea, wolfed down a couple of scones, found the morning newspaper and concentrated on shutting Tara out of his mind. She didn't deserve space in it and he wouldn't give it to her.

Having read everything he deemed worth reading, he was attacking the cryptic crossword when his mother returned to the conservatory, wheeling a traymobile loaded with lunch things. Liz trailed behind her, looking anywhere but at him.

'Well, we've worked everything out for the trip,' his mother declared with satisfaction. 'Do clear the table of that newspaper, Cole. And if you'd open a good bottle of red—Cabernet Sauvignon?'

'What are we eating?' he asked, hoping some mundane conversation would make Liz feel more relaxed in his company.

'Lasagne and salad and crispy bread, followed by caramelised pears. And we must hurry because Liz needs to do some shopping and it's after one o'clock already.'

'How much shopping?' he asked as he moved to the bar. 'Mum, have you been pressing Liz to buy a whole lot of stuff to fit what *you* think is needed?'

'Only a few things,' she answered airily. 'Liz didn't understand about the colonial night at The

Strand Hotel in Rangoon where the ladies are invited to wear white, and...'

'Surely it's not obligatory.'

'That's not the point, dear. It's the spirit of the thing.'

He frowned, wondering how much expense his mother was notching up for her companion—costs he simply hadn't envisaged. 'I didn't mean for Liz to be out of pocket over this trip.'

His mother gave him one of those limpidly innocent smiles that spelled trouble. 'Then you could take her shopping so she'll feel right...everywhere we go together.'

'No!' Liz looked horrified by the suggestion, stopping in her setting of cutlery on the table to make a firm stand on the issue. 'You're giving me the trip free, Cole,' she reminded him with vigour. 'And Nancy, I'll get plenty of use out of what I buy anyway. It's no problem.'

The line was drawn and her eyes fiercely defied either of them to cross it.

Cole felt the line all through lunch.

He was her boss.

She was here on assignment.

She would oblige his mother in every way in regard to the trip, but the block on any personal rapport with the man who employed her was rigidly adhered to. She barely looked at him and avoided acknowledging his presence as much as she could without being openly rude. It was very clear to him that what Tara had said about her—and him—was preying on Liz's mind.

It was even worse in the car travelling back into the city. She sat almost scrunched up in the passenger seat, making herself as small as possible, her hands tightly interlinked in her lap. No joy in riding in the Maserati this time, though Cole sensed she was willing the car to go as fast as it could, wanting the trip over and done with so she could get away from him.

It made him angry.

He hated Tara's power to do this to her.

Just because Liz wasn't built like Tara didn't make her less attractive in her own individual way. He liked the new hairstyle on her. It was perky. Drew more attention to her face, too, which had a bright vitality that was very appealing. Very watchable. Particularly her eyes. A lot of power in those sparkly green eyes. As for her figure, certainly on the petite side, but definitely feminine. Sexy, too, in the clothes she'd been wearing. Not in your face sexy. More subtle. Though strong enough to get to him this past week.

Cole was tempted to say so, but he wasn't sure she'd want to hear such things from him, coming on top of Tara's coupling them as she had. It might make Liz shrink even more inside herself, thinking he *was* about to make a move on her. It was damned difficult, given their work situation and her current fragile state.

'I'd appreciate it if you'll drop me off along Military Road at the Mosman shopping centre,' she said abruptly.

He glanced at his watch. Almost three o'clock. Most shops closed at five o'clock on Saturday, except in tourist areas, and Mosman was more a classy suburb. 'I'll park and wait for you. Take you home when you're through shopping.'

'No, please.' Almost a panicky note in her voice. 'I don't want to hold you up.'

'*You'll* be held up, getting public transport home. Apart from which, you wouldn't be shopping but for my mother making you feel you have to,' he argued. 'I'll sit over coffee somewhere and wait for you.'

'I truly don't want you to do that, Cole.' Very tense. 'It will make me feel I have to hurry.'

'Take all the time you want,' he tossed back at her, assuming a totally relaxed air. 'I have nothing in particular to go home to.'

And he didn't like the sense of her running away from him.

A compelling urge to smash the line she had drawn prompted him into adding, 'Actually, I think I'll tag along with you. Give an opinion on what looks good.'

That shocked her out of her defensive shell. Her head jerked towards him. The sunglasses hid the expression in her eyes but if it was horror, he didn't care.

'I will not let you buy anything for me,' she threw at him, a feisty pride rising out of the assault on her grimly held sense of propriety. 'You are not responsible for…for…'

'My mother's love of dressing up for an occasion?' he finished for her, grinning at the steam he'd stoked. 'I couldn't agree more. The responsibility is all yours for indulging her. And you probably don't need me along. Have to admit the clothes you've been wearing this past week demonstrate you have a great eye for what looks good on you.'

Got in that little boost to her confidence, Cole thought, and continued on his roll with a sense of triumphant satisfaction. 'But most women like a man's opinion and since I'm here on the spot, why not? More interesting for me than sitting over coffee by myself.'

'Cole, I'm your P.A., not your...your...'

Lover? Mistress? Wife?

Clearly she couldn't bring herself to voice such provocative positions. Cole relieved her agitation by putting their relationship back on terms she was comfortable with.

'As your boss, who instigated this whole situation, it's clearly within my authority to see that you don't spend too much on pleasing my mother.'

'I'm not stupid!' she cried in exasperation. 'I said I'd only buy what I'll make use of again.'

'Then you can't have any objection to my feeling right about this. Besides, I'll be handy. I'll carry your shopping bags.'

She shook her head in a helpless fashion and slumped back into silence. Cole sensed that resistance was still simmering but he was now determined on this course of action and he was not about to budge from it. Tara was not going to win over Liz Hart. One way or another, he was going to make Liz feel great about herself.

As she should.

She was great at everything she did for him.

Probably make a great mother, too.

Cole grimaced over this last thought.

Time he got Tara out of his head, once and for all. She'd left one hell of a lot of scar tissue but that was no reason for him not to move on. In fact, he'd told her he had, which had spurred the attack on Liz.

Well, at least he was moving on neutralising that— one step in the right direction.

CHAPTER NINE

LIZ'S heart was galloping. Why, why, why was Cole being so perverse, insisting on going shopping with her, foiling her bid to escape the awkwardness she now felt with him? Didn't he realise how personal it was, giving his opinion on what clothes she chose, carrying her shopping bags, acting as though they were *a couple?*

She took several deep breaths in an attempt to calm herself down. Her mind frantically re-examined everything he'd said, searching for clues that might help her understand his motivation. It came as some relief to realise he couldn't think she'd been making a play for him this past week. His comment on the clothes she'd worn to work had been a compliment on her taste, no hint of suspicion that they could have been especially aimed to attract *his* notice.

He'd said he had nothing in particular to go home to and tagging along with her would be more interesting than drinking coffee alone. But weren't men bored by clothes shopping? Brendan had always been impatient with any time spent on it. *That'll do,* had been his usual comment, never a considered opinion on how good anything looked on her.

Maybe with having a famous model as his wife, Cole had learnt some of the tricks of the trade, but thinking of Tara made Liz even more self-conscious about parading clothes in front of him. She couldn't compete. She didn't want to compete. She just wanted to be left alone to lick her wounds in private.

But Cole was already parking the car, pressing the mechanism that installed the hood, getting ready to leave the Maserati in the street while he accompanied her. She knew there'd be no stopping him. Once Cole Pierson made up his mind to do something, no force on earth would deter him from pursuing his goal. But what was his goal here?

Was it just filling in time with her?

She could minimise the shopping as much as seemed reasonable to him.

Reasonable might be the key. He'd said he wanted to *feel right* about what she bought. Which linked this whole thing back to indulging his mother. Nothing really personal at all.

The frenzy in her mind abated. She could cope with this. She had to. Cole was now out of the car and striding around it to the passenger door. Liz hastily released her safety belt and grabbed her handbag from the floor. The door was opened and once again he offered his hand to help her out. Ignoring it was impossible. Liz took it and was instantly swamped by a wave of dynamic energy that fuzzed the coping sector in her mind.

Thankfully he didn't hold on to her hand, releasing it to wave up and down the street, good-naturedly asking, 'Which way do you want to go?'

Liz paused a moment to orient herself. They were in the middle of the shopping centre. Mosman had quite a number of classy boutiques, but her current budget wasn't up to paying their prices, not after the big splurge she'd just had on clothes. She hadn't wanted to ask Diana for help with these extras for the trip. Her sister would inevitably pepper her with questions about her boss, and Liz didn't want to hear them, let alone answer them. There was, however, one inexpensive shop here that might provide all she needed.

'Across the road and to our left,' she directed.

Cole automatically took her arm to steer her safely through the cruising traffic to the opposite sidewalk. She knew it was a courtesy but it felt like a physical claim on her. She was becoming far, far too conscious of her boss as a man. It wasn't even a relief when he resumed simply walking side by side.

'Do you have a particular place in mind?' he asked, glancing at display windows they passed.

'Yes. It's just along here.' She kept her gaze forward, refusing to be tempted by what she couldn't afford. It was the middle of winter but the new spring fashions were already on show everywhere.

'Hold it!' Cole grabbed her arm to halt her progress and pointed to a mannequin dressed in a gorgeous green pantsuit. 'That would be fantastic on you, Liz.'

'Not what I'm looking for,' she swiftly stated, knowing the classy outfit would cost mega-dollars.

He frowned at her as she tugged herself loose and kept walking. 'What are you looking for?'

'A couple of evening tops to go with black slacks and something in white,' she rattled out.

'Black,' he repeated in a tone of disapproval.

'You're going into the tropics, you know. Hot and humid. You should be wearing something light.'

'Black goes anywhere,' she argued.

'I like green on you,' he argued back.

'What you like isn't really relevant, Cole. You won't be there,' she reminded him, glad to make the point that she wasn't out to please *him*.

'My mother would like what I like,' he declared authoritatively. 'I think we should go back and…'

'No. I'm going to look in here,' she insisted, heading into the shop she had targeted.

It was somewhat overcrowded with racks of clothes, but promising a large range of choice which was bound to yield something suitable. However, Liz had barely reached the first rack when Cole grabbed her hand and hauled her outside.

'A second-hand shop?' he hissed, his black brows beetling down at her.

'Quite a lot of second-hand designer wear,' she tersely informed him. 'Classy clothes that have only been worn a few times, if that. They're great bargains and perfectly good.'

'I will not have you wearing some other woman's cast-offs,' he said so vehemently Liz was stunned into silence, not understanding why he found it offensive. His hand lifted and cupped her cheek, his thumb tilting her chin up so the piercing blue eyes bored into hers with commanding intensity. 'I will not have you thinking you only rate seconds. You're a class act, Liz Hart. Top of the top. And you are going to be dressed accordingly.'

He dropped his hand, hooked her arm around his

and marched her back down the street before Liz could find her voice. Her cheek was still burning from his touch and her heartbeat was thundering in her ears. It was difficult to think coherently with his body brushing hers, his long stride forcing her to pick up pace to keep level with him. Nevertheless, something had to be said.

'Cole, I've…I've spent most of my spare money on…on…'

'I'll do the buying,' he cut in decisively. 'Consider it a bonus for being the best P.A. I've ever had.'

Bonus…best P.A.…top of the top…the heady words buzzed around her brain. The compliments were so extraordinary, exhilarating. And suddenly she recalled what his mother had said—*He cares about you.*

Her feet were almost dancing as he swept her into the boutique she had bypassed before. 'We'll try that green,' he told the saleswoman, pointing to the pant-suit on the display mannequin.

There was such a strong flow of power emanating from Cole, the woman virtually jumped to obey. Liz was ushered into a dressing-room and handed the garments in her size in double-quick time.

'I want to see that on,' Cole continued in commanding vein. 'And while Liz is changing, you can show me anything else you have that might do her justice.'

Wearing second-hand clothes had never bothered her, but Cole's determination to *do her justice* was too intoxicating to resist. She fell in love with the apple green pantsuit and his raking look of male appreciation and resounding, 'Yes,' set her heart fluttering with wild excitement. He really did see her as special…and attractive.

Next came a lime green cotton knit top, sleeveless but with a deep cowl neckline that could be positioned many clever ways. It was teamed with white pants printed with lime green pears, strawberries and mangos—the kind of fun item she'd never indulged in. But it did look brilliant on her and she was tempted into striking a jaunty pose when showing the outfit to Cole. He grinned at her, giving a thumbs up sign, and she grinned back, enjoying the madness of the moment. Both green tops would dress up her black slacks, she decided, trying to be a bit sensible.

'That's it for here,' he declared. 'We'll try somewhere else for the white.'

Somewhere else turned out to be a Carla Zampatti boutique, all stocked up with the new spring range from one of the top designers in Australia. With the help of the saleswoman Cole selected a white broderie anglaise skirt with a ruffle hem and a matching peasant blouse. The correct accessories included a dark auburn raffia hip belt featuring a large red, brown and camel stone clip fastening, long Indian earrings dangling with beads and feathers in the same colours, high wedge heeled sandals in white, with straps that crisscrossed halfway up Liz's calves.

The whole effect was absolutely stunning.

Liz couldn't believe how good she looked.

Fine feathers certainly did make fine birds, she thought giddily, waltzing out of the dressing-room on cloud nine. Cole's gaze fastened on her ankles and slowly travelled up, lingering on her bare shoulder where the saleswoman had pulled down the peasant neckline for *the right effect*. A sensual little smile was directed at the exotic earrings and when he finally met her eyes, she saw the simmer of sexual interest in his—unmistakable—and felt her toes curling in response.

'This strappy bandeau top in camel jersey also goes with that skirt,' the saleswoman informed, showing the garment.

'Yes,' Cole said eagerly. 'Let's see it on.'

It fit very snugly, moulding her small firm breasts, which didn't go unnoticed by Cole whose interest in dressing her as *he* liked seemed to gather more momentum. 'I like that filmy leopard print top, too,' he said, pointing to a rack of clothes.

'The silk georgette with the hanky hemmed sleeve?' It was held up for his approval.

'Mmmh…very sexy.'

'It teams well with the bronze satin pants, and the bronze tassel belt,' the saleswoman encouraged, seizing advantage of the obvious fact that Cole was in a buying mood.

Liz felt driven to protest. 'I don't need any more. Truly.'

'Just this one extra lot then,' came the blithe reply. He grinned at her. 'I know you've got bronze shoes. Saw you wearing them last week. And the jungle motif is definitely your style.'

He would not be deterred. Liz couldn't help feeling both elated and guilty as they left the boutique, both of them now laden with shopping bags.

'Happy?' he asked, triumph sparkling in his eyes.

'Yes. But I shouldn't have let you do that.'

He arched a cocky eyebrow at her. 'The choice was all mine.'

She heaved a sigh in the hope of relieving the wild drumming in her chest. 'You've been very generous. Thank you.'

He laughed. 'It was fun, Liz. Maybe that's what both of us need right now. Some fun.'

His eyes flirted with hers.

It was happening. It really was happening. Just as Diana had predicted. But could a classy appearance achieve so much difference in how one was viewed? It didn't seem right. Surely attraction shouldn't depend entirely on surface image. Yet Cole had *married* Tara Summerville, which pointed to his being heavily swayed by how a woman looked.

But he knows me, the person, too, Liz quickly argued to herself. We've worked together for three years. *Best P.A. I've ever had.* And he did like her. Trust and respect were also mixed in with the liking. So this suddenly strong feeling of attraction was acceptable, wasn't it? Not just a fleeting thing of the moment?

They reached the Maserati and Cole unlocked the boot to stow away the host of shopping bags. 'What we should do now…' he said as they unloaded themselves. '…is drop this stuff off at your apartment, then go out to dinner to celebrate.'

'Celebrate what? Your outrageous extravagance?'

'Worth every cent.' He shut the lid of the boot with an air of satisfaction, then smiled at her. 'Pleasure can't always be so easily bought, Liz, and here we are, both of us riding a high.'

She couldn't deny it, but she knew her high was fired by feelings that hadn't been stirred for a very long time, feelings that had nothing to do with new clothes. Not even fabulous clothes. 'So we're celebrating pleasure?'

'Why not?' He took her arm to steer her to the passenger side, opening the door for her as he added, 'Let's put the blight of our ex-partners aside for one night and focus on having fun.'

One night…

The limitation was sobering. So was the reference to ex-partners. As Liz stepped into the car and settled on the passenger seat, she forced herself to take stock of what these remarks could mean. She herself had completely forgotten the blight left by Brendan in the excitement of feeling the sizzle of mutual attraction with Cole. However, she did have three weeks' distance since last being with Brendan. Cole had been very freshly reminded of his relationship with Tara this morning.

Earlier, before the shopping spree, he'd said he had nothing to go home to. Tara had clearly left a huge hole in his life. Had he just been buying a filler for that hole? As well as some sweet private revenge on the woman who'd taken him for much more than Liz would ever cost him?

She glanced sharply at him as he took the driver's seat beside her. One night of fun could mess with their business relationship. Had Cole thought of that or was he in the mood not to care?

He switched on the engine and threw her a smile that quickened her pulse-beat again. 'How about Doyle's at Rose Bay? Feel like feasting on oysters and lobster?'

Oh, why not? she thought recklessly. There was nothing for her to go home to, either. 'Sounds good. But it's Saturday night. Will we get a table?' The famous seafood restaurant on Sydney Harbour was very popular.

'No problem,' he confidently assured her. 'I'll call and book from your apartment.'

No doubt he wouldn't care what it cost for the restaurant to *find* an extra table for two. Cole was on a roll, intent on sweeping her along with him, and Liz decided not to worry about it. Fun was the order of the night and there was nothing wrong with taking pleasure in each other's company.

Diana's advice slid into her mind.

Go with the flow.

For too much of her life Liz had been managing situations, balancing pros and cons, thinking through all the possible factors, choosing what seemed the most beneficial course. She wanted to be free of all that…if only for one night…to simply *go with the flow* and let Cole take care of whatever happened between them.

After all, he was the boss.

The man in command.

CHAPTER TEN

COLE had never thought of his P.A. as delightful, but she was. Maybe it was the influence of the champagne, loosening inhibitions, bringing out bubbles in her personality. It was the first time she'd ever drunk alcohol in his presence. First time they'd ever been away from their work situation, dining together as a social twosome. She was enjoying the fine dinner at Doyle's and he was thoroughly enjoying her company.

Aware that she liked travelling, he'd prompted her into relating what trips she'd like to take in future—the old silk route from Beijing to Moscow, the northwest passage to Alaska, the Inca trail in South America—places he'd never thought of going himself. He'd hit all the high spots—New York, London, Paris, Milan, Hong Kong—but they hadn't been adventures in the sense Liz was talking about—reliving history and relating culture to geography.

Watching her face light up with enthusiasm, her eyes sparkle in anticipation of all there was yet to see and know, Cole mentally kicked himself for allowing his world to become so narrow, so concentrated on the challenge of accumulating more and more money. He should take more time out, make a few journeys into other areas. Though he'd probably need Liz to guide him into seeing what she saw.

Future plans…he had none. Not really. Just keep on doing what he'd been doing. He looked at Liz, taking pleasure in her vitality, in her quest for new experiences, and a question popped into his mind—a question he asked without any forethought of what its impact might be on her.

'Does marriage and having a family fit anywhere in your future, Liz?'

A shadow instantly descended, wiping the sparkle from her eyes, robbing her face of all expression. Her lashes lowered to half mast, as though marking the death of her hopes in that area, and Cole mentally kicked himself for bringing up what must be a raw subject for her with Brendan having walked away from their long-term relationship.

Her shoulders squared. An ironic little smile tilted one corner of her mouth. Her eyes flashed bleakly at him. 'I guess I'm a failure at being desirable wife material. I haven't met anyone who wants to marry me,' she said in a tone of flat defeat.

Cole barely bit down on the urge to tell her she was intensely desirable in every way. Words were useless if they didn't match her experience. But they were true nonetheless. It had been growing on him all day…how different she was to Tara, how much he liked her, how sexy she looked in the right clothes.

His gaze fastened on her mouth. He wanted to kiss away the hurt that had just been spoken, make her smile with joy again, as she had this afternoon, twirling around in that very fetching white skirt. She'd felt all woman then, failing in nothing, and certainly stirring a few pressing male fantasies in Cole.

'What about you?' she asked. 'Would you come at marriage again?'

It jolted him into a harsh little laugh. 'Not in a hurry.'

'Bad experience?'

'Bad judgment on my part.' He shrugged, not wanting to talk about it. 'Though I would like to be a father again,' he added, admitting that joy and sorrow from his marriage.

She nodded, her eyes flashing heartfelt sympathy. 'I would hate to lose a child of mine.'

It had barely caused a ripple in Tara's life, which made her proposition today all the more obscene. He had no doubt Liz would manage motherhood better, probably dote on a child of her own. He recalled her speaking of a number of sisters to his mother and asked about her family, moving the conversation on.

She was an aunt to two nieces and nephews, had a big extended family, lots of affection in her voice. Good people, Cole thought, and wondered how much he'd missed by being an only child. His father hadn't wanted more, even one being an intrusion on the orderly life he'd liked. Though he had been proud of Cole's achievements.

His mother would have liked a daughter. Someone like Liz with whom she could really share things. Not like Tara.

Liz Hart...

Why hadn't he thought of her like this before?

Blind to what was under his nose.

Tara getting in the way, skewing his view, killing

any desire to even look at a woman, let alone involve himself with one.

Besides which, Liz had been attached—might still be emotionally attached—to the guy who'd used her for years, then dumped her. Though clearly she'd been trying to rise out of those ashes, firing herself up to make something else of her life. Still, she'd definitely been burned, thinking of herself as a failure in the female stakes.

It wasn't right.

And on top of that, Tara putting her down this morning.

So wrong.

The rank injustice that had been done to Liz lingered in Cole's mind, even as he drove her home from Doyle's. She was quiet, the bubbles of the night having fizzed out. Facing the prospect of a lonely apartment, he thought, and memories that would bring misery. He didn't like this thought. He didn't like it one bit.

It was just a one off night, Liz told herself, trying to drum it into her foolish head. And she'd probably talked far too much about herself, her tongue let loose by the free flow of beautiful French champagne, delicious food, and Cole showing so much personal interest in her.

But it hadn't been a two way street. Very little had come back to her about him, and on the question of marriage, Cole's instant and derisive reply—*Not in a hurry*—had burst Liz's fantasy bubble. In fact, reflecting on his manner to her over dinner, Liz decided he undoubtedly dealt with clients in the same fashion, drawing them out, listening intently, lots of eye contact, projecting interest. *Charm,* Jayne had called it.

It didn't *mean* anything.

He'd spelled it out beforehand—one night of fun. And now he was driving her home. Nothing more was going to happen. She just wished her nerves would stop leaping around and she'd be able to make the parting smooth and graceful, showing she didn't expect any more from him.

But in her heart she wanted more.

And trying to argue it away wasn't working. The wanting had been building all day. It was now a heaviness in her chest that was impossible to dislodge. A tight heaviness that was loaded down with sadness, as well. Crying for the moon, she thought. Which had shone on her for a little while this evening but would inevitably keep moving and leave her in the dark again.

Cole parked the car outside her apartment, switched off the headlights. Liz felt enveloped in darkness—a lonely darkness, bereft of the vital power of his presence as he left her to stride around to the passenger side. *Get used to it, girl,* she told herself savagely. *He's not for you.*

The door opened and she stepped out, not taking the offered hand this time, forcing herself upright on her own two legs because if she took that hand it would heat hers, sending the tingling message of a warm togetherness that wasn't true. Cole was her boss. He would do her the courtesy of accompanying her to her door and then he would leave her. Back to business on Monday.

She put her head down and walked, acutely conscious of the sound of their footsteps—the quick clacking of her heels, the slower thump of his. They seemed to echo through the emptiness of her personal life, mocking dreams that had never been fulfilled, recalling her mother's words—*The kind of man you want, Liz, is the marrying kind.*

Why couldn't she meet someone who was?

Want someone who was.

Someone who was at least…reachable!

Tears blurred her eyes as they started up the stairs to her apartment. She shouldn't have drunk those glasses of champagne, giving her a false high, making the down worse. It was paramount now that she pull herself together, get out her door key, formulate a polite goodbye to her boss who had done her many kindnesses today. Kind…generous…making her feel special…

A huge lump rose in her throat. She blinked, swallowed, blinked, swallowed, managed somehow to get the key in the lock, turned it, pushed the door open enough for a fast getaway, retrieved the key, dropped it in her bag, dragged a deep breath into her aching chest, and turned to the man beside her.

'Thank you for everything, Cole,' she recited stiltedly and tried to arrange her mouth into a smile as she lifted her gaze, knowing she had to briefly meet his eyes and desperately hoping no evidence of any excess moisture was left for him to see. 'Goodnight,' she added as brightly as she could. 'It was fun.'

Cole's whole body clenched, resisting the dismissal. He stared at her shiny eyes. Wet eyes. Green pools, reflecting deep misery. The smile she'd forced was quivering, falling apart, no fun left to keep it in a natural curve.

He should let her go.

They were on very private ground now.

If he crossed it, there'd be no going back.

She was his employee…

Yet he stepped forward, his body responding to a primal tug that flouted the reasonable workings of his mind. Raising a hand, he gently stroked the tremulous corner of her mouth, wanting to soothe, to comfort, to make her feel safe with him. A slight gasp whispered from her lips. Her eyes swam with a terrible vulnerability, fearful questions begging to be answered.

It laid a responsibility on him, instantly striking a host of male instincts that rose in a strangely exultant wave, urging him to fight, to hold, to take, to protect—the age-old role of man before current day society had watered it down into something much less.

A sense of dominant power surged through his veins. She would submit to it. He would draw a positive response from her. He sensed it waiting behind the fear and confusion, waiting to be ignited, to flare into hot fusion with the desire pounding through him.

He slid his hand over her cheek, felt the leap of warmth under her skin, the firm yet fragile line of her jaw, the delicate curl of her small ear. Even as his thumb tilted her chin, his fingers were reaching to the nape of her neck, ready to caress, to persuade, to possess.

He lowered his head...slowly, savouring the moment of impact before it came. She had time to break away. His hold on her was light. She stood still, as though her entire being was poised for this first intimate contact with him, caught up in a breathless anticipation that couldn't be turned aside.

His lips touched hers, settling over their softness, drawing on them with light sips, feeling their hesitant response, teasing them into a more open kiss, wanting an exchange of sensation, reining in the urge to plunder and devour. She was willing to experiment, her tongue tentatively touching his as though she wasn't sure this was right. It fired a fierce desire in Cole to convince her it was. He turned the kiss into a slow, sensual dance, intent on melting every inhibition. She followed his lead, seduced into playing his game, savouring it herself, beginning to like it, want it, initiating as well as responding.

Excitement kicked through Cole. This was so different to Tara's all-too-knowing sexual aggression. He had to win this woman, drive the memory of her lost partner out of her mind and supplant it with what *he* could make her feel. The challenge spurred him into sweeping her into his embrace.

Her spine stiffened, whether in shock or resistance he didn't know. Shock was probably good. Resistance was bad. Before he could blast it with a passionate onslaught of kisses, her palms pressed hard against his chest and her head pulled back from his—a warning against force that he struggled to check, sensing her need for choice here, even while gathering himself to sway it his way.

He felt the agitated heave of her breasts as she sucked in a quick breath. Her lids fluttered, lashes half veiling the eloquent confusion in her eyes. Satisfaction welled in him, despite the frustration of being halted. It wasn't rejection on her mind. She didn't understand what was going on in his.

'Why are you doing this?' The words spilled out, anxious, frightened of consequences that he should know as well as she.

The lack of any calculation in her question, the sheer exquisite innocence of it evoked a streak of tenderness that Cole would have sworn had died with his son. His own chest heaved with the sudden surge of emotion. He dropped a soft kiss on her forehead.

'Because it feels right,' he murmured, feeling the sense of a new beginning so strongly, his heart started racing at the possibility it was really true. He could move past Tara. Even past David. Perhaps it was only hope but he wasn't about to step away from this opportunity of taking a future track which might bring him all he'd craved in his darkest nights.

'But I'm not really a…a date, am I?' she argued, trying to get a handle on what he meant by kissing her.

'No. You're much more.'

She shook her head, not comprehending. 'Cole, please…' Anguished uncertainty in her eyes. '…we have to work together.'

'We do work together. That's precisely the point. We work very well together.' He stroked the worry line between her brows. 'I'm just taking it to another level.'

'Another level?' she repeated dazedly.

He smiled into her eyes, wanting to dispel the cloudiness, to make her see what he saw. 'This feels right to me, Liz. Don't let it feel wrong to you because it's not,' he insisted, recklessly intent on carrying her with him. On a wild burst of adrenalin he added, 'I'm damned sure I can give you more than Brendan ever could or would.'

'Bren…dan.'

The name seemed to confuse her further. Cole silently cursed himself for bringing it up. He didn't want to compete. He wanted to conquer—wipe the guy out, take the woman, make her his. He didn't care how primitive that course was. It burned in his gut and he acted on it, sweeping Liz with him into her apartment, closing the door, staking his claim on her territory.

Before she could even think of protesting, he threw off his leather jacket, needing no armour against the cold in here, nor any barrier to the enticing heat of her body, and he captured her within the lock of his arms, intent on her surrender to his will. She felt small against him, and all the more intensely feminine because of it, but he knew she had a backbone of steel that could defy the might of his physique. Triumph zinged through his brain as her spine softened, arched into him, and her hands slid up over his shoulders, around his neck, and she lifted herself on tiptoe, face tilted to his, ready to be kissed again.

The darkness of the room seemed to sharpen his

senses. He could smell her perfume, enticingly erotic. His fingers wove through the silky curls of her hair, revelling in the tactile pleasure of it. His body hardened to the yielding softness of hers. He was conscious of their breaths mingling as his mouth touched hers, touched and clung with a voracious need that demanded her compliance.

She kissed him back with a passionate defiance that challenged any sense of dominance over her. No submission. It was as though a fire had erupted in her and Cole caught the flame. It flared through him, firing his desire for her to furnace heat. The power of it raced out of control, taking them both, drawing them in, sucking them towards the intense thrill of merging so completely there could be no turning back.

He removed her jacket.

She lifted his sweater, fearless now in matching him step for step.

Discarding clothes...like walls coming down, crashing to the floor, opening up the way...the ravenous excitement of flesh meeting flesh, sliding, caressing, hot and hungry for more and more intimacy.

Kissing...like nothing he knew, sliding deep, a sensual mating of tongues, a fierce response generated in every cell of his body, the sense of immense strength, power humming.

He scooped her off her feet, cradled her against his chest, carried her, intuitively picking the route to the room where she had gone to get her scarf this morning. Her head rested on his shoulder, her face pressed to his neck, the whole feel of her soft and warm and womanly, giving, wanting what he wanted.

She made him feel as a man should feel.

Essentially male.

And all that entailed.

CHAPTER ELEVEN

Liz was glad of the darkness. It wasn't oppressive now. It was her friend and ally, heightening the vibrant reality of Cole making love to her while it hid the same reality in comforting shadows. It allowed her to stifle the fear of facing the sheer nakedness of what they were doing and revel in the incredible pleasure of it. She could even believe she was as desirable as Cole made her feel. In the darkness.

He laid her on the bed—a bed she had shared only with Brendan—and she felt a sharp inner recoil at the memory, not wanting it. Why had Cole referred to him? Brendan was gone. Long gone from her bed. And he'd made mincemeat of her heart—the heart that was now pounding with wild excitement as Cole loomed over her, so big and strong and dynamically male, as different as any man could be to Brendan.

Purpose…action…energy focused on carrying through decisions…and unbelievably that focus was now on her…a totally irresistible force that kept swamping the reservations that should be in her brain, but he'd blown them away as though they didn't count. And maybe they didn't at this level, wherever this level was taking them.

She could barely think. Couldn't reason anymore. His arms slid out from under her and the solid mass of him straightened up, substance not fantasy, Cole taking charge, wanting her with him like this. She saw his arm reach for the bedside lamp and reacted with violent rejection of the action he had in mind.

'No!'

The arm was momentarily checked. 'No what?' he demanded.

'No light. I don't want light.'

'Why not?'

'You'll see…'

'I want to see you.'

'It won't be right,' she argued desperately. Her mind was screaming, *I'm not built like Tara. My breasts are small. My legs aren't long. I don't have voluptuous curves.*

'I promise you it will be,' he said, his voice furred with a deep sensuality that did promise, yet she couldn't believe he wouldn't compare her body to that of the woman he'd married and find her wanting.

'I don't have red hair down there,' she cried frantically, clutching at anything to stop him from turning on the light. 'You'll see it and think of me as a little brown mouse again.'

'I never thought of you like that,' he growled. 'Never!'

It got him onto the bed, lying beside her, the lamp forgotten, his hand sliding down over her stomach, fingers thrusting into the tight curls below it. 'I always saw you as bright, Liz Hart. Bright eyes. Bright intelligence. And behind it a fire which occasionally leapt out at me. There's not an ounce of mouse in you.'

This emphatic string of statements was very reas-

suring as to her status in his eyes, but Liz was highly
distracted from it by the further glide of his fingers,
delving lower, probing soft sensitive folds, exciting
nerve ends that melted into slick heat.

'I thought this past week...she's showing her true
colours. Reflecting the real Liz instead of covering
her up,' he went on, still wreaking exquisite havoc
with his hand, caressing, tracing, teasing. 'You don't
need a cloak of darkness. You can't hide from me
anymore. I know the fire inside you. I can feel it...'

A finger slid inside the entrance to her body and
tantalisingly circled the sensitive inner wall, raising
convulsive quivers of anticipation for the ultimate act
of intimacy. He leaned over, his face hovering above
hers. She saw the flash of a smile.

'...and taste it.'

He kissed her, long and deeply, and the tantalising
fingertip plunged inward, stroking in the same rhythmic action as his tongue, a dual invasion that drove
her wild with passionate need, a need that swelled
inside her, arching her body in an instinctive lift towards his, wanting, yearning. He didn't instantly respond so she reached for him with her hands, turned
towards him, threw a leg over his, and her heart leapt
at the hard muscular strength it met. Huge thighs.
She'd forgotten how big he was, had a moment's trepidation...how would it be when he took her?

I promise you it will be right...

It had to be.

She didn't want to stop.

Not now.

Not when she was awash with a tumultuous

need to have him…if only this once. It was madness…dangerous madness…risking what should have been kept safe. But it was his choice. *She* was his choice. And feeling him wanting her—Cole Pierson wanting her—it was like being elevated above any other woman he could have had, above Tara, making her feel…marvellous!

He broke the kiss and moved, but not as she expected, craved. His mouth fastened over the pulse at the base of her throat, radiating a heat that suffused her entire skin. She heard herself panting, barely able to breathe. Her arms had locked around his neck, but his head slipped below their circle, his lips tracing the upper swell of one breast, shifting to its tip…

Her stomach contracted as the feeling of inadequacy attacked her again. Her breasts weren't lush. He'd be disappointed in them. Oh, why, why couldn't he just…

Sensation exploded through her as he drew the tense peak into the hot wetness of his mouth and sucked on it. Swept it with his tongue. Another rhythmic assault that moved in tandem with the caressing hand between her thighs, driving her to the edge of shattering. Her fingers scrabbled blindly in his hair, pressing, tugging, protesting, inciting.

He moved to her other breast, increasing her ache for him, and her flesh seemed to swell around his mouth, throbbing with a tight fullness that totally erased any concern about levels of femininity. He made her feel she was all the woman he wanted and he wouldn't be denied any part of her.

Again he shifted and her body jerked as his tongue

swirled around her navel, a hot sweep of kisses trailing lower, lower. Her hands grabbed ineffectually at the bunched muscles of his shoulders as fear and desire warred through her mind.

No hesitation in his. Ruthless purpose. Lips pressed to her curls, fingers parting the way, his tongue touching, licking. The intensity of feeling rocked her, drenched her with desire, rendered her utterly helpless to stop anything even if she'd wanted to. And she didn't. She was on fire and he was tasting her because he wanted to.

He wedged his shoulders between her thighs, lifted her legs, clamped his hands on her hips and held her fast as he replaced the caress of his hand with the incredibly intimate caress of his mouth, his lips encircling her, his tongue probing with such artful sensual skill, she couldn't breathe at all as the intensity of feeling grew, ripping through her. She tried to ride the tide of it, her hands gripping the bedcover, holding on, holding on, but a rush of heat broke through her inner walls, overwhelming her with a wave of excruciating delight. A cry broke from her throat as she lost all sense of self, falling into a deep well of pleasure that engulfed her in sweet, molten heat.

Then Cole was surging over her. She could see him, feel him, but her muscles were so limp, she was unable to react. Her mind was filled with awe that he had taken her this far before satisfying himself. Yet she sensed he was not unsatisfied with what he had done, but pleased, even triumphant, as though he'd found his feasting very much to his liking.

I promise you it will be right...

Impossible to deny it, feeling as she did.

Having set himself to enter her, he pressed forward, pushing into her slowly, letting her adjust to the thick fullness of him, a completely different sensation and one that re-electrified all her senses. He eased back, lifting her hips, stuffing a pillow under her.

'Put your legs around me,' he murmured.

Somehow she managed to do it, locking her ankles so that they wouldn't slip apart. This time his thrust was firm, pushing deep, deeper, filling her to a breath-taking depth, then bracing himself on his arms as he bent his head to join his mouth to hers, and the kiss was different, too, like an absolute affirmation of him being inside her, having him there, an intensely felt sensation of possessing and being possessed, exulting in it, absorbed by it.

'Now rock with me,' he instructed, flashing a smile as he lifted his head.

Joy rippled through her. He was happy with where they were. She was, too. It re-energised her body, making it easy now to move as he did, matching the repetitive undulation, even touching him, stroking him, encouraging him, running her hands over the warm skin of his back, inciting the rise of heat with each delicious rhythmic plunge.

It was a wild, primitive dance that she gloried in, flesh sliding against—into—flesh, fusing, yet still gliding with a strong, relentless purpose, friction building to ecstatic peaks, wave after wave of intense sensation rolling through her…so much to feel…flaring, swirling, pooling deep inside her, touching her heart, stirring indefinable emotions…too much to pin down…far beyond all her previous experience.

Rapture as he groaned and spilled himself inside her. She sighed his name as his hard body collapsed on her, spent, and she wrapped her arms around him, holding him close, loving him, owning him if only for these few precious moments in time. He'd given himself to her, all that he was, and she silently revelled in the gift, unable to see ahead to what came next, not caring, listening to his heart thundering, elated that he had reached a pinnacle of pleasure with her.

He raised himself to kiss her again, her name whispering from his lips as they covered hers, soft, lingering sips that demanded nothing, merely sealing a tender togetherness that tasted of true and total contentment. Then his arms burrowed under her and he rolled onto his back, carrying her with him so that she lay with her head under his chin, her body sprawled over his.

Done, she thought, and wondered where it would lead. But with no sense of anxiety. She felt too amazingly replete to worry about tomorrow. Only luxuriating in this blissful sense of peace mattered. As long as it lasted. It awed her that she had lived so many years without realising how fantastic intimacy could be with a man. With the right man. Cole…Cole Pierson. Was it asking too much to want him thinking the same about her?

Probably it was.

This could be just a timing thing with him—a backlash against Tara's assumption that she could rope him in again, making the alleged intimacy between him and his personal assistant real because it had been planted in his mind, and it was an act of defiance against any desire he might have left for his almost ex-wife.

People did do reckless things on the rebound.

Was he thinking of Tara now...mentally thumbing his nose at her?

Liz felt herself growing cold at these thoughts and fiercely set them aside. Cole was with her. He'd chosen her. She moved her hand, suddenly wanting to stoke his desire again, feel it burning through her, obliterating everything else with the intense sense of possession.

A long sensual caress from his armpit, down his rib-cage, over the hollows underneath his hipbones, his firm flesh quivering to her touch, pleasured by it. She levered herself to a lower position so she could close her mouth over his nipple, kissing it, lashing it with her tongue. His chest heaved, dragging in a sharp breath, reacting swiftly to the sexual energy that had roared around them and was sparking again, gathering momentum.

She reached further, her hand closing around him, fondling, stroking. He groaned, his whole body tensing as her thumb brushed delicately over the sensitive head of his shaft. Elated at his response, she seized him more firmly, felt the surge of rampant strength grow hard, harder...

Hands gripped her waist, lifting her. 'Straddle me,' came the gravelled command. 'Put me inside you.'

It was an even more incredible sensation, lowering

herself onto him, engineering the penetration herself, feeling her inner muscles convulse and adjust to the pressing fullness of him, loving the sense of taking him, owning him. His hands moved to her hips, helping her sink further as he raised his thighs behind her, forming a cradle for her bottom, a cradle he rocked to breathtaking effect.

'Lean forward.'

She wanted to anyway, wanted to kiss him as he'd kissed her when he was deep inside her. She placed her hands on his shoulders and merged her mouth with his, plunging into a cavern of wild passion, drawn into a whirlpool of need that he answered with ravishing speed, his hands on her everywhere, stroking, shaping, kneading, strong fingers clutching, gentle fingers loving, sensitising every inch of her flesh to his touch.

She lifted herself back and he rubbed his palms over her nipples, rotating the hardened buds, exciting them almost beyond bearing, then latching onto them one by one with his mouth, his hands back on her hips, moving her from side to side, up and down, stirring a frenzy of sensation that rocketed through her, shattering every last vestige of control.

Even as she started to collapse on him he caught her face, drew it down to his, and devoured her mouth again, a sweet devastating plunder that she could only surrender to, helplessly yet willingly because the intoxication of his desire for more and more of her was too strong an exhilaration to deny.

Then amazingly, he was surging upright, swinging his legs off the bed, holding her pinned to him across his lap, hugging her tightly, her breasts crushed so intimately against his chest, the beat of his heart seemed to pound through them, echoing the throb of her own. And he remained inside her, a glorious sensual fullness, as his fingers wound through her hair and his lips grazed over her ear.

'I have never felt anything as good as this,' he murmured, his voice furred with a wonderment that squeezed her heart and sent elation soaring through her bloodstream. He tilted her head back, rained kisses over her face, her forehead, her eyelids, her cheeks, his lips hovering over hers as he added with compelling urgency, 'Tell me it's so for you. Tell me.'

'Yes.' The word spilled out automatically, impossible not to concede the truth, and he captured it in his mouth and carried it into hers, exploding the force of it with a fierce enthralling passion, holding her caged in his arms, swaying to reinforce the sense of his other insertion, pressing the heated walls of the passage he filled, making her feel him with commanding intensity.

'So, good, it has to be right,' he said rawly as he broke the kiss and cupped her chin, his eyes burning into hers. 'So don't you doubt it tomorrow. Or on Monday. Or anytime in the future.'

Emphatic words, punching into her dazed mind. She wasn't sure what he was saying. Her brain formed its own message. 'Right…for one night,' she sighed, knowing she would never forget the feelings he'd aroused in her, was still arousing. She didn't care

if it was only one experience. It was the experience
of a lifetime.

'No.' His hands raked through her hair, pressing
for concentration. 'This isn't an end. It's a beginning.
You and me, Liz. Moving forward, moving together.
Feel it. Know it. Come with me.'

He moved his thighs, driving an acute awareness
of their sexual connection. He was still strongly erect,
probing her inmost self, demanding she yield to him,
and what else could she do? She wanted this deeper
bonding, wanted it to last far beyond now.

'Liz...' An urgent demand poured through her
name.

She lifted her limp, heavy arms and locked them
around his neck...for better or worse, she thought, her
mind aswim, drowning in the need for Cole to keep
wanting her, making her feel loved as a woman.

'Yes.' It was the only word humming through her
mind. Yes to anything, everything with him.

'Yes-s-s...' he echoed, but with a ring of triumphant satisfaction, powerfully realised.

One hand skated down the curve of her spine,
curled under the soft globes of her bottom, clasping
her to him as he rose to his feet and turned to lower
her onto the bed again, her head and shoulders resting
on the coverlet as he dragged pillows under her hips,
then knelt between the spread of her legs, leaning
over her, hands intertwining with hers, a wild grin of
joy on his face.

'We'll both come,' he promised wickedly, then began to thrust in a fast driving beat, rocking deeply
into her, and she felt her body receive him with an

exultant welcome, opening to him over and over again. And he claimed all she gave, imprinting himself so completely on her consciousness, her entire body was focused on the erotic friction he built and built…only pausing, becoming still when he felt the powerful ripples of her release, savouring them before he picked up the rhythm again, all restraint whipping away as he pursued his own climax, broken breaths, moans of mounting tension, climbing, climbing, bursting into a long, intense rapture, waves of heat spilling, swirling, fusing them, lifting them into a space where they floated together in ecstatic harmony.

And Liz no longer questioned anything.

A sense of perfect contentment reigned.

Sliding slowly and languorously into a feast of sensuality that lasted long into the night…the night that he said was a beginning, not an end.

CHAPTER TWELVE

COLE was gone when Liz awoke. She vaguely remembered him kissing her, murmuring he had to keep
an appointment. He'd been fully clothed, ready to
leave. She was almost sure she'd mumbled, 'Okay,'
before dropping back into a heavy sleep.

It came as a shock that her bedside radio now
showed 11:47, almost midday. There was only one
afternoon of the weekend left and she had washing to
do, food shopping. She bolted out of bed and headed
straight into the bathroom, cold wintry air hitting her
nakedness, making her shiver.

A hot shower dispelled the chill and soaping her
body brought back all the memories of last night's
intimacies with Cole…delicious, indelible memories.
If she wasn't in love with the man, she was certainly
in lust with him. He was an incredible lover. And he'd
made her feel sexier than she'd ever felt in her life.
Sexy, beautiful, special…

Her mind flitted to how it had been with Brendan.
Why had she accepted *so little* from him? Compared
to Cole…but she hadn't known any better at the time.
In fact, Brendan had been mean about a lot of
things—a taker, not a giver. Whereas Cole…the
beautiful clothes yesterday, the sumptuous dinner last
night, the loving…she felt wonderfully spoilt, as
though all her Christmases had come at once.

She desperately hoped it *was* right to have plunged into this intimate relationship with him. Her job was very definitely at risk if it turned wrong. Oddly enough, work security didn't weigh so heavily on her mind now. Losing him would be far more devastating. Which was the problem with being raised to giddy heights. The fall...

But she wasn't going to think about that.

Nor was she going to worry about Cole being her boss. As Diana had predicted, *he* had done the running, and Liz was now determined on *going with the flow,* wherever it took her. There really was no other choice, except dropping entirely out of his life. And why would she do that when he made her feel...so good?

The somewhat sobering recollection slid into her mind—he was in no hurry to marry again.

So what? she quickly argued. Did she have any prospects leaping out at her? Not a one. Besides, there was no guarantee of permanence with any relationship. It went that way or it didn't. Though everything within her craved for this new relationship with Cole to last, to become truly solid, to have it fulfil...all her impossible dreams.

As she stepped out of the shower, dried herself and dressed, a wry little smile lingered on her lips. Perhaps hope *was* eternal. In any event, it was a happy boost to her spirits. So was emptying yesterday's shopping bags, remembering the zing of parading the clothes in front of Cole as she hung them up in her wardrobe, knowing now that he did see her as a desirable woman—a woman he wanted.

She rushed through the afternoon, doing all the necessary chores, planning what she'd pack for the trip with Cole's mother, making sure everything was clean, ready to wear. She wondered what Nancy would think of her son becoming attached to his personal assistant. Better me than Tara, Liz cheerfully decided. Nancy hadn't liked Tara at all.

She was still riding a high when her telephone rang just past seven o'clock. She hesitated over answering it, thinking it might be Diana with another stream of advice. She didn't want to share what had happened with Cole. Not yet. It suddenly felt too precious, too fragile. And she didn't know how it might be tomorrow.

On the other hand, it might be her mother who wasn't pushing anything, only for her daughter to be happy about herself, and Liz was happy about herself right now, so she snatched up the receiver and spoke with a smile. 'Hi! Liz here.'

'Cole here,' came the lilted reply, warm pleasure threading his voice.

'Oh!' A dumb response but he'd taken her by surprise.

'Oh good, I trust?'

The light teasing note brought the smile back. 'Yes. Definitely good.'

He laughed. 'I've been thinking of you all day. Highly distracting.'

'Should I say I'm sorry?' It was fun to flirt with him, though it amazed her that she could.

'No. The distraction was very pleasurable.' He drawled the last words, sending pinpricks of excite-

ment all over her skin. 'I'm currently having to restrain myself from dashing to your door, telling myself I do need some sleep in order to function well
tomorrow.'

'You have a string of meetings in the morning,'
she said primly, playing the perfect P.A. while inwardly delighted that his restraint was being tested. It
spoke volumes about the strength of attraction he felt.
Towards *her*.

'Mmmh…I was wondering how to alleviate the
problem of people getting in the way of us.'

Us…such an exhilarating word. 'We do have work
to get through, Cole,' she reminded him, though if he
didn't care, she wasn't about to care, either.

'True. But you could wear that bronze dress with
the buttons down the front. Very provocative those
buttons. One could say…promising.'

Liz felt her thighs pressing together, recapturing the
sensations of last night when he'd…

'And wear stockings,' he continued. 'Not those
coverall pantihose. Stockings that end mid-thigh, under the skirt with the buttons. And no one will know
but you and me, Liz. I like that idea. I like it very
much.'

His voice had dropped to a seductive purr, and her
entire body was reacting to it, an exquisite squirming
that actually curled her toes.

'If you'll do that I think I'm sure to perform at a
high peak tomorrow,' he went on, conjuring up
breathtaking images that dizzied her brain. 'Won't
feel deprived at all during those meetings. There's
nothing quite like waiting on a promise.'

A shiver ran down her spine. Did he mean...after the meetings...at the office? He wanted sex with her there?

'Liz?'

'Yes?' It was like punching air out her lungs.

'Have I shocked you?'

'Yes...no,' she gabbled. 'I mean...I wasn't sure what you'd want of me tomorrow.'

'You. I want you. In every way there is,' he answered with a strength of purpose that thudded straight into Liz's heart, making her feeling intensely vulnerable about how he would deal with her in the end if she trod this path with him. Was it only sex on his mind? How much did she count as a person?

She couldn't find anything to say, her mind riddled by doubts and fears, yet physically, sexually, she was aware of an overwhelming yearning to follow his lead, to be the woman he wanted in every way.

'Remember how right it felt?' he dropped into her silence.

'Yes,' she answered huskily, her voice barely rising over a huge emotional lump in her throat.

'It will be tomorrow, too. That's my promise, Liz.' Warm reassurance.

'I'll come as you say,' she decided recklessly.

'Good! I'll sleep on that. Sweet dreams.'

The connection clicked off.

Goal achieved, she thought, then shook her head dazedly over the power Cole Pierson could and did exert. Being the focus of it was like nothing she had ever known before. In the past, she had always done the running, not very effectually where men were concerned. No truly satisfying success at all. In actual fact, a string of failures, probably because she'd tried to manage things to turn out right instead of them just being right.

She had no control with Cole.

He'd seized it.

Was still wielding it.

And maybe that was how it should be.

So let it be.

Cole sat at his desk in his office, his computer switched on, the screen flashing figures he should be checking, but he was too much on tenterhooks, waiting for Liz to arrive. He couldn't remember ever being this tense about seeing a woman again. Would he win or lose on last night's gamble?

He wasn't sure of her.

The sex on Saturday night had been fantastic. No doubting her response to everything they'd done together—a more than willing partner in pleasure, once he'd moved her past the initial inhibitions—storming barriers before she could raise them. Barriers that had undoubtedly been built during the Brendan era—damage done by a selfish lover who didn't have the sense to appreciate the woman he had.

Cole knew he could definitely reach her on the sexual level. It was what he was counting on to bind her to him. He'd moved too fast to take a slower route now, and be damned if he was going to let her slip away from him. He'd sensed her second thoughts during the telephone call. Perhaps the better move would have been to stay with her all yesterday. But her

apartment was her ground and she would have had
the right to ask him to go.

Best to keep the initiative.

She'd come to work this morning—his ground.
And after their conversation over the phone, she
would have gone to bed last night thinking of him,
tempted by the promise of more pleasure, remembering what they'd already shared, wanting more…

Cole dragged in a deep breath, trying to dampen
the wild surge of desire rising at the thought of what
she would wear today. Compliance or defiance? At
least the signal would be clear, the moment she
walked into his office. Yes…no. He fiercely willed it
to be yes. And why not? She had the fire in her to
pursue pleasure. He'd lit the flame. She wouldn't let
it go out…would she?

A knock on his door.

'Come in!' he called, his voice too terse, on edge.

She stepped into his office, wearing the bronze
dress with the buttons down the front.

His heart thundered as a lightning burst of triumph
flashed through his mind.

'Good morning,' she said brightly.

He saw courage in the red flags on her cheeks, in
the high tilt of her head, the squared shoulders, the
smile that wavered slightly at its corners. Courage
defying fear and uncertainty. It touched him to a surprising depth.

'I think it's a great morning,' he rolled out, his
smile ablaze with admiration and approval.

She visibly relaxed, walking forward, holding out

a Manila folder. 'I brought in the file for your first meeting.'

Straight into business.

Not quite yet, Cole thought. 'I seem to remember that the last time I saw you in that dress, there were several buttons towards the hem undone.'

It was a challenging reminder and she halted, looking down at her skirt in hot confusion.

'Three,' he said. 'I recall counting three undone.'

Her gaze lifted, eyes astonished. 'You counted them?'

He grinned. 'I'm good at counting.'

A little laugh gurgled from her throat. 'So you are.'

'And here you are all buttoned up today, which doesn't look right at all. I much preferred it the other way. I think you should oblige me and undo at least one button before we get down to serious business.'

'One button,' she repeated, her eyes sparkling at the mischievous nonsense.

Fun was the key here. There was never enough fun in anyone's life. She'd had fun trying clothes on during the buying spree on Saturday. What could be more relaxing and seductive than having fun with some knowingly provocative undressing?

'Okay. One button for now,' he agreed. 'Though I think it would relieve the pressure of these meetings if an extra button got undone after each session.'

'That makes four buttons.'

'I knew you were good at counting, too.'

She gave him an arch look, joining in the game he was playing. 'You might find that distracting.'

'No. I'll think of it as my reward for outstanding concentration.'

She placed the folder on the desk. Then with an air of whimsical indulgence, she flicked open the bottom button, straightened up, took a deep breath and boldly asked, 'Happy now?'

'We progress. Let's say I'm...briefly...satisfied.' He ran his gaze up the row of buttons from hem to neckline, then smiled, meeting her eyes with deliberately wicked intent.

She flushed, realising he had no intention of stopping anywhere. *And may she burn with anticipation all morning,* Cole thought as he drew the folder over to his side of the desk and opened it, ostensibly ready to familiarise himself with the financial details of the client who would soon be arriving.

He'd thrown his net, caught Liz with it, and he'd draw her closer and closer to him as the morning wore on. The whole encounter had sharpened his mind brilliantly. He felt right on top of the game.

An hour later, the first client had been dealt with. Without saying a word, Cole stared at Liz's skirt. Without a word from her, she undid a button, then handed him the next file.

Exhilarated by the silent complicity, Cole ploughed through the next meeting, sparking on all cylinders.

Another button hit the dust.

He could see above her knee now when she walked, the skirt peeping open far enough to tease him with flashes of leg. Was she wearing stockings as he'd requested?

Excitement buzzed through his brain. Restraint was

like a refined torture. He forced it over the desire simmering through him and satisfied the third client with a fast and comprehensive exposition on the state of the money markets. Even as he ushered the man out of his office, his gaze targeted the next button, wanting it opened, commanding it done…now…this instant.

He saw her hands move to do it as he walked his client through Liz's office. Anticipation roared through him. It was an act of will to keep accompanying the man to the elevator, farewelling him into the compartment before turning back to the woman who had to be wanting an acceleration of action as much as he did.

He'd planned the sexual tease. He'd meant it to go on all day, but here he was, too caught up with the need it had evoked in him to wait for tonight. To hell with work. It was lunch time anyway. Though his appetite for Liz Hart wiped out any thought of food. The energy driving him now did not require more fuel.

He strode into her office, locked the door against any possible interruption. She stood at one of the filing cabinets, putting the last folder away. The click of the lock caused her to throw a startled glance over her shoulder. Their eyes met, the sizzling intent in his causing hers to widen.

'It's all right,' he said, soothing any shock. 'We're alone. Private. And I want you very urgently, Liz Hart.'

She didn't move, seemingly entranced by the force of need emanating from him. Then he was behind her, his arms caging her, pulling her back against him, finding some solace for his fierce erection in pressing it against the soft cleft of her sexy bottom.

He heard, felt her gasp, kissed the delicate nape of her neck, needing to give vent to the storm of desire engulfing him. He was so hungry for her. His hands covered her stomach, pushing in, making her feel how much he wanted her. Then he remembered the buttons, stockings, bare thighs, and his desire for her took another turn. He dropped his hands, fingers moving swiftly, opening the skirt.

And yes, yes…it was how he'd envisaged, stockings ending, naked flesh above them, quivering to his touch, the crotch of her panties hot, moist, telling evidence of her excitement, boosting his.

He whirled her over to her desk, sat her on it, took her chair, spread her legs, lifting them over his shoulders as he bent to taste the soft, bare, tremulous inner walls of her thighs, kissing, licking, smelling her need for him, exulting in it, knowing she was his to take as he wanted.

Liz could hardly believe what was happening. He was spreading the silk of her panties tight, kissing her through the thin screen, finding the throbbing centre between her folds, sucking on it. Pleasure rushed from the heat of his mouth, sweeping through her like a tidal wave. She had to lie back on the desk to cope with it, though there was no coping, more a melting surrender to the flow of sensation.

And she had once thought him an ice man!

He let her legs slide from his shoulders as he rose,

seemingly intent on following her, bending over her, his eyes dark, ringed with burning blue—no ice!—and she felt the silk being drawn aside as the hot hard length of him pushed to possess the space waiting for him, aching for him.

The intense focus of his eyes captured hers, held it as he drove the penetration home. 'This is how it is…in the light,' he said raggedly. 'You don't need the dark, Liz. It's better this way, seeing, knowing…'

He withdrew enough to plunge again, and it *was* thrilling to see the tension on his face, the concentrated flare of desire in his eyes, to watch him moving in the driving rhythm that pleasured them both in ever increasing pulse beats of intense excitement. The final release was incredibly mutual, and instinctively she wrapped her arms around his head and drew his mouth to hers, kissing him with the sweet knowledge that his desire for her was very real, not some accident of fate because she was simply on hand at a time of need.

This was proven to her over and over again as the days—and nights—rolled on towards the date of departure for the trip to South-East Asia. For the most part, restraint ruled in the office, but then they would go to her apartment, his apartment, make wild needy love, proceed to a nearby restaurant for dinner, enjoy fine food and wine while they whetted their appetite for more lovemaking.

It was exhilarating, addictive, a whirlwind of uninhibited passion, and Liz was so completely caught up in it, she heartily wished she wasn't going off travelling with his mother…until Cole made an an-

nouncement over dinner on Thursday night that gave
her pause for thought.

'My divorce was settled this afternoon. I'm finally
a free man again.'

It was the relief in his voice that unsettled her, as
though his freedom had remained threatened until the
law had brought his marriage to Tara Summerville to
an end. It instantly brought to mind the confrontation
between them last Saturday, with Tara firing all her
guns to win a reconciliation, and Cole savagely denying her any chance of it.

Since then—apart from Sunday when he had been
occupied elsewhere—he had virtually immersed himself in a white-hot affair with the very woman Tara
had accused of a sexual connection to Cole. Had it
become so concentrated in order to keep Tara completely shut out? No space for her, not in his mind,
not in his life, ensuring the final line was drawn on a
marriage he'd written off as a case of bad judgment.

One could settle things in one's head that didn't
necessarily get translated into physical and emotional
responses. In a kind of reverse situation, Liz knew
she'd reasoned out a million things about Brendan,
trying to keep positive about their relationship, even
when her body and heart were reacting negatively.
The old saying, mind over matter, didn't really work.
It only covered over stuff that kept bubbling underneath.

Liz couldn't help wondering if Cole had chosen her
as the best possible distraction to take him through to
the finishing line with Tara. Yet the sexual chemistry
they shared had to be real. He couldn't perform as he

did unless he felt it. And he'd noticed how many buttons had been undone on the bronze dress last week, before that meeting with Tara. Which surely meant Liz could trust the attraction between them.

It was just that Cole had such a formidable mind. Once he decided something, he went at it full bore until the goal was achieved. And Liz didn't know what his goal was with her, except to satisfy a very strong sexual urge—made right because she wanted the same satisfaction. Although secretly she wanted more from him. Much more.

But nothing was said about any future with her. Too soon, Liz told herself. After dinner, Cole drove her home. This was their last night together for more than two weeks while she toured through South-East Asia with his mother. She had Friday off to pack and generally get ready for the trip so she wouldn't be seeing him at work tomorrow. It had been arranged for her to meet Nancy Pierson at the airport Holiday Inn at six o'clock for a tour group dinner and they would fly off early Saturday morning.

Cole stayed late, seemingly reluctant to part from her even when he finally chose to leave. 'I wish you weren't going on this trip,' he said with a rueful smile, then kissed her long and hard, passionately reminding her of all the intimacy they'd shared. 'I'll miss you,' he murmured against her lips.

In every sense, Liz hoped, silently deciding the trip was a timely break, giving them both the distance to reflect on what they'd done, where they were going with it and why.

She felt she'd been caught up in a fever-pitch compulsion that completely blotted out everything else beyond Cole Pierson. Distance might give her enough perspective to see if it truly was good...or the result of influences that had pulled them somewhere they shouldn't be.

Which wouldn't be good at all.

CHAPTER THIRTEEN

BY MIDAFTERNOON Friday, Cole found himself totally irritated by the temporary assistant taking Liz's place. He wasn't asking much of her. Why did she have to look so damned intimidated all the time? He hoped his mother appreciated the sacrifice he was making, giving her Liz as a companion for this trip.

Which reminded him to call his mother before the limousine arrived to transport her to the airport Holiday Inn, make sure she wasn't in a tizz about having everything ready to go. He picked up the telephone and dialled the number for the Palm Beach house.

'Yes?' his mother answered breathlessly.

'Just calm down, Mum. The limousine can wait until you're sure you haven't left anything behind.'

'Oh, Cole! I was just going around the house to check everything was locked.'

'I'll drive out tomorrow and double-check the security alarm so don't worry about it. Okay?'

A big sigh. 'Thank you, dear. There's always so much to think about before I leave. I did call your Liz and she assured me she's all organised.'

His Liz. A pity she wasn't his right now. In more ways than one. 'She would be,' he said dryly.

'Such a nice girl!' came the voice of warm approval. 'I rather hope we do run into her boyfriend at

Kathmandu. I can't imagine he's not having second thoughts about leaving her.'

'What?' The word squawked out of the shock that momentarily paralysed Cole's brain.

'You must know about him,' his mother said reasonably. 'Brendan Wheeler. He and Liz have been together for the past three years.'

'Yes, I know about him,' Cole snapped. 'But not that he was in Kathmandu. When did Liz tell you this?'

'Last Saturday when we were working out what clothes to take. It seemed wrong that she didn't have a boyfriend, so I asked her...'

'Right!' *Before he'd made his move. She couldn't want the guy back now...could she?* 'Brendan dumped her, Mum, so don't be getting any romantic ideas about their getting together again,' he said tersely.

'But it might have been only a case of him getting cold feet over commitment, Cole. If he comes face to face with Liz over there...'

'I am not paying for my personal assistant to run off with a guy in Kathmandu!' Cole thundered into the receiver. 'If you assist this in any way whatsoever...'

'Oh, dear! I didn't think of that. Well, I don't think she would actually run off, Cole. As you said, Liz is very responsible. I'm sure she'd insist on Brendan following her back home to prove good faith.'

'Better that the situation be avoided altogether,' he grated through a clenched jaw.

'You can't block Fate, dear,' his mother said blithely.

Fate was a fickle fool, Cole thought viciously, recalling how quickly Liz had agreed to the trip. He'd listed off Nepal as one of the destinations when he put the proposition to her. She must have instantly thought…Kathmandu…Brendan. And she'd played his mother brilliantly at lunch that day, clinching the deal.

No reluctance at the possibility of meeting him over there.

She'd even told his mother where the guy was.

'Mum, you keep your nose right out of this,' Cole commanded. 'No aiding and abetting. I'm telling you straight. Brendan was no good for Liz.'

'No good?' came the critical reply. 'Then why did she stay with him so long? She didn't have a child to consider…like you did with Tara. And Liz didn't do the leaving,' his mother reminded him with pertinent emphasis.

He wanted to shout, *Liz is with me, now,* but knew it would be tantamount to ringing wedding bells in his mother's ears and Cole was not prepared to deal with that.

'He repressed her. He put her down. He made her feel like a failure,' he punched out. 'I know this, Mum, so just let it be. Liz is better off without him. Okay?'

A long pause, then…'You really do care about her, don't you?'

Care? Of course, he cared. And he certainly didn't want to lose her to an idiot who hadn't cared enough to keep her. However, what he needed here was to seal his mother's sympathy to the cause of holding Liz away from Brendan.

'She's had a rough time, Mum,' he said in a gentler tone. 'I want you to ensure she enjoys this trip. No pain.'

'I'll do my best,' came the warm and ready promise.

Mother hen to the rescue of wounded bird.

Cole breathed more easily.

'Right! Well, I hope you have a wonderful time together.'

'Thank you. I'm sure we will. Oh, there's the limousine now. Must go, dear. Goodbye! Thanks for all your help.'

Gone!

He put the receiver down and stared at the telephone for several seconds, strongly tempted to call Liz, but what more could he say? He'd told her last night he would miss her, shown her how very desirable she was to him. There could be no possible doubt in her mind that he wanted her back, wanted her with him.

Surely to God she wouldn't throw what they'd shared aside and take Brendan back!

She couldn't be that much of a fool!

Or did he have it all wrong?

Cole rose from his chair and paced around the office, unsettled by the sudden realisation that much of what he'd told his mother comprised assumptions on his part. Maybe Liz had felt secure enough in her relationship with Brendan not to bother about feminine frippery, saving money towards a marriage and having a family…which had slipped away from her because… *He didn't like my style of management.*

That was all she had actually told him about the relationship.

He'd interpreted the rest.

What if he was wrong?

He'd steamrolled Liz into a hot and heavy affair, to which she'd been a willing party, but he didn't really know what was going on in her mind. Was it rebound stuff for her? An overwhelming need to *feel* desired?

What if she did meet Brendan in Kathmandu and they clicked again, as they must have done in the beginning? Would she count the sex with her boss as meaning anything in any long-term sense? Had he made it *mean* anything to her?

All he'd said was it felt right.

And it did.

She'd agreed.

But was it enough to hold her to him?

Cole didn't know.

But there was nothing more he could do or say now to shift the scales his way.

Besides, Kathmandu was a big city. The tour schedule was jam-packed. The likelihood of her running into Brendan was very low. She had a full-time job to do—looking after his mother—and he'd just ensured, as best he could, that his mother wouldn't let Liz skip out on her responsibility.

Cole took a deep breath and returned to his desk.

Liz would come back.

He was wasting time, worrying over things he had no control over, but that very lack of absolute control where Liz Hart was concerned made him...uneasy.

CHAPTER FOURTEEN

LIZ quickly found she had no difficulty in travelling with Nancy Pierson. All the older woman needed was a bit of prompting on where they had to be at what time, and when their luggage was to be put outside their hotel room to be collected by the Captain's Choice staff, all of whom were brilliantly and cheerfully efficient. Nancy accepted the prompting good-naturedly, grateful that Liz took the responsibility of ensuring they did everything right.

It was quite marvellous flying off on a chartered Qantas jet with almost two hundred other tourists, everyone excited about the adventure ahead of them. The party atmosphere on the plane was infectious, helped along by the champagne which flowed from the moment they were seated.

'Oh, I'm so glad you were able to come with me,' Nancy enthused, her eyes twinkling with the anticipation of much pleasure as she started on a second glass of champagne.

'So am I. This is great. But you want to go easy on the champers, Nancy. Don't drink it too quickly,' Liz warned, concerned about her getting tipsy.

Nancy laughed. 'I'm not a lush, dear. Just celebrating.' She leaned over confidentially. 'Cole's divorce was settled on Thursday. He's completely free of that woman now.'

'Well, I guess that's a good thing,' Liz said non-committally, unsure how she should respond.

'He'd make a wonderful husband to the right woman, you know,' Nancy went on, eyeing her with a spark of hopeful eagerness.

Liz could feel a tide of heat creeping up her neck and quickly brushed the subject aside. 'A failed marriage often puts people off the idea of marrying again.'

'But Cole absolutely adored his son. It was such a terrible tragedy losing David, and it's taken a long time for him to get over it, but I'm sure he'll want to have more children and he's not getting any younger,' Nancy argued.

'Men can have children any time they like,' Liz dryly pointed out. 'It's only women who have a biological clock ticking.'

'He doesn't want to get too old and set in his ways.' A sad sigh. 'His father—my husband—was like that, unfortunately. Didn't want more than one child. But I'm sure Cole is different. He loved being a father.'

'Then perhaps he'll be one again someday.'

This drew a sharp look. 'Do you want children, Liz?'

The flush swept into her cheeks. 'Someday.'

Another sigh. 'Someday I'd love to have a grandchild in my life again. Your mother must be delighted with hers.'

'Yes, she is. Particularly the twins, being boys, after having only daughters herself.'

Luckily, this turn of the conversation diverted

Nancy from pushing Cole as an eligible husband—a highly sensitive issue—and Liz was able to relax again. She didn't want to speculate on her new relationship with Nancy's son. It had happened so fast. She was banking on time away to bring some sort of perspective to it…on both sides.

When they arrived in Kuching, it was great to immerse herself in a completely different part of the world. Their hotel overlooked the Sarawak River with its fascinating traffic of fishing boats and sampans—smells and sights of the East. Kuching actually meant the city of cats and it even had a cat museum featuring an amazing collection of historical memorabilia on the feline species.

On their second morning, a bus took them to the Semengoh Orangutan Reserve where they were able to observe the animals closest to humans on the primate ladder, extinct now except here in Borneo. The orangutans' agility, swinging through the trees, was amazing but it was their eyes that Liz would always remember—so like people's eyes in their expression.

They also visited a long house where over a thousand men, women and children lived together in the old traditional way, with each family having their own quarters but sharing a large verandah as a communal area. No isolation here, as there was in modern apartment buildings, Liz thought. Ready company seemed to make for happy harmony, and sharing was obviously a way of life, clearly giving a sense of security and contentment in continuity.

It made her wonder how much had been lost in striving for singular achievement in western society.

She didn't want to live alone for the rest of her life, yet going back to her parents' home didn't seem right, either. She was thirty years old, had a mortgage on an apartment she was living in, but no one to share it with on any permanent basis. Her neighbours in the apartment block were like ships passing in the night. Where was she going with her life?

Would Cole ever think of marrying her?

Having a family with her?

Or was all this sexual intensity nothing more than a floodgate opening after a long period of celibacy?

It hurt to think about it. She knew the attraction had always been there on her side—suppressed because it had to be. Her boss was off limits for a variety of good reasons. Besides which, he'd shown no interest in her as a woman until…what exactly had triggered his interest? The new image? The fact that Brendan was no longer an item in her life, making her unattached and available? Simple proximity when he felt tempted by Tara's blatantly offered sexuality?

To Liz's mind, it wasn't something solid, something she could trust in any long-term sense. As much as she would like to explore a serious relationship with Cole, she wasn't sure it was going to develop that way, which made her feel very vulnerable about the eventual outcome.

She could end up in a far worse situation than when Brendan had decided enough was enough. Holding on to her job would be unthinkable, unbearable. Did Cole realise that? Had he even paused to think about it? What did *right* mean to him?

She wasn't at all sure that Diana's advice about

going with the flow was good—not if it led to a waterfall that would dash her to pieces. But there was no need to make any decision about it yet. Indeed, she didn't know enough to make a sensible decision.

The next day the tour group had a wonderful boat trip on the river to Bako National Park where they walked through a rainforest and swam in the South China Sea from a beautiful little beach. It felt like a million miles away from the more sophisticated life in Australia—primitive, sensual on a very basic level, simple but very real pleasures. Time slipped by without any worries.

They left Kuching and flew to Rangoon in Burma—or rather Yangon in Myanmar as it was now known. This had been one of the richest countries of South-East Asia and its past glories were abundantly evident. The Shwedagon Pagoda with its giant dome covered with sixty tonnes of gold and the top of the stupa encrusted with thousands of diamonds, rubies and sapphires, was absolutely awesome.

And the comfort of a past era was amply displayed in the old steam train chartered to take the tourists into the nearby countryside, through the green rice fields and the small villages where nothing had changed for centuries. Pot plants decorated the carriages, legroom was spacious, seats were far more comfortable than in modern trains, and provided with drink holders and ashtrays. The windows, of course, could be opened and it was fun waving to the people they passed, all of whom waved back.

'I feel like the queen of England,' Nancy commented laughingly. 'Such fun!'

Indeed, much of England lingered here, especially in the architecture of the city. The City Hall, Supreme and High Court Buildings, GPO, Colonial Offices—all of them would have looked at home in London, yet the city centre revolved around the Sule Pagoda which was stunningly from a very different culture, as were the temples.

On their last night in Rangoon a 'grand colonial evening' had been arranged for them at The Strand Hotel which had been built by an English entrepreneur and opened in 1901. It had once been considered 'the finest hostelry east of Suez, patronised by royalty, nobility and distinguished personages'—according to the 1911 edition of Murray's Handbook for Travelers in India, Burma and Ceylon.

The men were given a pith helmet to put them in the correct British India period, the women an eastern umbrella made of wood and paper printed with flowers. Everyone was asked to wear white as far as possible and as Liz dressed for the evening in the broderie anglaise peasant blouse and frilled skirt that Cole had bought for her, memories of their shopping spree came flooding back.

You're a class act, Liz Hart. Top of the top. And you are going to be dressed accordingly.

Cole hadn't been talking sex then.

If she really was the *top of the top* to him…but maybe that just referred to her efficiency as his P.A.

As much as she wanted to believe he could fall in love with her—was in love with her—Liz felt he only wanted sex, no emotional ties. And she'd been tempted into tasting the realisation of a fantasy which probably should have remained a fantasy. Except she couldn't regret the experience of having actually known what it was like to be his woman, if only for a little while.

'I just love that outfit on you!' Nancy remarked, eyeing her admiringly as they set off from their hotel room.

Liz bit her lips to stop the words, 'Your son's choice.' She forced a smile. 'Well I must say you look spectacular in yours, Nancy.'

She did. Her glittery white tunic was beaded with pearls at the neckline and hem, falling gracefully over a narrow skirt which was very elegant. In fact, Nancy had been right about the dressing on this tour. Casual clothes during the day, but there was very classy dressing at the evening dinners which were invariably a special event.

The compliment was received with obvious pleasure. 'Thank you, dear. We must make the most of this last night here. It's off to Kathmandu tomorrow.'

Liz didn't reply. Kathmandu conjured up thoughts of Brendan. Was he happy with *the space* he'd put between them? If by some weird coincidence they should meet, would he think she had pursued him? What would his reaction be?

Didn't matter, Liz decided with a touch of bitterness. She'd wasted three years on him and wasn't going to waste another minute even thinking about their past relationship. But was she doing any better for herself with Cole? Would she look back in a few months' time and wonder at her own madness for getting so intimately involved with him?

A bus transported them to the Strand Hotel, the men laughing in their helmet hats—a pukka reminder of the British Raj—the women twirling their umbrellas with very feminine pizazz, embracing the sense of slipping back into a past era. They walked into a spacious, very old-world reception lobby, two storeys high with marvellous ceiling fans and chandeliers, wonderful arrangements of flowers, someone playing eastern music on a xylophone. Many waiters circulated with trays of cocktails and hors d'oeuvres, the refreshments adding to the convivial mood.

Overlooking the lobby was an upstairs balcony, a richly polished wood balustrade running around the four sides. Nancy was taking it all in, revelling in the ambience of the superbly kept period hotel. Liz heard her gasp, and automatically looked to where she was looking, her whole body jolting in shock as she saw what Nancy saw.

'Good heavens! There's Cole!'

He was on the balcony scanning the crowd below. Even as his mother spoke, his gaze zeroed in on them. His mouth twitched into a smile. He raised his hand in a brief salute then turned away, heading for the staircase which would bring him down to where they were.

Every nerve in Liz's body was suddenly wired with hyper-tension. Her mind pulsed with wild speculation over why Cole was here? He hadn't once suggested he might catch up with them on this trip. Had he felt compelled to check on her for some reason? Didn't he trust her with his mother?

'Well, well, well,' Nancy drawled, her voice rich

with satisfaction. 'Cole has actually taken time off work to be with us. Isn't that wonderful!'

It jerked Liz out of her turbulent thoughts. 'Did you…invite him to join us?' she choked out, her throat almost too tight to force words out.

Nancy shook her head in a bemused fashion. 'I didn't even think of it.' A lively interest sparkled in her eyes. 'Though I do find it very encouraging that he's done so just before we leave for Kathmandu.'

'Encouraging?' Liz echoed, not comprehending Nancy's point.

'Oh yes, dear. It's a very good sign,' she said with a complacent smile.

Of what?

Liz didn't have time to ask. Cole was already downstairs and heading towards them. He cut such an imposing figure and emanated such powerful purpose, people automatically moved aside to give him a clear path through the milling crowd, heads turning to stare after him, women eyeing him up and down. He looked absolutely stunning dressed in a white linen suit, made classy casual by the black T-shirt he'd teamed it with. A man in a million, Liz thought, her heart pounding erratically at his fast approach.

He grinned, his hands lifting into a gesture that encompassed them both as he reached them. 'Definitely the two best looking women here!' he declared.

His mother laughed. 'What a surprise to see you!'

'A happy one, I hope.' His gaze slid to Liz, the piercing blue eyes suddenly like laser beams burning into hers. The grin softened to a quirky smile. 'One day in the office with your replacement was enough to spur me into taking a vacation. You are…quite irreplaceable, Liz.'

In the office or in his bed? Did this mean he'd decided he couldn't do without her? Excitement fevered her brain. 'Have you arranged to join the tour?'

'Only for this evening. I'm actually booked into this hotel for a couple of days. I thought I'd have this one night with you…'

One night…in this hotel…

'…share what appears to be a very special occasion and escort you both to dinner.' He turned back to his mother. 'Are you enjoying yourself, Mum?'

'Immensely, dear. What are your plans for the rest of your vacation?'

'I thought I'd take a look at Mandalay while I'm in this country. It's always had a fascinating ring to it…Mandalay…'

'You're not coming to Kathmandu?'

'No.' He flicked a quick probing look at Liz. Trying to assess her reaction to this decision? Was she okay with only one night here? 'But I am flying on to Vietnam,' he added. 'I might meet up with you there.'

'We're very busy in Vietnam,' his mother warned.

He laughed. 'Perhaps I'll catch up with you for another dinner together. Hear all your news.'

Another night.

Liz's heart squeezed tight.

Was Cole expecting to whisk her away from his mother for a while…fit in a hot bit of sex?

If so, she wouldn't be a party to it, Liz fiercely decided, her backbone stiffening. She would not have

his mother thinking there was some hanky-panky going on between her son and his personal assistant, just
as his ex-wife had suggested. Nancy might even leap
to a rosy conclusion that was not currently on the
cards—marriage and grandchildren!—and her happy
allusions to it would be horribly embarrassing.

Best that she didn't so much as guess at any intimate connection. There were another eleven days of
the trip to get through and every hour of it in Nancy's
company. As it was, she was happily raving on to
Cole about what they'd seen so far, accepting his
presence here at face value. *Let it stay that way,* Liz
grimly willed.

'What about you, Liz? Having fun?' he inquired
charmingly.

'Yes, thank you.'

'No problems?' His eyes scoured hers, trying to
penetrate the guard she'd just raised.

'None,' she answered sharply.

He frowned slightly. 'I haven't come to check up
on you, if that's what you're wondering.'

She managed an ironic smile. 'That would com-
prise bad judgment and a waste of time and money,
Cole.'

He returned her smile. 'As always, your logic is
spot on.'

'Thank you. I hope you enjoy your vacation.'

The distance she was putting between them was so
obvious in her impersonal replies, he couldn't possibly mistake it. His eyes glittered at her, as though
she'd thrown out a challenge he was bent on taking
up with every bit of ammunition at his disposal. Liz

burned with aggressive determination. Not in front of your mother, she wanted to scream at him.

'Time to move on to the ballroom,' Nancy announced, observing the people around moving forward, being ushered towards the next stage of the evening—dinner, entertainment and dancing in the Strand Hotel ballroom.

'Ladies…'

With mock colonial gallantry, Cole held out both of his arms for them to hook on to, ready to parade them in to dinner. His mother happily complied. Realising it would be rude to try avoiding the close contact, Liz followed suit, fixing a smile on her face and focusing on the people moving ahead of them, doing her level best to ignore the heat emanating from him and jangling every nerve in her body.

As they walked along, Nancy hailed various new acquaintances amongst the tour group, introducing her son, distracting Cole from any concentration on Liz, for which she was intensely grateful. It left her free to glance around the ballroom which was very elegant, panelled walls painted in different shades of pinky beige, huge chandeliers hanging from very high ceilings, a highly polished wooden floor, tables set for ten with white starched tablecloths and all the chairs had skirted white slip covers, adding to the air of pristine luxury.

Nancy insisted they sit at a table on the edge of the circle left free for dancing, saying she wanted to be close to whatever entertainment had been arranged for them. Cole obliged her by steering them to seats which had a direct view of the stage. Other people quickly joined them, making up the table of ten.

Liz was glad of the numbers. Although Cole had seated himself between her and Nancy, at least she had people to talk to on her other side, a good excuse to break any private tete-a-tete he might have in mind.

Even so, he shattered her hastily thought out defences by leaning close and murmuring, 'I look forward to dancing with you tonight.'

Dancing!

Being held in his arms, pressed into whatever contact he manoeuvred, moved right out of his mother's hearing for whatever he wanted to say to her...

Panic churned through Liz's stomach.

How was she going to handle this?

How?

CHAPTER FIFTEEN

Liz barely heard the choir of street children who had been rescued by the World Vision organization. They sang a number of songs. Another troup of children performed a dance. People made speeches she didn't hear at all. Food was placed in front of her and she ate automatically, not really tasting any of it. The man sitting beside her dominated her mind and played havoc with every nerve in her body.

A band of musicians took over the stage. They played a style of old time jazz that was perfect for ballroom dancing. A few couples rose from their tables, happily intent on moving to the music. Any moment now...

She could politely decline Cole's invitation to dance with him. He couldn't force her to accept. But given the level of intimacy there had been between them, he had every right to expect her compliance. A rejection would create an awkwardness that Nancy would inevitably rush into, urging Liz to *enjoy herself*.

She could say her feet were killing her.

Except she hadn't once complained about sore feet on this tour and Nancy might make a fuss about that, too.

Cole set his serviette on the table, pushed back his chair and rose to his feet. The band was playing

'Moon River', a jazz waltz which could only be executed well with very close body contact. Liz's stomach lurched as Cole turned to her, offering his hand.

'Dance, Liz?'

She stared at the hand, riven by a warring tumult of needs.

'Go on, dear,' Nancy urged. 'I'm perfectly happy watching the two of you waltz around.'

There really was no choice. Cole's other hand was already on the back of her chair ready to move it out of her way. Liz stood on jelly-like legs, fiercely resolving not to spend the night with him, no matter how deep the desire he stirred. It was an issue of... of...

She forgot what the issue was as his fingers closed around hers in a firm possessive clasp. An electric charge ran up her arm and short-circuited her brain. It seemed no time at all before his arm had scooped her against the powerful length of his body and his thighs were pushing hers into the seductive glide of the slow waltz.

He lowered his head and murmured in her ear. 'Why aren't I welcome, Liz?'

Her lobe tingled with the warmth of his breath. It was difficult to gather her scattered wits under the physical onslaught of his strong sexuality. The very direct question felt like an attack too, forcing her to explain her guarded behaviour with him.

'I'm with your mother,' she shot out, hoping he would see the need for some sense of discretion.

'So?' he queried, totally unruffled by any embarrassment she might feel about being pressed into some obvious closeness with him.

'It's not right to...' She struggled with the sensitivity of the situation, finally blurting out, '...to give her ideas...about us.'

'What's not right about it?' he countered. 'We're both free to pursue what we want.' His hand slid down the curve of her spine, splaying across the pit of her back, pressing firmly as his legs tangled with hers in an intricate set of steps and turns. 'I want you,' he said, again breathing into her ear. 'I thought you wanted me.'

She jerked her head back, her gaze wildly defying the simmering desire in his eyes. 'That's been private between us.'

'True. But I have no problem with making our private relationship public. And I can't imagine my mother would have any objection to it, either. She likes you.'

Resentment at his lack of understanding flared. 'That's not the point.'

He raised an eyebrow, mocking her contentious attitude. 'What is the point?'

Liz sucked in a quick breath and laid out what he apparently preferred to ignore. 'Nancy will want to think it's serious. She's already expressed her hope to me that you'll marry again and...and provide her with grandchildren.'

'And you don't see marriage on the cards for us?'

It sounded like a challenge to her. As though she had made a decision without telling him. And his eyes were now burning into hers with the determined purpose of finding out precisely what was on her mind.

Liz was flooded with confusion. 'You said…you said you had no intention of marrying again in a hurry.'

'Marry in haste, repent at leisure,' he quoted sardonically. 'Not a mistake I care to repeat. But I can assure you it won't take me three years to make up my mind.'

'Three…years?'

'That's what you spent on Brendan, Liz.'

She shook her head, amazed that he was linking himself in any way to her experience with Brendan. It was all so completely different. Why even compare a blitzkrieg affair to a long siege for commitment? In any event, it reminded her of a failure she preferred to forget. Surely Cole should realise that.

The music stopped.

The dancing stopped.

Cole still held her close, not making any move to disengage or take her back to the table. She dropped her hand from his shoulder, preparing to push out of his embrace. All the other couples were leaving the dance floor.

'Why didn't you tell me Brendan was in Nepal?'

'What?' Startled, her gaze flew up to meet his and was caught in the blaze of fierce purpose glittering at her.

'You heard me,' he stated grimly.

Her mind was whirling over knowledge he couldn't have…unless… 'Did Brendan try to contact me at the office?'

'Is that what you want to hear? Did you contact him with the news you were coming?'

'No...I...' She didn't understand what this was all about.

'Have you left a message for him to meet you in Kathmandu?' Cole bored in.

'It's over!' she cried, trying to cut through to the heart of the situation.

'Not for me, it isn't!' came the harsh retort.

She glanced wildly around the emptied dance floor. 'You're making a spectacle of us, standing here.'

'Then let's take the show on the road. You want private? We'll have private.'

Before Liz could begin to protest, he had her waist firmly grasped and was leading her straight to Nancy who was keenly watching them.

'I don't want private,' Liz muttered fiercely.

'I'm not going to let you take up ignoring me again, nor pretending there's been nothing deeply personal between us. Public or private, Liz. You choose.'

Aggression was pouring from him. He'd blow discretion sky-high if she insisted on staying at the table with the tour group. Liz frantically sought a way out of the dilemma Cole was forcing. Nancy was smiling at them, pleased to see them linked together. Liz inwardly recoiled from the interpretation she would put on their *togetherness* if Cole made it clear he was involved with his P.A. on more than a professional level.

Best to seize the initiative before he said something. Liz managed a rueful smile as they closed on his mother and quickly spoke up. 'Nancy, Cole and I have some business to sort out. Will you excuse us for a few minutes?'

'Might take quite a while,' Cole instantly inserted. 'Are you okay to get back to your hotel with the tour group, Mum?'

'Of course, dear.' She beamed triumphantly. 'I even have my room key with me. Liz always checks me on that.'

Trapped by her own efficiency.

'I'm sure we won't be so long, Cole,' she said, trying to minimise this *private* meeting.

'Best to cover all eventualities,' he smoothly returned. 'Given we run late sorting out this business, Mum, I'll escort Liz to your hotel and see her safely to your room, so no need to stay up and worry about her.'

Heat whooshed up Liz's neck and scorched her cheeks. Cole had to be planning more than just talk…

'Fine, dear,' came the ready acceptance to her son's plan. Nancy smiled benevolently at Liz. 'And don't you worry about disturbing me. It's been such a very busy day I'm sure I'll sleep like a log.'

Another excuse wiped out.

Cole picked up Liz's small evening bag from the table, taking possession of her money and her room key. 'Thanks, Mum,' he said by way of taking leave, then forcefully shepherded Liz towards the exit from the ballroom.

'Give me my bag,' she seethed through clenched teeth, determined not to have control taken completely out of her hands. If driven to it, she could arrange a taxi for herself.

'Going to do a runner on me, Liz?' he mocked.

'I don't like being boxed into a corner.'

'Right!' He passed it to her. 'So now you're a lady of independent means. Before you trot off in high dudgeon at my interference with your plans, I would appreciate your telling me what use I've been to you, apart from giving you a free ticket to Kathmandu.'

'What *use?*' She halted, stunned by what felt like totally unfair accusations. 'I didn't ask you for a free ticket!'

'This is not a private place.' To prove his point, he waved at the groups of smokers who had gathered out in the foyer to the ballroom. 'Since you don't want to cause gossip that might reach my mother's ears…'

He scooped her along with him, down the steps and through the passage to the hotel lobby, moving so fast Liz had barely caught her breath when he pressed the wall button beside an elevator.

'I am not going to your room,' she declared, furious at his arrogant presumption that she would just fall in with what he wanted.

His eyes seared hers in a savage assault. 'You had no problem with doing so last week.'

Liz's heart galloped at the sheer ferocity of feeling emanating from him. 'That…that was different.'

'How was it different? I'm making this as private as you had it then. Or was I just a stepping stone to boost your confidence enough to win with Brendan tomorrow?'

Brendan again!

The elevator doors opened while Liz was still shell-shocked by Cole's incredible reading of her actions.

He bundled her into the compartment and they were on their way up before her mind could even begin to encompass what he was implying. She stared at him in dazed disbelief. 'You think I went to bed with you to boost my confidence?'

'A frequent rebound effect,' he shot at her.

She was so incensed by the realisation he actually did think she had *used* him, the reverse side of that coin flooded into her mind. 'What about you, Cole?' she shot back at him. 'Quite a coincidence that on the very day Tara suggested I was obliging you in bed, you decided to make that true.'

He looked appalled. 'Tara had nothing to do with what I felt that night. Absolutely nothing!'

'So why do you imagine Brendan had anything to do with what I felt?'

'You didn't want the light on.'

'I didn't want you comparing me to your hot-shot wife. Finding me much less sexy.'

'You think I'd even look at a Tara clone after what I've been through with her?' he thundered.

Liz was stung into retorting, 'I don't know. She was the woman you married.'

'And divorced. As soon as it could be decently achieved after the death of our child.' A hard pride settled on his face. 'Tara is a user. She doesn't give a damn for anyone but herself. And believe me, that becomes sickeningly *unsexy* after you've lived with it for a while.' His eyes flashed venomously at her as he added, 'And I don't take kindly to being used by a woman I thought better of.'

'I didn't use you,' Liz cried vehemently.

'No? Then why the freeze-off tonight?'

'I told you. Your mother…'

'Not good enough!' he snapped, just as the elevator doors opened. He hustled her out into a corridor, jammed a key in a door, and pulled her into a private suite that ensured they'd be absolutely alone together.

Liz didn't fight the flow of action. The realisation had finally struck that this was not about having sex with her tonight. It was about sorting out their relationship and what it meant to them. And Cole was in a towering rage because he believed she meant to meet Brendan tomorrow, with the possible purpose of reigniting interest in a future together.

He released his hold on her as he closed the door behind them, apparently satisfied he had shut off all avenues of escape. 'Now…now I'll have the truth from you,' he said, exuding a ruthless relentlessness that perversely sent a thrill through Liz.

He cared.

He really cared.

Hugging this sweet knowledge to herself she walked on into the massive suite, past the opened door to a huge bathroom, past two queen size beds, through an archway to an elegant sitting room. She turned to face him in front of the large curtained window at the far end. He'd followed her to the archway where he stood with an air of fierce patience—a big, powerful man who was barely reining in violent feelings.

'I didn't tell you Brendan was in Nepal because it was irrelevant to us, Cole,' she stated quietly.

'Hardly irrelevant,' he gravelled back at her. 'Because of him you stopped hiding your light under a bushel and showed me a Liz Hart I'd never seen before.'

She shook her head. 'That was my sisters' idea. To brighten me up so that other men might see me as attractive. My mother insisted it would make me feel better about myself. Brendan was gone, Cole. I never thought for one moment of trying to get him back. It was over.'

'But then...having made me see you differently, which led to my proving how very desirable you were...you had a ticket to Nepal in your hand—the chance to show Brendan what he was missing.'

'We're going to Kathmandu. I have no idea where in Nepal Brendan is or if, indeed, he's still there. I don't care. If by some freakish chance I should run into him, it won't make any difference. I don't ever want him in my life again.'

He frowned. 'Is that how you feel about me, too? I've served your purpose of...feeling better about yourself?'

She lifted her chin in a kind of defiant challenge, telling herself she had nothing to lose now. 'You want the truth, Cole?'

'Yes.' Piercing blue eyes demanded it of her.

'I've always been attracted to you. But you were married. And I was no Tara Summerville anyway so it was absurd of me to even dream of ever having you. I guess you could say Brendan was a pragmatic choice for me and I tried quite desperately to make it work. Maybe that was what drove him away in the end…me trying too hard to make something that was never quite right into something I could live with.'

Another frown. 'You never indicated an attraction…'

'That would have been futile. And I liked working with you.'

He grimaced and muttered, 'My oasis in a desert.'

'Pardon?'

He managed an ironic smile. 'You helped make my life livable during its darkest days, just by being there, Liz.'

Her smile was wry. 'The handmaiden.'

'Oh, I wouldn't put you in that category. A handmaiden wouldn't talk back, put me in my place. More a helpmate.'

Liz took a deep breath and spilled out the critical question for her. 'Was I helping you to shut Tara out of your mind in those days—and nights—before your divorce was settled?'

He shook his head, clearly vexed by such a concept. 'She was gone. A lot longer gone than Brendan was for you, Liz. Part of me was angry because he'd made you feel a failure, made you feel less than you are. And Tara had put you down, as well. I wanted to lift you up…

'You took…*pity*…on me?' Everything within her recoiled from that idea.

'Good God, no!' He looked totally exasperated, frustrated by her interpretation, scowling as he gathered his thoughts to dispel it. 'I was angry that you felt so low, especially since you were worth so much more than the people who did that to you. I tried to tell you…show you….' He lifted his hands in an oddly helpless gesture. 'In the end, I couldn't stop myself from making love to you even though I knew I shouldn't risk our business relationship.'

'Making love…' She struggled to swallow the huge lump that had risen in her throat. 'It did feel like that, but then it seemed you only had sex on your mind. All the sex you could get.'

'With you, Liz. Only with you.' His eyes softened, warmed, simmered over her. 'You truly were like an oasis in the desert and when I finally got there, I wanted to revel in everything you gave me. It felt so good.'

So good… She couldn't deny it, didn't want to shade that truth by other things, but she needed to have all her doubts cleared away.

'To me, too,' she admitted. 'But I thought…maybe I was just handy and you were using me to…'

'No. Simply because you're you, Liz.'

'Tonight…when I saw you here…I decided I didn't want to be used like that. Not even by you, Cole.' She held tightly on to all her courage as she added, 'Though I want you more than any man I've known.'

His face broke into a smile that mixed relief with intense pleasure. 'Believe me. The feeling is entirely mutual.'

She let out the breath that had been caught in her lungs and an answering smile burst across her face. 'Really?'

'What do you think I've been fighting for?' He swiftly crossed the short distance between them and wrapped her in a tight hug, his eyes burning into hers with very serious intent. 'No pulling away from me now. We're going to see how well this relationship can work for us. Give it time. Okay?'

Not an impossible dream.

It was almost too much to believe. Her heart swelled with glorious hope. Her mind danced with future possibilities. She was being held very possessively by the man she wanted more than any other in the world. He'd left his work and flown to South-East Asia to fight anything that might part them, and now he was saying...

'Answer me, Liz.'

Commanding...

She loved this man...everything about him. Her arms flew up around his neck. 'Yes, Cole. Yes.' Joy in her voice, desire churning through her body. Mutual, she thought exultantly.

He kissed her, making *mutual* absolutely awesome.

They made love...wonderful, passionate, blissful love...long into the night. No inhibitions. Cole didn't have to sweep them away. Liz felt none. She believed she was the woman he wanted in every sense. He made her feel it. There was nothing she couldn't do with him, nothing she couldn't say to him. And she no longer worried about what his mother might think. Nancy would be happy for them.

It was almost dawn when Cole arranged for a car to transport them to the tour hotel. They'd both decided his mother might panic if Liz wasn't in their room when she woke up. Liz felt too exhilarated to sleep at all. She told herself she would have the opportunity later this morning, on the flight to Kathmandu.

Which reminded her…

'How did you know Brendan was in Nepal, Cole?'

'My mother told me, just before leaving on the trip.'

'Your mother?' Liz frowned over this unexpected source until she recollected having answered Nancy's questions on her ex-boyfriend. 'But why would she do that?'

Cole smiled. 'Maybe she guessed I cared about you and the suggestion that I might lose you was a prompt to action if I wanted to keep you.'

Liz sighed with happy contentment. 'Well, I'm glad you came.'

Cole squeezed her hand. 'So am I.'

She glanced down at their interlocked hands, suddenly recalling the horribly tense scene just after Tara had left the Palm Beach house and Cole had come to the conservatory to eliminate any distress she'd caused.

'Well, isn't that nice?' his mother had remarked. 'He cares about you, dear.'

Liz could now smile over the memory.

Maybe mothers knew best.

Cole did care about her.

And Liz certainly felt very, very good about herself.

CHAPTER SIXTEEN

Six months later…

LIZ and her sisters were in the kitchen, cleaning up after the Sunday lunch barbecue—an informal family celebration of her engagement to Cole who was happily chatting to her father and brothers-in-law out on the patio. Her mother and Nancy Pierson had their heads together in the lounge room, conferring about the wedding which Cole had insisted be held as soon as it could be arranged.

'That man of yours truly is charming. And mouth-wateringly attractive,' Sue declared, rolling her eyes teasingly at Liz. 'You have to admit it now.'

She laughed. 'He's improved a lot since we've been together.'

'Oh, you!' Sue flicked a tea-towel at her. 'You never give anything away. Still all buttoned up within yourself.'

'No, she's not!' Diana instantly disagreed. 'She's positively blossomed since we made her over. Best idea I ever had. And look what's come out of it.' She grabbed Liz's left hand out of the sink of washing up water and suds. 'Got to see your gorgeous ring again!'

It was a magnificent ruby, surrounded by diamonds. Liz smiled at the red gleams as Diana turned it to the light.

'That's the fire in you,' Cole had said when he'd slid it on her finger. 'Every time I think of you I feel warm.' Then a wicked grin. 'If not hot.'

'This is a very serious ring,' Diana decided. 'Definitely a *to have and to hold from this day forth* ring. High-powered stuff. I hope you realise what you're getting into with this guy, Liz.'

'I have known Cole for quite some time,' she answered dryly.

It evoked a gurgle of gleeful amusement. 'Nothing like marrying the boss.'

'What impresses me…' Jayne chimed in. '…is how good he is with the children. He's like a magnet to them. They're all over him and he obviously doesn't mind a bit.'

'He doesn't. Cole loved being a father.'

Jayne heaved a rueful sigh. 'So sad about the son he lost. Is he mad keen to have a family with you, Liz?'

'Definitely keen.'

'Liz…' her mother called from the doorway. 'Would you go and fetch Cole inside to us. Nancy and I need to talk to both of you.'

'Okay, Mum.'

Liz dried her hands on Jayne's tea-towel and headed for the patio. Behind her, her three sisters broke into a raucous chorus of, 'Here comes the bride…'

Liz was laughing at their high-spirited good humour as she stepped outside. It was so good to feel at one with them instead of shut out of their charmed circle, looking in. Not that they had ever shut her out.

Liz realised now she'd done that to herself, not feeling she could ever compete with them.

It was only with Cole that she'd come to understand that love had nothing to do with competition. Love simply accepted who you were. You didn't have to be like someone else...just who you were.

And she saw his love for her in his eyes as she walked towards him. It warmed her all through, made her feel special and brilliantly alive. She smiled, loving him right back.

'Our mothers want us in the lounge room with them. I think you've thrown them a bit, insisting on a quick wedding.'

'No way are we going to put it off,' he warned, and promptly excused himself from the company of the other men. He reached her in a couple of strides and wrapped an arm around her shoulders. 'We're standing firm on this, Liz. I want us married. I'm not waiting a day longer than I have to.'

'They won't be happy if they can't organise a proper wedding. And just remember, I only intend to be a bride once.'

He slanted a look at her that crackled with powerful purpose. 'I promise you, you'll have a proper wedding.'

Cole really was unstoppable when he had a goal in his sights.

Once they were in the lounge room, their mothers regaled them with the plans they'd made. A Saturday would be best for the wedding. Impossible to book a decent reception place at such short notice. Nancy had offered her home at Palm Beach, a marquee to be put up over the grounds surrounding the pool. Catering could be arranged.

'But, Liz,' her mother addressed her seriously. 'We really should have six weeks for the invitations to go out. People need that much time to…'

'No,' Cole broke in decisively. 'A month is it. If some invited guests can't make it, I'm sorry but we're not waiting on them.'

'What is the hurry, dear?' Nancy cried in exasperation.

His piercing blue eyes speared the question at Liz.

She nodded, feeling sure enough now to share their secret.

'Liz wouldn't agree to marry me until she was three months pregnant and feeling secure that everything was okay and she'd carry our baby full term.'

'Pregnant?' Her mother gaped at Liz.

'A baby!' Nancy clapped her hands in delight.

'If I'd had my way, we would have been married before she got pregnant,' Cole informed them. 'But Liz got this fixation about having a child…'

'*Our* child,' Liz gently corrected him.

He gave her a look that melted her bones. '*Our* child,' he repeated in a thrilling tone of possessive pride and joy.

'A grandchild,' Nancy said on a sigh of pleasure.

'And Liz doesn't want to look lumpy in her wedding dress,' Cole went on.

'Of course not!' Nancy happily agreed.

'Liz…' Having recovered from her initial shock, her mother rose from her armchair, shaking her head at her daughter as she came over to enfold her in a motherly hug. '…always bent on doing it your way. Congratulations, darling.'

'I'm so happy, Mum,' Liz assured her.

'As you should be.'

'And I'm so happy for both of you,' Nancy declared, leaving her chair to do some hugging herself. 'Liz is the right woman for you, Cole. I knew it the moment I met her.'

'Amazing how anyone can be blessed with such certainty at a moment's notice,' Cole drawled, his eyes twinkling at Liz.

'Mother's intuition,' she archly informed him. 'Maybe I'll get some of that myself in six months' time.'

'Mmmh…removing logical argument from our relationship?'

'More like shortcutting it.'

'This might be stretching my love for you.'

'You swore it would stretch on forever.'

He turned to his mother. 'You see, Mum? She's too smart for me.'

'Go on with you, Cole,' Nancy laughingly chided. 'You love it.'

He grinned. 'Yes, I do. And since we now have the wedding back on track, I'm going to whisk Liz off to show her how very much I love everything about her.'

And he did.

Six months later, Liz and Cole were the besotted parents of a baby daughter, Jessica Anne, whose tiny fingers curled around one of her father's and instantly enslaved him for life.

LUCA'S SECRETARY BRIDE

by

Kim Lawrence

Kim Lawrence lives on a farm in rural Anglesey. She runs two miles daily and finds this an excellent opportunity to unwind and seek inspiration for her writing! It also helps her keep up with her husband, two active sons, and the various stray animals which have adopted them. Always a fanatical consumer of fiction, she is now equally enthusiastic about writing. She loves a happy ending!

Don't miss Kim Lawrence's exciting new novel *Secret Baby, Convenient Wife* out in March 2008 from Mills & Boon® Modern™.

CHAPTER ONE

THE grateful mother had hysterics: the very loud, attention-grabbing variety. She certainly grabbed the attention of the shoppers, tourists and locals going about their business in the busy New York thoroughfare on the sunny late afternoon. A large crowd was gathering to hear her express her tearful gratitude to the man who had saved her baby's life.

The 'baby' in question added truculently that he was *not* a baby, he was nearly five, before kicking the man who had snatched him from the jaws of death on the shin.

Luca's fixed smile grew strained as he hung onto the kid who, even after his brush with death, had not made the connection between danger and moving traffic. As the screaming monster tried to bite him Luca found himself wondering just what the attraction of parenthood was. From where he was standing it wasn't exactly glaringly obvious.

Luca liked children as much as the next man, and of course it went without saying that any child of his would *not* try to bite people, but he felt no primal urge to get out there and procreate. Not that this was an issue as yet. Despite his reputation for being a bit of a maverick, Luca actually held some pretty traditional views, and in his book marriage and children came as a joint package. Though as he had never to this point in his life met a woman he would contemplate spending the rest of his life with, it was kind of academic.

Being of mixed Italian and Irish parentage, Luca had never been left with any doubt that one of his primary duties in life was to find a nice wife and produce babies...*no pressure*! That he had reached thirty without doing either did not go down well with his parents or, for that matter, his grandparents, aunts and uncles and cousins.

Luca's response whenever his single status was mentioned was to point out he had an elder brother who could carry on the family name. Clearly this subject came under the heading of the duty of the first-born, and what was Roman—thirty-two?

Luca himself would be more than happy to fulfil the role of doting uncle, something that would not require too many sacrifices, compromises or sleepless nights on his part. Unfortunately there were no likely candidates that he knew of on the scene to marry his brother right now.

Unless, he mused with a cynical grimace, you included the ever-present and incredibly faithful Alice, who would no doubt marry her boss like a shot if she ever got within sniffing distance of a ring.

Luca moved his head in an almost imperceptible negative gesture as an image of grey-blue eyes and pale silvery blonde curls appeared in his head.

The hardness that filtered into his eyes as he considered the question of his brother's indispensable blonde right-hand woman apparently communicated itself with the child he was restraining. Flashing the tall man a wary look, he ran back to his mother.

'I hate you!' the boy yelled from behind the protection of her skirt.

'I'm not wild about you either,' Luca responded absently. His thoughts were momentarily elsewhere.

His brother wouldn't actually consider marrying his blonde secretary, would he? He didn't love her, but as it seemed his brother had grown cynical in his old age and given up on love that might not be the obstacle it might once have been.

Just *how* jaundiced and disillusioned his brother had become had been revealed in a recent conversation. The occasion had been their parents' anniversary and their father had not wasted the opportunity of a captive audience to introduce his favourite theme.

Later that night they had been walking beside a lake on the extensive family estate in Ireland.

'Subtle, wasn't he?' Luca remarked ironically to his brother.

'As ever, but he might have a point, you know.' Roman, his expression unreadable, paused to skim a stone on the lake's still surface. 'It's all in the wrist,' he explained modestly.

'You don't say.' Luca punched the air in exaggerated triumph as his own stone outskipped that of his brother. The mocking enactment of the sibling rivalry that had once existed between them drew a smile from his brother. 'You're losing it, Roman,' he taunted before pressing curiously, 'Have you been holding out on me? Is there someone I don't know about?'

'*Someone…?*'

Luca spelt it out. 'Have you fallen in love? Will the parents disapprove of her? *That* would be interesting. God, she's not married, is she?' That would *really* put the cat amongst the pigeons, he thought.

'You think love is a good enough reason to get married?'

'I've not given it a lot of thought. I take it *you* don't.'

'Love is a form of temporary insanity,' his sibling informed him. 'Insanity is not a good basis for any contract I can think of, and when you get right down to it that's what marriage is…a contract.'

Luca didn't consider himself a particularly romantic man but he found this assessment of the institution of marriage chilling. 'Not a meeting of souls?'

'You need a soul mate to be complete? Do me a favour!'

'I feel pretty complete,' Luca agreed. 'But, can you imagine Da without Ma or vice versa?'

'There are exceptions,' Roman conceded grudgingly. 'I

tried doing the love and marriage thing.' The stone Roman flung sunk. 'In case it slipped your mind, things didn't go according to plan.'

Luca restricted his show of fraternal sympathy to a bang on the shoulder. 'You're not going to let a little thing like being dumped at the altar turn you into a lonely, bitter bachelor?'

'Oh, I'll get married, but *love* will not be high on my list of requirements. In fact it won't be on it at all,' Roman revealed with a cynical grimace of distaste. 'Marry now...marry in five years—what's the difference?'

What if this hadn't been an example of his brother's warped black sense of humour? What if he was on the lookout for a mother for his children? What if he wanted *Alice Trevelyan*?

Now wouldn't that be a joke? Joke or not, it didn't make Luca smile. Now the crazy idea had occurred to him Luca found it was one he didn't particularly warm to. It was patently obvious to him that Alice Trevelyan was *not* the wife for his brother.

There was any number of sound reasons to back up his conclusion—at least he was sure there would be had he chosen to work them out. Sometimes it was better to go on gut instincts and on this subject his guts were *very* definite.

The frown between his darkly defined brows deepened. There was propinquity to be considered, you couldn't underestimate the power of that, especially when the item you were constantly in close proximity to came attached to curves of a very superior quality.

The fact that his brother's secretary was easily the sexiest-looking woman Luca had ever come across had to be an influencing factor. She didn't flaunt it in revealing tops and short skirts, nothing clung, but somehow she managed to look more provocative in pearls and sensible shoes than another woman would have done naked.

Roman's Alice was the sort of female most men would not

be satisfied to simply look at…she was the sort who made a man want to touch. His sculpted mouth tightened into a grimace filled with self-mockery; he could personally testify to this. Not that he would go anywhere near a woman of his brother's even if watching her walk across a room could send his imagination into overdrive.

No way was he going to jeopardise his relationship with his brother to satisfy a fairly basic itch.

But he was assuming Roman wanted Alice. He never had figured out exactly what his brother's relationship with his secretary was. They certainly had a rapport in the office, Luca had seen it for himself, but did that rapport extend as far as the bedroom…?

He hadn't asked and he wasn't about to. If his brother chose to mix business with pleasure—a recipe for disaster in his book—that was Roman's business.

'Deserve a medal, pal…' Someone slapped him hard on the shoulder. Luca said something appropriately self-deprecatory. He didn't want a medal; he wanted out of there before someone produced a camera.

Damn…the crowd was starting to attract a bigger crowd.

Attention was the last thing Luca wanted. He spent what sometimes seemed to be an inordinate amount of energy avoiding attention, although, it had to be admitted, not always successfully.

He could see the headlines now…something to do with his old journalistic instincts? It was almost ten years since he had worked on the national broadsheet where he had cut his teeth straight from school, but he still possessed an insider's knowledge of how a journo's mind worked. Being able to occasionally anticipate the pack sometimes came in very handy.

Ironic, really, that if it hadn't been for his father's heart attack he might still be part of that pack. When Finn O'Hagan had been forced into early retirement it had been Roman, who had the financial expertise, who had stepped in to run the highly successful leisure and property side of the family-run outfit.

Before his heart attack Finn had been planning to offload the unprofitable Stateside publishing firm inherited from an uncle. It had only been sentiment that had made him continue to subsidise the loss-making operation this long. Luca had agreed to take a short sabbatical, step in, go through the books and generally put the place in good enough order to put on the market. He'd cleared his calendar for a couple of months.

Then something strange had happened. Luca had started enjoying himself and his enthusiasm had been contagious.

By the end of the first year they had been out of the red, had signed up a prolific new author who had not been out of the best-seller lists since his first week of publication and had attracted several established names. No longer the poor relation in the O'Hagan empire, they now had offices in Sydney, London and Dublin and Luca was still enjoying himself.

Luca gently but firmly detached the weeping woman from his shirt-front and scanned the gathering crowd as he smoothed the expensive fabric back into place. The action made him aware that he hadn't escaped unscathed from the incident. A slight frown formed on his lean, handsome face as he flexed his right shoulder experimentally and felt the burn of overstretched muscles.

Had some of the interested observers been privy to his private resolve to find time in his schedule to take more exercise, they would have been startled; Luca possessed a streamlined, long-legged muscular body—broad of shoulder, narrow of hip—that would have earned him a fortune advertising male swimwear.

The arrival of a man Luca assumed to be the kiddy's father was the cue for lots more tears. Greeted with the garbled explanation that his son and heir had escaped death by the narrowest of margins, the poor guy went into shock.

Luca decided to take advantage of the moment to slip away.

Melting into a crowd did not come easily for Luca. Being six four in his bare feet and the owner of a body that had come in the top three of a celebratory magazine poll of 'the man you would most like to see naked,' it was fair to say he stood out in a crowd.

He knew about the article because some joker in his Dublin office had pinned said article on the bulletin board along with the readers' letters in the next issue that contended the vote must have been fixed, and indignantly suggested that Luca had been robbed of first place.

Despite his natural handicaps he did manage to make a successful escape. Once he was out of sight and earshot of the crowd his phone rang. It was his brother, his single brother. Luca smiled in grim amusement when he realised that for a couple of minutes back there he'd almost had Roman locked into a loveless marriage.

Talk about letting your imagination run away from you.

Would it have run quite so far, and so fast, if the bride he had saying *I do* hadn't been Alice Trevelyan? He frowned as the unwelcome thought surfaced in his mind, and pushed it away.

'Are we still on for tonight?'

Luca glanced at his watch and grimaced. 'Sure thing, only I've still got to catch up with Hennessey. I could be a few minutes late.'

'And will the lovely Ingrid be with you?'

'Funny guy,' Luca said with a grin in response to the innocent enquiry.

'Tenacious lady, isn't she, and if ever there was a born self-publicist?'

'You put her onto me, didn't you?'

'*Me!* I'm heartbroken…my confidence is shot to hell, what man wouldn't be? Dumped for my own brother.'

'*Dio mio!* You're a devious snake is what you are,' Luca retorted.

'Give me a break, Luca. I had to do something, the woman kept planting stories about spring weddings. And it came to me…it's well documented that Luca likes blondes, especially tall Nordic ones. So I mentioned in passing that *you* get invited to all the A-list parties, and I let it drop that you're much more photogenic than me and infinitely more high profile, especially in the States.'

Luca couldn't help appreciating his brother's tactics. 'You knew she was gay, of course.'

A chuckle reverberated down the line. 'Did she sound you out on donating sperm at some future date too?'

'Yes,' Luca gritted with a shudder. 'Although she made it clear that would depend on me passing stringent medical screening.'

'And I thought I was special…' His brother sighed soulfully. 'About tonight, no problem, Alice and I are running late too. See you lat…by the way, I probably should warn you it's possible that Alice believes the tabloid version of you and Ingrid.'

Luca could hear the grin in his brother's voice. 'And you saw no reason to straighten her out?'

'Strangely enough that didn't occur to me. She thinks I'm being quite extraordinarily brave,' he confided.

'You're warped, you know that.'

'She thinks you're a heartless love rat,' Roman explained, not bothering to hide his amusement.

So no change there. 'Will Alice be there tonight, then?' he asked casually.

'Of course she will. Alice is almost family.'

Almost…? Luca slid the phone back into his pocket, a thoughtful expression on his face… *Am I being paranoid?*

Don't lose sight of the fact that, even if asked, Alice might say no to Roman, Luca told himself.

Sure, that's *really* going to happen. We are talking the

woman who without a second thought took a knife wielded by a raving lunatic to save her boss, he reminded himself.

So look at this another way. Would having Alice Trevelyan as his new sister really be so bad?

A spasm of distaste crossed his face. *Yes, it definitely would!* Well, if I can't find another bride for Roman, I might just have to marry the woman myself!

'Can I get you an aperitif?' the solicitous waiter asked.

Alice wasn't normally a drinker, but she felt that under the circumstances a little Dutch courage might not be such a bad idea.

All I had to say was no. Why was that so hard? She comforted herself slightly as she sipped slowly on her glass of white wine with the recognition that she wasn't the only person who found it hard to say no to her boss. Her employer had the enviable knack of getting people to do what he wanted.

Slow or not, in an hour and a half you could sip quite a lot, and there wasn't much else to do *but* sip as she sat conspicuously alone amongst the other people, or rather *couples*, dining in the exclusive New York hotel. It was at times like this a girl could be excused for thinking she were the only person left who wasn't part of a pair. She felt a flicker of pain as she reached unconsciously for the gold ring that she had worn on a chain around her neck since the day her worried mother had confided she was afraid her daughter wasn't letting go of the past.

You're young, Alice, and you know as well as I do that Mark would want you to get on with your life.

Discovering its absence made her feel more undressed than the low-cut dress that had forced her to remove it tonight.

With a pang Alice turned her head as the couple seated to her left touched fingers across the table. Not being a girl to dwell on the gloomy aspects of life, she reminded herself of the many benefits of not having a significant other.

If she had a lover she would have to worry about the hedgehog style her hair adopted when she woke up in the morning. She could sleep on whatever side of the bed she wanted—and right now the bed she occupied was a rather spectacular queen-size.

Roman was many things, she mused, but a stingy employer was not one of them. When she travelled with him it was always first class. She occupied a gorgeous room right next to his on the top floor.

Alice looked at her empty glass and hazily considered the possibility that she had had too much to drink. But didn't people who were drunk feel happy and carefree, prone to dancing on tables and breaking into song at the least provocation?

Alice felt no inclination to do either.

She had no illusions about it. At best the evening was going to be an endurance test of her self-control. The thought of spending a painful hour, or even *two*, trying to make polite conversation with someone who had enough ego in his little finger to sustain a small planet was something she was not looking forward to.

And when it came to filling the inevitable awkward silences she knew better than to look to her dining companion for help. He'd just sit there looking bored in that aggravatingly languid way he had with those eerily penetrating blue eyes of his giving the unnerving impression he could read her thoughts.

The irony of the situation didn't escape her. An intimate dinner with a single man who was universally acknowledged as being not only wealthy and smart but also unbelievably good-looking would have had most women turning cartwheels and here was she acting as if Judgement Day had arrived.

Of course most women, unlike Alice, didn't know what a pain in the rear Luca O'Hagan actually was. Given the choice

between root-canal work and dining by candlelight with her
boss's younger brother, Alice would have headed for the den-
tist's chair every time.

The problem was he was spoilt. Things came too easily to
the man, she decided, staring broodingly into her empty glass,
including female company, she thought disapprovingly.
Perhaps, she mused, he might have been more tolerable if
someone had actually ever said *no* to him. Having seen him
in action personally, she wasn't holding her breath! The title
'babe magnet' had never been more aptly bestowed.

Her soft but determined chin rose to a decisive angle. She'd
give him ten more minutes and then she was going to go back
to her room to order a sandwich. Feeling a lot better for having made the decision, she caught a waiter's eye and ordered
another drink.

At the same moment the voice of the *maître d'* drifted
across the room. 'Your favourite table…'

Alice's fingers tightened around the stem of her glass and
her slender back stiffened. Having worked for her millionaire
boss for the past five years, she immediately recognised the
warm 'very special person' welcoming tone.

What was it about some people that made other people fall
over themselves to be attentive? Alice would have liked to be
able to attribute the deference to money and power, but she
knew that even if you had robbed her boss and his brother of
those advantages they would still have been able to effortlessly command attention in any environment.

Impatient with the trepidation she was experiencing, she
turned her head and gave a smile befitting the efficient 'PA
cum secretary deputising for her boss's face.

There was a man standing there, but not the one she was
waiting for. Anticlimax sent the tense muscles of her stomach
into a lurching dive. She sighed, rubbed her nervously damp
palms against one another and, because she'd looked at most

everything else in the room and the newcomer was worth a second glance, she carried on studying him.

This one looked far more like the sort of man she would *prefer* to be waiting for, she mused wistfully. Tall but not *too* tall and well dressed. Youngish-looking, too, despite his distinctive head of silver hair. As her eyes connected with his the man gave a quizzical smile. Alice returned a lopsided embarrassed smile and looked away in case he got the wrong idea.

Her gloom intensified as she returned her attention to the wine list and pretended to study it, as if she couldn't already have written a dissertation on the hideously expensive bottles on offer! The man, like the entire room, including the overly solicitous staff, obviously thought she had been stood up. They weren't wrong.

Just as well this wasn't a real date.

The idea of her having a real date with Luca O'Hagan made her smile thinly. World peace by the weekend was a much more likely scenario!

She was making inroads into her fresh glass of wine when the discreet *maître d'* quietly informed her that Mr O'Hagan had left a message that he would be there presently.

'I can hardly wait.' Her dry rejoinder made the bearer of the glad tidings look slightly disconcerted. 'Thank you,' she added with a smile, trying hard to display a little of the gratitude the man obviously expected her to exhibit.

In reality the news had not made Alice feel exceptionally grateful, just exceptionally mad.

To be stood up by, not one, but *two* O'Hagans on one evening was enough to make anyone a little cranky.

'You stay, smooth things over with Luca for me,' her boss had cajoled persuasively before abandoning her. 'A night out will do you good. You deserve a treat.'

'Well, actually, I could do with an early night...' And you

could do with therapy if you imagine even for a tiny second that I'd class a night out with your brother as a treat.'

'Pity. I cancelled our meeting last month and I wouldn't like Luca to think I'm a sore loser.'

Alice was instantly sympathetic. 'Well, I suppose I could…'

'Excellent.'

What Roman had lost and Luca had picked up had been six feet one and blonde. The Swedish model in question graced the front covers of just about every glossy magazine Alice picked up at the moment. The elder O'Hagan brother had returned from a business trip to Prague to find that his girlfriend had left for the States with his brother.

Roman hadn't seem gutted; he had greeted the news with a philosophical shrug. Alice, indignant on his behalf, knew he was bravely hiding his true feelings. Bad enough to have your brother run off with your girlfriend, but for the story then to be splashed across the tabloids must have been truly shocking.

She really hoped her boss's feelings for the gorgeous lady hadn't run deep, but even if they hadn't it wouldn't have let the lecherous Luca off the hook in her eyes. For all he knew Roman might have been head over heels in love…no, Alice thought, he had behaved despicably!

Some things *nice* people didn't do, and pinching your brother's girl was one of them.

But then nobody had ever called Luca nice. Instead, they'd called him other things, including sinfully sexy!

While there was no denying he had something special in the looks department, Alice's personal taste ran to something far less in your face and obvious.

Her eyes wandered across the room to the quiet alcove the newcomer had been escorted to and found that coincidentally he was looking her way. She nodded slightly in acknowledgement and looked away. Maybe he'd been stood up too?

Although he didn't look like the sort of man that would happen to.

God, why did I let Roman talk me into this? Maybe Luca was right, maybe I am *Roman's doormat*. Even now, a long time after overhearing the contemptuous remark Luca had made, it still had the power to make her blood boil.

The notion that she was some sort of slave without a mind or will of her own was totally unfair. Luca's assessment of her relationship with her boss had been so far off the mark to be laughable.

For some reason Luca O'Hagan couldn't stand her and he didn't make any effort to hide the fact. The tight feeling in her chest got tighter as she contemplated the sneers and snubs, besides the despised 'doormat' jibe, she had been on the receiving end of courtesy of Luca O'Hagan. What had she ever done to him except bleed a bit on the upholstery of his car? Hardly a crime to justify a vendetta.

Her method of dealing with his sneers and him was polite indifference. You couldn't really start a slanging match with the brother of your boss, especially when he ran part of the family company. So Alice maintained a supernaturally serene front in face of his frequently provocative behaviour, a fact of which she was extremely proud. Fortunately their paths didn't cross too frequently as he spent most of his time this side of the Atlantic and her time was split between Dublin and London.

'Excuse me…?'

The Texan drawl startled Alice from her own thoughts. Her eyes widened when she lifted her head and saw the silver-haired new arrival standing at her elbow.

'I'm dining alone and I was wondering…?'

Alice, aware that his remark could be heard by fellow diners, felt her face flush. 'I'm waiting for someone.'

There was no question of her encouraging him, but the attention of an attractive man did make her feel a little less like a total loser sitting amongst the romantically inclined couples surrounding her.

He gave a rueful grimace. 'I never thought otherwise...but until then, would you like some company? I promise you I'm perfectly harmless.' His smile was as charming as the line was clichéd.

This claim wrenched an unwilling laugh from Alice. 'That I doubt. Actually I was just leaving.'

'You've been stood up?'

'It looks like it.'

'The man must be crazy.'

'No, just incredibly self-centred, insufferably rude and deeply obnoxious.'

CHAPTER TWO

EVEN without turning her head Alice could pinpoint the exact moment Luca O'Hagan walked into the place from the ten-second hush that descended on the candlelit room, followed by an interested low-voiced buzz of speculative comment.

She could visualise him in her mind's eye. He would act as if he didn't know his tall, imposing figure was the focus of attention as he wove his way with innate grace between the tightly packed tables, but he was. He knew *exactly* what effect he had on people and wasn't, she thought contemptuously, above exploiting it cynically when it suited him.

She smiled and tried to give the amusing tale the silver-haired Seth was relating the attention it and he deserved; it wasn't easy when she knew who was approaching. Seth paused expectantly and she laughed at the punchline…at least I hope it was the punchline, she thought.

An invisible presence and Luca was still a disastrously distracting person. Only if you let him be, she told herself sternly. There was no question of her own reaction to Luca being anything out of the ordinary; he was the sort of man who drew a reaction from people. Love or hate the man—she identified with the latter group—nobody ignored him!

Personally, the attraction of being the partner of a man who stopped conversations and drew covetous stares from other women when he walked into a room passed her by. Not a problem you're likely to have, the dry voice in her head pointed out cruelly.

She dragged her attention back to the man sitting opposite. He was telling her about an art exhibition he had attended the previous month. Actually he seemed one of the few people unaware of the buzz in the room that accompanied the tall man who came to stand by his shoulder.

'What have you done with Roman, then?'

There was no trace of the charm he was famed for in the terse, deep-pitched accusing enquiry. And you expected there to be, Alice? she asked herself. He reserved his *niceness* for people who mattered and clearly she didn't.

Alice didn't look up, but felt the familiar prickle of antagonism slide down her spine as her nostrils flared in response to the subtle male fragrance he sparingly used.

Experience had taught her that the first few moments of making contact with Luca O'Hagan were generally the worst; practically speaking this meant she kept eye contact to the minimum and didn't say the first or even *second* thing that came to mind. If she managed not to trip over her own feet or say anything too stupid in those first few seconds she could generally pass for someone who could bear to be in the same room as him without wanting to crawl out of her own skin.

'He's not here.' And I wish I weren't, she thought, picking up her glass to avoid focusing on him.

'That much I can see for myself.' There was the sound of a chair scraping the floor as he pulled one out from the table and sat down.

'He got called away…it was urgent.' There was an expectant silence, until belatedly she remembered her manners. 'This is Seth…Seth…erm?' She turned to her companion with an apologetic grimace. 'I'm terrible with names.' Before her entertaining companion could refresh her memory Luca spoke up.

'Chase,' Luca supplied. He nodded casually towards the older man. 'How are you, Seth?'

In Alice's eyes it counted in the Texan's favour that he didn't appear even slightly bothered by the perceptible coldness in Luca's manner. She was definitely inclined to think well of someone who wasn't blighted by Luca O'Hagan's disapproval. In her opinion there were far too many people—many of whom ought to know better—already willing to stand on their heads if it made him look at them warmly.

'Pretty good, thanks, Luca.'

She slid a sideways covert peek at Luca's classical profile; it looked like granite only not as warm. Her eyebrows twitched as she looked away. My, someone has got out of bed the wrong side today, she thought.

Whose bed? Was the model still his 'constant companion', as one of the gossip columnists had triumphantly revealed the previous week? she wondered sourly. Or had the woman seen the light?

She brought her speculation to an abrupt halt. Pathetic people with no life of their own got more excited by the love lives of celebrities than their own, she reminded herself severely.

Of course, I know this celebrity and I don't actually *have* a love life to speak of. But the principle is the same. It is pathetic.

Nobody watching as she looked from one man to the other would have guessed at how her stomach was churning. It had become a matter of pride with her *not* to react to Luca's volatile moods; the fact her stately calm irritated him was a plus point.

'You know one another?' she asked, trawling frantically through her memory to recall how she had described Luca to Seth. What she remembered made her cringe. The *one time I* speak my mind and get smart—now what were the odds on that? She just hoped that Seth would keep the joke to himself.

Luca's eyes skimmed her face; he looked faintly impatient. 'Obviously.'

'I met Luca a few years back when I was over in Ireland buying horses from his mother,' Seth explained. 'My dad wanted to introduce some new breeding stock.'

A glimmer of humour flashed in Luca's eyes as he said,

deadpan, 'My father was saying something similar to Roman and me only the other day.'

'He takes an interest in the stud?'

'Since Dad retired he has a lot of time on his hands. He uses it to *take an interest* in all sorts of things,' Luca returned smoothly.

'Likes to keep his finger on the pulse still, does he?' Seth sounded sympathetic.

'He's not quite got the hang of retirement yet,' Luca admitted. 'If it wasn't for Ma I think he'd still be behind his desk. How long have you and old Seth here,' he asked Alice, 'known one another?'

'About ten minutes,' she replied without thinking.

His dark-winged sable brows lifted in expressive unison. *'Amazing...'*

'Why amazing?' she queried suspiciously. Did he think she was lying? It required considerable self-discipline to smile serenely.

'I got the impression you were *old friends.*'

Not a liar, just a tart, she mentally corrected. Oh, that's all right, then. It was important on occasions like this to keep your sense of humour.

'What is this—an interrogation?' she wondered lightly.

More to the point, why am I feeling guilty? she asked herself angrily.

'Perhaps we were close in another life,' the American, who had been silent during their spiky war of words, spoke up.

His frivolity earned him a repressive frown from Alice before she turned her attention back to Luca. 'Seth took pity on me.'

'Pity wasn't my main motivating factor.'

'That,' Luca responded drily, 'I can well believe.'

Alice, her voice raised, interrupted this little male byplay. 'And if he hadn't I'd already be in my room ordering room service.'

Her pointed comment was wasted on Luca, who responded with an amused if cynical sneer. 'That's Seth all over—a regular Sir Galahad,' he drawled.

Her bosom swelled with indignation as she fought to control her temper. 'Something nobody is likely to accuse you of being.'

She saw the startled expression flash across Luca's face and felt a surge of reckless satisfaction.

Luca set his elbows on the table and said in a deceptively indolent drawl, 'I've read that inappropriate sarcasm often masks anger.'

This from the man who specialised in the cutting one-liner! She was an amateur compared with him; Luca's savage wit was as ruthless as a surgeon's scalpel.

'I'm sure you know much more about inappropriate sarcasm than I do.' Try guessing what this smile is masking, she thought, delivering a smile of brilliant insincerity.

'She's got you there, Luca.' Seth laughed. 'You know, before you arrived we were just—'

'Sure…whatever…' Actually it had been pretty obvious what they were *just*… The dull thud in Luca's temple cranked up another painful notch as he recalled the scene that had met him as he'd arrived.

He hadn't needed the directions given him to locate his table. He had heard her laughter the moment he had walked into the room, soft but huskily intimate.

He wasn't the only male whose attention was drawn to the sexy, inviting sound either. Half the men in the room were annoying their partners by risking a sly look. No doubt if the opportunity had arisen to do more than look they'd have jumped at it!

And you wouldn't? Being an essentially honest man, he couldn't dismiss the possibility he'd be tempted…all right, more than tempted. Especially in that dress, he thought as his eyes slid over the clinging fabric that revealed the full swell of her deliciously rounded breasts. His body reacted to her, so what? That just made him male and alive. That his basic— *very basic*—first impulse had been to throttle the life out of the man who was leering at Alice was not so easily explained away.

Roman might be prepared to accept a loveless marriage of mutual convenience, but no way would he accept a wife who when his back was turned flirted with any man who happened along. Luca doubted he and his brother were *that* different!

Alice was furious on Seth's behalf. Luca could not have made his boredom more apparent if he had yawned.

'How is the lovely Natalia?'

'She's fine. I think Seth thought that flirting with her would lower the price. He discovered it didn't; my mother,' he confided, 'takes no prisoners when it comes to business.'

'A family trait,' Alice muttered under her breath. The way Luca had turned the ailing publishing house into a dynamic, thriving business was an achievement that had earned him international respect. She knew for a fact that any number of well-known firms who had suffered financial setbacks had offered him indecent sums of money to work his magic for them.

'I flirted with your mother for pleasure, not profit,' Seth protested. 'She is a very beautiful woman.'

'Beauty runs in the family too, or so I've been told.'

I just bet you have, Alice thought.

'Damn, I thought I'd switched that off.' Seth grimaced and pulled a trilling phone from his pocket. 'Could you excuse me for a minute, folks?' he said.

'What runs in *your* family, other than blonde hair?' It took Alice, who was watching Seth's retreating back with dismay, a couple of seconds to realise that Luca had directed the question to her.

She pretended to consider his question before replying mildly. 'I think I'd have to say a dislike of people who can't look you in the face when they talk to you. You know the type I mean—shifty…sly…no manners…'

Luca, whose blue eyes had been unashamedly trained on her cleavage when he had mentioned her hair, and still were, gave a lopsided grin. He gave a shrug that acknowledged her hit and lifted his head.

Their eyes clashed.

The satisfyingly superior feeling, the product of having won a bout in this war of wits, evaporated about the same moment that her stomach muscles tensed with excitement. *Excitement…?*

'I thought you'd have been insulted if I hadn't noticed.'

If there had been even a hint of embarrassment, a trace of apology, in his attitude she might have forgiven him. Alice sucked in an angry breath. *Brazen!* she decided wrathfully. There was no other word to describe him…unless it was charismatic, beautiful and sexy.

'Insulting me has never bothered you before.'

'I didn't think you'd noticed.'

Unbelievable…did he think she didn't have feelings? 'I noticed.' Her lashes came down as it struck her forcibly that there was very little about Luca that she hadn't noticed. She frowned at this growing evidence of her unhealthy fascination.

Without turning his head, Luca halted the approaching waiter with a soft, 'no, we're not ready to order.'

Her spine stiffened with a snap and the jolt made her head spin—or was it the lack of food, or possibly that last drink? Her generous lips tightened into a disapproving and indignant line as she focused on the handsome face of her reluctant dining companion.

'*I* was ready to order two hours ago,' she informed him tartly.

One slanted sable brow rose as he scanned her flushed face and overbright sparkling eyes. 'I was unavoidably detained.'

'What was her name?'

Obviously she regretted this unwise comment the moment it had left her lips. She was uncomfortably aware that it was the sort of critical complaint a jealous girlfriend competing for his favours would have come out with.

Something she wasn't.

Actually Alice doubted that any girlfriend of Luca O'Hagan's who did complain, or demand to know where he had been and with whom, would retain that honour for very long. There would always be someone to replace her; Luca believed firmly in the theory of safety in numbers!

Alice decided to tack on an addition that would establish her disinterest in the subject of his love life, but instead heard with a deepening sense of dismay, *'Or didn't you ask?'* fall waspishly from her lips.

Oh, God…! She removed her stare from his darkly handsome face and made a detailed study of the bottom of her glass.

A short static pause followed her sarcastic jab.

'Actually I—'

'Spare me the details!' she cut in, her stomach muscles shifting nauseously at the prospect of him filling in the blanks in her imagination. *Still* she couldn't stop her runaway tongue. 'I suppose some men just never grow up.'

Luca looked at her with a worrying lack of expression. 'Am I to assume that you number me amongst these cases of arrested development?' A muscle in his lean brown cheek visibly clenched as their glances locked. 'Why is it you never lose an opportunity to look down that little nose of yours at me…?' He paused, a bemused frown drawing his brow into creases. Then unexpectedly he reached out to lightly graze the tip of the feature under discussion with his knuckle.

Alice, who literally jumped back in her seat, was too startled by the physical contact to register that the action had all the hallmarks of compulsion about it. She couldn't register much beyond the deafening thud of her heartbeat echoing dully in her ears.

Luca's sensually sculpted lips thinned into a cynical smile as his hand fell away.

'Why did you do that?' she asked.

'Damned if I know.' Not strictly true. He'd always wanted to touch her, to feel for himself if that alabaster-clear skin was actually as sensationally smooth as it looked; would his fingers glide over the silky surface?

Alice, who had been expecting some smart sarcastic response, found she couldn't meet his eyes. The direction of the conversation was seriously spooking her, as was the tension that weighed heavily in the air.

The uncomfortable silence seethed with things she didn't care to analyse until finally she could bear it no longer. 'Oh, and there's no need to apologise for being late. I've really had a lovely time sitting here for nearly two hours.' Angry, very blue eyes lifted from the depths of her glass and behind the anger lurked an awareness that she was blowing her years of supernatural serenity well and truly out of the water.

'I'm very sorry I'm late.'

She gave an unimpressed sniff. 'No, you're not.'

'*Per amor di Dio!* I think this is what you'd call a no-win situation.'

'It wasn't spontaneous…'

The scraping sound as Luca shifted his chair to give himself some extra leg-room made her jump nervously. Holding her eyes, he slowly crossed one ankle over the other.

'When I *spontaneously* admired your dress you didn't like it.' A slow, dangerous smile spread across his lean face. 'Or maybe you did?' Her angry gasp made his smile widen.

'It wasn't my dress you were looking at!' she countered huskily.

Luca's cerulean-blue eyes drifted downwards…

Alice bit her lip and endured the scrutiny even though she

felt like crawling out of her skin. She lifted her chin up, angry stare fixed straight ahead; no amount of will-power could prevent the rosy wash of warm tell-tale colour inexorably rise up her neck.

Grow-up, Alice, she told herself angrily, it's not as if he's actually *looking*. He's just trying to wind you up. This is probably his idea of a joke. That resentful theory fell apart when his glance lifted. There was nothing that faintly resembled humour in his expression.

'You're right, I wasn't,' he agreed sardonically.

Alice met his eyes and her breath snagged in her too-dry throat before she looked away again, deeply shaken by the predatory gleam in his fantastic eyes.

She pressed her hands against her thighs and took a deep restorative breath. Under the table her knees carried on shaking uncontrollably. If she had stood up at that moment she would have fallen flat on her face.

She knew that her reaction was way, *way* over the top. For starters she wasn't his type at all…heck, the man was probably *born* looking predatory. Far from finding her attractive, he probably wouldn't notice if she were sitting there stark naked.

A militant light sparked to life in her eyes. It wasn't that she wanted Luca to notice she was a woman, it was just the acknowledgement that she couldn't have made him notice even if she had wanted to that hurt her self-esteem.

My God, but there was no justice in the world, she thought, her temper uncharacteristically flaring. She hadn't actually expected the latest diet fad to turn her into a flat-chested clothes-horse, but after three weeks of self-deprivation it would have been nice to have lost a pound!

Not that anyone would have noticed, she thought with a self-pitying sniff.

'Anyway, we're not talking about my clothes sense, we're talking about your total lack of consideration.'

'*We* are? You should have said. Right, I'm *extremely* sorry I'm late.'

Luca's electric-blue eyes might not be what you expected of a Latin male, but everything else about him was—including his volatile temperament, off-the-scale insolence, and in-your-face sex appeal. It was pathetic really that he traded on his sexuality. Her deliberate attempt to view his tall, athletically lean six feet plus frame with amused condescension did not prevent the fluttery sensation in the pit of her stomach.

She cleared her throat; even so her voice held a husky rasp as she bowed her head slightly in grudging acknowledgement. 'Apology accepted.'

The pout was something he had not seen before, Luca registered, removing his eyes from the heaving contours of her generous breasts, which he *had* been conscious of on other occasions.

Several occasions, actually.

Even when she was in the less-revealing sexily discreet silk blouses she habitually wore during working hours a male's eyes were inevitably drawn to the full, feminine contours—even his, and Luca considered himself a pretty controlled sort of guy. If he weren't he would have told his brother the screamingly obvious fact that it was always a bad idea to have a personal relationship with someone who worked for you.

The line between Alice's feathery brows deepened as Luca leaned back in his chair with indolent grace. Her eyes were drawn to his hands as he laid them on the table; his long, tapering fingers were brown and shapely.

'Very gracious of you. Tell me, so that I know next time…do you always make the rules up as you go along?' he asked.

'At least I know that rules exist.' If ever a man had been born to push the constraints of society to the limit, it was Luca. He was a born risk-taker. As she turned her head to avoid contact with his compelling eyes she caught sight of something that made her eyes widen. 'Have you been fighting?'

Luca tilted his head and ran a hand lightly along the hard curve of his jaw. Almost imperceptibly he winced. 'You should see the other guy.'

Earlier in the subdued light Alice had missed the discoloured area extending from one sharp-edged cheekbone to his chiselled jaw. Now that she looked she could see there were also signs of faint puffiness in the skin around his sculpted lips.

'You think this is funny?' She didn't bother to hide her disapproval of his attitude. Violence was a subject upon which she held strong views.

In her opinion, no matter what the situation, an intelligent person—and there was no denying that Luca, for all his faults, had a mind like a steel trap—could *always* come up with a better solution than physical violence.

She was not even aware that her hand had come to rest on her midriff. The doctors had done a pretty neat job, but she would always bear the permanent reminder of the day that she had been the victim of an act of violence—the first day, coincidentally, that she had ever laid eyes on her employer's younger brother.

Memory triggered, she recalled the night he had carried her in his arms. Now it seemed like something that had happened to someone else...actually it always had. Her memories of the occasion were hazy, restricted to Luca cursing fluently in musical Italian when all she'd done was ask how Roman was. That and a series of impressions left in her head...warmth, lean hardness, strength, the male scent of his skin overlaid lightly with the subtle fragrance he had been wearing.

Perhaps it had been the relief, the instinctive knowledge at some deep level that here had been someone who would shoulder the burden of responsibility. She'd been able to let go, she hadn't had to be in control and strong. Maybe that was why these details remained so clear in her mind.

His prompt action had saved her life, they had said. Even if this statement had been a little over-the-top she would undoubtedly have been in trouble if he hadn't been there.

Though you could hardly compare the trauma of the two incidents, they were intrinsically linked in her mind. The day she had got in the way of a stalker's knife, not even her own stalker, and the day she'd first seen Luca O'Hagan.

'Have you seen a doctor?'

Luca, his eyes trained unblinkingly on her face, didn't respond to the querulous abrupt enquiry. Their eyes connected and she knew that in that uncomfortable way Luca had he knew exactly where her thoughts had been. Belatedly aware of the hand pressed to her middle, she let it fall self-consciously away.

His mouth softened slightly as he studied her downcast features. 'It was a minor accident, that's all, Alice.' Actually he had got the bruise from saving the child earlier.

Her gaze lifted. It wasn't very often he used her name, but when he did she always felt an odd insidious weakness work its way through her body. She worked very hard not to let him see that it was happening right now. 'Roman got called away.'

'So you said.'

'I did…?' she echoed vaguely.

'I suppose Roman standing you up explains the mood.'

'The mood? I don't have a mood.' Her frown deepened. 'Why,' she demanded, 'are you looking at me like that?'

'How many of those have you had?' His eyes touched the glass in her hand.

'Not nearly enough,' she told him sincerely.

His lips twitched. 'When was the last time you ate?'

Alice released a long, shuddering sigh as her eyes followed a splendid creamy confection topped by a lattice of calorific spun sugar being delivered to a nearby table. 'Three weeks ago,' she confessed.

Luca blinked. *'Three weeks ago…?'*

Alice nodded. 'Real food. I've been on a diet.' In her book powdered stuff that tasted of nothing when you mixed it with milk and as many grapefruit as you could stomach did not constitute food in the real sense of the word. 'Crazy, isn't it? Half the world are starving and the other half are trying to slim.'

'Diet? What on earth are you dieting for?'

Alice delivered a look of killing contempt. Only someone who wasn't carrying an ounce of surplus flesh on his hard-muscled frame could say something so spectacularly stupid. 'I'd have thought that was abundantly obvious,' she gritted. 'Especially,' she added gloomily, 'in this dress.'

She was viewing the despised curves of her body when it occurred to her that her comment had virtually invited his scrutiny. She closed her eyes tight as horror washed over her. Why do I keep mentioning this darned dress?

She hardly dared look up, but when she gathered the courage she discovered that he had not refused her invitation! She tried to act as if it didn't bother her that his eyes were super-glued to her body, but by the time he got back to her face her breath had increased to a degree she couldn't disguise. From where he was looking he must have been aware of the fact.

'It's *abundantly* obvious in that dress that most women would kill for the figure you've got. You have a body that would feature in nine out of ten men's fantasies,' he pronounced.

Alice gave a nervous laugh. *'Sure!'* she said.

'You don't think I'm serious?' He seemed perplexed by her attitude.

'People do not design clothes for women my shape.'

'That's because people wouldn't be looking at the clothes,' he immediately rebutted.

'Then what would they…?' She stopped and blushed darkly.

Luca grinned. 'Exactly,' he confirmed, looking amused by her embarrassment. 'Now, how about if we order?'

'I'm not hungry and, besides, it would be rude to order before Seth gets back.'

'You'll eat anyway, if only to soak up the drinks you've had, and Seth doesn't need to come back on my account.'

'Are you suggesting I'm drunk?' Alice demanded, indignant at the slur.

His lips curved in a sardonic smile. 'Aren't you?'

'Not saying what you want me to doesn't make me drunk.'

'I think when you review this conversation tomorrow morning you might want to revise that opinion.'

'Are you saying I'm talking rubbish?'

'You're talking. Normally you act as though—what do they say in the cop shows?—anything you say will be used against you. Though,' he added thoughtfully, 'you still get the message across. You have silent disapproval off to a fine art.'

'I have never assumed that anything I have to say would interest you. Now I know we can have nice long cosy chats.'

Her venom made his lips twitch. 'I can hardly wait.'

Alice saw the twitch and her own lips pursed as her eyes continued to linger on his mouth; it was extremely expressive. And sensual, she added, covertly examining the sculpted sexy outline. It was the mouth you expected someone who kissed really well to possess.

Did Luca kiss really well? If practice counted for anything he ought to, she reflected. An indentation appeared to mar the smooth perfection of her broad brow as she considered a small sample of the women he'd practised with. All were stunning, not just good-looking, but the sort of women who turned heads when they walked into a room.

It wasn't until her restless gaze clashed with Luca's that she appreciated how long she'd been sitting there staring at him, thinking about his mouth and kissing! A shamed warmth spread across her skin.

Good God, he's right, I must have had a bit too much to drink!

Nothing else could even begin to excuse her behaviour.

She lifted her hand and smiled at the figure who was approaching the table from across the room. 'Here's Seth. Will you *please* try and be nice?' she hissed.

'I'm always nice.'

This was so *not* true that she didn't even bother responding.

CHAPTER THREE

'PROBLEM?' Luca said as the other man approached.

Seth shook his head. ''Fraid so. I'm going to have to love you and leave you.'

'*Oh, God, no!*' Alice flushed deeply when both men turned to look at her. 'That is, we wanted you to stay and eat with us, Seth.' Her glare dared Luca to deny this assertion.

He did.

'*We* didn't.'

Alice shot Luca a murderous look, and he shrugged, which made her want to shake him. A physical impossibility, of course, considering his size. Not only was Luca tall, but his body had the toned development of an athlete, all lean muscle and whipcord strength.

Her breathing imperceptibly quickened as her eyes slid to his upper body. His jacket was open and she noticed for the first time that there was a slight rent in the expensive fabric through which she could see a section of smooth golden skin.

Normally he was immaculately turned out, not a hair out of place. Was it the minor accident he had lightly touched upon or had some over-zealous lover been a little too eager to remove his clothes?

In her head she saw eager hands ripping at his clothes and her concentration slipped. A secret little shiver of which she was deeply ashamed ran down her spine. Swallowing, she tore her eyes away.

As she turned to the Texan she put a few hundred watts of extra warmth into her smile. '*I'd* love for you to eat with us.'

'And I'd like nothing better,' Seth returned with a rueful sigh.

'Men like a woman to be direct,' her sister, who was happy and married and wanted Alice to be happy again, had explained on her last visit home.

'Direct women scare men off,' her brother, Tom, had corrected.

'Direct women scare *you* off. Men who are not immature and lacking in confidence are not scared by strong women who speak their mind,' her sister replied.

This provocative reply had been the start of a heated discussion. Now seemed as good a time as any to see which of her siblings had been right, despite her not really feeling attracted to Seth.

'Will I see you again?'

Encouraging. Seth looked surprised, but he wasn't running away.

'If you're still here at the end of the week I've got tickets for the opening night of Krebs's exhibition.'

'I'm not totally sure yet how long we'll be in town, but—'

'Roman keeps her pretty busy,' Luca inserted smoothly. His eyes were fixed on the hand laid against the smoother-than-silk contours of Alice's shoulder. As Seth's fingertips brushed casually against the hollow of one collar-bone, which was delicately defined without being unattractively bony, Luca stiffened.

Alice simmered silently. What was it with Luca? Did he begrudge her a social life?

'Ring me.' She softened the abruptness of her demand with a warm smile and added, 'I'd really love to go to the opening although I won't be able to afford to buy anything,' she admitted.

'I'm sure Seth will buy it for you if you look wistful enough,' Luca observed lazily.

Alice's hands clenched into fists under the table.

Luca watched the colour wash over her skin then equally

abruptly recede leaving a febrile spot of colour on each smooth cheek. One dark brow lifted.

'Calm down, I was just joking.'

Seth chuckled, apparently having no problem with believing him, but Alice was under no such illusion.

'Of course I'll ring,' Seth promised her. 'You're staying here?'

She nodded, all the while very conscious of heavy-lidded blue eyes watching her.

'Together…?' One brow raised, Seth's speculative look encompassed both Alice and Luca.

It was such an off-the-wall idea that it took several moments for Alice to catch his meaning. When she did her bewildered frown morphed into a look of stark horror. 'Me and…*Luca*?' she squeaked, shaking her head hard in a negative motion to the insulting question.

'You don't fight like friends, more like an old married couple…*or lovers.*'

Alice looked at him as though he were mad. Her own parents rarely raised their voices, let alone fought like cat and dog.

'We don't fight like friends, because we're not.' Trying to tear emotional strips off one another was not to her a sign of a close emotional relationship or for that matter—the thought made her skin heat—a *physical* one!

She turned her head, expecting to find Luca either laughing his socks off at the idea of them being an item or seeing the same revulsion she had experienced reflected on his face.

She found neither.

Luca was still, so still he appeared barely to be breathing. His glossy dark head, which in the candlelight gleamed blue-black, was tilted at an angle so that he appeared to be looking down at her. Through the thick dark mesh of his lashes she could see the gleam of his eyes, but nothing in his facial expression gave a clue as to what he was thinking. A sphinx would have given away more of his feelings than Luca, but the act of looking into those still criminally perfect frozen features set her heart off fibrillating like a wild thing in her chest.

'Sorry, folks, I got the wrong idea.'

Seth's amused apology broke the spell that bound her. 'Yes, you did,' she agreed. Did her smile look as forced as it felt? she wondered. 'Do I look like someone *he* would date?' she demanded in a voice that was the verbal equivalent of a shudder.

Seth appeared to find the question highly amusing. 'I thought maybe Luca here had decided to go for a bit of class for a change.' He slid the younger man a sideways twinkling look of challenge.

'I see you're a believer in miracles,' Alice retorted. 'And a sense of humour, I like that in a man.'

'I'm an easy man to like,' he promised her as he bent forward to kiss her lightly on the cheek. 'I'll be in touch,' he promised. 'Nice to see you again, Luca.'

Watching him go, Alice was suddenly filled with blind panic at the thought of being left alone with Luca, even alone in such a public place!

'I have a sense of humour,' Luca announced from out of the blue.

'No, you have a savage and cutting wit.' As someone who had been on the receiving end often enough, she felt qualified to respond on this score. 'It isn't the same thing,' she promised with feeling.

Luca shrugged but didn't respond to the accusation. 'I thought he'd never go.' He sighed, leaning back in his seat. 'We're ready to order now,' he said to the waiter, who had returned to their table.

'I'm not.' How come when *I* want a waiter there is never one around? 'I'm not hungry.' She was, but she felt like being stubborn.

'Sorry, the lady isn't ready to order…' The waiter nodded and vanished.

'Don't apologise for me,' she retorted spikily. 'You were unconscionably rude to Seth!' she hissed.

'I've had a bad day.'

'My heart bleeds.'

A look of fastidious distaste contorted his aristocratic and fabulously good-looking features. 'And my idea of winding down is *not* watching you and Seth making out,' he revealed.

'We were not making out!' she choked in outrage.

'Talk about all over one another!' he exclaimed in disgust. 'I thought I might have to throw a bucket of water over the pair of you.'

The hand Alice had been threading though her blonde hair fell away as her jaw dropped. It took her several moments to recover the power of speech; when she did her voice shook with anger.

'I won't ask what *your* idea of winding down after a bad day is,' she said with a scornful sniff. Even as she said it her wilful imagination was doing just that. Minus the tie; minus the shirt; minus…! She sucked in her breath and took control before he lost any more garments.

Luca planted his elbows on the table and, with his big body curved towards her, effectively cut out the rest of the room from her view. His breath caused the candles set in the middle of the table to flare and flicker as he planted his chin against the heel of his palm. The action, abrupt but elegantly co-ordinated, made her tummy flip. The feeling was intensified by the illusion they were alone. Luca's every action, even the most mundane, was performed with a fluid, almost animal, grace that was magnetically *male*.

There had been occasions in the past when caught unawares she had seen him walk across a room, knowing even at a distance who it was, and she would watch, helpless not to follow him with her eyes. Those occasions could unsettle her for the rest of day, though generally she succeeded in laughing off her weakness. Right now there was absolutely no question of laughing; he was too close and she was feeling strange.

'Why?' Alice blinked to clear her confused, disorganised thoughts as eyes deep and drowningly blue locked onto her own. 'Afraid you might discover we both like to wind down the same way?'

His taunt, low-pitched and huskily intimate, sent a shiver rippling through her body. Though she had no control over the heat that spilled out across her pale skin, pride stopped her lowering her eyes in confusion.

'That I seriously doubt.' Her scornful response wasn't quite as scornful as she'd have liked, which had more than a little to do with the images of him *unwinding* her overexcited imagination was predictably supplying.

If he had even the faintest inkling…?

Luca's eyes scoured her faintly flushed face and slowly the corners of his beautiful mouth lifted.

Inkling, girl…? It's written all over your face.

Mortified by her fatal weakness, Alice arranged her features in a careful blank canvas.

With a shrug of his broad shoulders Luca leaned back in his seat. 'What do you think Roman would say if he knew you went around picking up stray men in hotel bars?'

'*Roman…?*' She imagined that he would say *go for it*. Her boss was always complaining that she had no social life. According to him it made him feel guilty—not guilty enough to cut down on her workload, she had been tempted to retort.

'By the way, nice going with Seth.'

Alice gave a suspicious frown.

'You didn't know Seth's father owned half of Texas and he's an only child?'

It wasn't hard to see where he was going with this one. 'No, I didn't,' she gritted back.

'One of life's lucky chances,' he mused.

'It's true!' Alice hissed in frustration. She was hard pressed to decide which made her most mad: being called promiscuous or a gold-digger? Only *Luca* could manage to do both in the same sentence!

She focused on a point over his shoulder. 'Naturally now I do I will propose at the first opportunity.'

'I'm sure you wouldn't be so obvious.'

'A compliment…*gosh*! Also, this isn't a bar.' The cutting retort would have been more cutting if it hadn't taken her thirty seconds to think of it.

'*Semantics*: the last refuge of the guilty,' Luca suggested gently.

Alice took a deep breath and refused to take the bait. Unless you kept your wits about you when talking to Luca it took him about six seconds to tie a person in knots. 'And I did not pick Seth up.' She was quite pleased with herself for staying firmly focused.

'A moderately clever woman doesn't have to, she makes the poor dope think it was his idea.'

'I'm assuming when you talk about *clever*, you actually mean animal cunning of the variety that men like you assume all women have. You know, I had no idea that you were such a misogynist.' There was a fatal flaw in her coping strategy of focusing on a point over his shoulder—there was only so long she could keep it up!

Her eyes clashed with Luca's and she spoilt her clever rebuttal by adding in a loud, goaded voice, 'Oh, shut up!'

Colouring pinkly, she gave the couple at the next table an apologetic smile before turning her attention back to her persecutor.

'I didn't open my mouth.'

If she'd had the energy the innocence in his protest would have made her smile, but she felt totally drained. Talking to him was exhausting! As she tried to marshal her wits her eyes slid of their own volition to the sculpted outline of the lips he had referred to…

'But you were about to.'

He bowed his dark head in mocking acknowledgement.

'I knew this evening was going to be awful, I just didn't know *how* awful. And for the record if I had picked up Seth it wouldn't have had anything to do with his bank balance.'

'I didn't have you down as a girl with a thing for cowboy boots.'

A hissing sound of annoyance escaped through Alice's clenched teeth.

'It depends who's wearing them,' she rallied.

'Should I take that remark personally?'

'By all means,' she replied with a smile as insincere as his own. 'What's wrong, Luca? Are you feeling bitter and twisted because the girls are interested in your bank balance and not the *real* you? *Poor Luca!*'

Poor Luca gave her a smile that was one hundred per cent cynical charisma. 'You care—I'm touched, I really am.'

'In the head,' she muttered.

His lips twitched. 'Actually,' he explained, 'I tend to find it's my body that interests them most.'

'Just as I thought, you've started believing your own press releases,' she said. 'I'd be surprised if any of the women in that terrible article could spell their own name.'

'*Harsh!* How about sisterly solidarity? After all, you obviously read that *terrible* article too. Which terrible article was it we were talking about? There are so many,' he sighed.

The small gurgling sound of inarticulate disgust that emerged from her throat caused his wolflike grin to widen, revealing a perfect set of whiter-than-white teeth.

'Being a sex object is a burden, but…' another of his inimitable Latin shrugs '…I can live with it.'

Alice didn't respond. It wasn't easy; her facial muscles ached, as did the scream of sheer aggravation locked in her throat. It came so easily to him, she thought with frustration, all the sexual stuff that had every woman within a five-mile radius panting.

But not me!

Desperation and defiance…roughly a sixty-forty split? the ironic voice in her head suggested.

'Your fortitude and sense of duty does you credit, I'm sure.'

Infuriatingly he seemed to find her malice amusing.

'And for the record if I had decided to *pick up* Seth or, for that matter, anyone else,' she continued indignantly, 'I wouldn't care what you or Roman thought, because, strange as it might seem to you, working for an O'Hagan doesn't preclude having a personal life!' She lifted her hand to her mouth to cut off an unexpected yawn.

His all-encompassing gaze scanned her pale features. 'Tired?'

Holding his eyes, she placed the napkin she had been systematically folding and unfolding in her lap on the table. 'Extremely tired of this conversation.'

It wasn't until she actually got to her feet—thank God they didn't fold under her—that she knew what she was doing. She was doing something she ought to have done hours ago…getting the hell out of there! It wasn't in her nature to run from a fight. Her normal response to a difficult situation was to grit her teeth and tough it out, but this was one fight she couldn't win.

Luca's forceful personality she could deal with; it was his raw, rampant sexuality that she couldn't. Trying to maintain a semblance of normality when her imagination was busy spinning erotic fantasies was a humiliating experience. The unpalatable fact was she could fight Luca, but could no longer fight herself and the way he made her feel.

'So if you'll excuse me…' The longer she stayed, the more she would have to regret tomorrow.

His lean face was a study of astonishment as she got to her feet. 'What if I say I won't excuse you?'

'It will make no difference whatever,' she informed him simply before walking away, head held high, back straight. She got as far as the foyer before he caught her up at the same time as the effects of the stress of the evening from hell. She was literally shaking with reaction.

'I assumed I was meant to follow you.'

Alice stopped dead. It had been a terrible evening and this was the final straw. She hadn't retreated to get his attention, just to retain a little sanity. Dear God, Luca had a treble dose of male vanity.

Eyes narrowed, she swung to face the figure at her shoulder. Looking into his face meant she had to tilt her head back a long way. 'No, you're not supposed to follow.'

'Sorry, I'm a bit hazy on the rules governing women storming out.' The muscles along his taut jaw clenched. 'Not many women have stormed out of a restaurant on me…actually, none have.'

So that was his problem—*pride*. His precious ego couldn't take a woman walking out on him. Anger sent a rush of adrenaline through her body.

'Great, my place in history is assured. The woman who walked out on Luca O'Hagan. It doesn't get much better than that—except possibly being remembered as the woman who cured cancer, but still…' She lifted a hand to her aching throat as a shaky little laugh was drawn from it. 'Do you think they'll write a book about me?'

'I think they'll…' He drew in a shuddering breath through flared nostrils and glared down at her, his imperious features clenched into a tight mask of displeasure. 'That smart mouth of yours is going to get you into trouble one of these days,' he predicted grimly.

'Maybe. Then again, maybe it could also get me out of trouble. But then I forget—you prefer brute force, don't you?'

'I have not been fighting.'

'Whatever. I really couldn't care. Before I go to bed I'd like to get a couple of things straight. Three things, actually. Firstly, that wasn't storming, that was a dignified exit.'

'I stand corrected,' he conceded with a stiff bow of his dark head.

'Secondly, they may not have stormed out but—trust me— some must have wanted to, and thirdly…' She stopped. 'Actually there is no thirdly,' she admitted lamely.

She was too startled to resist when Luca suddenly caught her arm and drew her towards him. She opened her mouth to protest when she saw why he'd grabbed her. Though God knew how she hadn't noticed until now the laughing party of hotel guests in celebratory mood heading for the bar—they were making enough noise.

Luca, who muttered something harsh in Italian under his breath, made no attempt to move out of their path as they surged forward, but then she reflected he didn't need to. Luca was not the sort of person that anyone who wasn't insane or stupid jostled. *Or walked away from?* He had looked very angry.

Actually he still did.

As she looked at his fingers curled around her wrist she felt an enervating wave wash over her. The temptation not to fight it but to go with the flow was immense.

'I don't appreciate being…' A small grunt of pain escaped her lips as she received a glancing blow from an elbow in the ribs.

'Are you all right?' She angrily brushed away Luca's hand.

'I'm so sorry, I didn't see you there.' The woman she stepped back into looked concerned.

'I'm fine. It was my fault, I wasn't looking. Don't worry about it.'

'Are you sure?'

'Absolutely.' The fixed smile was still on her lips when the woman moved away.

Luca stood motionless while a shocking realisation swept over him.

He had chased after a woman.

Never in his life had he chased after a woman, but if he had done he didn't think it was too off the wall, too unrealistic to think that she might have been flattered! Any other woman but this one.

Luca waited until the middle-aged woman had moved out of earshot, waited until he could trust himself to speak calmly before he spoke.

'Well, far be it from me to inflict myself on you.' With a curt nod he turned back towards the dining room.

'Luca, I need to get outside—*now*!'

CHAPTER FOUR

IT WAS the hoarse, haunted note in Alice's barely audible voice that made Luca turn back.

'What's wrong? Are you ill?' He watched as she moistened her pallid lips with the tip of her tongue. The cold impatience in his eyes morphed into concern when he realised that every vestige of colour had gone from her face and her skin was covered in a thin film of moisture.

Alice shook her head. It required every ounce of her willpower to make her numb lips work. 'I just need some fresh air…now…*please*…'

She was looking straight at him but there was no recognition in her wide eyes. Just stark, chilling horror.

'Are you hurt? Alice, say something.'

Alice could hear her name and she tried desperately to respond. 'I think I'll just…' She began to lift one foot at a time but they felt as if they were nailed to the ground. Her knees shook with the effort to support her weight.

She could see Luca's lips moving but the words coming from his mouth made no sense. She had no ability to control the relentless kaleidoscope of images that flashed across her vision. Fear was a metallic taste in her mouth. She lifted a hand to her head and felt the clammy wetness of cold sweat.

It was happening again.

The doctor had given *it* a name. He had diagnosed post-traumatic stress disorder.

'But I haven't had a trauma,' she had replied, confident he must have the wrong notes laid out on the desk in front of him. This was the sort of thing that happened when you couldn't get an appointment with your usual doctor.

The doctor had looked quizzically at her over the top of his trendy designer spectacles. 'You were the victim of a knife attack, I understand? And you were also widowed...how long...?'

'My husband died some years ago,' she told him quietly. 'And the attack was a long time ago.' In the time since she had never awoken in the night in a blind panic. She had not suffered any flashbacks. She shook her head. 'Why should this be happening now?'

'Who knows?'

'Well, I rather hoped you would,' she returned drily.

The medic grinned. 'Good to see you've still got a sense of humour,' he commended heartily. 'I'm not an expert, but,' he added, handing her a card, 'I know someone who is. It's not unusual for this to happen some time after the event, years sometimes...a trigger, stress perhaps?'

'I'm not stressed—at least I wasn't until this started happening. I'm not sleeping.' She swallowed; the truth was she was afraid to sleep. 'It has happened twice now when I'm at work. I'm not sure how long I can hide it,' she admitted worriedly.

'And it's necessary for you to hide it? Your employer would not be sympathetic?' he probed.

'I don't want his sympathy...' Or, and which was more to the point, his guilt! It had been bad enough before. The way Roman had gone on after she'd come out of hospital, you'd have thought he had wielded the knife himself.

If her boss, with his overdeveloped sense of responsibility, ever got a sniff of her new problem he'd go off on another mammoth guilt trip and that was something Alice wanted to avoid at all costs. The hair-shirt period, while it lasted, had been pretty wearing, being considerate and reasonable just wasn't in Roman's nature!

'And I really don't want to involve anyone else,' she announced firmly.

'You might have no choice,' the doctor replied bluntly. 'This could get worse before it gets better,' he explained cheerily. He saw her expression. 'Then again...'

'It might not,' she finished heavily.

He shrugged.

'So actually you have no idea.'

The doctor continued to be frustratingly vague. 'It's not an exact science. The human mind is complex.'

'That doesn't help me much.'

'I could arrange that referral for you now if you like?' he suggested.

Alice got to her feet. 'Actually it might be better if I got back to you on that. I'll be out of the country for the next few weeks and—'

'There is no stigma attached to having therapy, Miss Trevelyan.'

Alice smiled. She had seen the address on the card; Harley Street did not come cheap. 'Don't worry, I'll get back to you after I've checked my diary.'

She didn't. Even if she could have afforded it the idea of a stranger poking around in her subconscious did not appeal to Alice. Weren't therapists for people who didn't have friends to talk to?

Alice had friends, but she didn't burden them with her problem; instead she looked up post-traumatic stress on the internet. Armed with as much information as any 'expert', she felt sure she could cope without resorting to therapists.

The turning point had been discovering what the trigger was. Sounds or even smells had been known to trigger attacks, this particular article had explained. In her case it had been an expensive bottle of perfume that she had received for her birthday...the same perfume Roman's stalker had been doused in! The woman whom she had just collided with also wore it.

If she had caught on sooner she could have saved herself

weeks of the flashbacks and awful episodes of inescapable blind, brain-numbing panic when her heart pounded as though it would implode and her body was bathed in a cold sweat. But who could know that a bottle of perfume of all things could be the culprit?

'Can you walk?'

She turned her head towards the voice; it came from some distant point above her head. 'Maybe.'

'*Madre di Dio*. I'm getting a doctor.'

'No...don't.' She took a deep breath. 'Sorry. Yes...yes, I can walk. It's passing.'

Luca's dark features clenched as he looked into the stricken, waxily pale face of the woman who stood swaying before him. She looked as though she was going to collapse.

He shook his head. 'I'm getting that doctor.'

'I don't need a doctor.' She gripped his arm tightly as the room tilted. 'Please, Luca,' she pleaded. 'I just need some fresh air and I'll be fine.'

Her relief when he slipped an arm around her waist was profound. With a sigh she sagged against him. 'Thank you. I'm very sorry to be a bother,' she murmured, tucking her head against his shoulder.

At the top of the sweep of elegant steps that led up to the entrance Luca gave up on the pretence he *wasn't* actually carrying her and scooped her up into his arms.

'You're shaking like a leaf,' he discovered as her soft curves melded into his hard angles. 'I knew I should have called that doctor.' His eyes darkened with self-recrimination; he had allowed her irrational pleas to influence his better judgement.

'Please don't do that, Luca.' Luca looked from the wide blue eyes to the small hand that tightened on his sleeve and back again.

Somewhere from the muddled mess of her thoughts a realisation that she was being carried for the second time in her life by Luca O'Hagan emerged.

'You're always around when I need carrying. Only twice in my life…obviously I'm not counting when I was a baby…' She just managed to bite off the flow of confidences before she revealed that he smelt extremely good.

'You're not a baby now.' The creature in his arms was all woman.

'Am I talking rubbish?'

'No more than usual.'

'Good.'

'I'm too heavy.'

'For what?' Under normal circumstances Alice might have taken note and wondered at his oddly thickened tone.

'For you.' Arms like steel bands effortlessly stilled her un-coordinated feeble struggles. 'I can walk.' It didn't necessarily mean she wanted to.

The lean brown fingers that framed her jaw left her no choice but to look up into the face of the man who held her.

'And even if you couldn't you'd prefer to fall flat on your face than let me carry you.' Eyes as keen as a laser and equally objective scanned her face. Whatever he saw must have satisfied him because he gave a grudging grunt and then set her down on the pavement.

Alice stood there taking big greedy gulps of fresh air while he arranged his jacket around her smooth bare shoulders. She was outside in the street and had only the vaguest memory of the events that had got her there.

'Right, you're not going to faint on me, are you?' he asked suspiciously.

'No, of course not.'

'There's no of course about it.'

Her glance dropped evasively from his searching scrutiny. 'I felt a little light-headed. I'm fine now,' she said, injecting a strained note of false cheer into her voice. 'You go back

and have your dinner,' she suggested. 'I'll take a little stroll.'
She had barely begun to shrug off his jacket when two heavy
hands landed on her shoulders, effectively anchoring it there.

'You have taken *stupid* to an entirely new level.' Luca,
being Luca, didn't see the need to lower his voice and several
people looked at them; a few stopped and stared.

'Please,' Alice hissed with an agonised look over her shoulder. 'People are looking at us. Let's walk.' Walking at least
they might blend in a little. When he didn't respond she
caught hold of his hand. 'Come on,' she urged.

For a moment she thought he wasn't going to co-operate,
then suddenly his fingers closed around hers. Her eyes widening as a tingling sexual shock sizzled through her body, she
almost missed a step, but somehow carried on walking as
though nothing had happened.

There was something quite surreal about it; she was walking hand in hand down the street with Luca O'Hagan. They
were still hand in hand when the flashes started popping.
Without thinking, Alice turned her head into Luca's chest. He
held her there until he said, in what seemed to her an amazingly disinterested fashion, 'He's gone.' Her face was framed
between big hands. 'You all right? You've got a bit more
colour in your face.'

'I'm fine. What was that?'

'A photographer.'

'Why was he taking our photo?'

'I would imagine that it was to go with the one of me
carrying you out of the hotel he took.'

'Oh, my God!' She angled a worried look at his profile.
'Will it be in a newspaper?' She hated the idea, but took
comfort from the fact that at least there was very little chance
of anyone she knew seeing it.

'Almost certainly.'

'I suppose you could explain to them that I was ill?'

Luca slid her an incredulous look. 'They'll assume you were drunk.'

On this occasion she couldn't work up enough indignation to complain that he was talking to her as if she were a child.

'That's the worst-case scenario...right?'

'No, them suggesting you were under the influence of illegal substances is the worst-case scenario.'

Alice would have fallen had his arm not shot out to steady her. 'But I wasn't. I'd had just a few drinks...and I've never...I don't do stuff like that.'

'You think the fact that it's not true will stop them printing it? *Dio mio*, what planet have you been living on, *cara*?'

'This is terrible. I'm so...so sorry. This is all my fault,' she said, chewing fretfully on her lower lip.

'Don't be stupid, it's nobody's fault. Unless you tipped him off that I'd be carrying a woman out of that particular hotel this evening?'

'Why would I do that?'

His sensual mouth twisted as he recognised the genuine bewilderment in her wide blue eyes. 'You'd be surprised,' he returned cryptically. 'It was just a lucky break for him. Don't stress.'

Easy for him to say, she thought. He was used to seeing his face plastered across newspapers.

He led her across the street. 'In case you were wondering, that was me being sympathetic and soothing.' He smiled into her startled eyes and urged her forward. 'Come on, it's at the next intersection.'

'What is?'

'Where we're heading.'

'Are we heading somewhere?' Silly question. Luca didn't aimlessly wander, he always had an aim and objective. And with his single-minded focus and determination he inevitably achieved it, she reflected.

'I didn't get my dinner and you haven't eaten for three

weeks,' he reminded her wryly. 'I know this great little Italian.'

'I can't let you buy me dinner,' she protested immediately.

'Saying no to anything I suggest is like a reflex with you, isn't it?' The corners of Luca's wide, mobile mouth lifted as he watched her open her mouth and close it again with a grimace. 'And anyway,' he added, 'who says I'm buying?'

Her lashes came down in a screen. 'But that's not what I meant…'

'I know,' he cut back impatiently.

A frown puckered her brow as she fretted. 'If Roman finds out you've bought me dinner somewhere he's going to think it's really odd.' He wouldn't be the only one.

'And do you normally ask my brother's permission before you go out on a date with someone?'

'Of course I don't,' she denied. Her frown deepened— surely he could see what she meant? 'It's just that it's—*you.*' She stopped abruptly, the colour rushing attractively to her cheeks. 'Obviously I know this isn't a date!' she added, anxious to let him know that she wasn't making any daft assumptions.

'Obviously,' he echoed as dry as dust.

She glanced up to see his expression was…well, actually he didn't have an expression. Despite this absence of anything she couldn't shake the feeling she had said something to make him mad.

'So now that we're in agreement on something,' he continued in the same tight, controlled voice, 'why don't you do us both a favour and just do as you're told? Just this once.'

'What happened to sympathetic and soothing?'

There was a perceptible thawing in his manner as his eyes brushed her indignant face. 'I'm cranky when I'm not fed,' he confessed.

'You're cranky full stop,' she retorted, happy if not relieved to accept this explanation for his intense mood.

'And when I've fed you,' he continued in a conversational tone, 'you can tell me what happened back there.'

Alice, caught off guard, stiffened. 'What happened back there?' she echoed, feigning ignorance.

Bad enough, she thought, inwardly cringing at the memory of him carrying her out of the hotel, to have made such an exhibition of herself in front of him, without going into the details. She couldn't imagine for a second that anyone as strong and seemingly invulnerable as Luca would not despise weakness in others.

'I can see how looking as though you'd just seen your worst nightmare and then almost losing consciousness might slip your mind, especially when it happened—what…?' He consulted his wrist-watch. 'Almost ten minutes ago,' he drawled.

'There is no need to be sarcastic.'

'Wrong, there is every need to be sarcastic…being sarcastic is the only thing stopping me from ki…strangling you.'

For a split second Alice had thought he was going to say kissing…*now how delusional was that*?

'Maybe I had too much to drink, but as you can see I'm fine now.' She gave a brilliant smile just to illustrate how fine she was.

Luca inhaled and closed his eyes. 'Clearly it was all a figment of my imagination.'

His scorching sarcasm made her wince. 'I've already explained.'

Expressive hands spread out before him in a dismissive gesture, Luca nodded, his face taut with annoyance. 'Let's just leave it, shall we?'

Alice, who was more than ready to leave it, gave a nod of sheer relief. She supposed that he did have some justification for being annoyed. She had gone out of her way to be unpleasant to him—something she might have to think about at a later date…*much* later—made him miss dinner, and he couldn't be too happy about the prospect of explaining away tomorrow's newspapers to the sublime Ingrid. Thoughts of the sublime Ingrid sent her fragile spirits plummeting.

The entrance to the tiny Italian restaurant was down a side street. 'Careful of the stairs—they're steep,' Luca warned as he preceded her down the steep flight. Presumably if she slipped he was going to cushion her fall.

Some people might think it worth a few bruises to land on top of Luca O'Hagan.

She took great care with the steps.

The interior of the unprepossessing building proved to be totally charming. The cosy room, decorated in a delightfully rustic style, was filled with warmth and laughter...and *people*! Lots of people! The place was literally heaving and the diners, like the mismatched and eccentric crockery, were a pretty assorted bunch, some dressed down in casual jeans, others dressed up to the nines.

There was absolutely no way they were going to get a table this side of midnight.

'It looks full,' she said as Luca slid the jacket off her shoulders.

'I'm sure they'll squeeze us in somewhere,' Luca responded with what seemed to Alice like wildly misplaced optimism.

'You're too big to squeeze in,' she retorted, her critical gaze lighting on his broad shoulders. Her stomach took an unscheduled dive. 'We might as well leave,' she added hurriedly.

'We've only just arrived.'

'You obviously have to book.' She sighed wistfully as a plate of something that looked and smelt delicious was placed in front of some lucky diners. Alice realised just how hungry she was. 'This is too cruel,' she complained.

Two minutes later they were sitting at a table for two in a concealed alcove. They couldn't have treated Luca with more warmth had he been the proverbial returning black sheep or visiting royalty. The owner, Paolo, who had kissed her soundly on both cheeks when Luca had introduced her, had taken their orders himself.

Not that she had had the opportunity to place her order; Luca had taken the unseen menu from her hand and handed it back to Paolo.

'We'll leave it up to you. That's all right with you, is it, Alice?'

Alice hadn't been left with much option but to nod.

As they were so busy Alice was resigned to a long wait, but about two seconds later a pretty girl who looked like a female version of one of the waiters appeared. 'Sorry to keep you waiting.'

'Do I detect a family resemblance?' Alice asked after she had deposited their meals in front of them.

'This is very much a family business; Gina is Paolo's granddaughter.'

'How do you know them so well?' Or was it just the pretty Gina he knew well? 'They don't seem like your...' She stopped and shook her head. 'They seem really nice and this,' she added brightly, 'looks delicious.'

Unfortunately Luca wasn't going to let her off the hook.

'They don't look like my what, Alice? My sort of people?' he suggested.

She coloured but didn't respond to his angry undertone. 'What *are* my sort of people? You think I'm some sort of élitist snob, don't you?'

She lifted her eyes from her plate. The conflict that she felt was tearing her apart was reflected in her troubled eyes. 'To be honest I don't know what you are,' she admitted with a spurt of candour. 'You're confusing.' Or should that be I'm confused?

For a long moment he looked into her face. Then with one of the startling changes of mood he was capable of he grinned.

A wide, incredibly charismatic grin that split his face. 'The first time I came in here I ended up washing the dishes.'

Alice's eyes were round with astonishment. *'You!'*

'I'd had my wallet lifted and I didn't discover it until I came to pay,' he explained. 'Paolo gave me a choice: the cops or the washing-up,' he recalled.

'You chose the washing-up?'

He nodded, looking amused by her open-mouthed astonishment.

Alice, her food forgotten, put down her fork. 'But the police would have been able to confirm that you weren't a con man,' she protested.

'I know.'

'Then why?'

'I hadn't been in the city for long and I didn't know many people. Actually...' his eyes held a gleam of self-mockery as they lifted from the prolonged contemplation of the ruby-red liquid in his glass '—I think it's possible I was lonely.'

Alice shook her head. 'You're teasing!' she accused. The idea of Luca O'Hagan washing up was hard enough to get her head around, but him being lonely! 'You expect me to believe you were reduced to sitting in your hotel room watching repeats on the television?'

Luca, who didn't immediately respond, leaned back in his chair and watched the play of expression across her flushed face. 'Haven't you ever felt lonely in the middle of a room of people, Alice?'

'Yes, I have,' she admitted, too startled by the soft question to prevaricate. 'But you're not—' She broke off, flushing in face of his sardonic smile.

'Capable of experiencing the same feelings you do, Alice?'

Alice, who felt there had been far too much discussion of feelings tonight, changed the subject. 'I don't expect your date was too pleased when you decided to wash up.'

'I didn't have a date that night.'

She picked up her fork. 'That was lucky.'

'Actually you're the first woman I've ever brought here,' he revealed, before turning his attention to the neglected food before them. 'Right,' he urged. 'Eat up. Paolo makes the best *fritto misto di pesce* in town and he'll be offended if you don't clear your plate.'

As Alice began to fork the fried fish, which was every bit as delicious as Luca had contended, into her mouth her thoughts were otherwise engaged. *No other woman*…that was what he had said. Of course she'd be daft to read anything into that…all the same…

CHAPTER FIVE

'I'M BEGINNING to feel a good deal of empathy for the animals in the zoo...'

Luca, his expression perplexed, shook his head.

'At feeding time,' Alice elucidated and he grinned.

That grin totally transformed the classically severe cast of lean features, banishing the stony reticence she was used to, and lending it an attractive warmth.

It was the most relaxed she had ever seen him, Alice realised. Her eyes flickered briefly to the discarded tie casually flung over the back of his chair and his elbows planted on the table. The steel had gone from his spine and the scorn from his expression as he slouched elegantly in his chair.

This was Luca with the charm and vigour but minus the snootiness and sneers—in short a pretty irresistible proposition.

'I like watching you eat; most women pick at their food.'

'Whereas I fall on it and devour it like a ravening beast?' she suggested, pushing aside the last portion on her plate with a regretful sigh. 'I feel so special...or should that be freaky?'

'Settle for different,' he suggested.

Her shoulders lifted. 'I can live with that,' she agreed amicably.

'What about that last bit?' he asked, pointing at the amount she had left on her plate.

'I'm not being polite. If I eat any more I'll burst. *Messy*,' she said with a grimace.

His mobile mouth quivered. 'Paolo will be hurt,' he contended.

61

'Fine, you eat it, then,' she suggested with a laugh as she speared a piece of squid onto her fork and held it out to him.

The smile died from his incongruously azure eyes as they collided with her own. In the space of a heartbeat the temperature soared by several degrees. She instantly responded to his abrupt change of mood and would have dropped the fork had his hand not come up to cover her own. Inside his fingers her hand was shaking as, without breaking contact with her wide eyes, he brought the fork up to his mouth.

A tidal wave of blind, uncontrolled lust swallowed her up like some heavy downy duvet. She didn't even try to fight it. Every cell in her body was tuned to him: his voice, his touch…the faint male scent that rose from his warm skin. He leaned across the table and she felt her skin prickle damply with heat.

'Delicious.' His voice was as velvety smooth as the sauce that had covered their food and infinitely more wicked.

Alice was mortified to recognise the low moan issued from her own throat. Luca heard and his eyes darkened dramatically; she felt his fingers spasm around her own.

'Alice.' He swallowed, the muscles in his brown throat visibly spasming. 'I think we both—'

'You enjoyed.' Paolo, oblivious to the atmosphere, beamed at them both. 'Now,' he announced grandly, 'you shall try my *pesche ripiene al forno*.'

Luca's hand withdrew. 'Baked stuffed peaches,' he explained for Alice's benefit.

'Oh, I couldn't. But they sound delicious,' she added quickly when Paolo looked crestfallen. If Paolo wasn't such an attentive host…another couple of minutes and they might have been in another place. Maybe it was just as well that he had interrupted. It was all very well to say she was a free agent, but this didn't alter the fact she still *felt* married. Look how guilty she felt simply acknowledging how attracted she was to Luca!

I'm not ready, she thought.

When their voluble host had gone Luca showed no inclination to take up where he'd left off; his manner was distant and he seemed to have something on his mind. Whereas earlier they had been talking non-stop, now there were inhibiting silences. Several times as she drank her coffee she caught Luca looking at her.

'I think I'd like to go now,' she said finally.

'Alice…'

She tensed expectantly as he dragged a hand through the thick glossy hair he wore longer than was fashionable.

'You were…' He stopped and inhaled deeply. 'Are you planning on seeing Seth again?'

'Seth?' She shook her head, then shrugged. 'I suppose so.'

'Then it doesn't bother you that he's married…or maybe you didn't know?'

Alice's eyes widened, her expression growing defensive as Luca surveyed her sternly from under the sweep of those preposterously sexy eyelashes of his with a look that said she was either a callous home-breaker or a total dope who believed any tale spun by a half-plausible stranger.

Not a person given to physical violence, she suddenly wanted to throw something at him.

'I think he did mention it…' She made a show of frowning as though she was trying to recall something and then smiled. 'Yes…Susan.' She directed a frowning look of enquiry at his taut face. 'Isn't that his wife's name?'

His expression remained veiled, but despite this he managed to project a silent but strong aura of disapproval. 'Yes, it is.'

'You've met her, then?' He acknowledged this with a curt nod. 'Is she very pretty?'

'Very,' he told her shortly.

Alice, who had been counting down from ten, reached four before he exploded.

'The fact he is married makes no difference to you?'

She affected surprise; she must have done it well because she heard the sound of his teeth grinding.

'Should it? It makes no difference to Seth,' she pointed out reasonably.

While Seth had discussed his marriage breakup she had wondered what it was about her that made men feel they could confide their emotional problems. Natural empathy, or did they think of her as a universal agony aunt? She supposed she should find the fact that Luca automatically assumed she was a tart with ulterior motives refreshing.

Presumably Luca didn't like the idea of his friend getting involved with a mere secretary. Ironically he needn't have bothered; Seth was nice, really nice, but she'd known within two minutes of being in his company that there was no spark between them. It wasn't that she was expecting a thunderclap when she saw *the one*, but it stood to reason in her mind that there had to be some chemistry from the first moment for love to stand a chance of developing.

'Have you no concept of self-respect?'

Alice could no longer disguise her feelings under a calm exterior. Her eyes flashed wrathful fire as she pinned him with a contemptuous glare.

'This amount of sanctimonious claptrap coming from a man who sees nothing wrong in seducing his own brother's girl-friend is rich…really rich.'

'Ingrid?' He threw back his head and laughed.

For a moment Alice was distracted from her objective by this inappropriate display of mirth. 'You think it was funny?' she condemned coldly.

'I think it was bloody hilarious,' he told her with eyes as cold as blue steel. 'But we're not talking about me or Ingrid,' he reminded her grimly.

'No, we wouldn't be, because, although you feel totally free to criticise me you'd be gobsmacked if I passed judgement on the way you live your life. No, we're talking about my total lack of moral fibre and principles, aren't we? A theme I sense is close to your heart!' she finished breathlessly. 'Tell me, Luca, how long is it since you touched base with Seth?'

'How should I know?' He looked impatient.

'How long?' she persisted.

'Six…ten months, maybe?'

What Luca needed was a major dose of humility and Alice decided that she was going to provide it.

'It's probably a little bit more than that because otherwise you would have known that Seth and his *pretty* wife are divorced. She ran off with a French count.'

'*French count!* My God, couldn't Seth do better than that? Mind you, I suppose he didn't need to. Did you always walk around with gullible idiot in neon across your forehead?' The angry finger he viciously dragged across his own forehead left a faint raised weal on his olive skin. 'Or is that a recent development?'

Alice found she couldn't take her eyes off the minor blemish. In truth she couldn't take her eyes off him. Every little detail, every tiny nuance afforded her endless fascination.

'I'm not about to apologise because I don't automatically assume someone's lying to me…unless of course they happen to be called Luca O'Hagan. Your problem is you believe everyone is as deceitful as you are,' she contended scornfully. 'The day I'm as cynical and twisted as you I hope someone's around to tell me to get over myself.'

White around the lips, Luca drew in a deep breath through his clenched teeth. 'Is that a fact?'

'Yes, it is. Besides, it's not the sort of thing Seth would make up, is it? I didn't even know there were any real counts in France,' she admitted. 'But apparently this one is the genuine article and poor Seth feels particularly gutted because she met him at a health-spa break that he arranged as a birthday treat.'

There was a degree of satisfaction in seeing Luca, for once
in his life, look taken aback. But not as much satisfaction as
she had expected.

'Are you actually serious?'

'Apparently the divorce was finalised last week.'

'So Seth is on the rebound. Congratulations. I suppose it
was inevitable. I mean, if Seth thought that marriage would
last for ever he was the only one.'

'I can see exactly why he didn't confide in you,' she
snapped in disgust. 'The supportive friend you are not.'

'I can see exactly why he confided in you,' Luca returned.
'A born bleeding heart. A suggestion of a tear in those spaniel
eyes and you'd be gagging to comfort him.'

She closed her eyes, almost weeping with anger. 'You are
disgusting, crude, vile and if you were sobbing your heart out
I wouldn't lift a little finger to comfort you.'

'I'd prefer to be crude than an idiot,' Luca retorted. '
wouldn't have trusted her as far as I could throw her.'

Alice's outraged glare focused on his lean face. How could
anyone be that unfeeling to a friend's tragedy?

'Kick a man when he's down, why don't you? That's just
typical of you,' she accused. 'You have all the empathy of a
Great White...' And, she decided furiously, he was just as
ruthless and single-minded. Actually, now that she thought of
it the analogy with the cold-blooded predator was extremely
apt. Luca was top of the food chain and he had no natural
enemies unless it was his own ego.

'I find it hard to empathise with a man who marries a
woman just because she's the woman that every other man
wants. She was the original trophy wife. But then Seth likes
to own beautiful things, as I'm sure you'll discover.'

'And you'd know this after meeting her, how many times?'

'Just the once.'

'Once! Oh, well, you could write the definitive character
analysis, then.'

'She came on to me,' he recalled in a matter-of-fact manner.

Alice blinked. *'She what?'*

'Do you want me to spell it out? She came on to me…made a pass.'

'Surely not!' she exclaimed, shaking her head.

'It has been known to happen,' he inserted drily.

Alice felt nauseous as she imagined the occasions he referred to. 'I meant she was married to your friend.'

He slanted an incredulous look at her face. 'I'm beginning to think you live in some little world all of your own where wives never cheat and everyone lives happily ever after.'

'Are you sure you're not the fantasist here?' she countered angrily. 'The poor woman obviously smiled at you and you assumed that she was offering herself. Why is it,' she asked, rolling her eyes, 'men think that every woman in the world fancies the pants off them?'

'Imagination, Alice, doesn't shove its tongue down your throat and its hand down your trousers.'

'She did?' The cynical sneer on his face deepened as she went bright pink. 'Did you…did you…?'

'Did I take her up on the offer? Actually, no, I don't like aggressive women. And even a total sleaze like me draws the line at sleeping with the wife of a friend. Also I'm allergic to silicone,' he admitted with a faint shudder.

Alice closed her mouth over the impulse to declare her cleavage unenhanced and sighed. 'Poor Seth… Fate is really cruel sometimes.'

'Fate?' Luca echoed. 'The same fate that makes two people's eyes meet across a crowded room?' His contemptuous sneer made Alice wince.

'I suppose you believe that people make their own fate?'

Luca looked at her with unconcealed irritation. 'I don't give a damn what *people* do.'

Alice smiled complacently into his dark, displeased face. 'I'm not wrong, though, am I?' she speculated.

'I can't deny it…Alice, you know me so well.' On any other occasion Alice would have responded to the danger in his silky response, but the extraordinary events of this night had imbued her with a strange recklessness.

She shrugged. 'You can be sarcastic, and I'm sure you *love* the idea of being enigmatic, but, let's face it, you're not exactly the most complicated of men ever to look in the mirror and like what he saw.' She saw the shock register in his electric-blue eyes and added innocently, 'No offence intended.'

The silence that followed his soft, *'Dio mio,'* lasted long enough for some doubts to creep in. He was everything she despised in a man, but was it such a good idea to tell him? Satisfying in the short term as it was, it was probably dangerous in the long term. Luca was not a man who let someone else have the last word!

He didn't.

'It's curious but I've noticed people who are eager to point out the faults of others are less eager to hear about their own. Of course, this doesn't apply in Alice's case because *she's* perfect.' He raised his glass in a mocking salute. 'Let's drink to perfect Alice.'

Alice was too angry to think straight. She was as close to *really* losing her temper as she had been in years.

'I'm well aware I'm not perfect,' she grated with a toss of her head.

'Such modesty.'

Her soft lips tightened at his mocking admiration. 'If we're talking compared with you, the answer is yes.'

Luca gave a very Latin shrug. 'So willing to flaunt it and almost perfect. Well, almost perfect is still much more than most of us can aspire to.'

Alice didn't know how she managed to smile through his satiric drawl when all she wanted to do was slap the smirk off his condescending face. 'It's certainly more than you can aspire to,' she agreed with a sweet smile.

Against his will an appreciative growl of laughter was wrenched from Luca's throat. 'I don't aspire to perfection; I always find paragons incredibly boring.'

She adopted an air of studied disinterest. 'How lucky that you don't drop off in my company.'

'There's always the possibility Roman was wrong about you. He's hardly what you'd call an objective observer, is he?'

'Well, he knows me a damn sight better than you do,' she retorted angrily.

'Granted. Or at least he *thinks* he does. Roman sees you as his indispensable PA and secretary.'

The dismissive note really got under her skin. In all modesty she was pretty indispensable. She hadn't appreciated until now that, despite all his egalitarian talk and washing dishes, Luca was actually a snob.

'I'm more than that.'

Though his tone was totally devoid of expression, there was unmistakable contempt etched in his dark lean face as he responded. 'I'm quite sure you're much, *much* more. Though maybe not quite as much as you'd like to be?'

The sly insinuation made her cheeks burn; anyone listening in would have automatically assumed that she was out to get her boss. Presumably that was the idea? Angrily she lifted her chin.

'Short of having the man's child,' she said with a soft, provocative laugh, 'I don't see how we could be any closer.'

Alice's provocative little smile faded, to be replaced by an expression of dawning horror. I as good as said I'm sleeping with my boss, and I said it to his brother…*oh, God*…!

She blinked as her eyes locked with Luca's. He really does have the bluest eyes I've ever seen. Blue and angry, *very* angry.

She gave her head a tiny shake; obviously she was not right in the head. It passed the bounds of ridiculous, considering the fact he was going out of his way to be even more insulting than usual, that she was wasting her time admiring the sheer unbelievable blueness of the man's eyes!

'That is, I mean—'

'I really don't need you to draw a diagram.'

Under his tan she saw that Luca had gone pale, and she realised that in her desire to score points she had gone too far. If she didn't want to have the unenviable task of explaining to her boss why she'd basically told his brother they were sleeping together, she had better set the record straight...and fast!

'Look, I don't know why I said that,' she admitted, trying for frank and open and achieving panicky and defensive. 'Any more than I know why you think I've got some sort of crush on your brother. But I'm not sleeping with him.'

To her dismay her earnest words appeared to make no impact on Luca. Her shoulders slumped as the nostrils of his narrow-bridged, masterful nose flared. He continued to act like a man who was having a tough time controlling his feelings.

'Working for Roman is always interesting and stimulating,' she added in a voice tinged with desperation. 'We have a very good working relationship...*professional*,' she emphasised. 'I like and respect your brother.' She swallowed as her voice thickened emotionally. 'But seducing him has never even crossed my mind.'

'You can bet it has crossed his. But you're wasting your time. You know Roman isn't in love with you.'

Alice's jaw dropped; mouth unattractively ajar, she stared back at him with stunned incredulity. The man was quite obviously out of his mind.

'Why do you imagine I'd *want* Roman to be in love with

me?' she demanded. The idea was so ridiculous that she began to grin. 'So what am I—some love-struck schoolgirl?'

There was obviously absolutely no point being sincere. He had made up his mind and nothing she said or did was going to change it. 'But you know, now that you've put it in my head I've got to thinking it might be interesting...mmm...' She pressed one finger to the slight cleft in her softly rounded chin and pursed her lips thoughtfully.

'It might be fun. After all, how many secretaries marry their boss? It's an acknowledged career path,' she reminded him. 'I think,' she mused, 'I'll go for something large and flash, ring-wise, that is. I mean, if you've got it, flaunt it, that's what I always say.'

'I'd noticed.' With an insolent half-smile on his mobile lips he perused the voluptuous curves of her upper body. 'So, I expect, has every other man in the place.'

Alice felt her nipples harden into burning life. She had no idea from where she found the strength to remain outwardly oblivious to his stare. Even the creamy contours of the cleavage he was crudely ogling flushed.

Alice's eyes narrowed angrily. 'Are there any family heirlooms locked in a vault somewhere? I've always seen myself in rubies.'

He looked at her for a long simmering moment. 'You're not, are you?'

Alice's eyes lifted from her bare left hand and swallowed. She and Mark had decided that a deposit on a house was more important than an engagement ring. But the night they had become officially engaged Mark had slid a plastic ring from a Christmas cracker on her finger.

'Not...?' she echoed blankly.

'You're not sleeping with Roman.'

She rubbed her bare left hand against her cheek. 'Of course I'm not,' she said, suddenly too weary to argue.

'I always thought...'

'You always thought what?'

He shrugged. 'Forget it,' he advised, gazing abstractly into the distance. He had spent so long wondering if his brother was bedding the most desirable woman he'd ever seen and all he'd had to do was ask.

'You realise that you're no longer off limits.'

Alice, who had been looking around to locate the ladies' room where she intended to lock herself in a cubicle and cry, focused on his face. 'Off limits to what?'

His nostrils quivered and his jaw clenched, drawing evenly toned skin that had a delicious golden sheen tight and revealing achingly perfect bone structure. 'Off limits to me,' he elucidated throatily.

Alice blinked. A flash-flood of heat passed through her body. 'This conversation is getting surreal.'

'You're not sleeping with my brother. Sleep with me.'

'Naturally such an offer is incredibly tempting,' she croaked hoarsely. She watched, her temper simmering gently as he ran a hand over his jaw where a dark fuzz of stubble cast a shadow.

'I assumed it would be.'

'I had no idea that it was an either-or option. If you're not sleeping with one brother you have to sleep with the other.' She pressed her face into her palms and shook her head. 'You really are unbelievable,' she breathed.

He inclined his dark head and smiled. 'Thank you.'

'It wasn't a compliment,' she said, pressing her palms tight together. 'What have I ever done to make you think for one second that I'd want to sleep with you?' she demanded scornfully. His mouth opened and suddenly she knew she didn't want to hear the answer to that question. 'And what,' she added hastily, 'did I ever do to make you think that I'm in love with Roman?'

'You took a knife meant for him. You don't risk your life for someone unless they're something special to you.'

CHAPTER SIX

THE knife had been in her hand when Luca had walked into the room. A knife, a beautiful blonde, and his injured—for all he knew at the time *fatally* injured—brother!

His mind had made the obvious connection.

'Luca, you're late,' Roman hailed him before closing his eyes. He was a deeply alarming shade of grey, but breathing, because Luca could see the rise and fall of his chest.

'Too late for the fun, it would seem,' Luca replied, approaching the beautiful blonde with caution, with several theories, most involving a lover's tiff that had gone *seriously* wrong, running through his mind.

After the initial shock when it didn't function at all, your mind, he discovered, worked very fast. A useful piece of information for anyone who walked into their brother's office looking to take him to the pub for a promised pint and finding a blood bath instead!

Before he could wrestle the nasty-looking weapon from her hand the blonde put it down on the desk with a small grimace. Scarcely acknowledging him, she moved towards Roman, who was standing with his shoulders braced against the wall. He had one gory hand pressed to his face, while blood was seeping through his fingers and dripping down onto his pale shirt.

Luca could see his brother's face remained scarily pale and his attitude dazed, but the fact his brother was standing was something that he took comfort from.

Luca faced a dilemma: take the knife or protect his brother from a possible second attack. His brother, dazed or not, was a good muscular twelve inches taller than the blonde so he went for the knife. Before he touched it the blonde gave an urgent cry of warning.

'Don't touch—the police will want it for forensics!'

His fingers poised above the blood-stained blade, Luca stopped. *'What?'*

'The police...I've phoned, they're on their way.' She began to fold the cardigan she had removed into a tight wad. Underneath she wore a snug-fitting sleeveless top. It passed through his mind that to notice a woman's body at a moment like this could indicate he was seriously disturbed.

The woman with the incredible figure scanned his face suspiciously. 'Look, if you've got a thing about blood maybe you should wait outside,' she suggested kindly.

'Wait outside?' he echoed.

'The last thing we need is you fainting.'

Luca, who had never been treated as though he was not just incompetent and irrelevant, but actually a bit of a nuisance too, was at a loss to know how to respond to this brutally frank observation.

'I won't faint.'

She looked mollified but not convinced. 'I'm glad to hear it.'

'Look, just who the hell...what the hell?' So she might not have attacked his brother, but someone had and he wanted to know who and why!

Her head turned, causing her silvery blonde curls to bounce attractively around her slender shoulders. There was a definite edge of irritation in her voice as she replied.

'Not *now*. And it's probably not a good idea for us to touch anything at all if we can help it.'

From this comment he deduced that she had decided that he looked stupid enough to go around contaminating the crime scene. Before he had thought of a response her attention had moved on. To his injured brother.

'Roman, let me look at it. Sitting down is good,' she added

as he slid gracefully down the wall. She knelt beside him. 'That's it, great,' she approved encouragingly as his hand lifted.

'Bad?' Roman asked.

At that moment Luca saw for the first time where most of the blood was coming from.

'*Dio*...your face, Roman!' he exclaimed, shocked by the sight of the deep cut that stretched from just below his brother's eye and extended halfway along his cheekbone.

'It's not nearly as bad as it looks.' The blonde had tilted her head to look at the gaping wound from several angles and said with an approving nod, 'No, not too bad at all.'

'*Not too bad!*' His brother was going to be scarred for life.

A look from those clear blue eyes silenced him. 'It's a good clean cut, which shouldn't leave much of a scar once it heals,' she announced in a tone that didn't invite debate.

At the time Luca hadn't believed her though for Roman's sake he hadn't said so, but in fact time had proved her prediction correct. His brother had been left with an interesting though not disfiguring scar, which the ladies found attractive.

'I'm going to press this against it, Roman, to stop the blood. I'm sorry if it hurts.'

'Go ahead, *cara*.' Roman smiled weakly. 'You all right?'

'I think so.' Her face creased in concentration as she applied the makeshift dressing to his cheek. 'It's not sterile but it is clean.' From her tone and attitude you'd have been forgiven for assuming she was engaged in selling jam at a village fête, not knee-deep in blood and knives!

'Luca, did you see her?'

Luca tore his gaze from the spookily composed blonde. 'See who, her?' he asked ungrammatically.

'My stalker.'

'You have a stalker?'

'Doesn't everyone? You could say she cut and ran. Ouch!'

he protested as the blonde applied some extra pressure to his bleeding wound.

'You shouldn't talk so much,' she reproached, huskily stern.

The huskiness and tiny catch were the only indications Luca had picked up so far that suggested maybe she wasn't as cool, calm and collected as she appeared.

'Luca, this is Alice, my assistant. Alice, this is my brother, Luca. You've not met, have you?'

'No.'

'Yes.'

They both spoke in unison.

'That is no,' Luca corrected himself.

What else could he say? You couldn't expect to be taken seriously if you said that you had recognised a person from a lavishly illustrated book your mother had read bedtime stories to you from when you were a child.

But he had.

The blonde curls, the heart-shaped face, the big blue eyes and rosebud lips…she *was* the princess in the tower, only in the flesh she didn't look as if she would hang around waiting for a passing prince to rescue her.

It had been his favourite story.

Luca had recognised straight off that this princess was a different proposition entirely. He was looking at a princess who would not only organise her own escape plan, but put together the most competitively priced package and bring in the project on time!

'What shall I do?' It went against the grain not to take charge, but when all was said and done Roman's bolshy princess secretary seemed to have things in hand.

Actually he didn't get to do anything because just then the police, closely followed by a team of paramedics, arrived. They were quick and efficient.

They looked disappointed when he admitted he'd not witnessed anything, but perked up considerably when Roman's princess, in that same calm and unhurried voice, supplied a detailed description of the attacker and the clothes she had been wearing.

She knew exactly what time the woman had arrived and left the building. Luca could see that she was a sort of witness superstar as far as the police were concerned.

'She thought Alice was my girlfriend,' Roman explained, pulling off the oxygen mask they had fitted to his face. 'She had a knife at Alice's throat and I tried to take it off her.'

'That was very unwise of you, sir,' the policeman observed. To Alice he explained they would need a full statement from her, but the morning would do if she didn't feel up to it to-night.

Somebody else said something about delayed shock and asked if there would be someone at home when she got there. Alice responded to all the questions and showed no signs of breaking down.

Stress! He'd seen people missing a bus display more stress! And Luca couldn't credit that she had actually had a knife held to that lovely throat, though there was a blood-stained nick at the base of her pale, graceful throat that said other-wise!

'Can I come along?' he asked the ambulance crew as they prepared to leave.

'No, Luca.'

'Please, sir, will you keep the mask on?' the sorely tried paramedic asked.

'In a minute...and I really could walk...' The professionals looked amused and Roman didn't push it. 'Luca, you stay. Tell Mum and Dad—I don't want them hearing about this second-hand. Tell them I'm fine.'

'I'll lie through my teeth,' he promised. 'Hang in there.'

'You shouldn't talk, Roman,' his brother's ministering an-gel quietly cautioned.

'The lady's right, sir. You shouldn't exert yourself,' the paramedic agreed.

Once his brother had been stretchered out Luca slipped into the outer office to ring his parents. He was glad it was his mother who picked up. His father had a volatile temperament and he didn't want to be responsible for him having a second heart attack.

His mother was upset but he managed to soothe her worst fears and promised to ring from the hospital with further news when he got there. He was half out of the door when he remembered the woman in the other room...*actually she wasn't easy to forget.*

He poked his head around the door; the promised forensic team hadn't arrived but everyone else had left. She was alone.

'Can I give you a lift anywhere? I'm on my way to the hospital.'

'The hospital,' she repeated vaguely.

Luca wondered if that delayed shock they had spoken of was setting in.

'Yes.' Her smooth brow creased in concentration as her eyes lifted to his face. 'Yes, that might be a good idea.'

He hovered impatiently at the door, but she made no attempt to follow him. 'I'm going now...if you're ready?'

'Right, I just...the thing is I don't think...'

In the split second before her knees folded he registered that blood that didn't belong to his brother was seeping through the fingers she had pressed to her abdomen.

'I think she must have nicked me,' she roused herself enough to say faintly as he fell on his knees beside her.

'God! Why the hell didn't you say something?'

'Didn't feel a thing.' She winced as he hefted her into his arms. 'Until now. I didn't even know she'd got me. Isn't that amazing?'

He figured if he was fast, he might catch the ambulance before it left. He didn't. There was a solitary uniformed bobby, no more than a kid really, standing beside the pavement that the ambulance had just pulled away from. His eyes widened when he saw Alice.

'Another casualty. Have you got a car?'

The young man shook his head. 'There was no room for me. I'll call an ambulance. I really don't think you should do that, sir,' he said as Luca slid the half-conscious woman in the back seat of his Mercedes.

'Maybe I shouldn't, but we've not got time to debate it. Can you drive?'

The young man nodded.

'Good.' Luca tossed the keys to him. 'Then drive...drive fast,' he added as he slid in the back and put the fair head in his lap.

Just before she lost consciousness she opened her eyes and murmured anxiously, 'Roman will be all right, won't he?'

It transpired that Luca's decision not to wait for an ambulance had been correct. Another few minutes and it could have been too late. Alice had lost part of her damaged liver, but not her spirit—that had remained firmly intact.

Luca was beginning to think that he had not escaped that evening totally unscathed himself.

'The knife thing was instinct or accident or most likely a bit of both. I would have done that for anyone...even *you*!' Alice said. 'Though I'm willing to bet there are a lot of people who would have paid me not to.'

As an image of Luca injured consolidated in her head, so did the bleak empty feeling. A world that didn't have Luca—infuriating, maddening and arrogant Luca—was shockingly unimaginable. But she had lost her husband and loss didn't get worse than that. So why did the idea of losing a man she didn't even like fill her with a dread that lodged like a solid object behind her breastbone?

The feeble voice from that night was now robust and angry,

the scared blue eyes now spitting fury. If Luca had been able to think humour when he recalled that night the contrast could have been comical, but it wasn't and he couldn't.

She got to her feet. 'Don't worry, I'm not going to faint this time, but I am going to leave and you're going to pay for a taxi to take me back to the hotel. I think that I deserve a free ride after putting up with your obnoxious company.'

To her surprise Luca didn't put up an argument. He made his farewells to Paolo, who became even more animated when Luca asked for the bill.

'You offend me!' Paolo declared.

'If it hadn't been for Luca here sorting out my accounts there would be no Paolo's.' He took Alice's hand and kissed it. 'And you will bring your lovely lady to see us again very soon.'

Luca's heavy-lidded eyes drifted towards her tense face. 'Very soon,' he promised in a voice that made her stomach flip.

Outside he put her in a cab, unfolded some notes from a wad in his wallet and gave the driver instructions. Without a word he walked away.

Alice was so wrapped up in her own thoughts that it was some time before it occurred to her the journey back to the hotel seemed to be taking an awfully long time.

'Is this the quickest route?' she asked the driver. 'It only took a few minutes to get here on foot.' All she wanted to do was get back to her room, lock the door, and indulge in a bout of unrestrained weeping.

'This is the best way to avoid the roadworks, lady,' he replied and Alice didn't have much choice but to take his word for it. She comforted herself with the reflection that if he was ripping anyone off it was Luca. And to her way of thinking anything that caused Luca O'Hagan a moment's annoyance could only be a good thing.

She closed her eyes and leaned back in her seat. Damn Luca O'Hagan!

The relief she felt when they finally drew up outside the hotel was short-lived. It actually lasted until she stepped out of the glass-fronted lift and saw the tall figure of a man standing down the farthest end of the hallway. The man had sleek dark looks and the sort of inbuilt air of assurance that made him stand out from the crowd. Only there was no crowd, just the two of them.

Alice's heart climbed into her throat. Her firm light step faltered, but she carried on walking. What choice did she have? This couldn't be happening. But it was; there was no mistaking the arrogant angle of Luca's dark head.

As she approached Luca levered himself off the wall. His relaxed manner was a striking contrast to her dry-mouthed discomfort.

'You're not here?' she protested in more hope than anticipation of him vanishing in a puff of smoke. 'It's not possible. I left before you.'

'The impossible is not so very difficult to achieve if you bribe the driver to take the scenic route.'

His casual confession made her stiffen with anger. *'Why?'*

'Because you'd have kicked up a fuss if I'd tried to get in the cab with you.'

'And you *so* hate to draw attention to yourself.'

'You noticed that? Not everyone realises that I'm a shy and unassuming guy at heart.'

Anger flared in her eyes. 'If you came here to be smart, Luca, go away.' She lifted a weary hand to her head. 'Actually go away anyway, Luca.'

'I'm not going anywhere. We've got some unfinished business.'

'You mean you've thought of some other way you can insult me.' She vented a bitter laugh and swallowed, willing the tears she felt stinging her eyelids not to fall. 'Surely not.'

The hard lines of Luca's bronzed face tightened at her sarcasm. 'I think you gave as good as you got,' he retorted. 'But enough of that…you were ill. For all I know you still are, and don't tell me it was having a few drinks that did that.'

'I wasn't about to because, quite frankly, I don't owe you any explanations.' Her defiant eyes collided with his and as their glances locked and lingered an emotional thickness developed in her throat.

'We'll have to agree to disagree on that one,' Luca said regretfully.

Expelling a long sigh, he rubbed a hand along his hard chiselled jaw. There was no trace of the regret he claimed in his face, just sheer bloody-minded determination as, hands thrust into the pockets of his tailored trousers, he sauntered forward.

Alice hardly registered his inflammatory comment. His jacket had swung open and her eyes were glued to his chest…the chest against which she had recently been closely held. Beads of perspiration broke out across her forehead as she recalled the sense of deprivation she had experienced when he had released her.

To walk into his arms…feel them close tight about her, lose herself in that male hardness… There was a rushing sound in her head as she tried to subdue the crazy compulsion to act out those forbidden cravings. *What would he do if she did?*

The concern in Luca's eyes deepened as he followed the flicker of emotion on her face.

'Are you feeling unwell again?'

As she lifted her eyes to his face the shatteringly erotic image of hands—her own hands—moving over the naked, gleaming flesh of his bare chest surfaced from some corner of her subconscious.

'Ill!' She gave a strange, bitter laugh. 'I wish I was. *Stupid*…stupid, stupid!' she gritted before turning stiffly away.

With any luck he'd assume the scornful slur had been directed at him, not herself. *How crazy am I? The sexual stuff was bad enough but this!*

'There's something wrong with you and I think I know what it is.'

Her back stiffened. 'Haven't you got anything better to do than follow me?'

'Probably.'

'I could call Security.' *Now that should be interesting. What should she tell them? Take this man away he's making me fall in love with him.*

'True, you could.'

Colour heightened, Alice slung him a discouraging look over her shoulder. It didn't discourage.

Hand on her chin, he turned her face up to him. 'You look terrible.'

She flashed him a tight, resentful smile and pulled away. 'I really needed that.'

'I'm just trying to show a bit of concern.'

Alice eased her shoulders against the wall and closed her eyes. '*Concern?* Well, you can see how that would throw me after tonight.'

'Would you have preferred I had said you looked beautiful?' The dark fan of his incredible eyelashes cast a filigree of shadow along his prominent cheekbones as his glance dropped. 'That's so like a woman.'

She bristled angrily at the amused note in his voice. She only just repressed an impulse to tell him that some men found her pretty.

'You lie to women! Surely not?'

His eyes lifted and infuriatingly he looked appreciative of her acid jibe. *God, why did he never react the way she expected?*

'Are you on some sort of medication?'

'No, I am not on medication!' she retorted indignantly.

'I wasn't accusing you of being a junkie. I meant prescription drugs.' Eyes that were far too penetrating for her liking swept across her face. 'Have you seen a doctor recently?'

'No, I have not seen a doctor.'

One dark brow lifted. 'Will you?'

'Yes,' she hissed from between clenched teeth.

He laughed. 'You're a very bad liar.'

'I'm also very fed up with ridiculous cross-examination. For the last time,' she yelled, 'I am not ill, I'm just…'

He stilled, his vivid eyes narrowing suspiciously. *'Pregnant?'*

There was a palpitating silence.

Alice's small hands clenched into fists at her sides. Of all the extraordinary explanations, Luca had to come up with one that made her look bad. She attempted to treat the accusation calmly. 'No, I am *not* pregnant!'

'Who is the father?' he asked, acting as if she hadn't spoken, which was Luca all over. He wasn't interested in anyone else's opinion…well, not mine anyhow, she thought. This quality might make him a force to be reckoned with in the business world, but when it came to a personal level it made him a total pain!

'Didn't you hear me? Oh, silly me, I forgot, you're far too fond of the sound of your own voice to listen to what anyone else says!'

As someone who broke out in goose-bumps every time she heard that distinctive velvet drawl, she felt pretty uniquely qualified to discuss his voice.

Luca's attention, which had been fixed on his shoes, suddenly switched back to her face. 'It would explain your over-emotional erratic behaviour,' he contended. 'Your hormones are obviously all over the place.'

She exhaled and closed her eyes…wasted breath did not

cover this! 'For the last time I am not pregnant!' she repeated, her voice tight with frustration.

His sensual lips twisted in a cynical smile. 'Would you tell me if you were?'

'Only if you happened to be the father.'

CHAPTER SEVEN

SOMETIMES I don't believe the stuff that comes out of my mouth...!

Luca being the father of her baby would require that they had... Inhaling sharply, Alice bit her lip as she was helpless to control the tide of heat that washed over her fair skin.

'That is of course good to know, but as I do not indulge in unprotected sex that would be unlikely.'

'Neither do I!' No sex at all was about the safest you could get! 'And,' she choked, 'you're not going to indulge in any sort of sex with me!'

'Imagine my devastation,' he said drily.

Alice's eyes glowed with dislike as she glared up at him. 'You're the very last man in the world I would have sex with.'

'Which is why you shake every time I touch you.'

Alice didn't even dignify this taunt with a response. 'Let me say this slowly, so that even someone of your limited mental capacity can understand. I am not pregnant. I don't actually carry a medical certificate to that effect concealed about my person—'

'I think it would be physically impossible, given what you're wearing, to actually conceal anything about your person.'

To her horror she felt her body react to his scrutiny. 'Then you'll just have to take my word for it.'

Mortified, she quickly turned away; the darned dress left her precious few secrets, she thought as her nipples pressed stiffly against the silky fabric. The friction created as she moved to open the door was almost painful.

'Permit me.'

'You make it sound as if I have a choice,' she snarled sarcastically as she was forced to stand by and watch him smoothly open the door with the card he had appropriated from her shaking hand.

'So if you're not pregnant, what are you?'

'Very tired…goodnight.'

She was fast, but not fast enough. The door closed, only Luca contrived somehow not to be on the side she wanted him to be when it clicked shut.

He looked around the room. It had no distinguishing features that made it different from any other bedroom in a five-star hotel. 'Nice room.' One brow lifted. 'Nice knickers,' he added admiringly.

Alice took a wrathful gasp and grabbed the pile of clean undies that had been lying on the bed and dropped them into her open case. Straightening up, her face flushed, she closed the lid with her foot.

'What do you think you're doing?'

'I'm still waiting…' he explained with infuriating calm.

She shrugged. 'For some reason you're acting as though I owe you some sort of explanation.' She disguised her discomfort with the fact that he was in her bedroom with a disdainful toss of her head.

'And you don't think you do? I'm the one about to have my face splashed across the tabloids because I came over with a fit of gallantry.'

The reminder made her tummy squirm queasily. 'It's my face too and there's no great secret. I felt slightly faint…' He looked openly sceptical. 'The room was hot and…I had too much wine.' She couldn't tell him the truth.

'I don't believe a word you're saying,' he divulged, folding his arms across his chest.

Alice's frustrated eyes clashed with deep shimmering blue. 'Don't turn your back on me!' she said, catching his arm as he turned towards the phone, which had begun to ring.

A flicker of shock appeared in her eyes as her fingers closed over the expensive fabric of his jacket. If she had been the sort of person who was impressed by a set of iron-hard perfectly developed biceps she would have been *very* impressed; she had felt steel bars with more give than his upper arm.

Luca's brilliant azure eyes travelled from the small shapely hand on his arm to her angry, agitated face. It wasn't until her dazed eyes meshed with his that Alice realised that, not only had she not let go, her fingers were exploring the hard contours of his upper arm.

She gave a shaken gasp and tucked her hands behind her back.

His darkly handsome head tilted slightly to one side as he looked at her. 'Are you going to pick that up?'

Alice blinked like someone waking from a dream, then, mortified, sent him an angry look and moved towards the phone. As she extended her hand it stopped ringing.

'Frustrating.'

Alice ignored the mock sympathy. 'Will you please just leave?' she begged. 'It's late and I have to work in the morning.'

'Ever the efficient assistant,' he mocked. 'As a matter of fact, you could give Roman a message if you see him before me.'

'Of course.' Alice couldn't believe her luck—he was actually going to go.

'Ask him if he knows why I had to carry his assistant out of the dining room.'

A horror-struck expression spread across Alice's face. 'You can't tell Roman what happened!' she protested shrilly. 'You *mustn't* tell him.' It was only when her own eyes automatically followed the direction of his gaze that she realised that in her desire to communicate the urgency of what she was saying she had grabbed hold of his arm again.

She heard herself stupidly mutter, *'Sorry,'* as she rubbed

her palms in a circular motion against her legs. The action caused a static build-up that made the dull, satiny fabric cling to the firm lines of her thighs.

'Why must I not tell him?'

'Don't sit there!' she exclaimed in horror as he made himself comfortable on her bed.

He ignored her…*he was good at that.* 'Why must I not tell Roman that you are ill?'

There was no diverting the man once he got his teeth into something.

And if that something was you…your neck…stomach…? Alice felt a rash of prickly heat break out over the exposed sensitive skin of her throat. Maybe he's right, maybe I am ill, she thought. Only a seriously deranged mind could come up with a thought like that.

'I'm not ill. Or,' she added with a grim smile, 'pregnant.' She heaved a heavy sigh. 'I'm…' Her eyes dropped and she shook her head mutely. Opening up about something that was so personal to Luca of all people…she just couldn't do it.

'You're what?' he prompted impatiently.

The crest of dark lashes lifted from her cheeks as she turned her frustrated glare on him and shook her head. 'I'm nothing.'

Something clenched hard in her belly as she watched him uncoil on the bed. She thrilled to the sheer male vitality he projected.

Iridescent eyes sealed to hers, he gave a smile that left his incredible eyes determined. 'You will tell me,' he promised.

'There's nothing to tell.' She pushed her fingers into her hair, unwittingly drawing his attention to the upward tilt of her breasts outlined in the strapless bodice of her evening gown. As the silky blonde threads of hair slipped through her fingers Alice lowered her arms and fixed her unfriendly eyes on his face.

'What are you going to do?' she enquired sarcastically.

'Bring out the thumbscrews? Send me to my room without supper?' Her mocking laugh had a strained sound.

His lashes lifted; the thin line of colour along each cheekbone accentuated the sharp, sculpted contours. 'You're already in your room, and so am I.'

He had mentioned what she had been trying very hard not to think too much about. Alice gulped as her stomach went into a crash dive. Arms crossed over her chest, oblivious to the uplifting effect this had on her full breasts, she rubbed her damp palms nervously over her upper arms. The smooth flesh was covered in goose-bumps.

'Yes, and I've already had my supper, so I don't suppose it was a terribly apt analogy,' she admitted prosaically.

'I find I can usually fit in a midnight snack.'

Alice pretended not to hear the suggestive purr in his voice and responded to his comment at face value. 'I'm sure you can, but is it a good idea?' she asked with a little shake of her head.

'You don't think it is?'

'Well, you know best, but I've heard that after a certain age those midnight snacks have a habit of catching up with men in the waistline department.' She patted her own stomach and looked sympathetic.

'Thanks for the advice,' he said, looking amused as only someone who didn't carry on ounce of surplus flesh could afford to as he placed his hand flat against his washboard-flat belly.

Her eyes followed his complacent action and her pulse rate kicked up several notches.

His voice dropped to a low, disturbingly intimate level as he throatily added, 'You're the big believer in fate. Could be that this is something that is fated.'

Their combative eyes connected and locked, sexual inertia slammed through her body. Alice was nailed to the spot. She had never in her life experienced the sort of blind lust that could literally paralyse; she couldn't even blink. Her mental faculties were equally traumatised.

The last time I saw that colour, she thought, I was lying on my back on the sugary soft sand of a Mediterranean beach. On that occasion she had needed to shade her eyes to cut down the dazzle from the cerulean sky. Luca was advancing inexorably towards her when she rediscovered her power of speech.

'I think you should leave now.' She almost winced to hear the thread of hysteria in her voice.

Luca winced. 'There's no need to yell, woman.' Along with the irritation that gleamed in his eyes there was another, less easily identifiable emotion, something darker, something infinitely more dangerous. It was the other thing that was responsible for the spill of liquid heat low in her belly.

She looked into his beautiful face and her breath snagged painfully in her throat. It frightened her to realise how powerless she was to control her response to him.

Alice felt a sharp flare of panic; Luca knew about women. She could just about live with him realising she was sexually attracted to him…she didn't think she could bear it if he realised that her feelings went deeper…a lot deeper. Pride became very important when you didn't have much else left.

She was going to have to be very careful about what she said and did. 'Ouch!' She hadn't even been aware of backing away until the back of her knee made painful contact with the corner of a table.

'Are you hurt?' His voice was rough with concern as he caught her arm to steady her.

'Like you'd care!' she retorted childishly.

A hissing sound of exasperation escaped from between his clenched teeth. 'Before tonight I always thought you were the most practical person I had ever encountered.'

'Is that why you generally treat me like part of the office furniture?'

'I have never treated you like a piece of furniture.'

'No, you treat furniture better,' she heard herself accuse ridiculously. 'I suppose you prefer women who are decorative, but can't change a plug.'

'The relevance of that statement passes me by,' he admitted. 'Right now I'd settle for boring. *Dio*, woman…you're not fit to let out without a keeper. *Can* you change a plug?'

'Of course I can.' She saw his expression and flushed. 'Don't be ridiculous!'

'*Me* ridiculous? You're the one who picked up the first guy who smiled at you regardless of the fact he could have been a mad axe murderer.'

Alice's eyes grew indignantly round at this gross distortion of the facts. 'Which would have been one up from you! Will you let go of my arm, please!'

With a muttered imprecation he released her. He watched as she rubbed the area.

'Sorry.'

'You should be.'

His response made it obvious her attempt to make him feel guilty was wasted.

'So sue me,' he suggested callously.

Tears sprang to her eyes, her lower lip quivered…she *never* cried. 'I hate you.'

'They do say that hate and love are closely related.'

For a split second she froze, then loosed a peal of caustic laughter. 'In this case *they* would be wrong,' she promised, seeing him through a mist of tears.

'Personally I think hate and lust are much closer related,' he revealed.

Alice's heart started beating like a wild bird in her chest. She bent forward to pick up a cushion that had been knocked to the floor, glad of the opportunity it gave her to school her features.

'If it makes you happier to think I am fighting a base urge

to rip off your clothes, go ahead,' she offered, clasping the cushion protectively against her stomach.

'I like it when you talk dirty.'

From somewhere she discovered hidden reserves and didn't react. 'If you think that's dirty you really have led a very sheltered life.'

He gave a wolfish grin. 'I think you know I haven't, Alice, but if you feel you could further my education…?'

'Did I somehow give you the idea I was interested in how many notches you have in your bedpost?' Or that I'd want to be one of them?

'Not up until now, no.'

It wasn't until the cushion fell from her nerveless fingers to her feet that she was aware she had been standing there, for God knew how long, staring at him.

'My God, you really do love yourself, don't you?' she choked.

'I'm a self-sufficient sort of guy.'. The mocking light died from his eyes. 'But as much as I like talking about me…'

'You don't,' she inserted, surprise at her discovery reflected in her expression. Despite his celebrity status, what did she actually know about the *real* Luca? Giving a little was what he did to stop people looking any deeper.

'We have that much in common, it would seem, but like they say sometimes it's good to talk and I think you need to…I'm here…'

Alice looked at the hands he held palm up in front of her. After a fractional pause she laid her own hands on top of them.

Now why did I do that?

His long, lean fingers, very brown against her own, tightened as he drew her forward. She must have responded because moments later she found herself sitting on the bed. Luca was on his feet.

'You talk, I'll listen.' When a mulish expression spread

across her face he added simply, 'You talk to me or you talk to Roman. The choice is yours.'

Alice took a deep breath and simulated an interest in her shoes. 'I get flashbacks to the…a…attack.'

A stunned silence followed her stuttering admission.

'And that is what occurred earlier?'

She nodded.

'What form do these flashbacks take?' There was no discernible inflection in his voice.

'I don't get them any more…' Her mouth twisted. 'Or I didn't,' she corrected, lifting her head. 'I see the knife…I feel powerless.' She swallowed and closed her eyes. 'But it tends to be muddled,' she added, wrapping her arms tight across her middle as a shudder ran through her body.

'Here.' She looked up surprised as Luca placed a wrap that had been draped over a chair across her hunched bare shoulders. 'I get the feeling you're leaving a lot out.'

The blood, the noise of the ambulance, the hospital smell and the lights in the corridor shining in her eyes and Luca…

'But essentially we're talking a post-traumatic disorder? I have a friend who resigned his army commission because of it,' he added in response to her startled expression.

'Did he, your friend…did he get better?'

Luca studied her upturned features. 'You've never met the guy, but you really care, don't you?'

'Anybody would care.'

Luca shook his head and looked at the top of her fair head. 'Actually, no, they wouldn't. Martin is fully recovered and in his element running an Outward Bound centre for executives who want to bond while building rafts. You said that it had stopped.' She nodded. 'What made it happen again tonight? Was…was it something I did?' he suggested.

'Something you did?' She was genuinely startled by the suggestion. 'No, of course not. It was the perfume,' she explained.

He looked at her blankly.

'Smells can be very evocative,' she told him.

A flicker of something she couldn't identify moved at the back of his dramatic eyes. 'I know.'

She nodded. 'The literature I read explained that things trigger the attacks sometimes...a sound...a word...*smells*. I had some perfume as a present—I started using it just before the first attack.'

His jaw clenched. 'The stalker was wearing it?'

Alice nodded.

'*Dio!*' he exclaimed, looking shaken.

'It wasn't a very nice perfume really. It was too heavy for me—' she tried to joke.

'Who else knows about this?' he cut in, scanning her face.

She shook her head. 'Nobody.'

Unbelievable! It was unbelievable that she should cope with that alone. Nobody there when the nightmares came. Nobody to share her fears with. Luca decided he must have misunderstood.

'You've coped with this all alone? But your family knew?'

'You have no idea how upset they were when I was in hospital. I couldn't put them through that again.' Her slender shoulders lifted. 'It was my problem.'

His unblinking appraisal began to make Alice feel unaccountably guilty. She tilted her chin.

'*All right?*' She immediately regretted the belligerent outburst; it made it sound as though she needed his approval for her actions.

A hissing sound of exasperation escaped through his clenched teeth. 'There is self-sufficient and then again there is bloody stubborn. Do I need to say which heading you fall under? If one of your family was in trouble would you want them to lick their wounds alone in a corner? Or would you want them to turn to you for help? Didn't it occur to you that they would be very hurt if they thought you couldn't come to them when you needed support?'

'I don't like a fuss,' she protested weakly.

He rubbed his index finger along the frown line between his brows as though he was trying to figure something out. His eyes narrowed as they focused on her face. 'Alone? You said Roman doesn't know about this?'

'No, and I'd like it to stay that way,' she told him quickly.

Luca shook his head incredulously. '*Madre di Dio*. How is that possible?' he demanded.

'I didn't tell him.'

'Why the hell not?'

The only part of his body moving was the muscle along his jaw, which was pulsing. His stillness had an explosive quality to it.

'Isn't it obvious?' She really couldn't see what he was getting so het up about.

'Not to me.'

'Your brother thinks it's his fault I got hurt in the first place. He feels guilty.' She sighed—from his blank expression it seemed that she was going to have to point out the obvious...Luca wasn't normally slow on the uptake. 'If he knew about this he'd feel simply terrible! You have no idea how he was afterwards; if I'd asked for him to write me a blank cheque he would have.'

Luca unclenched one white-knuckled fist and dragged it through his dark hair. 'So the secrecy is to protect Roman from feeling "simply terrible".'

'He may not show it, but the whole thing was *awful* for him,' she told him reproachfully.

'I hate to be the one to break this to you, Alice, but my brother is not a sensitive little flower. He's a big boy now. But then you've already noticed that, haven't you?'

'I've already told you I don't think of Roman that way,' she retorted primly.

'And do you think of me that way?' Their eyes collided and the raw sexual hunger stamped on his hard, dark features made her mind go blank.

Alice looked at the floor, but she only managed to resist the draw of his earthy masculinity for a matter of seconds before her head lifted. She swallowed to lubricate her vocal cords. 'I try not to think of you at all,' she admitted hoarsely.

'Do you succeed?'

Her face twisted in an anguished mask. 'Luca,' she begged. 'Don't do this.'

'You do think about me, don't you? Maybe as much as I think about you.' His eyes burned into hers and her heart skipped several beats. 'I think about you in your modest skirts and sensible shoes. The silk shirts, do you buy them in bulk?'

'I...I...' The fact that Luca could recite what she wore to work so accurately was another amazing revelation on a night when revelations were the norm. 'You're very observant.'

His lips twisted. 'Yes, aren't I? But you're not wearing your pearls tonight.' An abstracted expression slid across his face as his restless blue glance came to rest on the pulse spot at the base of her throat.

Agonisingly conscious of her own body, Alice lifted her hand in a protective gesture. 'They didn't go with this outfit. They were my grandmother's.' And he really wanted to know this. 'I don't know whether she was right, but she always said you should wear pearls or they lose their sheen.' Her voice faded to a whisper in face of his slow-burning, dangerous smile.

'Their sheen fades into insignificance beside your skin.'

Alice swallowed. 'Don't say things like that.'

He tilted his head to an arrogant angle. 'Why not?'

'If you had an ounce of sensitivity you wouldn't ask and I wouldn't need to tell you.'

Luca's tall loose-limbed frame grew taut. Like a man who had just completed a marathon, he was breathing hard and deep. The rhythmic rise and fall of his chest had a hypnotic quality.

'I may not be sensitive but I think I'd have noticed you've been to hell and back over the last few years if you'd been working for me,' he revealed, grinding one clenched fist into the palm of the other.

Alice, watching him with wide eyes, was acutely conscious at that moment of what a physically powerful man he was. Shaken and excited, she lowered her smoky eyes.

'He must be blind!' The exclamation emerged like a pistol shot.

Eyes fixed on her clasped hands, Alice heard the sound of footsteps as he paced across the room and then back.

'Who?' she asked, bewildered.

'How could he not notice? If tonight was anything to go by it's hardly the sort of thing you can hide.'

'You mean Roman?'

'Who else?'

'Roman doesn't watch me like a hawk waiting for me to do something he can sneer at,' she countered defensively.

'I don't sneer,' he denied immediately.

'Luca, you could give a master class in sneering,' she told him when she had stopped laughing bitterly.

An abstracted expression slid into his eyes as they travelled the length of her body. 'You must be accustomed to being watched.'

'Are you suggesting I'm an attention seeker?'

'I'm saying you're an extremely beautiful woman,' he rebutted in a husky drawl that vibrated through her body.

Heart beating fast, she looked away from the heat in his smouldering eyes. 'Well, Roman did notice something once or twice,' she admitted. 'But I told him it was a migraine.'

'And he swallowed that?'

'There was no reason for him not to.'

'Because you never lie to him.'

His sardonic drawl brought a flush to her cheeks. 'There's no need to be facetious. I suppose *you've* never been economical with the truth.'

His eyes narrowed. 'I'm not sure you could cope with the truth.'

'Try me.'

'Every time I see you wearing one of those provocative silk shirts buttoned up to the neck...I want to...'

'They're not provocative,' she protested.

'They provoke me.'

'I don't button my shirt up to the neck.'

'Don't be pedantic, woman.'

'What do you want, Luca? To call the fashion police and have me arrested?'

'I want to watch you take it off for me. That's what I've always wanted.'

CHAPTER EIGHT

ALICE froze. Every cell in her body just came to a dead stop for the space of several heartbeats. When things began functioning again she started to shake.

'Always...?' She shook her head from side to side in a negative motion.

Luca nodded.

A wispy little sigh emerged from her lips. 'You never said so,' she whispered.

His glittering eyes were filled with self-mockery as they settled hungrily on her face. 'I thought I'd be treading on Roman's toes. Would it have made a difference if I had?' he challenged, scanning her flushed face.

'We'll never know now, will we?'

He sucked in a deep breath. 'We could still find out?' he suggested thickly.

Alice swallowed. 'How?'

Luca held out his hand and she took it. Holding her eyes, he pulled her to her feet.

'Where do we go from here?' she asked.

'Let's play it by ear, shall we, *cara*. Does that suit you?'

She looked directly into the feverish blue glitter of his eyes and swallowed. *Suit me!* The driving desire for him crowded every other thought from her head. Relentless flames of lust licked her body, hardening her nipples to tight, aching buds, melting the secret core of her. Making her ache.

Breathing hard, she caught her lower lip between her teeth. Then she admitted in a throaty whisper, 'Anything you want suits me.'

The blood rushed to Luca's face as a hoarse, incredulous groan escaped through his clenched teeth.

'I want you.'

'Luca...' she moaned.

As he took her face between his big hands his intent was clearly written in the lean, darkly dangerous lines of his face and the suffocating heat in his smouldering eyes.

Her own breathing had become painfully irregular; her hand went in a fluttery motion to her throat to loosen constricting clothing only to find bare skin exposed by the low-cut gown she was wearing.

The movement momentarily diverted Luca, who took hold of her wrist and unpeeled her tightly clenched fingers one by one.

Like petals of a flower.

As Luca touched his warm lips to the centre of her exposed palm his heavy lids lifted, revealing eyes as hot as an Italian summer sky. Alice couldn't tear her eyes away from the mesmeric heat.

She heard a raw half-sob escape from her throat; it was closely followed by a throaty purr of male satisfaction.

He took her hand and laid it against his chest. Alice's eyes widened to their fullest extent as she looked at her own hand, pale by comparison to the dark fingers that imprisoned it.

'This is crazy.' It's my lips moving but whose is that voice? she wondered, hearing the throaty whisper.

Luca's hand fell away but her own stayed in place against his chest. The heat of his hard body was seeping into her stiff fingers; she could feel the slow, steady vibration of his heartbeat through her splayed fingertips.

'Crazy is good,' he told her.

She nodded her head. 'Kiss me, Luca; I'd really like you to kiss me.'

'Tell me you want me first. I want to hear you say you want me.'

Want…! It was possible that she had never wanted anything more in her life than she wanted this! She wanted to know what his lips felt like against her skin; she wanted to know the taste of him, the heat, the hard male strength of him. The depth of her sheer wanting made her head spin.

'Luca, I want you.'

Anticipation made Alice shake; her breath came in a series of short, shallow gasps as she felt his tantalising tongue slide between her parted lips. Her insides turned to warm molten honey as he slowly probed the moist recesses. As the deep, drugged kiss lengthened she stretched upward, her slender back arching as she strove to increase the erotic penetration, and Luca cupped the back of her head with his hand.

When the kiss stopped they remained as they were with his head to one side so that their noses touched, his forehead resting against her own. Alice felt his breath fan the downy skin of her cheeks.

'Bella mia,' he rasped throatily, running his thumb along the swollen curve of her lower lip before tugging the tender skin sensually with his teeth.

Alice gave a fractured gasp. *'Oh, God!'* Her eyes snapped open as he lifted his head. 'Don't stop!' she pleaded in the grip of a raw need that was outside her experience.

'Stop?' he said thickly. *'Cara*, I haven't even started yet.' To back up his claim he curved his hands around her bottom and drew her pliant body hard up against him.

Her eyes widened as she felt the brazen swell of his erection against her belly. He grinned wickedly as she mouthed a breathless, *'Oh…!'*

The grin made him look so incredibly gorgeous that she found the corners of her own mouth lifting.

'I've made you smile at me…a first.'

She tilted her head a little to one side as she trailed her fingers along his sleeve and felt his muscles tense. Love for this incredibly gorgeous man made her heart race as she watched the shift of expression play across the strong planes and intriguing angles of his face.

'Tonight seems to be a night for firsts. Have you any idea how badly I want you?'

'You shall show me,' he promised.

She shuddered with pleasure and closed her eyes as he bent his head and fitted his mouth to hers. The heat in her blood ignited and she was kissing him back with a desperate starved intensity.

The abruptness with which he released her left Alice gasping quite literally and she began to shake with fine tremors that shook her entire body. Her big eyes were fixed with bewildered reproach on his face.

'What's wrong? Did I do something?'

A spasm contorted his lean features. 'You're beautiful.' His eyes slid from hers as he dragged a not-quite-steady hand through his hair. 'You have been drinking...you were ill.' So what's your excuse, Luca?

Alice listened to him with a growing sense of frustrated disbelief.

'I've had a drink; that isn't the same thing as being totally drunk or incapable!' she protested. 'I'm quite able to make my own decisions.' Even really bad ones like kissing Luca O'Hagan.

Dear God, what was I thinking of?

Silly question, I wasn't thinking, I was just acting like a sexually starved idiot!

'Alcohol can affect a person's judgement,' he recited gravely. 'The hospitals are full of young men who made the decision to drive after a skinful.'

'Are you trying to tell me that the consequences of sleeping with you are likely to land me in hospital?'

'You know exactly what I was saying, Alice.' Luca massaged his temples and revolved his athletic shoulders. Neither action released any of the tension that was tying his body in knots.

'I know you won't let a little thing like the facts ruin a good sermon.' She scrubbed angrily at her tear-stained cheeks with her clenched fists and sucked in a tremulous breath. She suddenly buried her face in her hands.

'Tomorrow...'

Her head lifted.

'If you say I'll thank you for this tomorrow I'll kill you!' she warned. 'How dare you tell me I'm being reckless? I'm *never* reckless; I reckon I'm due a bit of reckless. And who would I be hurting? Tell me that.'

'There's no need to act as if you are the only one who's suffering, Alice. This isn't easy for me either,' Luca pointed out with what, when you considered the ache in his groin, was in his opinion admirable restraint.

Pity you hadn't shown some of that restraint five minutes ago, the voice in his head suggested drily.

Was she meant to offer him sympathy? 'Good!' She wanted him to suffer...suffer lots. 'And who says I'm suffering?' she added defiantly.

Consciously controlling his breathing, Luca prized his eyes away from the pouting outline of her full, luscious lips. His mobile mouth twisted as their eyes met.

'My mistake.'

'I can't believe it happened.' Alice wasn't even aware she had voiced her dismay out loud until Luca responded.

'I wouldn't try and figure it out; sexual chemistry doesn't follow a logical pattern.'

Alice studied him with an expression of seething dislike as he moved to the other side of the bed. He couldn't have made it much more obvious he was deliberately putting distance between them.

'Don't worry, I'm not going to jump you!' She felt the hot sting of tears and blinked. She had never felt so mortified in her entire life. 'And for the record there is no chemistry here, sexual or otherwise.'

Luca's expressive shoulders lifted in a shrug that revealed his irritation. He looked at her big tear-filled eyes and quivering lips and his expression softened.

'I'm not drunk, I'm mad! As for you coming down with a case of principles...' she released a hoarse laugh '...just how likely is that?'

Much more likely, she thought, now in full self-pity mode, he had realised whom he was kissing. The incomparable Luca O'Hagan kissing a glorified office dogsbody? That would never do.

'You don't think I have principles?'

'The truth?'

He shrugged. 'Why not? It has a novelty value at least.'

'I think you'd sell your mother for a profit,' she flung back recklessly. 'And...put that down!' she yelled, flinging herself across the room in her haste to snatch the framed photo he was studying out of his hand. She glanced down at the snapshot of Mark and a younger her before glaring at him and clutching it protectively against her heaving bosom.

'Who is he?'

'Mark.'

'*Mark*...my, you do get around, don't you? And where is this *Mark* while you're trying to get me into bed?'

'He's dead.'

The sneer died from his face. 'I'm sorry,' he said abruptly. Electric-blue eyes travelled over the contours of her face, dwelling longest on the softness of her lips still swollen from his kiss. He was very aware of the sweet taste of her mouth still on his tongue. 'He was someone special to you?' he asked thickly.

She nodded mutely. 'Very special; Mark was my husband.'

A look of total astonishment swept across his lean face. 'You were married?'

Alice gave a tight shrug. She didn't want this conversation. Not with Luca, of all people. 'People do get married, you know.'

People, but not Luca, she thought, sliding a covetous look at the tall, lean figure beside her. Luca had never displayed the slightest inclination to settle for one woman. His idea of a long-term relationship was two weeks.

Now that she thought about it, in all but one very important detail he was the sort of man her sister-in-law said she really needed at this point in her life. Alice tried and failed not to recall some of the qualities her blunt sister-in-law had said were essential when looking for a suitable man to make her feel like a woman. 'He's got to be hot in the sack and generous, if you get my meaning?'

It was generally pretty hard *not* to get Rachel's meaning!

At the time an amused Alice had doubted this sex god who could turn your bones to water *and* make you laugh existed outside her sister-in-law's fertile X-rated imagination. Now Alice knew differently! She almost could have been describing Luca.

'So I've heard. When did you get married?'

She replied and he swore softly in Italian. 'Six years ago; you must have been very young.'

'So was Mark.'

Luca narrowed his gaze on her wide, wary eyes. 'How long were you married for?'

Ridiculously the sexy rasp in his voice made her tummy flip. 'Three months.'

His chest lifted as he inhaled deeply in shock. 'Three months!' he repeated. *'Madre di Dio!'* He scanned her averted face. 'Was he ill?' he probed gently.

'Mark got pneumonia, which developed into septicaemia.'

Luca wondered how often she'd been forced to explain these bleak facts, being scrupulously careful not to display any emotion that might embarrass the other person. The Latin and Irish blood running through his veins made him unable to see anything good about the English stiff upper lip. In his view emotions were there to be expressed, not repressed.

The owner of a volatile temperament and strong views, Luca had got into trouble expressing his own in the past. Trouble included losing a job for refusing point-blank to write a juicy story that would have hurt a politician's family, and getting beaten senseless as a thirteen-year-old for telling a group of bullies four years older than him exactly what he thought of them!

Hell, it had to be frustrated lust that was making him see Alice jumping into bed with every man she spoke to...and now he was jealous of some dead guy! His hands clenched into white-knuckled fists as his guts churned with self-contempt.

'He was dead within forty-eight hours.' She connected with his eyes and registered the flash of shock and warmth of sympathy in the startling depths. 'I know, I didn't think that young, fit people died of pneumonia either, not with modern drugs. Well, that's what I thought...' she admitted huskily.

Luca watched her slender shoulders lift; the pragmatic gesture hid a world of hurt. He could only imagine what it must have felt like. The surge of fierce protectiveness that surfaced from somewhere deep inside him froze Luca to the spot; it was one of the strongest, most primal responses he had ever experienced.

'But apparently they do.' For a long time she had been bitter and angry but this had lessened over the years.

'Three months isn't long to get to know your husband.'

'Mark wasn't a complicated person.' Unlike you, she thought. Her husband had been caring and mild-mannered; it was actually hard to think of a man more different from the complex, difficult one who stood beside her. Mark had been a gentle man and theirs had been a gentle love, not a wild,

breathless passion, and she had liked it that way. The thought
had a defensive quality that made her brow pucker.

'Anyhow,' she added, 'how long does it take to fall in
love?' And when did it happen to me?

She was so white he thought for a split second she was
going to pass out, then suddenly as she exhaled shakily her
cheeks filled with colour.

'You're asking the wrong man.'

'Haven't you ever…?' She bit off her impetuous question
and, blushing deeply, she shook her head. 'It's none of my…'

One dark brow slanted sardonically. 'Have I ever been in
love? That sort of depends on how you define love, doesn't
it?'

'Oh, God, you're not going to give me a body count, are
you?'

He saw her grimace of distaste and his eyes darkened with
anger. 'Oh, I stopped counting years ago.'

His satiric drawl made her shift uncomfortably but she
added defiantly, 'No little black book?'

'In these days of computers? Haven't you heard print is
dead?' he asked her ironically. 'Just what the hell have I done
to make you think I'm some emotionally shallow bastard?'
Before Alice could think about responding to this bitter demand he added abruptly, 'How long did it take for you to fall
in love, Alice?'

'Me?' Flustered, she pressed a hand to the base of her
throat. She tried to look away but those curiously intense eyes
had her held tight. She couldn't even blink. 'I, well…'

'Was it love at first sight?'

'I'd known Mark all my life. He was the boy next door,
literally. Well, the farm next door, to be precise.'

'You married your childhood sweetheart?'

To Alice's sensitive ears he sounded disapproving. 'I suppose I did.'

Luca watched through heavy-lidded eyes as she went over

to a drawer and opened it. Carefully she slid the framed photo between the layers of clothes inside.

'Do people know you were married?'

Alice repressed the urge to go back and open the drawer. It was stupid to feel disloyal for closing a drawer. To see anything symbolic in the gesture, she told herself, was just plain crazy. Mark was still part of her life; he always would be. This was Luca's fault. If it weren't for him she wouldn't be feeling this way.

When she swung back to face Luca her expression was borderline belligerent. 'It's hardly a secret.'

'I didn't know.'

'Well, we never exactly reached the cosy-chat stage, did we?' Even *thinking* cosy in the same breath as Luca seemed wildly inappropriate.

'No, we just got straight down to ripping off each other's clothes.'

Alice gasped, her eyes filling with hot tears of humiliation. 'I'm trying to forget.'

Breathing hard, Luca placed his hand palm-flat against the wall and spread his fingers until the sinews stood out in his hand. 'Having any luck?' he asked throatily after an interval of several long, laboured breaths.

'No!' she wailed miserably.

Luca straightened up and, hands linked behind his head, dragged his fingers down his neck, where he began to massage the tight tortured knots of muscles. 'Six years is a long time to be celibate.'

'I'm sure it is to someone who can't go for six minutes without sex!' she flared.

'So you've had lovers?'

'You're unbelievable!' she gasped, staring up at him incredulously. 'Just what makes you think you've got any right to ask me something like that?'

His eyes narrowed on her angry face. 'So you have.'

'Even if I'd had as many lovers as you have, it wouldn't make any difference to what I shared with Mark. Sex is just sex; the love we shared was something else entirely. Mark will always be part of my life.' Her voice thickened. 'And I'll never be alone.' Her eyes flashed as she lifted her chin.

The silence that filled the room after her impassioned declaration seethed with loud emotions.

If Alice hadn't been busy feeling disgusted with herself for using her relationship with Mark like some sort of shield to disguise what she was feeling for Luca, she might have noticed the beads of sweat across his brow and the unhealthy grey tinge to his olive skin.

'That will make your bed crowded for any man who wants to be part of your life now.'

'That's a totally *horrible* thing to say!'

'Sometimes totally horrible things need saying,' he retorted coldly. 'It's very easy to idealise someone when they're dead, especially when you conveniently filter out all the things that irritated you about that person.'

'Well, with you that wouldn't leave much else, would it? Beside a massive ego.' He inclined his dark head sarcastically as though acknowledging a compliment and her lips tightened. 'Mark didn't *irritate* me; he was kind and funny. We didn't fight.'

A nerve beside his wide mobile mouth spasmed. 'Always gave in to you, did he?'

Alice, her hands clenched tightly at her sides, glared at him with loathing. 'You'd like to spoil my memories, wouldn't you?' she accused wildly. 'But you can't. We had a happy marriage, we thought alike, we agreed on almost everything.'

'And that is your formula for a happy marriage?' he questioned incredulously.

'It worked for us.'

His expression was shuttered as his brilliant eyes swept her flushed, impassioned face. 'So you had something you don't expect to recapture and in the meantime you make do with casual lovers.' Ironically, a day earlier that would have made her his ideal woman. At what point tonight had he realised he wanted more from Alice...much more?

'And why *shouldn't* I have lovers?' Alice demanded truculently. 'Not everyone finds me as repellent as you do!'

'Repellent?'

'I'm so glad you find this funny,' she told him witheringly. Actually, as much as she tried not to notice, it was impossible not to recognise he had a quite amazingly attractive laugh even when it was bitter.

'You have no idea, do you?' he said.

Alice flicked a nervous hand through her hair, drawing the end of one curl absently into her mouth. 'No idea about what?' she queried suspiciously.

'No idea that everything you do is...' he raised his expressive hand and prescribed an undulating curve in the air '...*seductive*,' he rasped huskily. 'You have more sex appeal in your little finger, than any woman that ever drew breath,' he announced with the embattled air of a man who had been pushed too far. 'Look, I can't do this now. We'll talk about this.' He shook his head. 'But not now.'

'I don't want to talk. I want to go to bed with you.'

'*Per amor di Dio!*' he groaned, grabbing his thick dark hair in agitated handfuls. 'You are...killing me!'

'That's not what I want to do to you.' She kept changing from hating him, to wanting him!

Luca never knew where he got the strength to get out of that door, but from somewhere he discovered hidden reserves.

Sitting in the cab, because frankly he didn't trust himself behind the wheel of his car, Luca basked in the saintly glow of knowing he'd done the right thing for... Actually, he didn't bask at all! He doubted he had ever felt this lousy in his entire life.

Halfway home he decided that he had proved his point. Alice could be in no doubt now that he had principles. There was no need to push it. If she wanted a casual lover he would be that casual lover. Why not? It was a pride thing, nothing else. His middle name was casual, so why change now? And, he thought, his eyes narrowing grimly, he would make her forget every other lover she had ever had!

'Mate,' he called out to the driver. 'Change of plan—take me back to the hotel.'

The driver was sympathetic. 'Left something behind?'

'Yes, something pretty important.'

The black coffee he had ordered at the desk reached the room just before he did. Luca watched as the young man knocked politely at Alice's door. The door swung inwards and he called tentatively through the gap.

Luca stepped forward. 'I must have left it open. Thanks, I'll take it from here,' he said, pressing a note into the boy's hand.

'Thank you, sir…' His eyes widened as he saw the colour of the note. 'Thank you *very much*. Anything else you want, just call.'

'I think I can manage from here,' Luca returned.

He felt nervous… *This wasn't just any woman; this was Alice.* Alice who from day one had got under his skin like no other woman born.

His footsteps silent on the deep pile of the carpet underfoot, he walked into the room. He could hear the soft sound of weeping before he actually saw the figure hunched in an attitude of abject misery. Alice, her knees drawn up to her chest, was sitting on the bed rocking gently to and fro. Her glorious hair fell in silvery bangs hiding her face from his view, but her distress was obvious.

Automatically Luca took a step towards her. It was then that he saw what was clutched in her hands: the photo of her husband.

He turned and walked away, quietly closing the door behind him. The people he met as he walked through the hotel gave the tall, grim-faced figure a wide berth. Luca was oblivious to the wary looks. It shook him to realise that for a minute there he'd been willing to go to Alice, take her in his arms, make love to her, even though he knew that he would be a substitute. She would close her eyes and think of her husband.

Were fools born or made? It was an interesting question.

What had she said? Sex is just sex. All his adult life that had been true for Luca, but this time sex was not going to assuage the ache in his loins. He wanted Alice to love him…he loved Alice. If he was going to show Alice that it was possible to find true love more than once, he was going to have to stifle his natural inclinations and take things slowly. It might kill him, but he was going to be patient.

After Luca had left her, Alice wept long and hard. Then after the tears stopped she lay on the bed and, shading her puffy eyes against the electric light overhead, did some good, hard, and, it had to be admitted, overdue, heart-searching.

What had Mum said…life had to go on? Something along those lines. Ironic, really—she'd been avoiding living hers all this time because she had never wanted to feel the sort of pain she had experienced when she had lost Mark, and now she had fallen for a man who aroused feelings far stronger than she had thought she was capable of.

When she thought how much Luca could hurt her if she let him it terrified her, but when she thought about never knowing what it felt like to be loved by him it terrified her even more.

She didn't delude herself, she knew a man like Luca would only be interested in a casual relationship. An expression of determination spread across her face. Well, if casual was what he wanted she would show him just how casual she could be, she decided, levering herself into a sitting position.

She looked at the photo in her hand and kissed the smiling image. She accepted that it was illogical to feel she was being disloyal to Mark for falling in love with another man. She would always love Mark, but he was the past and she had to look to the future. Mark had loved life and her and he would be angry if he thought she was using his memory as an excuse not to live life to the full.

With an expression of sad resolve she took the ring on the gold chain and placed it with the photo.

'Time to move on, sweetheart,' she whispered.

CHAPTER NINE

ALICE stood in for the absent Roman at the next morning's meeting. Armed with a confident smile and copies of a comprehensive independent report on the impact of the proposed development on the local flora and fauna, plus attached recommendations to protect the above-mentioned, she took her place at the table.

'I'm deputising for Mr O'Hagan. I hope nobody has a problem with that?'

The spokesperson of the conservation group caught up with her as she was leaving the building. 'Excellent meeting,' he congratulated her.

Alice, professional-looking in her grey tailored suit and silk blouse, smiled as he shook her hand. 'Yes, it did go well, didn't it?'

'Refreshing in this day and age to deal with a developer who doesn't put profit ahead of the environment,' he commended.

Alice stepped into the cab feeling pretty pleased with her morning's work, but by the time she had reached the hotel the warm glow of achievement had cooled considerably. The concerns that she'd managed to push to the back of her mind while she'd been having to field questions, not all friendly, resurfaced.

Or rather *one* resurfaced, the one being what had almost happened the night before. It had been Luca who had called a halt and for some reason that made her frustration a million times worse. Alice knew she *ought* to feel grateful to him for showing restraint.

At least it wasn't lack of interest that had motivated him,

she thought with a surge of relief not untinged by complacency. Her skin got hot and her stomach muscles clenched as she recalled the raw hunger in his incredible eyes as he'd looked at her. No man had ever looked at her that way or made her feel so feminine and desired. And no comprehensive independent report ever commissioned was going to cure the gnawing knot of need in the pit of her stomach!

Nothing except showing Luca that his desire was fully reciprocated was going to do that.

He might have guessed, the ironic voice in her head drily suggested.

The previous night now seemed like some erotic dream. Thinking of the frankly wanton things she had done, and said, made Alice get even hotter, and the thing was she couldn't *not* think about them!

How was she going to act when she saw him again? She knew he had a mental image of her trying to rip his clothes off…well, as good as! She was going to seduce Luca O'Hagan; the questions were how and where, as her experience of seducing men was severely limited.

What she needed was to focus. When she needed to think she often swam. Maybe this sort of thinking called for a more extreme form of exercise? She had already used the hotel pool a couple of times that week. Normally Alice had very little interest in breaking the pain barrier, but she knew the hotel also boasted a particularly well-equipped state-of-the-art gym. Perhaps a visit was called for?

After emailing the boss with the results of the meeting she stripped off her working gear and donned a pair of joggers and a tee shirt. Stuffing her swimsuit in a bag, she headed for the hotel spa.

Glancing through the glass wall of the gym at the sweaty bodies and high-tech equipment, Alice grimaced. The atmosphere seemed a bit too testosterone-packed for her and the females who were there were all wearing Lycra that clung to every taut muscle of their beautifully toned, lissom bodies like a second skin. This was the sort of place where you probably had to pass a midriff test before they let you in—tanned and taut only!

Maybe a swim first would be a good compromise; it was excellent aerobic exercise. And she might get inspiration without resorting to lifting weights, getting red in the face on a treadmill and standing out like a sore thumb in her baggy top and joggers.

She was negotiating her way around a lavish arrangement of flowers balanced on a Grecian-urn-type marble display stand when the glass doors of the gym slid open allowing the blast of loud music from inside to spill out into the sitting area. Alice automatically turned her head in the direction of the sound. At that exact second the person she wanted to run into more than anyone else on the planet walked through.

She was only dimly conscious that the two women sipping a herbal tea while earnestly debating the merits of a new wonder cream for cellulite had stopped mid-sentence as the tall figure dressed in a vest and shorts stood framed in the open doorway. A tidal wave of lust and longing washed over her.

'*Oh, boy!*' Alice heard the soft exclamation but didn't look to see who had made it. She couldn't; her feet were glued to the floor.

Luca, still breathing hard from his workout, had a towel looped casually around his neck. As she watched he dabbed the towel across his face before crumpling the paper cup he was carrying. As he turned he gave a perfunctory smile to the two women sitting there; the smile was still there as his eyes moved past her and then almost immediately back.

The smile vanished.

She saw his chest lift as he inhaled, shock flaring for a split second in his eyes. Then the smile was back, not so impersonal this time and tinged with caution.

It didn't take a genius to figure out why he viewed her

presence with caution. He probably thought she was about to
take up where she'd left off. Is she going to act as if last night
was the start of something deep and meaningful? Alice could
almost hear the thought going through his head.

As he came towards her she took a deep restorative breath
and smiled. You could say a lot with a smile and body language and she was aiming for something unclingy with hers.
If he picked up on 'I really am interested', so much the better.

'Alice.'

You're staring…say something. *Put on some clothes* was
not an option, so she settled for a safe, if uninspired, 'You
look hot.'

'That's the general idea.'

She tore her eyes from the drop of sweat running down the
side of his neck and gave a flustered smile. 'Of course it is.'

'I didn't expect to see you here.'

If it was immediately obvious to him that she didn't work
out it was equally obvious to her he did! It was all she could
do to keep her eyes on his face. She had never before associated sweaty with sexy but the sheen of perspiration that
made his sleek bronzed body gleam made her quiver.

Face the facts, girl, you're incapable of looking at Luca
without wanting to touch.

'I thought I might as well make use of the facilities.'

To her immense relief, even though her throat felt dry and
achy her voice emerged sounding passably normal. Her
arched brows lifted in enquiry. 'Are you staying here?' she
added, unable to hide her hope.

'No, I'm not.' His lips twitched faintly as her lips turned
down at the corners. 'The building where I live is doing some
renovations; our pool and gym are out of action this month.
The residents' group have worked out an arrangement with
the spa here,' he explained.

'Great.' At least she now had a legitimate reason not to go
to the gym for the rest of her stay.

He looked around, brows lifted. 'No Roman?'

Alice shook her head. 'No, he's had to go to Boston for some pet project of his. He flew out last night.'

Luca was acting as if nothing had happened. From his perspective it probably hadn't; nothing that couldn't be dismissed with a shrug anyhow. Oh, God, did I misread the signals that badly? she thought.

'Did he miss his meeting this morning? It sounded important when we spoke.'

'I stood in for him.'

'Really!' He sounded surprised.

Her chin lifted. 'You don't think I'm up to it?'

'You obviously are; my brother wouldn't delegate responsibility on account of your blue eyes.' The militant sparkle in the blue eyes in question faded slightly at this conciliatory observation. 'You must admit that it's a lot of responsibility for a secretary to take on.'

'A lot of secretaries have very wide-ranging responsibilities,' she informed him. 'Not all of them get paid for their extra duties.'

'But you do?'

'Very well. I'm well aware of my worth.'

'I'm sure you are.' But presumably oblivious to the youth who had been ogling her through the plate-glass partition all the while they had been talking. Luca casually stepped a little to one side, effectively blocking the young admirer's uninterrupted view of Alice's rear, before enquiring casually, 'So you haven't seen him today, then?'

She shook her head. If my skin gets any hotter I'm going to end up a greasy puddle on the floor, she thought, staring fixedly straight ahead.

'Are you feeling better today?'

Her glance lifted. 'If you mean have I been drinking, no.'

He ran a hand through his damp dark hair and fixed her with an exasperated glare. 'That's not what I meant.'

'No?'

'No more flashbacks?'

'What? Oh, no.' She found that she didn't know how to react to the genuine concern evident in his expression. 'I'm sure that was just a one-off.'

'A therapist might be able to put your mind at rest.'

Her jaw hardened at this piece of blatant interference. 'My mind is at rest.'

'Nevertheless it would be sensible to seek professional advice, especially as you quite obviously feel unable to confide in your friends or family,' he observed. 'I've made a few enquiries,' he revealed casually. 'And it seems the best person—'

Alice, her cheeks pink, interrupted. 'I thought you wanted to sleep with me, not offer me therapy, because I should tell you the first interests and the second doesn't.'

After his audible intake of breath there was a charged silence.

Alice took a deep interest in her trainers. If it had been possible to die from sheer toe-curling embarrassment she would be stretched out on the carpet right now. She'd tried for bold; trouble was she'd gone overboard big time.

The warmth in Luca's eyes deepened as he looked down at the top of her head. This woman was born for him—she just didn't know it yet.

'That is good to know and I hope you always feel able to tell me what you want,' he told her in all sincerity. 'Were you just on your way in?'

Alice lifted her head just as he casually gestured towards the gym. Maybe it happened to him so often that he took women telling him they wanted to take him to bed in his stride?

'I changed my mind. I thought I might go for a swim instead.' She pulled her swimsuit from her bag to back up the story.

'Excellent. That's where I'm heading. I'll see you in there. Take care,' he added, touching her arm to prevent her colliding with the two women who were no longer sitting, but were now engaged in some extremely advanced-looking stretches.

Alice had been dimly aware of their exhibition, though unfortunately for them the person the graceful display was aimed at seemed totally oblivious to their contortions.

'No!' she blurted, nursing the arm he had touched against her chest; the brief contact had left her skin tingling in a disturbing way.

In the act of turning away he swung back. 'No...?'

'I can't...can't...' There was nothing more alarming to read in his deep blue eyes than mild enquiry, yet the moment they locked onto hers Alice couldn't string a sentence together.

I look at him and I lose my mind. The things she wanted to say and do to Luca couldn't be said or done in a public place.

'You can't swim.' He nodded in an understanding way.

'Well...I'm...no, I can't.' Why did I say that?

'Are you afraid of the water?'

'No, I just can't swim.' Alice thought guiltily of the medals sitting proudly on her parents' bureau and added in a forced voice, 'That is, I *do* swim, only not very well.'

'Don't worry, I'll teach you.'

Was he serious? 'I really couldn't impose.'

'It's a matter of confidence really,' he told her.

'In that case you must be a very good swimmer.'

He acknowledged her sly jibe with a lopsided grin. 'I'm a very good teacher also.'

'So I've heard.'

He gave his head an admonitory shake. 'You don't want to believe everything you hear, Alice.' Leaving her to wonder about the meaning of his cryptic comment, he sauntered away. As he disappeared around the corner the two women straightened up.

The frustrated glares they gave Alice were hostile.

As she walked away she heard one of them say, 'She's not even slim.'

'God knows,' came the baffled response.

Alice took a couple more steps, then stopped. While she normally didn't engage in debate with ignorant, rude twits, these two hadn't even bothered to lower their voices. With an impish grin and dancing eyes she turned and walked back to them, emphasising the natural sway of her hips.

'I may not be slim but, between you and me, I'm exceptionally good in bed,' she explained.

The sight of their shocked faces and open mouths made her chuckle softly to herself as she walked to the changing room.

Alice slipped into the shallow end of the pool, having first ascertained that Luca was not there yet. Her efforts to break all speed records getting changed had worked.

When he did appear all thoughts of simulating cramp and having to leave the pool were forgotten. She just stared. He was quite simply perfection in motion!

Her eyes darkened and her breath quickened as she watched him with hungry, covetous eyes. There was not an ounce of spare flesh on his magnificent torso, his legs were long, his belly washboard-flat and his shoulders powerful and broad. Her glazed half-closed eyes were drawn to the light dusting of body hair on his olive-toned tanned chest. It narrowed to a directional arrow of dark fuzz on his belly until it disappeared beneath the waistband of the shirts that he wore low across his narrow hips.

The way her nipples suddenly hardened and tingled could have had something to do with the temperature of the water, but the cause seemed more likely to be the image in her head after following that arrow to its source.

She gulped and looked away. Ducking beneath the surface

of the water until her lungs burned didn't decrease the raw
visceral feelings twisting in her stomach.

A hand like steel suddenly wrapped around her middle.
Alice was so surprised to find herself hauled bodily upwards
that she took a startled breath. When her head emerged she
immediately began to cough. Her head went forward onto the
chest of the man who held her as she coughed and spluttered.
A firm hand did some soothing stroking of her bare back as
she was convulsed by noisy spasms that racked her entire
body.

'What the hell did you think you were doing?' he blazed.

The soothing stops here, she thought. Luca had barely
given her time to catch her breath and he was yelling.

'*Me* doing?' she squeaked, seeing his dark irate face
through a mist of tears. '*Me?*' she repeated, her voice rising
a quivering decibel or two.

'You could have drowned.'

Alice sighed. It was clearly time to fess up. 'No, I really
couldn't...' Her voice faded as his incredible eyes darkened
and she felt a shudder run through his body.

'Oh, yes, you could. Have you any idea how long you were
down there?' Luca had and each second had lasted half a
lifetime for him. 'If I hadn't seen you go under have you any
idea what could have happened? Then when you didn't come
up I...' She saw the muscles in his brown throat work as he
swallowed convulsively.

'Why the hell didn't you wait for me to arrive? And where
the hell was the lifeguard?' Without waiting for her to respond, he added in a voice that shook with anger, 'It's crim-
inal negligence!'

'I didn't drown, Luca.'

Her quiet words seemed to have a soothing effect on him.
'No. Did you get cramp? Have I said something funny?'

She shook her head and bit her trembling lower lip. 'I
didn't have cramp. I was just messing around really.'

'Messing around?'

'Oh, for heaven's sake, if you must know I was fine until you nearly drowned me.'

If she hadn't been busy nearly drowning she would have noticed before now that nothing much more than a drop or two of water separated her lightly clad body from his bare torso.

They were effectively sealed from shoulder to thigh. She was painfully aware of how hard his hair-roughened flanks were against her smoother skin.

She unwound her arms from around his neck and, hands flat against his chest, tried to push herself free but his grip didn't slacken.

'I saved you,' he rebutted grimly.

'My hero,' she intoned with shaky sarcasm.

'I didn't expect gratitude, but...will you keep still or you'll drown us both.'

She gave a scornful snort. 'In five feet of water?'

A muscle along his jaw quivered. 'People have been known to drown in five inches of water. We should get you checked over by a doctor.'

'I'm actually fine. Look at me. Do I look like I'm in need of medical attention?'

Luca accepted her invitation and looked. He loosed his arm from about her waist and, retaining a grip on both her hands, took a step back himself.

Alice noticed that the face so disturbingly close to her own was pale beneath the tan and, though he was looking right at her, there was an odd, unfocused look in his eyes as though he wasn't seeing her.

'I wasn't drowning, you know. I'm actually quite a...competent swimmer,' she admitted guiltily.

'Sure you are.'

His patronising tone made her teeth clench. 'I am.'

'Like I said, it's all about confidence.'

'Perhaps you could tell me what I'm doing wrong?' she suggested innocently.

'All right, then,' he agreed. 'And don't worry, I'm here.'

She secured the goggles that had been hanging loose about her neck across her face. 'Knowing you're here makes me feel so safe.' Then, arms stretched in front of her, she dived cleanly beneath the water. Surfacing a few feet away, she began to swim, settling immediately into the familiar rhythm as her body cut a clean, streamlined swathe through the water.

She reached the far end exhilarated but not out of breath. She trod water waiting for him to reach her. It didn't take him long; she was technically a better-than-good swimmer but he was much more powerful.

'*Actually*, it's all about timing, technique and breath control.'

'You little witch!' he cried, brushing the water from his eyes with the back of his hand. 'That was your idea of a joke?'

Hair slicked back that way, he reminded her of a sexy seal. 'I tried to tell you,' she reminded him defensively. 'But you were so patronising I couldn't resist.'

'Patronising! I thought you were scared of the water when all the time you swim like an Olympic contender.'

'I'm not *that* good,' she protested modestly. 'The Commonwealths maybe?'

He shook his head, covering everything in the immediate vicinity in a shower of water droplets. 'Damn it, you swam competitively, didn't you?'

Guiltily she nodded. 'It was a long time ago and I'm terribly out of shape these days.'

'You don't look out of shape to me.' His burning glance licked down the full feminine curves of her body attractively displayed in clinging black Lycra.

'Luca…' Her agonised whisper only made him grin.

'Why did you tell me you couldn't swim?'

Without replying Alice lay on her back and with a couple of lazy kicks reached the side where, with a sigh, she flipped over onto her stomach.

'I didn't mean to, it just came out,' she admitted miserably.

Luca, shoulder-deep in the water, curled a hand over the grab rail. 'For any particular reason?'

'Well, you said…and I thought…if you thought then I wouldn't have to swim with you…but…'

'Stop!' he pleaded, holding up his hand. 'You didn't want to swim with me so you lied? Does that about cover it?'

Not meeting his eyes, she nodded.

'Couldn't you have simply just said no?'

Her eyes widened. 'Have you any idea how hard it is to say no to you?' she demanded.

'Do you find my company so distasteful, Alice?'

'*I wish!*' she exclaimed unthinkingly.

'Then you like my company?'

'Oh, for God's sake, Luca, don't you understand? I can't string two words together when you're fully dressed,' she revealed incautiously. 'I *knew* I'd do or say something really daft if I saw you like…' Her eyes met his and she groaned before sinking once more beneath the surface.

Alice opened her eyes and found herself looking into Luca's lean dark features. Her lips parted in a startled 'O' of shock.

As she kicked for the surface Luca grabbed her shoulders, his mouth sealed tight to hers preventing the bubbling air escaping. Alice twisted her arms tight around his neck and wound her long legs around his hips. Tightly entwined that way they slowly rose upwards.

As their heads broke the surface they both reacted simultaneously, gasping hungrily for air.

Luca, his chest still heaving with the effort to replenish his oxygen-starved lungs, was the first to recover.

'That gives an entirely new meaning to mouth to mouth.'

His eyes slid to her full lips and lingered on the lush pink softness. 'You know, you have the most indecently seductive mouth I have ever seen,' he imparted throatily.

Without a word Alice took his water-drenched face between her hands and lovingly stroked the dark hair from his face before pressing her lips hungrily against his.

'You are so beautiful it makes me want to weep,' she confessed against his mouth. 'I simply can't bear it...I...' She broke off as his hands curved around her buttocks, drawing her body towards his.

Luca's eyes dwelt on the vulnerable, exposed length of her slender neck. He sucked in a deep, painful breath before pressing his mouth to the base of her throat. Slowly he worked his way lovingly upwards until he reached her lips.

They kissed, both driven by the same unspoken desperation, deep, drowning kisses that made Alice's vision blur and her heart ache.

The pool attendant cleared his throat for the third time before the couple noticed he was there.

'Is there anything I can do for you?'

Luca responded to such exquisite tact with an appreciative smile. 'Actually we were just leaving.'

The young man looked relieved.

Alice slid her fingers into the wet hair at his nape and touched her thumbs to the strong angle of his jaw. She gave a discontented pout. *We are?*

'He was tactful, but that poor guy was basically saying *get a room*. Didn't you hear that?'

Alice shook her head from side to side. 'I was distracted,' she admitted.

Luca's tongue darted out to touch the finger she ran across his lips. 'You're distracting. But about that room?'

'I have a room,' she recalled happily.

'So you have. Do you think it might be a good idea to continue...this there?'

'Anywhere you like.' And shockingly she meant it. If Luca had wanted to make love to her there and then she would have had no objections.

'Right then, perhaps?' He extended a hand.

Alice ignored his hand and, palms flat on the Italian-tiled poolside, levered herself out with an agile twisting motion that left her seated on the poolside with her toes dangling in the water. Aware that Luca's eyes were closely following everything she did, she gathered her long hair in one wet hank over one shoulder and twisted until the excess moisture dripped onto the floor.

'You've done that before.'

Alice gave her head a flick that sent her hair flying backwards. 'It's a matter of confidence,' she confided, smiling.

'Witch,' he accused huskily. Then as his eyes slid over her voluptuous dripping form he corrected himself. 'No, mermaid.'

She held out her hands to him. 'Aren't you getting out?'

'I think it might be better for all concerned if I waited until I cooled off.' In response to her baffled frown his eyes dropped significantly.

'Oh!' she gasped, scrabbling to her feet. 'I see.'

'You, I don't mind seeing,' he admitted. 'Maybe I'll do a few lengths?'

'Excellent idea, I'll see…that is, I'll…later.' As she headed for the women's changing room she heard the sound of his husky laughter.

CHAPTER TEN

'ARE you going up?' Luca asked from within the lift.

The elderly couple who reached the lift before Alice nodded to Luca. 'Very kind,' the woman murmured as he stepped aside to let them enter.

'And, Alice!' He affected shock as he saw her approach. 'Now this is just spooky. I was only thinking about you…well, not five minutes ago. How are you?'

'Fine.'

'You look marvellous.' He appealed to the couple already established in the lift. 'Can we fit another little one in?'

'Of course.'

She squeezed past him into a corner to mutter with a pleasant smile fixed firmly on her face, 'If you don't shut up I'll kill you.'

In her experience awkward silences were the norm for lifts, but the short one that followed her gagging order had a life of its own! His whistling didn't help either. For the benefit of their interested audience and her nerves she made a valiant attempt to initiate a normal conversation.

'I understand you're renovating a place in Tuscany, Luca,' she said in a bright, slightly too loud voice.

His eyes flickered in her direction. 'Yes.'

Her teeth grated as he started whistling again. 'And Roman says your family have owned property in that valley for generations. He says it's very beautiful.'

Luca scanned her frustrated face. 'Are we going to have a conversation about property?'

'That's the sort of thing people talk about in lifts,' she whispered.

The lift stopped and the couple got out but three more people got in.

'Roman's right, it is very beautiful, but if you're angling for an invite I'm afraid—'

The first sniff of rejection and her defences sprang into life. '*Me* angle for an invite from *you*!' She injected a double dose of scorn into her laughter. 'I don't get many holidays and when I do I like to spend them with like-minded people whose company I enjoy. People,' she added pointedly, 'I can relax around.'

One dark brow lifted. His eloquent eyes sparkled with malicious mockery as they skimmed her flushed, antagonistic face. 'You can't relax around me?' His glance dropped to her tightly clenched hands. 'I can see we'll have to put some work in on the relaxation front. But actually,' he continued, 'I was about to explain that the facilities are primitive as yet.'

'*Oh!*'

'Actually the facilities are non-existent,' Luca admitted. 'No running water, no electricity—'

'You've had problems with your contractors?' It was some comfort to know that things didn't always go Luca's way. He had problems with tradesmen like normal people.

'No, I'm doing most of the work myself.'

Her eyes grew round with astonishment as they focused back on his face. '*You!*'

His wide, sensual mouth curved into an amused smile that widened to reveal a set of perfectly blindingly white teeth.

Attractive smile, she immediately registered.

'It must be the peasant in me.'

Alice blinked to clear the distracting image that immediately entered her head of Luca stripped to the waist revealing tautly muscled golden flesh glowing with the honest sweat of labour. She swallowed convulsively and, aware of their audience, arranged her features into an expression of bland interest.

'Sorry, I'm boring you.'

Too bland.

'No, actually, I am interested. My sister is a furniture re-storer...on a small scale. She and her husband renovated an old granary and she said that finding craftsmen who could recreate the original artisan's work was the hardest part of it.'

Luca nodded. 'That's true, but it's not why I'm doing the work myself. I get a kick out of building with stone.' He narrowed his eyes as though he could see the stone he spoke of and made a descriptive fluid gesture with one hand.

Her eyes were drawn to the long, tapering length of his brown, infinitely elegant fingers. A shiver traced the tingling path of the imaginary caress that travelled the length of her spine and was followed by a second wave of heat that left her fair skin washed with rosy colour.

The lift stopped yet again, disgorging and taking on pas-sengers. Did nobody take the stairs any more? Carrying on a normal conversation when her entire body was tingling with arousal, when her head was filled with erotic images, was not easy.

'Roman says it will be quite a show place when it's fin-ished.'

'It's a long-term project but sometimes things are worth waiting for, don't you think?'

No longer caring about keeping up appearances, she gave a deep sigh. Just looking at him made her ache with longing. 'If I have to wait much longer...I'll...'

Luca pressed a finger to her lips. 'Keep it together, *cara*,' he whispered into her ear. 'We're nearly there.'

To see this incredibly beautiful woman almost fainting with lust for him was one of the most arousing experiences of his life...second only to the underwater kiss. The next project in Tuscany would be a very large pool.

When the lift finally reached her floor Alice all but fell out in her haste to escape.

'Do you and my brother have a lot of conversations about me?'

She blinked as her eyes connected with his blissfully blue eyes. *Blissful blue?* Oh, God, this is just what I need! Why is it we women insist on falling in love with and weaving our sexual fantasies around the most unsuitable men we can find? she wondered. Her attempt to trivialise what she was feeling didn't help. She wanted Luca with every fibre of her being and she loved him with an equal intensity.

'You're hardly out of our thoughts.' The truth, even though she hadn't admitted it to herself before, was that once she'd realised that she was milking her boss for information about his brother she had made it a rule not to mention him at all.

Sexual fantasy was fine, she reminded herself. But that was not what this was; this was real. Was she ready for real?

'That might have been the longest few minutes I have ever spent,' he said. 'All I wanted to do was kiss you senseless. Have you ever made love in a lift?'

She swallowed and asked hoarsely, 'No, have you?'

'The things I haven't done could fill a book, but it wouldn't be as thick as the book filled with the things I've imagined doing to you.' Luca watched her lips part in a soundless sigh and he lowered his head.

The depth of her response shocked Alice and, from the look in his eyes when he lifted his head, she thought maybe it had shocked Luca too.

He ran a hand over her still-damp hair, trailing his fingers in the soft, fine ringlets around her face. 'You're incredible,' he said, short of breath.

'So are you.' He reached for her but she stepped back, shaking her head. 'Come on, we'd better go to my room or we could get arrested. Now that would make the headlines.'

'You could be right. My sense of decorum goes out of the window when I'm around you.'

Approaching the door, Alice turned her head. 'About the headlines… Our photo wasn't news, after all.'

'No.'

Something in his voice made her query. 'Do you know something about that?'

'I called in a few favours,' he admitted, stepping through the door behind her.

Alice gulped when she heard it click closed, but didn't turn around.

'Alone at last.'

She felt him walk up behind her, she felt the long, lean, hard length of him up against her, and with a purr that was part sheer relief she leaned into him.

Luca leaned down and pushed her hair back. 'I love the way you smell.' Her head fell back against his shoulder as he kissed her neck.

'I like that.'

'We like the same things,' he rasped huskily. 'Do you like this too, *cara*?'

Alice gasped as his big hands came up to curve possessively over her incredibly sensitised breasts. Unable to speak, she nodded. Her eyes closed as his fingers slid down the loose neck of her top caressing the smooth upper slopes. With unerring accuracy he located the front fastening catch. She gave a stifled moan as his fingers moved over her aching flesh.

Her spine arched when he located her nipples. She lay there passively while ripple after ripple of hot sensation swept through her as he teased the rosy peaks. When she could bear his clever caresses no longer she twisted around and wrapped her arms around his neck.

Luca's eyes burned with a dark fire that made her quiver with anticipation as he caught her wrists and held them above her head. Then, still looking into her hot, aroused face, he took the hem of her top and pulled it over her blonde curls.

Very carefully he pushed the lacy fabric of her loosened bra back to expose the full proud swell of her breasts.

His fierce gasp was audible. 'You're incredible! Perfect.'

Alice gasped his name out loud as he dropped to his knees in front of her. Her teeth were chattering helplessly with re-action to what was happening. 'What are you doing?'

In reply he placed one hand in the small of her bare back. The lightest application of pressure brought her towards him. The first brush of his tongue over one erect rosy nipple and she was lost. The contact sent a surge of pleasure like nothing she had ever known through her body.

'My God!' Her entire body shuddered in reaction. She knew the erotic image of him kneeling there before her would never leave her.

'You like that?' he asked in a whisper.

In reply Alice slid her fingers into his lush dark hair and shut her eyes tight as he went exactly where she guided him. The sensual touch of his hands and mouth made her skin burn with desire until her skin felt as though she were literally on fire. Her entire body was so sensitive to his touch that the lightest caress made her squirm and moan.

When his fingers slid under the waistband of her trousers, skating lightly over the soft curve of her belly, the feral moan lodged in her throat escaped in a long, low, keening cry.

Luca's head finally lifted. The strain he was under was etched in the tenseness of his features and the blazing heat of his darkened eyes.

She ran her fingers down the curve of his cheek. 'Please, Luca.'

His lips curved in a slow, sensual smile, then without say-ing a word he rose in one fluid motion and almost casually lifted her into his arms.

He lowered her on the bed, carefully pausing to smooth her hair around her face. Kneeling over her, he ran his tongue over her quivering lips before plunging deep inside her mouth…again and again.

Her hands slid off his shoulders as he levered himself away from her and Alice opened her eyes. In the grip of wild and uncontrollable emotions she cried out. 'I love your mouth…'

'That,' he said thickly, 'makes me happy.'

Eyes half closed, she ran a finger along the swollen outline of her own full lips. 'Good, I want to make you happy.' *Because I love you.*

He didn't respond to this husky confidence, but the hands that were sliding her trousers down her legs developed a tremor.

Moments later she was completely naked.

'You're beautiful.' The primitive need stamped on his features made the breath catch in her throat.

'Even with this?' She moved her hand to cover the ugly scar faded now to a thin white line on her abdomen.

'What are you—?' she cried out in startled confusion as both her hands were imprisoned either side of her head. Luca's big body curled over her. His eyes blazed angrily down at her.

'Never try to hide yourself from me, Alice.'

She felt overwhelmed and excited by this masterful display. 'I won't.'

He scanned her face, then, apparently satisfied with what he saw, grinned. 'I feel pretty overdressed.'

She watched—how could she not?—her heart beating fast as he fought his way out of his clothes with flattering urgency and a total lack of self-consciousness.

He was every bit as breathtakingly magnificent as she had imagined. A flush ran over her skin as she lowered her eyes and swallowed; he was very aroused.

The mattress gave as Luca joined her on the bed. He laid his hand on the curve of her hip as he stretched out beside her until they lay thigh to thigh.

Alice turned her body towards him as she laid a tentative hand on his flank. She was shaking. 'I've wanted to touch you for such a long time.'

A sigh shuddered through Luca's body and she felt the vibration through her fingertips.

'Then touch me, *cara*,' he rasped, kissing the side of her mouth.

Alice accepted his invitation until his painfully aroused body could bear no more. He slid his hands between her smooth thighs. A keening cry of pleasure left her throat as his exploration deepened.

'Is that for me…?' he asked thickly as his fingers slid into her moistness. She shook her head mutely and pushed against his hand, moaning.

'You're so tight…so hot…'

'Oh, God…Luca…' she cried, her face twisted in anguish. 'Please…'

Luca's eyes were fixed on her face as he slid between her thighs and entered her in one smooth upward motion into the slick heat.

'You're so…so…I…' she cried brokenly, almost sobbing as she felt him fill her. When he began to stroke inside her she lost all sense of anything but the man who possessed her and the pleasure that stretched her senses to the utmost limit.

Her hands curved over the firm contours of his tight buttocks and her legs locked tight about his waist as he began to move faster and harder. Finally, when she thought she could bear no more, her body was convulsed by a shatteringly sweet climax at almost the exact moment she heard Luca cry out and felt his body shudder.

CHAPTER ELEVEN

LUCA considered time his most important commodity; he didn't participate in endless meetings where pieces of paper were pushed around the table and no decisions made. He had no problem with people who disagreed with him; in fact he encouraged a lively exchange of views. One of his pet hates were people who sat on the fence.

This afternoon's meeting had by his own criteria been a total waste of time and the only person he could blame was himself! He had been totally unable to focus on the problem in hand...not only that but he didn't care!

His ability to ruthlessly compartmentalise his life had deserted him with a vengeance. Physically he had been in the meeting but in every other way he had been elsewhere...no prizes for guessing where!

Leaving a warm bed and the arms of an even warmer woman had required every ounce of his not-inconsiderable will-power. Alice had simply looked mildly surprised when he had suggested cancelling his meeting.

'Don't be silly, Luca. You wouldn't expect me to cancel a meeting for you, would you?' she'd reproached, stroking his cheek.

Yes, I damned well would!

He'd stopped himself saying it, but only just. How could she treat what had passed between them as a casual coupling?

The supreme irony of his outraged thought suddenly struck him forcibly. He threw back his head and laughed out loud, a grim, harsh sound that made a nervous temp walking by stare at him.

Luca O'Hagan, the man who was a renowned commitment-

phobic, was feeling badly done to because a woman had not
acted as though her world would come to an end if he didn't
call back. Actually from the way she'd acted it was difficult
to imagine her losing an hour's sleep if he vanished off the
face of the earth!

A taste of your own medicine, O'Hagan?

Alice had been his dream lover made flesh and blood in
bed—warm, soft flesh, giving, warm and wild. Out of bed?
Well, if she hadn't shown him the door, she hadn't seemed
too damned bothered when he had gone through it! His jaw
clenched as he recalled her response to his suggestion he ring
her later.

'That would be very nice, Luca, but don't worry if you
can't,' she had told him with an absent smile that had suggested her thoughts had already been elsewhere.

Nice!

Luca had swallowed his anger and salvaged a little pride
simulating the indifference Alice was displaying.

'Well, actually I've got a full day.'

Had the flicker of hurt he'd seen in her eyes been wishful
thinking? Certainly her practical shrug and cheerful smile had
not suggested she would be hanging around waiting for him
to call. Deciding he could wait until she realised she needed
a flesh-and-blood man, not a dead hero, was fine in theory;
in reality he frankly didn't think he could handle it.

One of the joys of being the boss was when you decided to
take a walk in the park...*literally*...nobody was going to say
a word. The fresh air might clear his head. It sure as hell
needed clearing.

He reached the park and it began to rain, which made him
think of home—Ireland. Luca, who considered himself cos-
mopolitan, a city boy through and through, experienced an
unaccustomed pang of homesickness for the green isle of his
youth.

By the time he sat down on a bench the sun had come back out. He brushed some of the excess moisture from his hair with a careless sweep of his hand as he stared into the distance, an abstracted expression on his handsome face. A couple walked by oblivious to the rain. Looking at their linked hands made his chest tighten. What the hell is happening to me? he thought.

Whatever it was he had to share what he was feeling…and that was definitely a first!

When he got back he cancelled his appointments for the rest of the day and caught a cab to the hotel. The manager saw him crossing the lobby.

'I'm afraid your brother isn't here at the moment, Mr O'Hagan.'

'Pity.'

'I understand he won't be back until the morning.'

'Has Miss Trevelyan gone with him?'

'No, I believe the young lady is still here. Shall I have them ring her and say you're on your way up?'

'Don't bother, I'll surprise her.'

There was a purposeful spring in his step as he approached the door. He went to knock when a maid carrying linen let herself out of the room. Luca nodded and stepped into the room past her. His lean body tensed as he heard the sound of Alice's voice; she was obviously on the phone.

He was in the act of revealing himself when he registered what she was saying. The blood drained from his face.

'Yes, pregnancy test…that's right. Sure I'll hold…'

Luca could hear her humming softly under her breath as she waited. He raised a hand to his temple and massaged the spot where a vein visibly pulsed beneath the golden sheen of his skin.

'And there's no doubt it's definitely positive… Right, thank you very much.' Alice, punching in her sister-in-law's number, didn't see the tall figure who slipped silently from the room.

The phone was picked up immediately. 'It's positive— you're going to be a mum.' Alice couldn't stop grinning. 'The nurse at the doctor's sent her congrats and said you should ring for an appointment to see her and the doctor. I explained you were going back to England tomorrow.'

'I'm going to have a baby...' The sound of soft sobs echoed down the line.

The shock and wonder in the older woman's voice made Alice's own eyes fill up. *Relax* had been the doctor's advice to her brother and his wife when all the tests had given them both a clean bill of health. That had been ten years ago; no wonder her sister-in-law sounded gobsmacked.

'You're *sure* they said it was positive?' Rachel hesitantly asked after a lot more sniffing.

'Totally sure.' Alice wasn't surprised that Rachel sounded as though she couldn't believe it. After three false alarms her distrust was hardly surprising.

'Oh, God, I don't know what I'd have done if you hadn't been over here,' admitted Rachel, who was on a visit to her parents in Long Island. 'I couldn't tell Mom until I was sure— not after last time.'

Alice gave a sympathetic murmur. The 'last time', by the time Rachel had realised the home pregnancy kit was not as foolproof as it claimed, she had given half her friends and family the glad tidings. She had then had the horrid task of telling them she wasn't pregnant after all.

'I know you must have thought I was crazy when I asked you to phone the doctor's office, but after all the other times I was just *so* nervous. Oh, God, what will Ian say? Why isn't he here?' she added in the next breath. 'That would make everything perfect.'

'Well, he's due home next week, isn't he?' Alice comforted the wistful mother-to-be.

'Tuesday morning.'

'How long since you saw him?' Alice had boundless admiration for her sister-in-law, who coped stoically with her husband's long absences.

She wasn't sure she would have coped as well as Rachel if she had been married to a navy officer. His own wedding was about the only family occasion her brother had made it to in the last ten years!

'Three months. What's the betting he won't be around for the birth?'

'I'm sure he'll try to be.'

'Well, if he's not…I hope you don't mind me asking this, Alice, but would you mind being there as my birthing partner? Well, actually, I'd like you to be there even if Ian is there. You know how bossy he gets—he'll probably put up the backs of everyone at the hospital.'

This unexpected request made Alice's eyes fill with emotional tears again. 'Are you sure it's me you want?' she queried, incredibly touched to be asked.

'There's absolutely nobody I'd prefer,' Rachel replied firmly.

'If you want me I'll be there. I don't know that I'll be much use,' Alice warned. 'But I'll be there with bells on if you want me,' she promised eagerly. She privately resolved to read up everything she could on the subject.

'Always supposing that sexy boss of yours can spare you.'

'Roman? If I added up all the overtime I've put in for that man he owes me a *year's* holiday.' Alice frowned when there was no response. 'Rachel…Rachel…?'

'Sorry,' came the breathless reply seconds later. 'I was just dancing around the table.' Her voice dropped to an awed whisper. 'God, Alice, I'm going to have a baby! Isn't it incredible?'

'Absolutely,' Alice agreed fondly.

'What were you saying?'

'Nothing, I just said leave the boss to me,' she recapped quickly. 'When is the great day? Have you worked out when you're due?' Rachel told her and her eyes widened as she made a quick mental calculation. 'That makes you almost four months gone!' she exclaimed.

'I know. Ironic, isn't it? I spend years getting excited if I'm half an hour late and when I actually fall pregnant...' she gave a burble of euphoric laughter '...I don't even realise it until I'm almost four months! And if Mom hadn't remarked on how much weight I'd put on I'd probably still think I had indigestion.'

'What are you going to call indigestion? Do you want a boy or a girl? Gosh, what if it's twins?'

The two women spent a happy half-hour talking baby names and somehow, Alice wasn't sure how, but as often happened when two women chatted, they got onto the subject of men.

Alice thought she was being incredibly discreet until Rachel said, 'Does he have a name, this man we're talking about?'

'I was talking hypothetically.' She was glad that her sister-in-law couldn't see that she had gone the same colour as her freshly painted toenails—scarlet had seemed appropriate under the circumstances. 'You didn't think I was talking about me?' Sometimes she forgot that Rachel actually *listened* and in doing so often heard the things you *weren't* saying.

'Sure you weren't.'

'I wasn't!'

'It sounds to me like you're pretty smitten.'

'Good God, no, it was just casual.' *For him at least*, and she had tried, she had really tried, to follow his lead even though she had wanted to lock the door and tell him he couldn't possibly leave.

It was irrational, she knew, to feel bitter. It wasn't as if he had offered her anything but sex. She ought to be grateful that he hadn't lied to her the way some men did. At least this way they both knew where they stood.

At least she hadn't done anything terminally stupid such as tell him of her undying love! When she recalled how close she'd come her blood ran cold.

'Then we are talking about you.' Rachel sounded smug. 'I thought so. About time too,' she approved. 'Now tell me all— who is the lucky guy? Is he incredibly gorgeous?'

'I don't even like him,' she lied.

'So it's pure animal lust. Well, that can be fun too.'

Alice had no intention of discussing animal lust with her embarrassingly outspoken sister-in-law. 'Great fun,' Alice agreed unhappily.

'Is there a problem?'

'No problem, we just…we don't actually have much in common.'

'So this isn't a meeting of minds. Does that matter if the sex is great? It's not like you're planning to marry the guy, is it? Like I keep saying to Ian, Alice got married so young, she never really let down her hair and did the crazy, irresponsible, single-girl bit.'

Alice's lips quivered as she imagined how her protective big brother would have reacted to the opinion his little sister should be crazy and irresponsible.

'You need to test-drive a few men, compare and contrast. You know what I mean?'

'I get your drift, Rachel.' The sparkle of humour died from her eyes as an image of Luca came into her head. Luca with his incredible eyes sparkling with sexual challenge, his sensual lips curved into an insolent smile. Compare and contrast? Luca was quite simply incomparable!

The only way to go after Luca was definitely down. Though down might be less exhausting, both emotionally and physically, than Luca.

'The sex *is* great, I take it?'

Alice blinked. Eyes half closed, she recalled the way her treacherous body had responded to Luca's touch, his raw masculinity. Even thinking about his voice made her tummy muscles clench.

'*I* thought it was.'

The sound of Rachel's exasperated sigh echoed down the line. 'Sometimes British self-deprecation is kind of sweet, other times it's just plain irritating! Who is this guy, anyway? Have you known him long?'

'I've known him but we haven't...that is, Lu...he...we...'

'Good God, Alice, you're not talking about Luca O'Hagan, are you?'

'I might be...' There was a definite edge of defiance in Alice's response.

'Luca O'Hagan. My God. He's a total stud, but, no offence, isn't he a bit *deep end* for someone like you?'

Alice appreciated her tact, but she needn't have bothered. She was perfectly aware that the likes of Luca wouldn't normally look twice at someone like herself. But he had looked, and more, hadn't he? And furthermore he'd acted as if he enjoyed looking.

'Alice, be careful won't you?' she heard Rachel say worriedly as she tuned back into the conversation.

It could be too late for that, Alice admitted as she forced herself to concentrate on what Rachel was saying.

'I'd hate to see you get hurt. His reputation—'

'I know all about Luca's reputation, and, don't worry, I can take care of myself. It's not likely it's going to happen again.'

'Do you mean that?'

'Of course I mean it.' I mean it right up to the moment he walks through that door. If, she thought bitterly, he can drag himself away from his meeting. She could almost see his tall, athletic figure, framed in the doorway.

'You sound as if you're sorry about that.' Alice blinked

away the imaginary Luca and her sister-in-law continued. 'Was he *that* good?'

'*Rachel!*'

A wicked-sounding chuckle echoed down the line. 'My husband's been at sea for three months. The only sex I have is vicarious,' she excused herself.

Despite herself, Alice grinned. 'Let me put it this way: chocolate is good, but you'd get bored if you had it for every meal.' Wasn't chocolate addictive?

'That good, huh?' came the impressed response.

No wonder Rachel had been so shocked, Alice thought as she stood under the hot needles of the power-shower spray. Me and Luca—what am I thinking of falling for a man who changes his women the same way most men change socks?

Be careful, Rachel had said, and she doubted her sister-in-law had been talking birth control when she had said that! No doubt she assumed that when you were talking to a twenty-eight-year-old, well-educated female who ought to know better this wasn't the sort of thing that needed discussing!

Luca had probably thought the same thing. No doubt he had taken it for granted that she had taken precautions. Though given his claim to never have unprotected sex it did strike her as slightly unexpected that he hadn't done something about it himself. Of course the chances were…what…even given her erratic cycle…*minimal*…?

I can't think about that now!

She had to focus her thoughts and energy on the things that she *could* control…like being good at her job and not acting like a total idiot when she saw Luca again. If they were going to have a sexual relationship she would have to accept some very brutal truths and keep some very difficult secrets. She had serious doubts when it came to her ability to disguise the depth of her true feelings.

She selected a pair of jeans that made her hips look relatively slim—her bottom might be generous but at least it was firm—and topped it with a white designer tee shirt and tailored jacket. She had some free time and if her credit-card limit was not going to allow her to literally shop until she dropped she was hoping that the retail therapy would still be therapeutic. If she didn't think about Luca for half an hour it would be worth the expense!

After a final check of her reflection in the mirror she stepped out into the corridor where she almost walked into someone standing outside the door. She raised her hands to stop herself colliding with the stationary figure.

'Sorry.' She lifted her head and the breath rushed out of her lungs in one sibilant sigh as she found herself looking up into a pair of electric-blue eyes. 'Luca...you here... now...how?' She bit down hard on her lip. Me Jane, you Tarzan would have been a step up from that disjointed gibberish.

Start again. From somewhere she dredged something that passed for self-possession.

'Luca...' Good tone, casual and relaxed, but not too relaxed. It gave no hint of the tumultuous state of her pulse or the mortifying condition of her nervous system, which was what counted.

'You remembered my name, I'm touched.'

Alice was too occupied repressing her basic instincts to pick up on any undertones beyond casual sarcasm in his comment or his strained attitude.

'What are you doing here? I was just on my way out.'

His dark brooding features hardened perceptibly. 'Then you can change your plans.'

It was several seconds before she realised she ought to object to his masterful behaviour. 'Well, really, that's...' Her legs felt hollow and weak as, with shaking fingers, she smoothed down her hair.

One dark brow lifted. 'You have a problem with that?'

A tiny fractured sigh escaped her parted lips as she recalled with perfect clarity the way it had felt to run her hands covetously over the surface of his skin.

'No problem,' she whispered, mentally teasing her fingers into the dark fuzz of silky hair on his chest.

Resisting the abrupt and almost overwhelming urge to rip off his shirt and expose that golden expanse of hard flesh beaded her upper lip with sweat. She felt dizzy.

'What are you thinking about?'

The truth sprang to her lips. 'Touching you.'

His bronzed features clenched. 'I like your hands on me. I like you touching me.'

Her insides melted as a shard of sexual energy blasted through her feeble defences. 'And I *love* touching you,' she admitted in a small breathless whisper.

Her heart was thudding so loud that she could hardly hear her own voice. 'But, Luca, I think it isn't really a good idea...under the circumstances.'

'To hell with the circumstances!'

'Easy for you to say.'

'No, actually, it isn't.' His ironic laugh held a bewildering degree of bitterness. 'Not easy at all. Open the door, Alice.' He planted his hands palm-flat on the wall either side of her shoulders.

Alice instantly lost the ability to think or even breathe. His fingers slid into her hair, loosening the clip that held it in a casual twist on her head; it fell down into a silky sheet around her shoulders. He cupped her chin in his hand and tilted her head up to him.

'You want me. Say it!' he demanded fiercely.

Alice shuddered and closed her eyes as surrender flooded through her body. 'I want you, Luca.'

CHAPTER TWELVE

ALICE placed the item on the neatly packed suitcase and sat down on the bed. She felt her small self-congratulatory smile was well deserved; she hated packing with a vengeance and couldn't understand people who happily lived out of a suitcase. It was definitely not the lifestyle for her.

Of course the travelling she got to do with work had seemed very glamorous at first to a girl who had never been on a plane until she was twenty. She had not been a cool teenager, and family holidays when she was young had been a seaside boarding house in Cornwall, before it was a trendy destination. She had shared a room with her sister and slept in a bottom bunk that wouldn't have accommodated a plump Cornish kipper let alone a growing girl!

She had recollections of lots of rain, compulsory board games in the evening, and a fair number of family squabbles. All memories she treasured. Basically she was a girl who needed roots and that was where she was headed for a fortnight's holiday in the bosom of her family to recharge her depleted batteries.

Her expression softened as she thought of her home. Her father had been retired for several years. Not as spry as he once had been and with no son or daughter who wanted to work the land, he had sold all but a few of his acres off to a neighbour several years earlier. However, the half-timbered farmhouse with its odd-shaped rooms, low ceilings and passages that led nowhere was still the place where the brood returned and Alice was no exception.

This time was different. The tug of her roots was still as strong as ever, but she knew that the moment she walked through the door her mother would *know*. There was no *maybe* involved. It was spooky, but her mother always knew about these things. Her husband laughingly claimed she would have been called a witch in an earlier century.

Alice wasn't sure she wanted her feelings for Luca to be poked and prodded even by her liberal-minded mum. How was she going to admit that she had fallen in love with someone who had forgotten she even existed?

Her mother had been the only one to express concern when she and Mark had announced their engagement.

'I know you both like the same films and support the same football team. I'm sure you're as compatible as hell, sweetheart, but is he the love of your life?' she asked Alice on the evening of her engagement party. 'Are you sure you're not marrying because everyone expects you to?'

Alice was hurt by the question. 'Don't you like Mark, Mum?' she asked.

'Of course I like him. That's not the question; he's a very likeable boy. Do you love him? That's the only question that counts.'

'Of course I do,' she responded and at the time she believed it, but now Alice knew there was more than one way to love a man. Comparing what she had felt for her husband with what she felt for Luca was like comparing a gentle summer breeze to a full-scale hurricane warning.

It was a warning she ought to have heeded!

Though Mum ought to approve, Alice thought. I did what she always told me I ought to—I followed my instincts!

And where did it get me?

It had been three whole days since their last passionate encounter, and it had meant so much to Luca he hadn't even picked up a phone to call her since. She knew because she'd been waiting for it to ring…her heart racing every time she leapt to answer it and her spirits plummeting when she didn't hear his voice.

Her expression hardened as she gazed bleakly into the distance. Luca's method of giving the brush-off was brutal but efficient and he didn't even have to do anything, just make himself unavailable. Alice had got the message loud and clear. She just wished she had got it before she had rung his office number and got through to a nervous-sounding temp.

Alice could understand why she sounded nervous; she didn't see Luca as being an easy man to work for. Perfectionists rarely were, in her experience.

'Miss Trevelyan...sorry, you're...bear with me, I'd better check. Hold on a sec.'

Alice heard a few rustles and bangs and realised the harassed temp had obviously left the receiver lying on her desk.

'There's an Alice Trevelyan on the line asking for you?'

Alice winced and held the phone a little way from her ear as the voice continued loudly. 'Shall I put her through?'

Alice was looking at the tickets in her hand, wondering what she'd do if Luca hated the ballet, when down the line she heard a door slam.

'This is the intercom...next time use it.'

Alice winced in sympathy at the cutting derision in Luca's exasperated voice.

Despite that, I could listen to his voice all day, she found herself thinking.

'Sorry, sir, I just...sorry. Shall I put Miss Trevelyan through?'

'No.'

The contemplative smile that lifted the corners of Alice's wide mouth snuffed out. She lifted her hand to her mouth and a chill spread through her body as every last vestige of colour leeched from her face.

'What shall I say?'

'Use your imagination, but I don't want to speak to her. Is that clear?'

'Yes, absolutely, you don't want to speak to Miss Trevelyan.'

Alice replaced the phone down on the cradle with exaggerated care; she was shaking with hurt bewilderment. With stricken eyes she stared at the silent phone.

Oh, yes, she had got the message all right.

Was he more interested in the chase than anything that might follow? It certainly looked that way and she had made a terrible mistake. She had believed that what had passed between them was more than great sex. She had been misguided enough to imagine what they had shared was special...she was special.

What was she feeling? Humiliation, pain, anger and regret? Did she regret what had happened? Would she actually play it differently if the choice were offered her now?

Would she *not* have that memory?

God, why am I doing this? she wondered. The man didn't even have the decency to dump me and I'm obsessing about him. Would it have been so hard for him to issue some face-saving platitude like 'I think you're a lovely girl and we've had a great time but this isn't going to work out' in person?

'I'm doing it again!' she cried out loud. 'Say this after me, Alice...I will not think about Luca O'Hagan. He is not worth wasting one second of one minute on.' She gave a decisive nod and picked up the control for the TV while she finished packing.

She was flicking between a cartoon channel and a documentary on volcanoes when there was a knock on the door. Tucking a stray strand of hair behind her ear, she pulled it open with one hand while still looking at the screen.

'Hello, Alice.'

The voice made her freeze. She dropped the remote and poked her head around the door. Her eyes widened to their fullest extent. 'Oh, God, no!' she gasped and ducked back inside.

Standing with her back to the wall, she pressed her hand
to her head and released a silent groan.

I can't believe I did that!

I could have spent a week figuring out how to look a total
idiot and not come up with something that good. She turned
her face to the wall and rested her forehead against the neu-
trally painted surface. A slick one-liner, that's what I need. A
glib phrase that will leave me with a crumb of self-respect.

'Go away!' she heard herself growl.

That wasn't the line.

'You were very much nicer to me the last time we met.'

She could hear the nasty tone in his voice. Anger made her
feel courageous. Chin up, eyes blazing with anger, she
stepped into the doorway. 'I must have been drinking,' she
choked. Even though she knew it had meant nothing to him,
the memory of their lovemaking was precious to Alice. That
he could use it to mock her hurt her beyond measure.

'Next you'll be saying you didn't know what you were
doing.'

'I knew what I was doing,' she agreed quietly. 'The same
way I know I'm not going to do it ever again.'

She definitely hadn't known what she was doing when she
made the mistake of looking directly into his eyes. Normally
expressive, his blue eyes were flat like a bottomless lake,
nothing in them but her own reflection. It took all of her not
inconsiderable will-power to break the hypnotic pull of those
impenetrable orbs.

'So you no longer want me?' His expressive brows quirked.
'You want us to have a platonic relationship?'

Breathing hard, she gazed at the shiny surface of his leather
boots while she tried to collect her thoughts. As her glance
climbed over his long legs and muscular thighs clad in faded
denim and moved upwards to his taut midriff and broad chest,
so did her heart beat until it was pounding so hard she felt
light-headed and breathless.

'I don't want us to have any sort of relationship.'

His nostrils flared. 'You think you can dismiss me the way you do your one-night stands?'

'One-night stands!' she gasped.

He looked into her wide eyes filled with bewilderment and stifled the irrational urge to comfort her. 'Don't look like that.' Voice harsh, he lowered his eyes. 'Sex is sex, you said.'

'I did no such thing...oh...!' Alice broke off, her eyes widening as her face flushed with colour. She did have the distinct recollection of saying something not dissimilar. 'I didn't mean—'

Luca cut her off with an imperative gesture. 'I know you probably don't think about it in those terms,' he conceded heavily. 'I suppose in your own peculiar way you think you're staying faithful to the memory of your dead husband. But the bottom line is avoiding involvement is—'

'Something you'd know all about,' she supplied, white with fury. 'A lecture on morals from you of all people. Do me a favour!'

There was a short static silence. Their eyes locked. 'That's exactly what I intend to do,' he said, before barging past her into the room.

Alice stayed where she was, her hand curled over the door handle; she wasn't too proud to run away. In fact the longer she considered the option, the more appealing it seemed. She kept her wary eyes trained on him as he sauntered across the room.

The navy cashmere sweater he wore had designer written all over it. It made his eyes look even more startlingly blue than usual...if that were possible! He had casually pushed the sleeves up, revealing the light sprinkling of dark hair on his sinewed forearms.

The stab of lust she experienced was so all-consuming that she was literally paralysed with longing. The paralysis was not just physical; she couldn't think...she couldn't breathe...

How long was I standing there eating him up with my eyes?

The truth was she didn't have the faintest idea. It could have been half an hour or seconds but she sincerely hoped it was closer to the latter estimate!

Tiny muscles along her delicate but firm jaw quivered as she inhaled.

He ran a hand over his aggressive jaw, drawing Alice's attention to the dark designer stubble that covered the lower half of his face. Fairly predictably the almost piratical look it gave him was wildly attractive.

'It's a new look for you,' she said, simulating amusement. 'Very moody and if you're sporting it I'm sure it's all the latest fashion.'

His hand fell to his side. 'You think I'm a fashion victim?'

'I'm sure you couldn't give a damn what I think,' she returned with a carelessness she was a long way from feeling.

'I didn't come here to play word games.'

'Why did you come?'

So far her own efforts to figure this one out had not been productive. This could have something to do with the fact she was on some sort of intellectual hamster wheel. Her thoughts were stuck in a nightmare loop and nothing that was happening made any sense to her.

Luca, who was looking at the luggage neatly stacked on the bed, didn't appear to hear her question.

'You going somewhere?'

'Yes.'

His questioning glance didn't waver. 'Home,' she supplied reluctantly. 'I'm booked on the nine-thirty flight. So if you don't mind I need to finish—'

'It's lucky I got here in time, then, isn't it? Have you told your family?'

She gave a puzzled nod. 'I planned this holiday last year.'

'That's not what I was talking about and you know it,' he contended grimly.

'I don't know anything!'

Her heart-felt protest made him turn back towards her, and the light from the east-facing window fell directly across his face. Alice's stomach tightened. Whatever else Luca was, she thought as her eyes moved over the strong, powerful contours of his amazing face, he was beautiful.

Swallowing, she lowered her pain-filled gaze.

'Look, Luca, I can see how you might think my door and my bed is always open to you when your plans for the evening have fallen through.' She caught her lower lip between her teeth, hating the embittered note in her voice. 'We had a nice time, but trying to recreate a mood is, in my experience, all too frequently disappointing. Let's keep the memory.' An inspired response if I say so myself.

She was too miserable to take any pleasure from his confounded, furious expression.

'We managed to recreate the *mood* pretty successfully once. Or were you *disappointed*?'

Her teeth clenched. She would have loved to wipe that smug, self-satisfied expression from his face. 'You know I wasn't,' she admitted with painful honesty. 'But please don't run away with the idea you could *recreate* anything again with me.'

'Actually I didn't come here to recreate any mood.'

The anger in his face extinguished any unrealistic hopes she had been nursing that this scene was going to follow the same format as one of her romantic fantasies. The ones that ended up with him telling her he had realised she was the only woman for him.

She gave a small derisive sniff. 'Well, why don't you tell me why you came before I lose the will to live?'

'I said I *didn't*, not that I *couldn't*. We both know that I could.'

'God knows what I ever saw in you!' she yelled.

'My incredible modesty?' There was a redeeming hint of

self-mockery in his arrogant suggestion. 'Or my giving nature?'

'Will you take your giving nature and go away? I'm trying very hard to be polite. I can't guarantee I'll stay polite,' she warned him darkly. 'You know, I think I'd quite enjoy a scene right now.'

He folded his arms across his chest and trained his glittering gaze on her angry face. Alice's rigid spine felt as though it would snap. 'Bring it on, girl. Conflict is mother's milk to me—my mother's Latin and my father's Irish. Communication is always loud and dramatic in our house…especially loud.'

'That sounds tiring,' she said, almost as distracted by the picture his words conjured as she was by trying not to breathe in the musky scent of the fragrance he used. 'I hate arguments. I didn't know your parents' marriage wasn't…'

'*Solid?*' he suggested, looking amused. 'It remains a beacon of hope in these days of disposable marriages. Some people thrive on conflict, but, yes, I agree it's not relaxing. But Dad's heart attack means they have calmed things down. These days they count to ten before they let rip with the four-letter words. But I didn't come here,' he said grimly, 'to talk about my parents.'

'For heaven's sake, you keep saying what you didn't come for! Why did you come here?'

'I'm getting to that…' he promised, dragging a hand through his hair. A spasm of irritation crossed his face. 'Will you come in here and close that damned door? Maybe you don't mind sharing your business with the world but I do.'

Alice's expression hardened at his brusque demand. If it hadn't been for the maid outside her room who had dusted the same spot six times she would have ignored him.

'Door closed.' She flashed him an insincere smile. 'Now say your piece…not that I can imagine anything you say will be of interest to me,' she observed.

Luca studied the floor, tracing a pattern with the toe of his shiny boot in the deep pile of the carpet. Exhaling deeply, he lifted his eyes. 'I've been thinking about this situation and I think it would be the best solution all around if we got married.'

Not interested? Oh, boy, when I'm wrong about something I'm *really* wrong!

The seconds ticked away while she stared at him in open-mouthed disbelief.

'You think that we should get married?' The fact Alice's voice held no emotion was a reasonably fair reflection of her feelings; she was simply too numb to feel anything.

Luca's mouth twisted impatiently as he gave a curt nod. 'Isn't that what I just said?'

The knife-edged steely stare that accompanied this testy reply had very little of the desperate lover and a hell of a lot of anger. Even if you allowed for the fact Luca might not be a man particularly in touch with his feminine side, his attitude was not that generally expected of a man proposing.

Alice braced her shoulders against the wall as a wave of desolation of breathtaking intensity washed over her. She reached out blindly and her hand closed over the back of a chair; she was grateful for the support.

'Is this some sort of joke?' For one brief, blissful moment she had thought his proposal was for real...that he was here to tell her that he loved her. How much of a fool does that make me? she asked herself. 'Or have you discovered you can't live without me?'

Ironically that was exactly what he had discovered. In fact after three days he had accepted that bringing up another man's child as his own was preferable to living without this woman. His nostrils flared as his eyes ran over the ripe curves of her body. The fact he had no control whatever over the primitive response of his own body brought an angry rasp to his voice.

'*Hardly...*'

'So, the living without me you can manage, but you want to marry me? Curiouser and curiouser...' In stark contrast to her amused tone Alice felt physically sick when she realised how close she had come to making a total idiot of herself.

She cringed when she imagined what Luca's reaction would have been if she had followed her first impetuous instincts and flung herself at him. Now that would have been embarrassing!

'This is so unexpected,' sheer nerves made her flippantly trill.

'I'm sure some people appreciate your infantile sense of humour, but I am not one of them.'

'In that case I definitely can't marry you. The man I marry will definitely have to laugh at my jokes.'

'Shall we be serious?'

'Not easy...'

'This is not a decision I make lightly. Marrying me would solve a lot of problems for you.'

'You being the matrimonial catch of the century?' she suggested.

'You being an unmarried mother.'

Alice eyes widened. *Mother!* Slowly she shook her head. She held up her hand and hoarsely protested, 'Back up there! You think I'm pregnant?' *I'd have to eat an awful lot of cheese to get a nightmare this surreal:*

'We could waste time pretending, but this seems pointless. I'm assuming the father doesn't want to know? Have you told him or anyone else? I know you haven't told Roman. Presumably you'd planned to tell your family face to face?' He looked at her expectantly.

Alice stared at him, unable to believe what she was hearing. 'You told Roman I'm pregnant?' she said blankly.

'Of course I didn't tell him,' Luca responded with an irritated frown. 'I just asked a few leading questions and it was obvious he didn't have a clue, but he did confirm that you're not in a relationship.' For the first time Luca's rigid poise showed signs of cracking. 'It was also clear from what he said that you do have plenty of offers.'

A choking sound escaped Alice's white lips. 'How dare you discuss me with your brother?'

'Now listen, this is important. Alice, are you paying attention?' he rapped.

Alice's bloodless lips parted, then closed again. She shook her head. 'Oh, you have my full attention,' she promised hollowly.

Luca, his expression grave, nodded and ran a hand over the dark growth that covered his lean cheek. 'Does anyone but me know that you're pregnant?'

She shook her head. 'Not a soul,' she told him truthfully.

Some of the tension went out of his shoulders as he began to pace the room. 'Right, and it can stay that way.' He flashed her a look as if he expected her to protest. When she didn't he inclined his head. 'I'm glad you're going to be sensible about this.'

'You are?'

'As far as the world is concerned this baby is mine.'

'Why would you want people to think that?'

'I suppose you know my father had a heart attack some years ago?' Alice nodded. 'And it's important he doesn't subject himself to undue stress?'

'I really don't see what this has to do with—'

'My father is an old-fashioned man in many ways, deeply religious and proud of the family name,' Luca revealed gravely.

Alice, who had gathered as much from things that Roman had let drop, nodded cautiously.

'He has this thing, bordering on obsession actually, about continuing the line...the pride of the family name and all that. You probably know that Roman had a near miss marriage-wise. That broke Da's heart,' he admitted. 'He's been getting really worked up about the unmarried-sons-no-grandchild situation lately. So much so that Ma is seriously concerned about his health.'

Luca saw no need to explain that Natalia's concern hadn't prevented her expressing her opinion with fiery Latin bluntness that, the more her husband nagged, the less likely it became that she would ever have a grandchild because *his* sons were just as pigheaded and stubborn as their father.

'I'm sorry about your father, but I—'

Luca's expression became grave. 'His last check-up was not what anyone was expecting.' The consultant had been so amazed that he had taken his patient off almost all his medication.

'That's sad, but—'

'The fact is one of us has to get married.' Alice's eyes widened at this drastic solution. 'With his history, Roman is out; that leaves me.'

'You plan to get married to—'

'If you could make some small sacrifice that would save your father's life, wouldn't you make it?'

'Of course I would but—'

'Then why shouldn't I do the same?' he asked. 'I need a wife and baby, you are having a baby that needs a father. You must see the advantages of marrying me. Obviously we will draw up a pre-nup that protects your interests.'

'What more could I want?'

'You mean sex.'

'No, I damned well don't!' she rebutted furiously. 'Sex is all you ever think about.'

'I think that's what people in the trade call transference.'

'My God, get over yourself!' she advised with a caustic laugh. 'The person that is in urgent need of psychiatric care around here isn't me. I'm very sorry your father is ill, but your idea is totally crazy.'

'I'm assuming that mood swings and irrational behaviour are to be expected when you're pregnant. Let's calm down and deal in realities.'

'I'm perfectly calm!' she gritted through clenched teeth.

'It's tough bringing up a baby alone and my wife would lead a very comfortable life.'

'Pretty poor compensation for having to see you every day.'

'There will be no need for us to live in each other's pockets. There are many successful marriages where the partners lead separate lives.' His sensual lips curled. 'In fact they might actually be the most successful ones.'

Her hands clenched into fists as she listened to him outline what he obviously imagined were selling points of this proposed union...or should it be merger? she wondered bitterly.

'Gosh! When you put it *that* way how can I say no?' Her expression of brainless adoration morphed into one of hard-eyed anger.

'I really don't think you're in any position to cut off your nose to spite your face.'

'Thank you for the reminder.'

'There are not just your feelings to consider,' he reproached.

'Yes, but maybe I'm terminally selfish. Or maybe I don't like moral blackmail. You know, the longer I'm in your company, the more attractive being a single parent seems.' Suddenly Alice had had enough of this farce. 'You stupid man, there is no child!' She pressed her hands flat against her belly. 'I may look pregnant compared to those rakes you normally see naked, but I'm just fat and if I was having a baby I wouldn't lumber it with a father like you!'

Luca gave a derisive snort. 'For God's sake, woman, stop lying. I was standing outside the door when you rang for the test results.'

'Test results, but not *my* test results. You heard me ringing the clinic for my sister-in-law. The only thing I'm expecting is a niece or nephew. And for your information you're the only man I've slept with other than my husband and we actually waited until our wedding night. I'd like to say it was worth the wait, but we were both pretty clueless and it took us a couple of months to get the hang of things.' She stopped, appalled by what she had said.

Luca was staring at her, a hand pressed to the side of his head; he looked like a man who had just received a blow to the head. His eyes dropped to her middle. *'You're not pregnant?'*

'Finally...' she breathed.

'And you've not had any other lovers?'

'No.' She gave a bitter smile.

For a long moment he studied her with blank, stunned eyes. Then abruptly and with none of his usual natural grace he turned and walked to the window. The lines of his back screamed with tension.

When he turned back his face was wiped clean of emotion. 'It would seem that I made a mistake.'

'Not nearly as big a mistake as I made.' I fell in love with you, she nearly said.

His eyes slid from hers. 'Maybe we can retrieve something from this situation.'

'Like a lifelong friendship? I don't think so.'

'Then you wouldn't consider marrying me anyway?' Through the sweep of his lashes his brilliant eyes blazed.

She froze...marry him anyway? This had to be some twisted joke. He had loved her, left her, thought he could buy her, insulted her in every way possible and now this...! She drew a deep breath and fixed him with a look of loathing.

'Marry *you*? I think you're the most loathsome man I have ever met. I hate you! Marriage isn't about *sacrifice*, it's about *love* and I'm sure your father would agree with that if you asked him.'

Luca inclined his head. His face was like a slate wiped

blank. 'He probably would,' he conceded. 'But you do things you might not otherwise consider when you love someone.'

'I appreciate you love your father, but if you need a wife I'm sure you won't have a problem finding someone other than me to say *I do*.' The day that advert appeared they'd be lined up around the block!

'I don't want anyone else.' The vehemence of his raw revelation made her blink. 'I want you, Alice.'

Alice closed her eyes. 'I don't want you,' she lied. He didn't love her.

'I slept with you when I thought you were carrying another man's child.' She heard his impassioned voice continue. 'I thought about not smelling your skin, you see, not feeling you quiver when I touch you, and I knew I had to have you one last time.' She heard a sound and imagined him raking his hand through his dark hair. 'I'm not proud of it. I spent too long successfully not touching you...' If he had touched her then she would have melted but he didn't. 'And now that I have I can't seem to stop. You're like a drug in my bloodstream.'

Alice opened her eyes to tell him she felt the same way and found she was alone.

CHAPTER THIRTEEN

ALICE couldn't let things stand that way. She had fully intended to contact Luca, and ask him if he had actually meant what he had said.

She rang New York as soon as she got home and discovered that nobody knew where Luca was; he had effectively vanished. Maybe he'd eloped, someone had laughingly suggested and Alice had felt sick...she'd been feeling sick a lot, actually. By the time he resurfaced, unmarried as it happened, she had discovered a complication.

Just a few months after she had told Luca that she wasn't pregnant, and she was. It was sometimes hard to think that the father of her child had a reputation for perception that bordered on the supernatural.

People might have noticed by now if the morning sickness hadn't been so bad, but rather than put on weight in the early weeks Alice had dropped over a stone. To her relief things were looking up and a glass of water no longer made her heave, so she knew it was only a matter of time before she started showing.

The fact she had to tell Luca soon was with her constantly. She didn't even have the excuse that she hadn't had the opportunity—she had. She still worked for Roman and Luca ran half the company; there had been any number of occasions when she had picked up the phone and heard his voice. In fact if anything she was forced to speak to him more often than usual, a circumstance that had made her seek out the bathroom on more than one occasion, not to throw up, but to cry her eyes out.

A couple of times she'd actually begun to tell him, but his

curt response had always been so cold and impersonal that she hadn't been able to go through with it. It would have been like telling a total stranger you were carrying his child, especially when you had recently denied you were even pregnant. It sometimes seemed to Alice like another life when he had proposed and she had rejected him.

If Luca had ever been addicted to her it seemed to a miserable Alice that he had discovered the cure. She only wished she knew his secret.

Her normally super-observant boss hadn't picked up on any of the obvious signs, which wasn't like him. But Roman wasn't himself, due mostly, Alice suspected, to a new woman in his life.

She had known for sure that this Scarlet was something special when Roman had said he wouldn't be flying out to Ireland with her on Friday. He would, he'd explained, be on the ferry. When Alice had expressed her surprise at his choice he had explained, somewhat defensively, that Scarlet didn't like to fly.

'You'll like Scarlet,' he told her abruptly.

'I'm sure I will.'

'And Sam.'

'Her little boy…?'

'My son, actually.'

Having dropped the bombshell, he calmly walked into a meeting leaving her staring open-mouthed. Maybe this was why Luca was still unmarried? His father had the grandchild and, if she read the signs correctly, the marriage he had wanted too. That let Luca off the hook.

Alice ended up flying out to Ireland first class and alone. She was met at the airport by a chauffeur-driven limo and whisked away in style to the O'Hagan family estate. She had been here a couple of times before with Roman on working weekends but on those occasions she hadn't been carrying the O'Hagans' grandchild!

She was positively racked with guilt when Natalia went out of her way to make her feel welcome. She wondered if the welcome would have been quite so warm if she had known the truth. Mothers were notorious for siding with their sons and Natalia's pride when she spoke of hers was obvious.

'Make yourself at home, my dear. I know you like to walk and apparently this dry spell is set to last into next week. We're not expecting Roman until later. We're very excited,' she confided, confirming Alice's suspicion that there was a celebratory mood in the air.

Deciding to take her hostess's advice, she put on some walking shoes and a jacket intending to take a walk. She was actually opening the front door when the phone started ringing. Nobody appeared and it stopped, but almost immediately started up again.

Alice picked it up and before she had a chance to identify herself the person on the other end began to speak.

'Da, is that you?'

Alice almost dropped the phone. She stood there staring at the instrument in her hand for a long moment, shaking so hard that she almost dropped it. She swallowed past the dry constriction in her throat. 'No, it's me.' She closed her eyes and winced—he wouldn't know who *me* was.

He did.

'Alice...Alice, is that really you?' There was a crackling on the line and then his voice. 'Damn thing, it's cutting out and my flight...whatever you do don't...'

'Luca, I can't hear you. What are you saying?'

'Just don't do *anything* daft until I get there. I'll be there tonight. Alice, *cara*, promise me you won't do anything.'

'I promise,' she said without the faintest idea what she was promising.

Before the event Alice had been determined not to put a damper on things during dinner. So much for good intentions!

She decided afterwards that it was that empty seat that had done it—made her lose it.

She had been wildly ambivalent about the news Luca was arriving, her mood swinging from wild hope to deep depression, but every time she looked at that empty seat where he ought to be sitting her eyes filled. It reached the point where she found it hard to breathe past the knot of misery lodged like a stone behind her breastbone.

After she had applied cold water to her tear-stained face following the short, frustratingly cryptic call she had received earlier from the airport, Alice had told his parents that Luca would be there for dinner.

She had been dreading their questions but beyond a, 'How lovely, all the family together,' Natalia, being extremely diplomatic, didn't pry further. Neither did her husband, though Alice suspected his silence was more to do with a discreet but well-aimed kick on the shins than diplomacy.

'I tried him earlier, but there was no answer on his mobile,' Roman said when Luca didn't show. 'I'll try him again.' He left the dinner table. When he returned he was shaking his head. 'Still no luck.'

'Well, there's no point waiting for him,' Finn O'Hagan, who had displayed none of the signs of infirmity Alice had been anticipating, said. 'I don't know what's got into him. Last night he cut me off right in the middle of a conversation. Cut me dead!' he added, shaking his head incredulously. 'If he's not got the manners to inform us he'll be late, he doesn't deserve the lovely meal your mother's organised.'

Natalia smiled her charming smile. 'But don't panic. When Finn says *organise* he doesn't mean I actually touched the food. I organised by nodding when Cook told me what she was making. Experience has taught me that if I do anything else she throws an artistic hissy fit and resigns.'

There was a ripple of amusement across the table.

'Mother is not renowned for her culinary skills,' Roman

explained to the two young female guests. 'It takes dedication to burn water the way she does.'

As Alice stared at their laughing faces with disbelief, the distracting buzzing in her head got louder. Why was she the only one taking this seriously? The tight feeling in her chest continued to expand until she couldn't restrain herself any longer.

'Isn't anyone worried about where Luca is?' Pent-up anxiety made her voice loud and accusing. As a bottle stood poised above her wineglass she covered it with her hand and shook her head.

All eyes turned to her in response to her question.

'Knowing Luca, he could be anywhere,' his brother joked.

'He'll turn up,' his father predicted. Then added with a chuckle, 'The young devil always does, like the proverbial bad penny.'

This display of parental callousness fed the flames of Alice's growing anger.

'Oh, Cook will put aside some food for him, my dear,' Natalia said, stretching across the table to place a pat on Alice's hand.

Alice looked at the beautifully manicured hand covering her own and blinked. She couldn't believe what she was hearing. Hadn't it occurred to *any* of them that Luca could be in trouble?

'But he said he'd be here,' she reminded them, forcing a quick tight smile.

'Perhaps you misunderstood,' Roman suggested.

Scarlet, seated beside him, nodded. 'That's easily done,' she agreed.

'Maybe he meant tomorrow?' Roman ventured.

Their inability to appreciate the urgency of the situation made Alice want to scream. 'Or maybe he didn't ring at all. That's probably what you're all thinking,' she accused wildly.

Somewhere in the dark, dim recesses of her consciousness

she knew she had already said too much, she knew she was making a total idiot of herself, but she couldn't stem the flow.

'But he did ring,' she choked. 'And he said he'd be here tonight.'

'Maybe he just changed his mind,' Roman suggested tentatively.

Alice shook her head positively. 'Luca doesn't say things he doesn't mean.' She scanned the faces around the table and appealed, 'Hasn't it occurred to anyone that he may have had an accident?'

The colour drained from her overheated face as she envisaged Luca's lifeless body lying in an overturned car or worse, almost, he might be hurt and need her and she wasn't there!

'We should call the police!' She pressed her hand to her mouth as acid rose in her throat.

'My dear girl...' Finn began. He subsided when his wife pressed a warning hand to his arm. Slowly she shook her head before murmuring something in her native tongue to her eldest born, who nodded back.

'And so we shall, my dear,' she soothed.

Alice heaved a sigh of relief.

'If we don't hear from him before, we'll call them directly in the morning.'

'But—!' Alice began heatedly.

Natalia held up her hand, her expression kind but firm. 'They won't do anything unless someone is missing for twenty-four hours, you know, and the chances are he'll walk through that door any moment now.'

Alice bit her lip and, after a short pause, nodded. She looked around the table and realised that she had firmly established herself as the mad woman in their midst.

'I just thought...' She took a deep breath. 'I might have overreacted,' she conceded.

'And then some,' Finn agreed with feeling before his wife

silenced him with a frown, but not before a mortified flush had spread over Alice's pale skin.

It was Scarlet who smoothly came to her rescue.

She turned to her prospective father-in-law, who was not immune to the charm of her teasing smile. 'The trouble is, men lack imagination, and so they don't understand the curse of having an overactive one.' She forestalled the predictable male protest with an imperious wave of her hand. 'Whereas I can definitely empathise,' she admitted ruefully. 'Sam doesn't have a tummy ache, he has a burst appendix; he doesn't have a high temperature, he has meningitis. That's the way my mind works when it comes to Sam. I tell you, our doctor dreads hearing my voice and the practice nurses have coded me an NOPM...neurotic over-protective mum.'

Laughter and a general lessening of tension followed her droll disclosure. Alice mimed a thank-you across the table and Scarlet wrinkled her nose and gave a conspiratorial wink.

Alice smiled her way through the rest of dinner. She even managed to make a cheerful contribution when the after-dinner conversation turned to babies and weddings. Every time she replayed her spectacular loss of control she cringed and wished the floor would open up and swallow her, but she managed to hold it together until she said goodnight to Scarlet and Roman.

In fact, if she hadn't paused and turned back to make her last husky comment she would have got through the door with her smile intact.

'I'm so happy for you both,' she declared before bursting into tears.

'You can tell how happy she is, can't you, *cara mia*?' Roman observed, watching the tears stream down the cheeks of his cool and collected secretary.

'*Roman!*' Scarlet reproached, enfolding the sobbing woman in a comforting embrace.

'S...sorry,' Alice hiccuped as she wiped the moisture from her face and sniffed. 'I'm just...'

'No need to explain,' Scarlet interjected. 'I know *exactly* how you feel.'

'Is someone going to let me into the secret?' Roman enquired.

'Don't be so dense, Roman!' Scarlet chided impatiently.

'I'm assuming this has got something to do with my brother. If you've got any problems with him, come to me, Alice,' he suggested. 'I'll sort him out.'

'God, she's not that desperate!'

Alice had to look away...

Roman and Scarlet represented everything she wanted and would never have...*couldn't* have, unless Luca loved her—and, no easy way to say this, he didn't!

Self-pity, Alice, she reproached herself sternly, is not an attractive thing. Besides, she had other priorities now; like the child she was carrying. She had to tell Luca; on this subject at least there was no option.

She'd been through this in her head a million times before and a few barely intelligible words on the phone didn't change anything. She was pretty sure she knew how Luca would react when he knew about the baby. Luca called his father old-fashioned and proud of the family name, but he was just as proud; he was an O'Hagan.

He'd want to marry her for the sake of the baby.

There was no escaping the fact that Luca *was* the love of her life—and Luca would be resenting the fact he was tied to the mother of his child.

She sucked in a deep breath. 'No, I'm not that desperate,' she agreed quietly.

'Honestly, if you're worried about Luca, don't be,' Roman advised earnestly. 'He's got more lives than a cat,' he reflected. 'And he has a *very* well-developed sense of survival.'

She nodded. 'I'm sure you're right,' she agreed, on the outside, at least, calm.

'If you need me, you know where I am.' Scarlet, her pretty face a study of concern, caught Alice's arm.

Alice reminded herself that it had always been a long shot that anyone was going to swallow her show of disinterest close on the heels of her hysterical breakdown.

'I know,' she agreed, doubting that Roman would appreciate it if she took Scarlet up on the offer.

A glance at the grandfather clock ticking away in the hallway revealed it was still relatively early. The lure of another sleepless night and an intensive study of the wallpaper—no matter how tasteful—held a limited attraction for Alice. She responded to the plaintive cry of a sleek cat who had escaped from the kitchen and unbolted the grand front door.

The moggy vanished without a backward glance into the night and Alice stood there inhaling the sweet night air redolent of night-scented stock that someone had filled the tubs outside the door with.

Why not? she thought.

Feeling rather like a schoolgirl daringly ignoring a curfew, she pulled a jacket casually slung over the back of a chair in the hallway over her shoulders and went outdoors.

As she stepped outside the heavy door swung closed behind her with a decisive clunk. She shrugged; it wasn't as if she were locked out in the literal sense. Nobody here seemed to feel the necessity to lock anything. She could quite easily let herself in the side kitchen door after she had had a walk in the moonlight.

The night was simply magical…no street lights, just a moon and the smell of green growing things. Alice felt her mood lift.

The moment she stepped on the neatly trimmed lawn her high heels sank into the soft ground. After stumbling her way a couple of hundred yards, she slipped the shoes off and stuffed them in the jacket pockets.

Back to nature, she thought as she enjoyed the squidgy feel of the wet grass. Experimentally she wriggled her toes and discovered it was not actually unpleasant. An owl hooted eerily in the distance as she turned her face to the warm soft breeze that sprang up. Lost in thought, she walked until the lights from the house were a distant twinkle.

She reached a slight rise ahead as the parkland became woodland proper, and she stopped to catch her breath, realising for the first time how far she'd gone from the neatly manicured lawns. She began to wonder if she had maybe had enough of nature for one night. Maybe she ought to make her way back now?

Just as she was reflecting how easy it would be to imagine yourself the only person in the world out here a cloud drifted across the silver face of the full moon. It almost immediately lifted. Alice had lived in the City so long she had almost forgotten that dark in the country was not the same thing as dark in the town! Not by a long chalk!

Standing there, she rediscovered that the countryside at night was not actually quiet. If you listened as she was it was filled with sounds—soft, sinister rustling sounds, sounds made by things she couldn't see.

Now that she thought about it, she wasn't sure she wanted to see them. Come to think of it, what was she doing in the wilds of Ireland, alone, in the middle of the night?

It seemed a good idea at the time. That was probably what all the victims of mad knife-wielding psychopaths said, or *would* have if they hadn't been dead. She brushed aside her morbid fancies.

'A torch would be good!' She spoke out loud to steady her nerves. They stayed steady until the moon ducked once more behind a cloud at the same moment her hair snagged on a low branch.

Alice lost it. She let out a high-pitched scream and began running barefoot. By the time exhaustion made her stop she had lost her bearings totally.

Don't panic. What's the worst that can happen? *Excluding psychopaths!* She forced herself to think logically. She could get blisters, scratches and scare the odd sheep. It was a warm night so she wasn't going to get hypothermia. Gradually her racing heartbeat slowed.

Tomorrow she would laugh about this.

Despite her determinedly upbeat attitude tomorrow seemed an awful long way away.

She slid the shoes back on her dirty feet and cautiously now continued through the trees heading towards high ground, calculating that from that vantage point she might be able to see where she was.

Despite her efforts to spot landmarks around her, nothing around looked familiar. If I'd been a girl-guide this would have been a different story. Talk about wisdom in retrospect, she thought. The only survival tips she seemed to have picked up involved digging a hole in the snow and wrapping yourself in clingfilm…or was that tinfoil? Well, as she had neither, or for that matter snow, it wasn't terribly helpful.

'A trail of breadcrumbs is what I need,' she muttered as she gingerly picked her way around a bramble bush. Emerging unscathed the other side, she felt quite pleased until without warning she collided with a large warm body. A warm body that had hands, ones that grabbed her.

Instinct took over and she immediately tried to pull free, struggling frantically against her captor, whose grip lessened momentarily when she released a scream an Irish banshee would have been proud of.

During the short, frantic struggle that followed several of her wild blows and kicks found their target and she had the satisfaction of hearing her assailant grunt in pain more than once.

'I know karate,' she warned. 'I don't want to have to hurt you.'

'Congratulations, you're hiding your reluctance really well so far. Alice, *Madre di Dios*, will you calm down? I'm not going to hurt you.'

CHAPTER FOURTEEN

ALICE froze… She would have recognised that voice amongst a thousand others. In a split second she tumbled headlong from extreme terror and misery into total bliss!

'*Luca?*'

'Were you expecting someone else?'

The relief that flooded through her was profound as she collapsed weakly against him. He felt solid and deliciously real. Too real to be a dream.

'I can't believe…'

For a moment she saw his dark lean face, dappled by moonlight that shone through the leafy canopy overhead, before his mouth came crashing down. With a soft, muffled cry against his lips, she wound her arms around his neck; resistance didn't even enter her head.

There were tears running down her cheeks when he eventually lifted his head. He blotted them gently with the back of his hand.

'Believe now?' he said, breathing against her cheek.

She might have interpreted his tone as complacent if she hadn't been in a position to know that he was shaking, racking his greyhound-lean frame with fine tremors.

She sighed and cupped her hand around the side of his face. 'That was quite a hello.'

He turned his face into her hand and kissed the centre of her palm, sending a delicious shiver all the way to her bare toes. 'I'm known for my hellos.'

'So that was nothing special?'

His fingers tightened around the delicate bones of her wrist. 'Very special. I've been thinking about it for a long time. I wasn't sure about how welcome I'd be. But you seemed to be moderately glad to see me?' Luca's attempts to read her expression were frustrated by the shadow that lay over her face.

A plea for reassurance from Luca?

'Moderately glad, yes,' she agreed with overdue caution. 'How did you know I was here?'

'I didn't know, at least not that it was you, but I heard you from half a mile away. I thought you were a particularly noisy poacher.'

'I'm not a poacher.'

'That's good. You have no aptitude for it.'

'I was thinking about you,' she murmured, pressing her face into his chest. The feeling of intense relief was mingled with an overpowering sense of coming home. 'And you came,' she sighed softly. Nothing had ever sounded as good to her as the thud of his slow, steady heartbeat.

Luca held her as though he'd never let her go.

For several minutes she stood there as he stroked her hair, letting the mellifluous stream of passionate Italian that spilled from him wash over her.

When she finally lifted her head she saw that he was looking strained; his lean face in the moonlight was all stern, strong angles and fascinating shadows. Her breath caught in her throat... *Oh, my God, but he's beautiful!*

'You're really here?' She sighed happily.

'We'd already established that, *cara*. If we carry on covering old ground we could be here all night.'

'I just still don't understand how or why...' She looked around the leafy glade. 'Where is here?'

'You don't know?'

'I went for a walk; I got lost.'

'You thought that going for a walk in the middle of the night was a good idea? What the hell were they thinking of,' he snapped, 'letting you go out? They should have found you by now.'

'Nobody's looking. I didn't ask permission, Luca, and I doubt if anyone even knows I'm not in bed.'

'So you could have fallen and broken your leg and nobody would have been any the wiser.' She could hear the anger in his voice as he slid a finger inside the lapel of the borrowed jacket. She shivered as his fingertip slid along her collar-bone.

'I thought the fresh air would make me sleep. I lost a shoe,' she discovered. 'They cost a fortune.'

'Be grateful that's the only thing you lost!' he retorted harshly. 'When I think—' He broke off and cursed softly when he saw the glint of tears on her cheeks.

'I was lost,' she revealed plaintively. 'And scared, so don't shout at me.' With a shiver she cast a scared look over her shoulder. 'Is it far back to the house?'

Without replying he took her hand and led her to the top of the small rise; below them was the house illuminated by strategically placed spotlights.

'I thought I was miles away!' she gasped. 'When all along—'

'All you had to do was follow your nose,' he interjected, looking amused. 'And a very beautiful nose it is too.' He kissed the pink tip of her nose.

'You can laugh, but you were lost too.' Actually Luca wasn't laughing, he was looking at her as if he was committing every detail of her face to memory. Her erratic pulse rate kicked up another notch.

'Me…?' His deep voice held a dry satirical lilt but he still didn't smile. 'I swerved to avoid a loose horse and ended up in a ditch.'

The breaths nagged painfully in her throat. Without realising it she grasped his shirt, dislodging in the process the jacket draped around her shoulders.

'Were you hurt?' Her eyes ran down the lean, taut lines of his body but she could see no obvious signs of injury.

He shook his head. 'Would you have cared?'

She didn't respond to his soft taunt; the rampant hunger in his eyes was less easy to ignore. 'You didn't ring. We waited to have dinner.'

'But not long?'

She conceded the point with a shrug.

'The old man doesn't like to eat late,' he said drily. 'I suppose he wasn't happy...?'

'Actually everyone was pretty happy.' Except me, she wanted to say, but didn't.

'So nobody missed me?'

'We managed to muddle through without you.'

'That's good.'

Alice gave a snort of exasperation and pulled out of his arms. 'Would you prefer I said that I was worried sick...that I had a *totally* terrible night? If you must know I made a total fool of myself.' She pushed her fingers in her hair and shook her head back and forth in weary disbelief. 'Your parents think I'm a lunatic.' She arched a brow. 'Does *that* make you any happier?'

'Looks like I missed quite a night. Are you hugging that tree?' he asked as she walked over to a large oak and laid her face tiredly against the bark.

It stops me hugging you.

'Don't worry, you didn't miss that much.' Besides my disintegration into a raving lunatic. 'You'll be able to catch up on the wedding arrangements; nobody is talking about much else.' In the darkness she couldn't see the colour leave his face.

'There isn't going to be a damned wedding.'

'W...what are you talking about? Of course there's going to be a wedding; everyone's so excited.'

'For God's sake, woman, you promised me you wouldn't do anything!' he groaned.

'And I haven't.'

'You call saying you'll marry my brother nothing? You're both insane if you think I'm going to let that happen. You can't settle for second-best. I know you think you'll never feel the way about anyone like you did your husband,' he admitted. 'And Roman's got this crazy idea he's never going to find love after being dumped. Dad's been getting to him lately, but believe me he's a lot tougher than he looks.'

'But…Luca…I'm…'

'I know I behaved like an idiot. I know I messed up big time when I proposed, but the idea of you bringing up a baby alone just…I just couldn't let that happen.'

'Why were you willing to bring up another man's child?'

'It wasn't an easy decision to make,' he admitted. 'But once I realised the important thing was that it was *your* child too, I knew what I had to do,' he explained simply. 'These last few weeks have been hell. You must have realised half those calls I put through to the office were just so that I could hear your voice.'

'They were?' she gasped, enchanted by this revelation.

'You sounded so cold and distant,' he accused.

She pressed her hand to his lips. 'Stop it, Luca, I'm not marrying Roman.'

'Damn right you're not,' he growled, kissing her finger.

'He's got engaged to Scarlet.'

'Scarlet?'

'You'll like her,' Alice promised. 'And Sam.'

'Who the hell is Sam?'

'Sam is Roman's son.'

'Dio mio,' he breathed in a shaken voice. 'I have missed a lot. I knew you were here, and when Da said on the phone that I was off the hook because according to Mum the chances

were Roman was finally about to tie the knot...' He appealed to her. 'What was I supposed to think?'

'On past experience, something really stupid. Luca, darling, I'm only crazy about one of the O'Hagan brothers.'

'I got on the first flight I could,' he revealed in a harsh, driven voice. Alice stood there in the darkness, tears streaming down her face, *feeling* the pain she heard in his voice. 'When I reached London I rang...you answered and it seemed like my worst fears were confirmed. If only I'd had the guts to come out and tell you how I actually felt.' He stopped abruptly, his lean body stiffening.

'What did you just say?' he demanded in a raw voice. 'What did you call me?'

'*Darling*. Luca, you asked me to marry you once and I said no...'

'You said more than that, *cara*.' His hand moved to her cheek. 'You're still crying?'

'I didn't mean what I said. I was hurt and angry and I've regretted it so many times since,' she admitted.

'I deserved it,' he said. 'I suppose you realise by now that Da is in no danger of dropping dead if I don't get married. I was wrong.'

'You were a manipulative snake.'

He didn't offer any excuses. 'Listen, I *totally* accept that Mark was an important part of your life,' he told her urgently. 'But you have to move on...'

'I have moved on. Luca, will you marry me?'

The silence stretched until Alice, who had been serenely confident about what she was doing moments earlier, started to think she'd made a terrible mistake.

'What did you say?' His voice was barely recognisable.

'I said will you marry me, Luca?'

'Why?'

She closed her eyes, took a deep breath and stepped right off the cliff. 'Because,' she replied in a clear, confident voice,

'I love you. I love you more than I thought was possible.' The breath whooshed out of her lungs as he enfolded her in a satisfyingly hungry, rib-crushing embrace.

Luca kissed her until she forgot where she began and he ended. While it lasted the rest of the world ceased to exist for Alice.

'Is that a yes?' she asked shakily when they finally surfaced.

Luca ran a finger down her smooth cheek. 'What do you think?'

'I think I'd like to hear you say it.'

'Yes, of course yes, you idiot woman. And of course I love you, Alice, my first and last true love. Why else would I have done what I did tonight? I mean, what sane man would throw his phone over a hedge when the batteries run low and hike ten miles cross country?'

'Gracious,' she exclaimed. 'Is that what you did?'

'Damn right I did.'

'You could have got lost.'

'No. Roman and I know this place like the back of our hands. We used to camp out here—' he gestured towards the sinister-looking craggy peak silhouetted to the north '—and fish through the night on the lough.'

'I can understand your desire to recapture your youthful exploits as a wilderness man but—and I know I'm a tenderfoot, but wouldn't it have been easier to go to the nearest house and use the telephone?'

'Most probably, but you forget you're talking to a man in love here and all I could think about was getting to you.'

'And now you're here.' She couldn't stop smiling. 'Luca, there's something I haven't told you…'

'And what might that be?' he asked lovingly. 'Is something wrong?' he added, suddenly picking up on her tension.

'I don't think so and I hope you won't think so either. I didn't tell you before because—'

'If there was someone else while we were apart I'll understand. It's probably my fault,' he gritted. 'But I don't want to know any of the details.'

'Of course there was nobody else!' The cloud lifted from the moon and she saw the intense relief on his strong face. 'If you must know, I've spent the last few weeks with my head down the toilet.'

He shook his head. 'You've been ill...you are thin...'

'Not ill, Luca, having a baby, your baby.' She pressed her hand to the gentle swell low on her belly and smiled. 'Our baby. I really am pregnant this time.'

If she had had any doubts about his feelings, the look of sheer, incredulous joy and fierce pride that blazed across his face would have put them to rest.

'I knew you'd marry me because of the baby,' she explained quietly. 'I just wanted to know if you'd marry me for me, Luca.'

His electric-blue eyes darkened. 'I'd marry you in a heartbeat.' He took her face between his hands and pressed a long, lingering kiss to her lips. When he pulled back he sighed. 'I'm over the moon about the baby, Alice, but you're the centre of my universe and you always will be.'

Moved beyond words, she felt tears sting her eyelids.

'Hormones...?' he queried, touching his thumb to a solitary tear rolling down her cheek.

She shook her head. 'Happiness,' she corrected huskily.

With an instruction to, 'Hold on tight,' he suddenly scooped her up into his arms. 'Come on, let's go and tell everyone the news.'

'You can't carry me all the way back.'

'I can not only carry you all the way back, I can leap tall buildings.'

'My superhero,' she sighed, looping her arms about his neck. 'Luca, you're not really going to tell everyone now, are you?'

'Of course I am. I want everyone to know how lucky I am.'

'But, Luca, it's the middle of the night and they'll all be asleep.'

He looked unimpressed by this argument. 'Not after I wake them up, they won't be,' he observed with a complacent smile.

'I appreciate you want to shout it from the rooftops, but just for tonight can it be just you and me?'

'It's going to be you and me for the rest of our lives, Alice.'

His blue eyes were filled with so much love that she gasped. Alice suddenly saw the future...their golden future together stretching ahead of them. Could one person have this much happiness...?

'No, you're right,' she said with an impish grin. 'Let's wake up the house!'

And they did. The O'Hagans were proud and stubborn, but wow did they know how to party!

HIRED BY MR RIGHT

by

Nicola Marsh

Nicola Marsh has always had a passion for writing and reading. As a youngster, she devoured books when she should have been sleeping and later, kept a diary whose contents could be an epic in itself! These days, when she's not enjoying life with her husband and son in her home city of Melbourne, she's at her computer creating the romances she loves in her dream job.

Visit Nicola's website at www.nicolamarsh.com for the latest news of her books.

Don't miss Nicola Marsh's exciting new novel *Executive Mother-to-be* **out in February 2008 from Mills & Boon® Romance™.**

CHAPTER ONE

SAMANTHA PIPER needed this job, more than she'd ever needed anything in her entire twenty-five years. OK, so maybe she'd tampered with the truth, changed her surname and taken a crash course in subservience, but it would be worth the price. In fact, she would have done a lot worse to gain employment as Dylan Harmon's butler.

'So, what do you think?' Sam pirouetted in front of her best friend, Ebony.

'Honestly? I think you're nuts.'

'Why? Doesn't the uniform fit? Does it make my backside look too big?'

Ebony rolled her eyes and snorted. 'Oh yeah, like anything could make you look huge! Puh-lease!'

Sam sat down on the part of anatomy in question. 'You're probably right. I am nuts but this is what I want to do. The least you can do is support me.'

Ebony wrapped an arm around her shoulders and squeezed. 'Hey, who's been your biggest fan all these years? And who gave you a crash course in ''bowing and scraping, butler-style''? Not to mention a glowing reference.'

Sam smiled. 'Point taken. Let's just hope that I remember your tips when it comes to the crunch.'

'Oh, when's that? When the dashing Dylan asks you to hold his warmed towel as he steps from a hot shower, water sluicing down his great bod, from his broad shoulders to his—'

'Stop!' Sam clamped a hand over her friend's mouth. 'If I wasn't nervous before, now I'm petrified.'

'Since when has any guy intimidated you? Supergirl Sam, able to leap tall men and their hang-ups in a single bound.'

'If you're referring to my archaic father and his cronies, yeah, I can usually handle them. I hope Dylan Harmon proves to be just as easy.'

Ebony chuckled. 'I'm sure your five hunky brothers would love to hear you describe them as cronies.'

Sam wrinkled her nose. 'To you, they're hunks. To me, they're major pains in the rear end.'

'Whatever.' Ebony glanced at her watch. 'Isn't it time you left? Wouldn't want to miss your flight and be late on your first day.'

Sam noted the time on her bedside clock and grimaced. 'Wish me luck. I'm going to need it.'

Ebony hugged her. 'You'll be fine. Just remember everything I taught you and it'll be a cinch.'

'That's what I'm afraid of.'

Since when had her life been easy? Sam had bucked the system for as long as she could remember, ignoring the old-fashioned views of her parents who were still caught up in the ancient fairytale of their royal blood. So she was descended from Russian royalty? Big deal. The more her family treated her like a princess, the more she wanted to rebel. When her five older male siblings joined her parents in reinforcing her 'duties' as the only princess in the family she'd been pushed over the edge. And the result? A three-month contract in Melbourne as Dylan Harmon's butler, as far as she could get from Queensland, family constraints and their expectations.

What better way to shun family ties and prove her independence than accept a position as some rich boy's servant? Not that she'd told them that. Instead, she'd spun them some lame story about meeting a prospective husband through her friend Ebony and they'd bought it. In fact, her parents had practically pushed her out the door when she'd mentioned the possibility of matrimony to such an influential man as Dylan Harmon. After all, what better way to ensure royal heirs than matching their

princess daughter with the prince of Australia's
landowners?

'Good luck, honey, you'll be fine. And remember, ring me if you need anything.' Ebony blew
her a kiss as she walked out the door, leaving Sam
alone with her thoughts.

Picking up her bag and scanning the room one
last time, Sam hoped to God her best friend was
right. Everything would be fine, as long as she kept
her mind on the job and Dylan Harmon didn't treat
her like the rest of the females in his sphere. She'd
had enough of egotistical, overbearing men to last
her a lifetime and she had it on good authority that
he was one of the best. Defying her brothers was
one thing, gaining the upper hand with one of
Australia's most eligible bachelors would be another entirely. Not that his good looks would in-
timidate her. She loved a challenge in any shape
or form and handling the likes of Dylan Harmon
shouldn't be a problem.

Now all she had to do was believe it.

Dylan Harmon stepped from the shower, wrapped
a towel around his waist and reached for a razor.
While shaving, he heard the bedroom door slam
and assumed it was the new butler his mother had
hired. Not that he'd needed one but Liz Harmon

seemed hell-bent on making his life easier these days.

'Is that you, Sam? I'll be out in a minute.'

Splashing aftershave on his face, he wondered what sort of man his mother had deemed suitable. Sam Piper must be a jack-of-all-trades, as his mum believed he needed someone to lend him a hand in all facets of the business. If he hadn't been so pig-headed, she'd have hired someone a long time ago. They'd argued about his workload for far too long and he'd finally given in, knowing that his mother's interference sprang from concern rather than any great desire to rule his life.

Strolling into the bedroom, he came face to face with a woman. Not just any woman, but a delicate waif wearing a navy blue uniform with the Harmon coat of arms over her left breast. Once his gaze strayed to her chest he had a tough time wrenching it back, for the evidence of her femininity, combined with the uniform, could only mean one thing.

'Hi. I'm Sam Piper. Pleased to meet you.' The woman held out her hand and he continued to stare, taking in her short blonde curls, wide green eyes and heart-shaped face. He wouldn't call her beautiful but there was something he glimpsed in those eyes, some indefinable quality he recognised as class.

He shook her hand, surprised at the firmness of her grasp. '*You're* the new butler?'

She gave a quaint little bow. 'At your service…sir.'

He noted the cheeky pause, the twinkle in her eye. 'Call me Dylan. Though it won't be for long.'

She straightened her shoulders. 'Why is that?'

'Because you're fired.' He turned away and headed for the wardrobe, wondering what had possessed his mother to pull a stunt like this.

'If you're looking for the charcoal suit, white silk shirt and maroon tie, they're hanging on the back of the door.'

He stopped midstride and turned around, surprised that she seemed unperturbed by his putting an abrupt end to her employment. In fact, she hadn't moved an inch and didn't seem at all concerned, when most women he knew would be cowering in the face of the famous Harmon wrath. 'How did you know?'

She shrugged and he noticed the stubborn set of her shoulders, the clasped hands in front of her body. 'You're a man of habit. You always wear that combination on a Wednesday.'

His eyes narrowed. 'Been studying me, have you?'

'Call it research. All part of the job, sir.'

'Don't call me that!' he snapped. He strode across the room and picked up the clothes, wondering when he'd become so predictable. 'What are you still doing here? Didn't you hear me before?'

'I heard you but I'm not going anywhere.'

He stared at the waif. Rather than being intimidated, as most people were around him, she met his gaze directly, not flinching an inch when he moved towards her. 'Care to repeat that?'

Sam squared her shoulders and silently wished for an extra few inches. It was difficult to look threatening when she had to tilt her head back to stare her new employer in the eye, though it provided her with the perfect excuse to stop ogling his near-naked body. Her gaze had been drawn to his towel too often for her liking and she needed something, anything, to distract her. 'You can't fire me. I've signed a three month contract.'

A dangerous glint shone from his eyes, the colour of molten chocolate, and she mentally chastised herself for comparing them to her favourite food.

'Contracts can be broken.' He took a step closer, making her all too aware of his broad, bare chest merely centimetres from her own.

Resisting the urge to run her hands over his muscular pecs and see if they felt as firm as they looked, she struggled to maintain composure. 'I had an intensive interview. I'm sure your mother can vouch that I possess all the necessary skills for this job.'

His gaze perused her body, leaving her in little doubt as to what skills he thought she possessed. 'So, you think you've got what it takes to be my butler?' He quirked an eyebrow, as if daring her to agree.

Sam bit back a smile. Dealing with Dylan Harmon would be child's play after facing her brothers' inquisitions for the last umpteen years. 'If you're after someone with the right attitude, the right qualifications and a genuine love of the job, then yes, I'm your woman.'

Her breath hitched as he smiled at her and she wondered where the helpless, fluttery feeling deep in her gut had come from. She'd never reacted to any man like this, especially one who obviously turned on the charm when it suited him.

'Okay, Miss Piper. Consider yourself on trial for the next three months.' He tipped up her chin and stared directly into her eyes. 'But if you make one wrong move, you're out.'

Sam battled the urge to shut her eyes and block out the hypnotic intensity of his stare. Instead, she took a steadying breath, wishing her erratic pulse would calm down. As a waft of expensive after-shave hit her she clenched her teeth, wishing her traitorous senses would stop misbehaving. So the guy had a great body, soulful eyes, a killer smile and smelled good enough to eat? She'd dated bet-ter and come away unscathed.

Then why the jittery feeling that just wouldn't quit?

'Call me Sam.' She turned away before she did something stupid, like manhandle her boss on the first day.

'Samantha.'

She knew that tone, the one that most males got when they've been beaten and don't want to give in too easily. So he wanted to prove a point by calling her Samantha? No big deal. At least she'd survived his attempted sacking and it had proved to be a lot easier than expected.

'Can I get you anything?' She fiddled with the clothes he'd laid on the bed, hoping he'd send her on an errand that involved being as far away from him and his skimpy towel as possible.

'Actually, yes. Your first job can be to reorgan-ise my underwear drawer. I want it colour coded, neatly arranged and segmented for every day of the week.' His accompanying smirk, casual stance and

quirk of an eyebrow left her in little doubt as to
the challenge he'd just laid down. He wanted to
make her squirm and, strangely enough, the idea
of touching his underwear was doing exactly that.

Heat flooded her cheeks, though she bit back a
host of retorts that sprang to mind about what he
could do with his underwear. 'Fine.'

'Oh, while you're at it, please choose me something to wear today. *Under* my suit, that is.'

Sam risked a glance over her shoulder. She
could have sworn he was laughing at her.
However, he stood in the middle of the room,
hands clasped over the front of his towel, trying
his best to look innocent. She almost snorted at the
thought.

Sam stalked across the room, opened the top
drawer of the dresser and rummaged around. To
her surprise, the first undergarment she laid her
hands on was a thong. Leopard print, no less!

Stifling a grin, she hooked it with her index finger and held it out to him. 'Perhaps this would be
suitable for today?'

His jaw dropped. There was no other way to
describe it, for she'd never seen a guy with so
much poise look so totally and utterly shocked.
'But that's not mine!' he said, a look of distaste
marring his handsome features.

'Oh? It's in your drawer.' The corners of her mouth twitched as she struggled to maintain composure.

'Are you calling me a liar?' He placed his hands on his hips and glowered as the towel around his waist slipped an inch.

The action distracted her and, for one horrifying yet thrilling moment, she thought it might slide down his legs and pool on the floor, along with what was left of his dignity.

Before she could reply, he hitched the towel up, strode across the room and snatched the offending garment out of her hand. 'Give me that! Meg's been up to her tricks again.'

Sam should have known. Meg was probably five-ten, of perfect proportions and had just stepped off the pages of Vogue. 'One of your conquests?' she couldn't resist adding, though what he did in his private life shouldn't concern her in the slightest. Funny though, it did.

'My wayward niece,' he snapped, 'who takes great delight in tormenting me.'

'Way to go, Meg,' she mumbled, thrilled at the thought of any woman getting the better of her suave boss.

'I beg your pardon?'

Resisting the urge to imitate his plummy tone,

Sam schooled her face into what she hoped was a mask of respect. 'Nothing. Should I get started on my first assignment?' She pointedly stared at the thong in his hand.

'Forget it.' He scrunched and flung it across the room, where it landed neatly in the bin. 'As of now, your duties will consist of business affairs only. I'm more than capable of taking care of myself. Consider this room off-limits.'

Fine with her. The less time she spent around the semi-naked tyrant, the better. In fact, everything about the job had worked in her favour to date and she hoped her luck would hold out.

Fixing a placating smile on her face, she nodded. 'Certainly. Where would you like me to start?'

He stared at her for an interminable moment, before turning away and heading to the bathroom. 'Meet me in the study in fifteen minutes. We'll discuss today's agenda then.'

Feeling suitably dismissed, she gave a mock salute behind his back and headed for the door.

'Oh, Samantha. There's one more thing.' His commanding tone halted her and she swivelled to face him. 'Lose the uniform.'

'Now?' The response slipped out before she knew it, typical of the feisty banter she was used to exchanging with her brothers' friends, who were like family. However, Dylan's response was far from familial.

He strolled across the room and leaned a hand on the door, effectively barring her escape. 'Since when did the hired help get so provocative?' His gaze skimmed her face before dropping lower, sending her heart galloping at breakneck speed.

'Since when did the employer think he could ask questions like that?' She stilled as he reached towards her and ran a finger down her cheek, sending her nerve endings haywire in the process.

'Didn't your mother ever teach you not to answer a question with a question?' His finger dropped away as it reached her jaw and, strangely, she missed his brief touch.

'No, but she taught me to stay away from men like you.' She tilted her chin up, determined not to let him see how he affected her.

'Men like me?' He folded his arms, drawing attention to his broad, naked expanse of chest.

Her mouth dried as her gaze strayed to his pecs, noting a light smattering of dark hair that attracted rather than repelled. Swallowing, she looked him in the eyes, hoping her interest didn't show. 'You know. Egotistical, over-confident, world-beaters. Used to getting what they want and letting nothing or nobody stand in their way.'

He smiled, the self-satisfied grin of a cat toying with a mouse. 'Didn't know I was so transparent. Lucky my butler has a degree in psychology as well as servitude. What other talents are you hiding?'

Sam bit back a host of retorts. Thankfully, her mouth and brain had finally decided to work in sync. 'None. Now that we've got you sorted out, perhaps I should make a start on the rest of that servitude stuff and organise breakfast in the study for our meeting?' She had to escape and soon. Having her sexy, bare-chested boss standing too close for comfort was doing strange things to her insides. Not to mention addling her brain.

The warmth drained from his face in an instant and she wondered at the abrupt change. 'Fine. See you there.'

He opened the door and she brushed past him on her way out, wishing he didn't look and smell so darn good. Just her luck that her new boss would be thirty-something and gorgeous rather than ancient and decrepit like most of the rich landowners in Australia.

'One more thing, Samantha.' His serious tone stopped her.

'Yes?' She turned to see him framed in the door-

way, looking every bit the consummate millionaire, even without clothes.

'Welcome to the Harmon world.'

Before she could respond he closed the door,
leaving her with a distinct feeling that while he'd
welcomed her to his world, he'd just turned hers
upside down.

Dylan stalked into his mother's sitting room after
a brief knock on the door.

Liz Harmon looked up from the newspaper she
had spread across the table. 'Good morning, darling. Sleep well?'

With a perfunctory nod, he sat opposite her. 'I
met the butler.'

His mother's face lit up. 'Isn't Sam wonderful?
She came highly recommended.'

'From where? Butlers-R-Us?'

'Don't take that tone with me, young man. What
seems to be the problem?'

Dylan fiddled with the knife-edge crease of his
trousers. 'She's totally unsuitable. Too young, too
feisty, too—'

'Beautiful?' Liz interrupted. 'You did notice,
didn't you, or has all work and no play made you
a dull boy?'

A vision of Sam flashed into his mind, those

startling green eyes staring at him as he'd touched her silky-soft cheek. Thankfully, she'd been looking at his face and not lower, where the evidence of how she'd affected him would have been plain to see beneath the cotton towel.

'I noticed,' he said, wondering if it sounded like the understatement of the year. 'Though what her looks have to do with it, I'll never know. It's her qualifications I'm interested in.'

Liz nodded and gave him one of those knowing smiles, the kind she'd been bestowing since he'd eaten his first bug against her instructions and thrown up, at four years of age. 'She came highly recommended. I spoke with Ebony Larkin, her main referee.'

His eyebrows shot up. 'She's worked for the Larkins?'

Liz nodded. 'Trust me, darling. I wouldn't have hired just anybody to be your butler. I know how much you need the help.'

'I'm doing fine on my own, Mum.'

'No, you're not. Between running the business, inspecting the lands around Budgeree and looking after the family, you're worn out.' She paused and he waited for the inevitable reference to his single status. Predictably, his mother didn't disappoint. 'Besides, you never have time for fun any more.

When are you going to meet a nice young woman to make your life complete?'

'My life *is* complete and I like it just the way it is, thanks very much.' He ignored the swift rising bitterness whenever the subject of women entered their conversations. He'd tried the relationship merry-go-round and had hopped off as soon as humanly possible, managing to get his heart trampled in the process. As far as he was concerned, women and serious commitment didn't belong in the same sentence, especially with females who looked good, had the right family credentials yet lied through their expensively-capped teeth to get what they wanted. Which, in his case, happened to be the Harmon name and fortune.

And he'd worked too damn hard to let his family's wealth fall into unscrupulous hands.

'You don't have to prove anything to anyone, Son. You've taken this business to the next level all on your own.'

'But Dad would've wanted more.' Hell, his ambitious father wouldn't have stopped till he owned the whole of Victoria and then some.

'He would've wanted you to be happy, not running yourself into the ground.' She didn't have to add, like he did.

His workaholic father had taken the word 'work'

to new levels, driving himself to skyrocketing profit margins but into an early grave in the process. Dylan still missed him after ten years.

'Besides, don't you think you're taking the role of family protector a tad too seriously? Most of us can take care of ourselves, you know.'

Dylan rolled his eyes. 'Yeah, sure. Then why is Meg running around placing racy underwear in my drawer? And why is Allie traipsing round the world like a lost soul?' He stared at his mother, noting her wrinkle-free skin, the clear eyes, the black hair with barely a grey streak. 'Not to mention *you*.'

The corners of Liz's mouth twitched. 'Your nieces are more than capable of taking care of themselves. Besides, what have I done?'

He tried a frown and failed. 'You're trying to matchmake yet again. And I'm not interested.'

His mother smirked. 'I'm not trying anything. If you've got romantic thoughts where the new butler is concerned, that's not my doing.'

'The *butler*?' Sam Piper and him, romantically linked? Not a hope in hell. He shook his head, trying to ignore her alluring image again. 'No, Mum, I was talking about Monique and that dinner party you've organised. Didn't you think I'd see through the ruse?'

This time Liz laughed outright. 'You're getting paranoid, love. There's no ruse, no hidden agendas. I just thought it was time we got together with our oldest family friends. If you find Monique attractive, that's up to you.'

Funnily enough, the thought of spending a sophisticated evening dining with the exquisite Monique Taylor and her parents didn't hold half the appeal it once had. He'd grown up with the leggy brunette and had dabbled in a kiss or two once they'd reached their late teens, but he'd never been interested in taking it further. Though Monique was beautiful, educated and attuned to his world, there was no spark to light his fire. Not that she hadn't tried, many times.

Dylan relented. 'Okay, it will be nice to catch up with the Taylors but, just to let you know, there won't be any romance between Monique and I, ever. She isn't my type.'

His mother was no slouch when it came to matchmaking her only son and she latched on to his last words in a flash. 'Oh? Then what is your type?'

A petite woman, with short blonde curls, green eyes he could drown in and a cheeky smile that just wouldn't quit. The thought popped unbidden into his mind and, for the umpteenth time in the last half hour, he wondered if he'd lost a grip on reality since he'd laid eyes on his new butler.

He stood quickly and made for the door. 'Bye, Mum. I have a meeting scheduled.'

Liz smiled knowingly. 'Run all you like, Son, but you can't hide from love for ever.'

Dylan refrained from answering. The day he fell in love would be the day he surrendered his sanity and he had no intention of doing that. He had too much to do yet to fulfil his dad's wishes, the one driving force that kept him going these days.

Him, in love? No way.

CHAPTER TWO

SAM paced the study while waiting for Dylan. She couldn't believe the way she'd reacted to him—stupid, stupid, stupid! She'd known what she was letting herself in for when she had applied for this job. After all, she'd heard about Dylan's charms firsthand from Ebony, whose family had known the Harmons for ever. Ebony had extolled high-and-mighty Dylan's virtues for a full hour before Sam had covered her ears and yelled 'la-la-la'. If she'd heard one more word about the rich, handsome, responsible, caring man soon to be her boss, she would've thrown up.

So, she'd steeled herself for the challenge at hand, knowing that Dylan's looks would have little effect if she set her mind to doing a good job to prove a point to her snobby family. She'd focused all her energy on taking a crash course on butler etiquette, Ebony-style. Thankfully, her best friend had come through for her in every way, going as far as giving her a fake reference when Liz Harmon had called after the gruelling interview she'd endured.

Now that she was here at the Harmon mansion in the posh Melbourne suburb of Toorak, she should be ecstatic. If she could last the distance in this job it would prove to her family once and for all that she could eke out an existence for herself, without their prehistoric expectations for her to marry and produce heirs to continue the royal line. Not that her title meant anything here in Australia; in fact, most of her Russian ancestors had reneged on their royal heritage a century ago, but not her family. They were hell-bent on resurrecting the past and restoring glory to the Popov name. Strangely, many historians here were interested in the Popovs too, which was why she'd had the sense to change her surname when applying for this job.

'So much for obeying orders.'

Sam jumped as Dylan's voice interrupted her musings and she whirled to face him. 'I'm here on time, I've kept out of your bedroom and breakfast is waiting.' She gestured to the sideboard. 'What else did you want?'

He strode across the room and helped himself to a piece of toast and a cup of coffee before sitting behind a large mahogany desk. 'I thought I told you to lose that uniform.'

She frowned, as memories of their intense

exchange in his bedroom flooded back. 'I don't think we agreed on that.'

'You're right. We didn't get to finish that conversation, did we?' He stared at her over the rim of his cup and she could have sworn she read desire in his eyes.

Great. Despite her mental pep talk a few minutes earlier she still harboured ridiculous fantasies where her spunky boss was concerned. He could have any woman in the world and she thought *she'd* captured his interest in half an hour? Yeah, right.

'I thought all your staff wore uniforms.' She tried her best to look demure, clasping her hands behind her back. How she'd last more than a week in this subservient act, she'd never know. For some strange reason this man brought out the worst in her. She felt compelled to trade quips with him, to ruffle his oh-so-suave feathers, to get the better of him in any exchange.

He placed his cup on the desk and rested steepled fingers on his chest. 'Not my personal assistant.'

'I'm your butler, not your PA.' Somehow, the title of PA conjured all sorts of vivid images of how personal she could get with the delectable Dylan.

'You've just been promoted. If you're up to it, that is.'

He'd done it again, known exactly how to push her buttons. As if she would ever back down from any challenge he threw at her.

'So you're that impressed with me, huh?'

He shook his head. 'No need to fish for compliments, Samantha. I've read your résumé and I'm intrigued. Why would a woman with a degree in economics want to work as a butler? And, even better, work for a man with a reputation for being a hard taskmaster?'

She squared her shoulders and hoped that the little white lies she had to tell to keep this job wouldn't show on her face. 'I enjoy a challenge. Working for someone with your vast experience in the business world will be a bonus, if and when I decide to enter that field.' She hoped her answer would satisfy his curiosity—when in doubt, flatter.

He quirked an eyebrow. 'You're not some kind of spy, are you?'

Sam sighed. 'Your mother checked out my credentials and I'm sure you've discussed my appointment with her by now. What do you think?'

'I think that if you're half as good as your résumé says you are, you'd be perfect as my PA. So, what do you say?'

Okay, she wasn't completely stupid. Being
Dylan's personal assistant would be a heck of a lot
more interesting than bowing and scraping to him
and a lot less damaging. After all, she had a lot
less chance of seeing him almost naked as his PA
than as his butler. 'I accept. Thanks for the opportunity.'

He nodded his approval. 'Good. Now that's settled, let's get started. I need to dictate some letters
that need to be sent ASAP. While I do that, you
can sort through this pile of invoices. In monthly
and alphabetical order please, with the most urgent
bills to be paid uppermost.'

She took the pile and seated herself opposite
him, thankful for the huge desk. No chance of accidental contact across a great divide of mahogany,
though there'd been nothing accidental about the
way he'd caressed her cheek earlier that morning.
Though she tried to concentrate on the task at
hand, she couldn't resist sneaking a peek as he
spoke into a Dictaphone, his low tones soothing
her. He'd dressed in the outfit she'd predicted earlier, though it looked a heck of a lot better on the
man than on a hanger.

Visions of their morning interlude drifted into
her mind and, before she knew it, she'd mentally
undressed him down to the skimpy towel he'd

worn as he'd strolled into his bedroom looking a million dollars. How she'd managed to maintain composure, she'd never know. At least those boring drama classes at high school had been good for something. Old Mrs Lincoln would have been proud of her You don't affect me one bit performance she'd given Dylan that morning.

At that moment, the man in question hit the 'stop' button and looked up.

'Having trouble keeping up?' He pointedly stared at the pile of invoices in front of her and raised an eyebrow.

Fighting a losing battle with a rising heat that flooded her cheeks, she shook her head. 'Sorry. I was just thinking.' Lame, even by her standards, but what could she do when the object of her lustful fantasy was glaring at her with those dark eyes that screamed, Come and get me?

'About what? Some old boyfriend you've left behind in Sydney?'

'I'm not from Sydney.' She responded without thinking and, predictably, he pounced on her answer.

'But I thought you'd been working for the Larkins?' His stare intensified, leaving her squirming like a bug under a ten-year-old's magnifying glass in the sun.

Crossing her fingers behind her back, she hoped her voice remained steady. 'I was, but I'm from Brisbane originally.'

'Ah.' Before she could breathe a sigh of relief, he continued, 'So, what about the boyfriend?'

For a moment, she hoped he was asking out of interest in her as an available woman, before reality set in. The likes of Dylan Harmon would never be interested in the hired help, unless it was for one thing. And she had no intention of making that bed or lying in it.

'You're my boss, not my owner. My private life is none of your business.' She folded her arms in a purely defensive gesture, wishing she could ignore that probing stare. Unfortunately, her action drew his stare downwards before he quickly returned his gaze to her face.

'That's where you're wrong. You'll be spending a lot of time travelling between our outback property and Melbourne, with little time off for socialising. I need to know that you're one hundred per cent committed to this job. Otherwise, I'll find someone else.' He picked up a pen and tapped it against the desk, as though impatiently awaiting her answer.

Though it went against the grain, she had to tell him about her private life—or lack of one. She needed this job and she hadn't come this far to lose it now. 'There's no one special in my life at the moment. You'll have my entire focus for the time I'm employed.'

His face softened at her response. 'Good. I need all your attention…for the tasks at hand.'

His pause, combined with the subtle change in body language as he leaned towards her, sent her imagination spiralling out of control again. She stared at him, caught in the hypnotic intensity of his smouldering eyes, wanting to look away yet powerless to do so. If she didn't know better, she could have sworn that he felt the bizarre attraction she'd conjured up out of thin air too.

'Are you free tonight?'

She blinked and resisted the impulse to nod like a schoolgirl being asked out on her first date. 'That depends on you.'

He smiled, the rare flash of brilliance illuminating his face and sending her heart hammering in her chest. 'Oh, really? How so?'

Ignoring her pounding pulse and wondering how she could control her treacherous reactions to her handsome boss, she said, 'I didn't know the hours I'd be expected to work. Your mother suggested I discuss it with you.'

'So, if I say I need you tonight, you're mine for the evening?'

Oh-oh. She didn't need this sort of encouragement. Her overactive imagination was doing fine on its own, thank you very much, without help from his innuendo.

She cleared her throat. 'As your butler, I would've expected to work evenings. As your PA, I thought most work could be accomplished during the day.'

His smile broadened, if that were possible. 'Not for what I have in mind.'

Thankfully, the intercom buzzed on his desk, saving her from answering. She took a deep breath and wondered if he played word games with all his female staff. Was he actually flirting with her or was her limited experience with men rearing its head?

Dylan hit the speaker button. 'Yes, Mum?'

Liz Harmon's voice filtered through the intercom. 'I was wondering if you could spare Sam for a moment? I need to discuss a few things with her.'

He looked up at his new personal assistant, who had her head bent over the stack of invoices and was sorting them into several neat piles as if her life depended on it. 'Sure, as long as it doesn't take too long. I've upgraded her position from butler to

PA and we have a mountain of work to get through.'

His mother chuckled. 'This, from the man who said he didn't need help?'

He studied the way Sam's hair fell in loose curls around her face, the slight frown that marred her smooth forehead, the flicker of her tongue as it darted out to moisten her top lip. He'd noticed she'd done that earlier, when he'd first strolled out of the bathroom and seen her standing in his bedroom, and several times since; he assumed it was a nervous reaction, though it sure as hell drove him crazy every time she did it. How could such an innocuous movement elicit the wayward thoughts he'd been experiencing about what the gorgeous Sam's tongue could be doing to him?

'Dylan, you still there?'

Wrenching his thoughts out of the gutter, he replied, 'Yes, Mum. I'll send Samantha right up.'

'Thanks. Oh, and by the way, you're welcome.'

He smiled as his mother's chuckles petered out and he disconnected. 'Leave those for now. You can get back to it later.'

Sam looked up and, once again, the luminous green of her eyes hit him like a blow to the solar plexus. It wasn't the colour so much as the clarity that shone like a beacon, beckoning him to chal-

lenge her, taunt her, flirt with her, anything to get
her looking at him with more than a passing interest from an employee for her boss. That was what
had prompted him to offer her the job as his personal assistant—the more time she spent in his
company, the more chance she might look at him
with the spark he'd glimpsed when he'd caressed
her cheek that morning. That one, fleeting flare of
fire in her eyes had aroused him more than any
other woman had in a long, long time.

She stood up and he had a chance to admire the
snug fit of the uniform. He had a real hankering to
see her without it—hell, he wished he could see
her trim body with nothing at all—but, right now,
he'd settle for anything else in her wardrobe. For
some strange reason she had too much poise, too
much class, to be wearing a uniform and he didn't
need any reminder of her status as his employee.
If he had his way she'd be far more than that by
the end of her three month stint; it had been far
too long since he'd had a lover.

'About my working hours?'

He resisted the urge to shake his head; ever since
she'd walked into his life this morning, his mind
had been enveloped in a fog that clouded his every
thought. Even now, he could barely remember

what they'd been discussing before his mother had interrupted.

'We'll discuss it later.' He waved her away, noting the stiffening of her shoulders, the straightening of her spine. Once again, it hit him that she didn't like taking orders and he wondered what on earth had prompted her to take this job. Something about Sam Piper didn't ring true and, lovely as she was, he had every intention of finding out exactly what secrets she hid behind that sexy façade.

'Fine.' She nodded before turning on her heel and walking towards the door, giving him free rein to ogle her slim legs and tantalising butt.

Though she'd said everything was fine, he seriously doubted it. Her rigid posture screamed that it wasn't, not by a long shot. And, if his confused libido were anything to go by, he'd have to agree.

Sam slowly exhaled as she closed the study door. She must be insane to contemplate going through with her plan if she couldn't even last the morning in Dylan's company. Heck, could he see how she practically swooned when he smiled at her? And, as for his asking if she was free tonight, she'd had to restrain herself from leaping over the desk and straight on to his lap!

Men had never affected her this way; she'd al-

ways managed to keep her relationships strictly
platonic, preferring male friends to the groping
Neanderthals that some of her dates had turned into
at the slightest encouragement. Even some of the
'pillars of society' that her brothers had set her up
with had turned out to be marauding sex maniacs
and she'd managed to avoid their embarrassing ad-
vances with aplomb. So maybe that made her naïve
when it came to men, but did it totally explain her
over-the-top reaction to Dylan?

What made him so special that every self-
preservation mechanism she'd ever used seemed to
malfunction whenever he so much as looked at
her? Whatever it was, she needed to get a handle
on it quick smart. Heck, that was all she needed,
her new boss to think she had some childish crush
on him.

Taking a deep breath, she knocked on the door
to Liz Harmon's sitting room.

'Come in, Sam.'

Sam opened the door, wondering what the older
woman could want. After the initial interview they
hadn't crossed paths, though she'd taken an instant
liking to the elegant Liz.

'You wanted to see me, Mrs Harmon?'

Liz waved towards a chair. 'Take a seat, child.
And please, call me Liz.'

Keeping her surprise from showing, Sam perched on the overstuffed chair and folded her hands in her lap.

Liz reached for a leather-bound book on a nearby table and opened it. 'I know all about you, dear.'

She fixed Sam with a piercing stare, leaving her in little doubt as to what she meant. Sam clenched her hands till the knuckles whitened, trying to buy valuable time to compose an answer that wouldn't incriminate yet sounded honest at the same time.

However, Liz continued before she had the chance to speak. 'There was something about you that looked familiar at the interview, so I followed a hunch. I'm a great fan of history, you know.'

In that instant, any hope Sam harboured that the older lady was just fishing for information vanished. Schooling her features into a polite mask, she said, 'I can explain—'

'Please.' Liz held up her hand. 'Indulge an old lady for a moment.' She flicked a few pages before stopping at what looked like a family tree and tracing a line with her finger. 'You must be Princess Samantha Popov. Am I correct?' She looked up expectantly, not a trace of anger on her face.

Sam didn't know where to look, an embarrassed heat flooding her cheeks. She'd been caught out in her lie and on the first day! She nodded, not quite understanding the excited look on the other woman's face. 'You're right. I'm sorry for lying to you but I really needed this job.' She stood quickly, wishing the Persian rug beneath her feet would disappear and the ground underneath would open up and swallow her. 'I'll pack my things and be out of your way as soon as possible.'

Liz slammed the book shut, sending a cloud of dust into the air. 'Don't be hasty, child. We have so much to talk about.'

Sam shook her head in bewilderment. If Liz had appeared excited a moment ago, she now looked downright ecstatic. 'I don't understand. You want me to stay?'

Liz waved her back to the chair she'd just vacated. 'Of course. I'm sure you had a very good reason for lying to obtain this job and I want to hear it. I also want to hear every last detail of your story, without a single omission.'

'So, I'm not fired?' Sam held her breath, praying for a miracle yet knowing they rarely happened, at least to her.

'Fired? My dear, you've just made my day.'

'How so?'

Liz grinned, the expression on her face rivalling that of a child on Christmas Day. 'If my son thought finding an attractive woman as his butler was a surprise, wait till he finds out I chose him a princess to boot!'

Sam's heart plummeted. If Dylan found out her background she'd be out of the Harmon mansion so fast her head would spin. She needed to stay, at least till the trial three months were up. Anything less and her family wouldn't be convinced she could make it on her own and she'd be back to square one, enduring their rigid conditions and stipulations regarding her life.

Right now, she needed to convince Liz Harmon that keeping her identity a secret was the best thing for all concerned, even if it meant keeping it from her precious son. Taking a steadying breath, she looked up and met the older lady's gaze directly. Seeing the twinkle in her eye, she hoped to God that Liz wanted in on the secret, otherwise she'd be back in Brisbane and pledged to some ancient groom before she could blink.

Tied to some fossil in matrimony because it suited her royal parents and their antiquated ideas? Uh-uh.

Liz leaned forward. 'Start at the beginning, dear. And tell me everything.'

Resisting the urge to grimace, Sam did as she was told.

CHAPTER THREE

SAM hated confusion. She preferred order, precision and being in control. However, as she joined Dylan for a late night supper in his study so they could continue working, she knew that her preferences had flown straight out the window following her meeting with his mother. Rather than berating her for lying and sacking her, as she'd expected, Liz Harmon had almost clapped her hands in glee as Sam regaled her with a truthful account of her life to date. In fact, the older woman had been only too pleased to keep Sam's secret so she could continue in her farcical role as Dylan's PA.

But why? Sam needed to know people's motivations; it was the only way to stay one step ahead. However, she had no intention of giving Liz Harmon the third degree when the woman had done her a huge favour. In fact, for someone who barely knew her, Liz had accepted her version of events with few qualms. In her place, Sam knew she wouldn't have been as trusting.

'Daydreaming again?'

Sam jumped as Dylan strode into the room and wondered if she'd ever get over the fluttery feeling in her gut whenever her boss came within ten feet of her. In over a week, her absurd physical reaction to the man hadn't dimmed one iota. If anything, her responses made her want to do all sorts of wild and wicked things, such as strip off and lay across his desk! Maybe then she'd have some hope of grabbing his attention, for that was all he seemed interested in—the endless stream of paperwork crossing his desk, taking up every minute of his day.

She must have imagined his flirtation and innuendo on her first day, for he'd lived up to his reputation as a cold, calculating business tycoon ever since. In fact, his love for the family business bordered on obsession and she wondered if he ever loosened his tie, took off his shoes and took a stroll barefoot in the lush gardens surrounding the mansion. By the serious look on his face as he glared at her, she doubted it.

'Daydreaming is healthy. You should try it some time.' She noted the tense neck muscles, the lines around his mouth, the smidgen of dark rings under his eyes and hoped that her banter might lighten his mood.

He piled a plate with club sandwiches and

grabbed a caffeine-laden soft drink from the sideboard before responding. 'Who says I don't?'

'You don't look like the type to indulge in fanciful dreams.' Heck, he couldn't look any more uptight if he tried. He wore a different suit, shirt and tie for every day of the week, each outfit expertly tailored but boringly conservative and she'd yet to see him with a hair out of place. Except that first morning in his bedroom—though she'd managed to effectively block out that provocative memory.

He quirked an eyebrow. 'Daydreams are wasted. Maybe I prefer to *indulge in fanciful dreams* at night?'

Sam looked up quickly, wondering if she'd imagined his lowered tone, the slight husky edge. He stared at her, dark eyes unreadable, as he took a casual bite out of a tuna and mayonnaise sandwich. She swallowed, trying to ignore the sudden wish that she could replace the sandwich as his supper. She wouldn't mind him nibbling on her, not one little bit.

Spurred on by the urge to match wits with him, she took a sip of her coffee and feigned innocence. 'What you do at night is no concern of mine.'

'Would you like it to be?'

Damn, he was good. Just when she thought

she'd got the better of him, he sent her a loaded comeback like that.

Resisting the urge to grin, she said, 'Depends. I thought I'd worked enough nights lately. There's only so much typing, filing and bookkeeping a girl can take.'

'I wasn't talking about work.'

'Oh?' Her heart hammered in her chest as she tried to hide behind her coffee mug. She loved playing games, especially with a man as sharp as Dylan and she wondered how far she could push it, though every ounce of common sense urged her not to match wits with her boss.

'You've been doing a great job, Samantha. I'm pleased with your work and you've hardly had a night off since you started. How would you like a tour of Melbourne by night?' He devoured the last of the sandwiches, concentrating on his plate as if her answer meant nothing to him. However, she noticed he ran a finger around the inside of his tight collar, a gesture she'd noted only when he seemed rattled.

She smiled, her heart threatening to burst out of her chest. 'Sounds great. Know any good tour operators?'

He looked up and fixed her with a piercing stare, the chocolate depths of his eyes drawing her in, deeper than she'd ever been or intended to go. She could drown in those eyes, spend a lifetime floundering in their mysterious warmth.

'Why settle for good when you can have the best?'

'You're that confident, huh?'

'You'll just have to try me and find out.' He smiled, that killer smile she'd rarely glimpsed since the first day, yet her response had intensified tenfold.

She knew accepting his invitation wasn't a good idea. It sounded suspiciously like a date and she had no intention of getting involved with her boss. As if her life wasn't complicated enough. However, she did want to see Melbourne and what better way than a personal tour with a man who set her pulse racing? If the scenery bored her, she could always cast surreptitious glances his way.

'Okay. I'd like that.' Who was she trying to kid? She almost had to sit on her hands to prevent herself from clapping like an excited child.

'Good. I'll make the arrangements and let you know.' He stared at her for a moment and, from the intense look in his eyes, she thought he might say something else. However, he merely cleared his throat and picked up a stack of contracts. 'Let's get back to these. Now, where were we?'

Masking her elation proved difficult, though Sam managed to keep her mind on the job. She had plenty of time to fantasise about her evening out with Dylan once she reached the confines of her bedroom later that night. In the meantime, she'd better continue doing a good job, for she had no intention of letting him renege on his offer. A night out on the town with a gorgeous guy? It had been far too long…

Dylan sighed in resignation as he straightened his tie. Though he'd been looking forward to catching up with the Taylors, the planned dinner had lost some of its appeal when he realised it would keep him away from the office for the evening. He hadn't felt so alive in years, ploughing through reams of work all day and into the nights, relishing the sense of achievement, Sam by his side…

Suddenly, an unwelcome thought insinuated its way into his brain and he wondered if his renewed enthusiasm for the job had anything to do with the actual work or everything to do with his stunning personal assistant. He shook his head, trying to dislodge her image and his disturbing thoughts from his mind. So what if she'd been by his side, working into those long nights? He'd barely had time to notice her, he'd been so hell-bent on putting the finishing touches on a contract to acquire more land in northern Victoria.

Sure. He hadn't registered the slim ankles, the trim waist, the curve of her breasts, the lightly-glossed mouth… He groaned, wrenching his way-ward thoughts away from her glorious pout and what she could do with it—to him. He couldn't believe he'd been so stupid, insisting she ditch the uniform. At least he'd managed to keep his mind somewhat on the job when her lithe body had been encased in boring navy. Now, with the array of suits she wore each day, his imagination had taken flight, wondering what a stray button undone or removing a lacy camisole would reveal. Though she didn't dress provocatively, he wished he'd kept his big mouth shut. And now he'd invited her on a night out—Lord only knew what outfit she'd pro-duce to add to his sleepless nights.

Another strange phenomenon—since Sam had entered his life, his ability to sleep through the loudest thunderstorm had mysteriously vanished. Instead, night after night, her image filled his head in an erotic kaleidoscope, making slumber impos-sible. He hadn't had such vivid dreams since his teenage years and it rattled him. He shouldn't be having *those* thoughts where Sam was concerned. Dammit, she was his employee! And a valuable one at that. He couldn't bear the thought of losing her so early into her contract. He'd just have to keep his thoughts under control.

A loud knock interrupted his musings and for a second he wished it were Sam, back in her role as butler. Thankfully, he'd had the sense to change that little arrangement—the thought of facing her in his bedroom as he had the first day sent his self-control spiralling downhill. He may be strong-willed but he wasn't a saint.

'Come in.'

His mum stuck her head around the door. 'Ready, darling? The Taylors have arrived.'

He nodded and followed her out. 'Remember what I said, Mum. No matchmaking.'

He didn't like his mother's sly grin. 'Wouldn't dream of it, darling.'

Sam towel-dried her hair, donned her oldest jeans and a cutoff top and settled down to watch a movie. Though she'd enjoyed working late with Dylan most evenings, having a night off was a welcome relief. He'd told her he had old family friends coming to dinner and she'd leaped at the chance to spend some quiet time alone. Since his invitation their working relationship had become fraught with a weird kind of tension. She'd caught him staring at her several times, an unfathomable expression in his eyes. If she hadn't known any better she'd almost think he felt the same bizarre attraction she did, though perhaps it was just a figment of her over-stimulated imagination?

That had to be it. Her last date had been ten months ago and had ended like the rest of them, with her fending off groping hands. So Dylan had invited her out? No big deal. He'd made it clear that it was thanks for the work she'd done, not a date. She'd been the foolish one to put that connotation on it.

Wishing she could stop thinking about him, she reached for her bag of supplies. She'd walked to the local shops earlier and stocked up on her favourite 'stay-in' food: chocolate biscuits, dried apricots, cashew nuts and Turkish Delight. Ebony shared her weird taste in snacks and they'd spent many nights curled up on the couch, watching horror movies and scaring themselves silly.

She missed her best friend, their weekly phone chats not the same as sharing every piece of their lives, as they usually did on a daily basis and had since they'd met at boarding school all those years ago. Thank goodness Ebony had moved to Brisbane permanently after school had finished; who else would have kept her sane all these years if she hadn't had a friend to off-load her family dramas to?

When her hand came up empty, Sam searched around the room before realising she must have left the bag of goodies in the kitchen when she'd grabbed a light dinner earlier. Thankful that the Harmons would be busy entertaining their guests and no one would see her outfit, she darted down the hall towards the kitchen. However, as she rounded a corner near the guest bathroom, she almost collided with Cindy Crawford's double.

'Watch where you're going!' the sultry brunette spat out as she smoothed a hand over her shiny, shoulder-length locks.

'Sorry,' Sam murmured, feeling like one of the ugly stepsisters standing next to Cinderella at the ball.

The beauty wrinkled her nose. 'Who are you anyway?'

Resisting the urge to wipe her hand down the front of her jeans before she offered it, she replied, 'Sam Piper. I'm Dylan's personal assistant.'

Predictably, the other woman's eyebrows shot up. '*You're* the PA he's been raving about?'

Pride filled Sam, though it was quickly replaced by some strange emotion she could easily label as jealousy. This supermodel look-alike could only be one of the Taylors, the 'old' family friends Dylan had told her about. Funnily enough, when he'd said old she'd assumed he referred to their ages as well as the length of their acquaintance.

Sam squared her shoulders, though she fell inches short of the towering woman in front of her. 'Yes, I'm very good at what I do.'

'And what's that?' The haughty tone of Cindy's double echoed in the marble hallway.

Sam didn't like being spoken down to, she never had, and she responded in impish fashion. 'I'm there for Dylan in whatever capacity he needs me. After all, that's the service a *personal* assistant should provide, don't you think?'

The woman's beautiful features contorted into ugliness in a second. So Sam's barb had hit home? That meant that the woman had more than a friendly interest in Dylan and, strangely enough, the realisation filled her with dread. There was no way she could compete with this stunner—not that she had any intention of doing so. The sooner she realised that fantasising about her boss was off-limits, the easier this job would become.

'I think your work speaks for itself, Samantha.'

Sam jumped as Dylan's voice rang out. Mortification filled her as she wondered how much of their conversation he'd overheard. Raising her eyes to meet his, she was unprepared for the appreciative glow in his gaze as it skimmed her faded jeans with the tear above one knee to the expanse of skin exposed by her skimpy top.

'Thank you.' She didn't know if her gratitude stemmed from the verbal compliment or the approval in his stare. 'I'll leave you two to get back to dinner.'

'So, you've met Monique?'

Sam shook her head. 'Not officially. We sort of ran into each other.'

'Oh?' Dylan stared at her, intense, probing, and she had the sudden feeling that he could look into her very soul and see her animosity for the other woman just simmering below the surface.

Monique laughed, a fake sound to match the rest of her. 'Yes, it was quite amusing, actually. No harm done, Miss Piper?' As the brunette laid a possessive hand on Dylan's arm, Sam wasn't so sure about the harm bit.

Right now, she had a distinct urge to harm someone and she was looking straight at her. Instead, she schooled her face into a polite mask. 'Nice to meet you. Enjoy your dinner.'

She hurried down the hallway and into the kitchen without a backward glance. If that was the type of woman Dylan wanted, he could have her.

She would ignore his mixed signals, stop reading more into them than was necessary and do what she had come here to do. Losing sight of her goal at this early stage into her employment would be disastrous. She still had a long way to go to prove a point to her family and getting 'ideas' where her spunky boss was concerned would only prove detrimental.

As the memory of his simmering stare returned, she knew that focusing all her attention on her goal and less on Dylan was going to prove a lot harder than she had initially thought.

Sam snuggled deeper into the cushions, ignoring the incessant pounding that threatened to disrupt the delightful dream she'd been having about her two favorite film stars fighting over her. However, the noise intensified and she reluctantly struggled back to consciousness, vowing to watch that DVD again in the hope of rekindling the dream.

Glancing at her watch, she was surprised to see she'd dozed for over an hour and it was well after midnight. Padding across to the door, she opened it, rubbing sleep from her eyes.

'What do you want?' She frowned up at Dylan, knowing she sounded like a recalcitrant child.

She'd never been any good on wakening, whatever time of day or night.

'I needed to see you.'

She stepped away from the door, letting him into the small sitting room. 'Now?'

He picked up the DVD cover from the coffee table and pointed to the picture. 'Yes, unless you were expecting him?'

Her cheeks flooded with heat. 'Don't be ridiculous.'

He laughed, a warm, rich sound that reached out and enveloped her in an intimate cocoon. 'Someone's got a crush.'

'I have not!' She folded her arms and glared at him, wishing he would leave her alone. It was hard enough spending time with him in the study each day; having him in her room, standing there as if he owned the world and knew it, was not conducive to her peace of mind. Maybe she did harbour fantasies about film stars, but they were unattainable—unlike the living, breathing fantasy before her, who she could reach out to and…

'Are you all right?' He closed the distance between them, his signature aftershave washing over her in a sensuous wave.

She inhaled, infusing her senses with the smell, knowing the potent combination of aftershave and pure Dylan couldn't be good for her health yet doing it anyway.

'I'm just tired,' she murmured and turned away, not ready to face his tenderness. She preferred his bossy, tyrannical side to this gentle caring, which could undo all her good intentions in a second.

'I've been working you too hard, haven't I?'

To her amazement, he reached out to her, laid his hands on her upper arms and turned her around to face him.

'N-no,' she managed to stammer out, as her skin burned beneath his touch. Though he hadn't stroked or caressed, the nerve endings in her body had taken on a life of their own beneath his scorching hands and were firing all sorts of mixed messages to her overheated imagination.

'You're telling me the truth?'

Oh, heck. If he only knew. 'I'm fine, Dylan. How did the dinner party go?' She had to move on to safer ground, grasping for any topic that would wrench her mind away from the reaction of her treacherous body to his touch.

He dropped his hands, leaving her hankering for more. Though she knew it wasn't right, she wished he'd slid his hands around her, wrapped her tight and kissed her senseless. 'The usual get-together. Fine food, fine wine, boring small talk.'

Sam tried to keep the bitterness out of her voice as the image of Monique rose before her. 'Really? Seems like you and Monique would have loads to talk about. Sharing childhood anecdotes, making plans for the future...'

He stared at her, the corners of his mouth twitching. 'Are you jealous?'

'Of course not! She just seems to be the perfect woman for you.'

'And how do you know that?' The twitching had broadened to a smirk and she wished her attention wouldn't keep focusing on his lips.

She shrugged. 'Call it intuition.'

He took a step closer, once again invading her personal space and sending her pulse racing. 'Monique is not my type.'

Sam knew he was baiting her. She knew she shouldn't ask the next question. However, with his dark eyes hypnotically boring into hers and his body standing so close she could feel the heat radiating off it, she went ahead and did it anyway.

'What is your type?' she asked, soft and breathy, flicking her tongue out to moisten her top lip.

He didn't answer her question. Instead, his head descended with infinite slowness, his lips brushing hers with skilled patience. She sighed and melded into him, his muscled chest brushing against her breasts, setting her body alight. Resistance was a fleeing thought, quickly discarded, as his mouth closed over hers and he kissed her expertly, leaving her breathless, clinging and yearning for more. He tasted of port, rich and sweet, and she longed to prolong the kiss, the moment, for as long as possible.

For this was no ordinary kiss. Sam knew from the minute his lips touched hers that the fiery reaction of her body, the urge to take this to the next level so quickly, the total loss of self-consciousness, had everything to do with the man giving her the toe-curling kiss of a lifetime. She'd never experienced anything like it before and, damn him, she'd be spoiled for any future experiences.

She pulled away, needing to refocus before she lost complete control and dragged him into the bedroom. Though her sexual experience was extremely limited, Dylan and his earth-shattering kiss had awakened a latent passion she hadn't known existed.

'We shouldn't have done that,' she whispered, reluctant to break the silence that enveloped them.

He stared at her, his passion-hazed gaze doing little to still her hammering heart. 'Probably not.'

He ran a finger down her cheek, feather-light. 'Though at least we've established one thing.'

Her breath hitched as his finger followed a lazy trail along her jaw line before dropping to her collarbone. 'What's that?'

'I know what my type is.'

Sam struggled not to gape as he smiled and walked out the door.

CHAPTER FOUR

DYLAN knew he shouldn't have kissed Sam. Apart
from being totally unprofessional, irrational and in-
explicable, it made sleep impossible for the next
week. Every time he closed his eyes, her provocative image danced before him, faded denim hugging her lean legs and some sort of short top that
should be banned barely skimming her flat, tanned
midriff. The minute he'd seen her standing next to
Monique he'd had a hard time tearing his gaze
away from that bared expanse of flesh that just
beckoned to be touched.

So what had he done? Made up some lame excuse about needing to see her and barged into her
room, manhandling her in the process. Not one of
his smarter moves. But then, nothing he'd done
since Sam had entered his life made much sense.
He'd never needed a personal assistant before, yet
she'd insinuated her way into his business, making
herself seem indispensable. Hell, he hardly made a
move these days without asking her opinion.

Since when did he need anyone's help? He'd run

the family business with little assistance from anybody all these years and done a damn fine job. He knew his dad would have been proud, though, funnily enough, it didn't ease the burden, the endless drive of proving that he was the man of the family. From an early age, his dad had drummed the ideals of loyalty, responsibility and family obligation into him and he hadn't forgotten a single lesson. In fact, he'd spent most of his life living up to his dad's values and hadn't regretted a single moment.

Until now.

Somehow, Sam's presence in his life had opened a void he hadn't known existed. Though he couldn't put his finger on it, she made him feel ancient, as if he'd lived a lifetime yet had nothing to show for it. Stupid, considering he owned one of the largest tracts of land in Australia.

Shaking his head, he shrugged into his jacket and headed for the door. So much for trying to ignore her; he'd invited her on a personalised tour of Melbourne and, though he didn't want to go through with it, he had no choice. By his own warped sense of duty, he felt he owed her. And, if there was one thing his dad had taught him, he always paid his dues.

*　　*　　*

Sam tried on and discarded several outfits before settling on black evening trousers and a ruby top. She rarely wore skirts on a first date.

First date? Where had that come from?

She wrinkled her nose at her reflection, wishing she hadn't been looking forward to this evening so much. No matter how much she'd tried to convince herself this was just a night out as repayment for her hard work, she couldn't forget Dylan's kiss or the way he'd stared at her every day since. Though she'd tried her utmost to concentrate on her work, whenever she looked up and found him staring at her she lost all train of thought and struggled to give one hundred per cent to her job.

And now, she had to spend a whole evening in his company without the safety net of pen, paper or endless invoices. No hiding behind business questions or typing dictated letters. Instead, she'd be forced to make small talk and, God forbid, face possible interrogation about her personal life. Not to mention the more daunting prospect of facing Dylan at his charming best. If he flashed her that killer smile and stared at her with those chocolate-brown eyes for more than ten seconds, she'd be a goner.

Dashing a slick of gloss across her lips, she hoped she had more willpower than she'd shown that night he'd come to her room. She should have pushed him away and given him a verbal barrage in the process. Instead, she'd submitted to that mind-blowing kiss with all the fierceness of a purring cat. All she'd needed to do was roll over and beg for her tummy to be rubbed, an action she'd been perilously close to doing before she'd pulled away.

As if on cue, a knock sounded at her door. Straightening her shoulders and taking a deep breath, she opened it, doing her utmost to appear nonchalant.

'Hi. Ready to go?'

Ready and raring.

Dylan smiled and, for a horrifying second, she wondered if she'd spoken aloud. However, he continued to stare at her, obviously awaiting her answer.

She nodded, wishing her heart would stop hammering a staccato beat. 'Lead the way.'

'The view's that good, huh?' His grin broadened and she wished she'd had the sense to refuse his invitation.

Fighting a rising blush and losing, she brushed past him and stalked ahead. 'I wouldn't know. Haven't really checked it out.'

His chuckles followed her down the hallway and

out to the car, where she leaned against the door and tried her best to look nonchalant.

'By the way, you look great.' He opened the passenger door for her, a waft of woody aftershave washing over her and sending her already reeling senses spiralling dangerously out of control. 'And, from where I stand, the view is sensational.'

Sam didn't reply, knowing she'd say something incriminating, like, Take me, I'm yours. Instead, she muttered her thanks as he slid into the car and she fished around for a safe topic of conversation.

'So, where are we off to?'

'Dinner at Southbank, a cruise up the Yarra, coffee on the observation deck of the Rialto. And anything else that takes your fancy.'

She risked a quick glance at his face, noting the relaxed lines, the slight smile tugging at the corners of his mouth. She'd never seen him this laid back and it scared her; if she couldn't resist him at his stern, business best, she had no hope with this new, appealing Dylan.

'Let's just take it as it comes, okay?'

'Sounds good to me.'

He drove with the expertise of a man used to handling the large recreational vehicle and she wondered if he was bad at anything. She'd never met a man who exuded such charisma, such confidence, in everything he did. If he ever turned his expertise to seducing her, she'd be a pushover.

He pointed out several landmarks as he drove, saving her from making conversation. Not that she could have strung more than two sensible words together; if she thought working in the confines of a study was hard, being enclosed in a motor vehicle with a man who smelled good enough to eat was doing strange things to her insides.

Unfortunately, once they were settled at an intimate table for two at a plush seafood restaurant, had ordered their meal and had their wine glasses filled, he refocused his attention on her.

'So, tell me the Samantha Piper story.'

Almost choking on her wine, she cleared her throat and made a lightning-fast decision to stick to as much of the truth as possible. 'Not much to tell. I come from a fairly conservative family, with five brothers who are major pains. I've done a degree but I'd prefer to get some hands-on life experience before I pursue a career in the field.'

'Five brothers? Bet your dates got a rough time.'

She rolled her eyes, remembering the painful interrogations, the endless probing for information that the few guys she'd dated had to endure. 'Don't remind me.'

'So how many dates were there?' He pinned her

with a fierce stare, as if trying to drag her darkest
and deepest secrets from her.

She shrugged and bit back a grin. 'I lost count
after the first fifty.'

'*What?* You can't be serious?'

'Deadly.' She smiled and mentally counted the
men she'd had the misfortune to go out with on
one hand. None had measured up to the man sitting
opposite her and for one brief second she wished
they'd met under different circumstances. For there
was no way she could let anything develop between them, not when her presence in his life was
based on a lie. 'Why are you so interested in my
life story anyway?'

'It pays to know who I'm working with.' He
avoided her eyes and Sam knew he was hiding
something. Someone had burned him before and
obviously the memory still lingered, intensifying
her guilt at deceiving him tenfold.

'Speaking of work, when do we leave for
Budgeree?' She tried to sound casual, thankful to
move the topic of conversation on to safer ground.

'In the next few weeks.' He sipped at his wine
and leaned back, the earlier tension while he'd
been grilling her gone. 'Funny, I didn't pick you
to be the outback type. Sure you're ready for the
barren plains?'

She bit back a grin. 'There you go again, trying to figure out what "type" I am. So tell me, what is the outback type? Brawny women in flannel checked shirts and jodhpurs, cracking whips and rounding up their men along with the cattle?'

He rolled his eyes. 'Nice stereotype. I just picked you to be a city girl. Something in the way you dress…' He trailed off as his gaze skimmed her top, lingering a second too long on her cleavage, before returning to her face.

Sam tried not to squirm, the intensity of his stare sending her pulse skyrocketing. Thankfully, she was saved from answering by the arrival of their meals and quickly focused her attention on the plate of steaming scallops in front of her. As she speared one of the plump molluscs and bit into its juicy freshness, he notched up the heat by reaching across the table towards her.

'You have some parsley right about there.'

She looked up, trapped like a deer in oncoming headlights as he brushed his thumb across the corner of her mouth and let it stray to her bottom lip. She stilled, resisting the powerful urge to turn towards his hand and nibble on his finger. Lord, if he didn't remove his hand this second, she'd do something they would both regret.

'Thanks,' she mumbled, bowing her head and

wishing for longer hair to shield the dazed expression she knew must be spread across her face.

'No problems.' His voice sounded strangely husky and she wondered if he had any idea of the sort of effect he had on her. She'd never experienced such a profound sense of confusion when it came to a man, the jittery nerves, the racing pulse, the hollow stomach. If she didn't know better, she'd swear these were the symptoms of the fabled 'love' that Ebony was always raving about, the emotion that she'd scoffed at and swore to permanently avoid. Heck, if her best friend could see her now, she'd laugh till her sides hurt.

As she mopped up the last of her garlic sauce with bread, Sam risked a glance at Dylan. Relishing the luxury of studying his impressive profile as he turned to gesture at a waiter, she didn't notice the man walking purposefully towards them. Until it was too late.

'Hey, Princess. Fancy seeing you here.'

Sam's attention snapped back as her heart sank. Quade Miller, her eldest brother Dimitri's best friend, towered over their table with a smug look on his face as he glanced from her to Dylan and back again.

She clenched her hands under the table, wondering how much Dimitri had told Quade about her journey to Melbourne and wishing that he wouldn't call her princess. All her brothers and their mo- ronic friends had called her that for as long as she could remember, delighting in the fact that she hated it.

Pasting a bright smile on her face, she made the necessary introductions. 'Hi, Quade. How are you? By the way, this is Dylan.'

Quade's grin broadened as he shook Dylan's hand. 'Nice to meet you. Heard a lot about you.'

'Oh?' Dylan quirked an eyebrow and gave Quade the same supercilious look she'd seen on his face countless times before, the one reserved for people who displeased him in some way.

'Yeah, Sam keeps her family informed of her goings on.' Quade sent another cheeky grin her way. 'Way to go, Princess. So everything I've heard is true?'

Please don't blow it, she silently wished, know- ing that one wrong word from Quade could send her plans straight to hell, with her lying soul along with them.

'Possibly, though you know how that brother of mine loves to gossip.' She deliberately kept her response light, knowing he would report back to Dimitri and her family, who thought she was head over heels in love with Dylan Harmon, her prospective husband, as she had implied to them.

Quade winked and jerked his head in Dylan's direction. 'Well, in this case, I think he's hit the nail on the head. Seems like all the speculation is correct.'

Dylan continued to glare daggers in Quade's direction and Sam knew she had to get rid of the other man fast. So far, so good, but all it would take was one stray word...

'Nice seeing you, Quade. Though, if you don't mind, we'd like to finish our dinner.' She sent a warm smile in Dylan's direction, hoping Quade would get the hint.

Thankfully, he did. 'Sure thing. You have fun.' He nodded at Dylan. 'Nice meeting you, Dylan. I'm sure I'll be seeing more of you in the future.'

Sam swore she heard Dylan mutter, 'Not if I can help it' under his breath as Quade walked away and joined a large party at a table across the room.

'Who was he?'

She noted the tensed jaw muscles, the thinned lips and wondered why Quade had made Dylan so uptight. If anyone should have been uncomfortable, it was she. She'd been so sure Dylan would read something into her rigid posture and stilted answers, yet here he was, looking like an actor who'd forgotten his lines on opening night.

'An old friend.' She sipped her water, suddenly thankful for the opportunity Quade had presented her. Though she'd spoken to her family over the phone and tried to convince them that her continued absence meant she was growing closer to her prospective 'husband', Quade's back-up story that he'd seen her having a cosy dinner with her intended would be just what she needed to keep their prying noses at bay.

'Boyfriend?' Dylan almost spat the word out and she wondered at his sudden turnaround.

'Jealous?' She almost chuckled at the notion, but the strange look that flitted across his face made her wonder.

'Of *him*?' He made it sound as if taking on Quade and winning would be child's play. 'Of course not. Just curious, that's all.'

Eager to put the whole episode behind them and get the evening over and done with as quickly as possible, she said, 'Quade's a friend of my brother. We practically grew up together.'

This time, she definitely saw relief in Dylan's face and wondered at the reason behind it. She'd only been teasing about his possible jealousy. Surely he couldn't care about her? No way. She was the one prone to lively fantasies around her delectable boss and if he showed one inkling of interest in return she'd have a hard time keeping them locked where they belonged—in her fanciful head.

'Let's finish up here and take that cruise.' Thankfully, he seemed just as eager to ditch the subject of Quade and the meal ended peacefully, with mundane small talk scattered between the courses.

However, just as she'd managed to replace the lid on her fantasies surrounding Dylan, he went and did something that pried it open.

He kissed her. Again.

CHAPTER FIVE

DYLAN had known this evening would end in disaster yet he'd gone ahead anyway, consequences be damned. From the minute he'd laid eyes on Sam in her slinky black trousers and shimmering red top his caveman instincts had risen to the fore and all he'd wanted to do was drag her back to his room and make long, slow love to her all night long. Ridiculous, really, as he'd never had that urge with any other woman in his past.

Sure, he'd done the dating rounds, but each and every relationship had soured when the women had revealed their true colours. They'd never been truly interested in him, the major attraction being marrying into the Harmon name and fortune. Since the last disaster over three years ago, he'd sworn to avoid lying women. Perhaps that explained his attraction to Sam?

She was a refreshing change from the contrived, artificial women that usually graced his path, from her tousled blonde curls to her quirky sense of humour. She teased him, reeling him in with a beguiling openness that had him hankering for more.

And what had he done about it?

The one thing that he'd sworn he wouldn't do again. He'd kissed her. Correction, he'd devoured her till they'd both been breathless and in dire danger of being tipped into the icy Yarra River. Rather than berating him, she'd had the audacity to laugh!

'Stop it. It's not funny.' His mouth twitched with the effort of trying not to laugh.

Peals of laughter rang out, drawing curious glances from other couples drifting along the river in nearby gondolas.

'Sam!'

Her chuckles petered out and she stared at him with those wide green eyes that had bewitched him from the first minute he'd seen her.

'That's the first time you've called me that.' She'd sobered up quickly and managed to wriggle away from him, putting as much distance between them as possible, no easy feat in the narrow boat.

'What?'

'Sam. You usually call me ''Samantha'' in that plummy accent of yours.'

'I don't have a plummy accent.'

'Do so.'

'Do not.'

She smiled, the moonlight glinting off her teeth.

'Who would've thought, the high-and-mighty Dylan Harmon reduced to bickering like a child?'

'Must be your influence.' He poked out his tongue like a ten-year-old trying to prove a point.

Her expression sobered as she stared at his tongue, her intensity reviving memories of the scorching kiss they had just shared moments before.

It had started so innocently, with her excited jiggling rocking the boat and he'd admonished her, reluctantly admitting that he couldn't swim. She'd proceeded to rock the boat even more, till he'd seriously thought they might tip into the river. So he'd done the first thing that entered his mind to stop her; he'd reached for her and held her within his arms. However, he hadn't planned the part where she tilted her head up with that playful smile tugging at the corners of her mouth, merely inches from his own.

He'd lost it then, his lips crushing hers before he'd known what he was doing. Her response, startling in its eagerness, had only served to fire his libido and they'd kissed like two teenagers, barely coming up for air. In fact, he would have taken things further if the violent swaying of the boat hadn't brought him back to the present and he realised their predicament. If common sense wasn't a passion-dampener, maybe a dip in the cold depths of the Yarra would be?

And what had she done? She'd laughed at him, loud, infectious chuckles that just begged him to join in. So much for keeping his distance where his luscious employee was concerned. He'd landed himself smack bang in the middle of a situation he had no idea how to extricate himself from. Thankfully, she seemed to have more common sense than he did at the moment.

'At the risk of rocking the boat, how about that coffee you mentioned earlier?' She smirked and all he could do was stare at the slight dimple that flashed in and out at the corner of her mouth.

He folded his arms, wishing that the simple defensive gesture could hold his wayward emotions at bay. 'Sounds good to me. I think you've done enough boat rocking for one night!'

'Spoilsport,' Sam murmured, watching him as he used the pole to manoeuvre them towards shore. She'd never been on a gondola before, believing that Venice had the monopoly on them. She'd been pleasantly surprised when their cruise on the Yarra entailed a trip in one of the long, narrow boats, until Dylan had sat next to her on the padded seat and she realised exactly how small the boat was. If she'd had a hard time controlling her imagination at dinner, she had no hope in the confines of a boat with his muscular body pressed up against her, radiating enough heat to spontaneously combust her on the spot.

And what had she done? Behaved like a mischievous imp in the hope her antics would distract from the urge to snuggle into his arms. Instead, they'd backfired, sending her straight to the place she'd wanted to avoid. Not that the experience had been unpleasant—far from it. If she thought their first kiss had been mind-blowing, this one had been earth-shattering and more. Boy, did the man know how to kiss? Dylan managed to ignite sparks that quickly exploded into fireworks, leaving her dazed and seeing stars.

She floated through the rest of the evening, barely noticing the stunning views of Melbourne from the top of the Rialto building while sipping a creamy latte. Though she'd done her utmost to convince herself this wasn't a date, it had been one of the best evenings she'd spent with a man in a long time. In fact, on a scale of one to ten, it scored a twelve.

It wasn't till later, when she'd thanked him for a 'nice' evening with a polite nod of her head, that it struck her. Despite their strong working relationship, the main common link they shared, they hadn't discussed business once tonight and her intentions of maintaining a professional distance from her hunky boss had taken a serious nosedive. And, to make matters worse, she had no idea how to re-establish the boundaries again.

As the sprawling homestead came into view Sam tried not to bounce on the leather seat in excitement.

'Welcome to Budgeree,' Dylan said, audible pride in his voice.

'It's breathtaking.' Understatement of the year, thought Sam. The surrounding landscape had held her enthralled for most of the trip, yet nothing Dylan said could have prepared her for the beauty of his family's property.

As the car swept up the circular drive to the front porch, she admired the wide verandas, French doors and floor to ceiling windows that dominated the huge house. Despite its size, it didn't detract from the beauty of the land beyond, towering eucalypts dotting the landscape between native Australian flora.

'Since when did you get to love the outback so much?' He'd switched off the engine and turned towards her, curiosity evident in his face.

'I've been to my fair share of remote areas in Queensland.'

'I thought you were from Brisbane?'

Guilt flooded her; she hated having to lie, especially to a man like Dylan. 'I've travelled a fair bit.'

He quirked an eyebrow. 'You've done a lot for someone so young. How did you manage to fit it all in?'

Heck, how could she tell him that she'd lived most of her life in Queensland, making regular trips to her family's outback properties whenever she could? She'd woven a tangled web and the closer she got to Dylan the more likely she was to tear down the whole deception.

She shrugged and reached for the door handle, eager to escape the confines of the car and Dylan's probing questions. 'Hey, I'm a woman of many talents. Haven't you worked that out by now?'

His eyes glowed as the sun set, bathing them in a kaleidoscope of fiery colour: burnt orange, deep purple and shocking magenta. 'Oh, I'm well aware of your talents, Samantha.' The burning intensity of his gaze scorched her, eliciting an excited shiver that started at the nape of her neck and travelled all the way to the tips of her toes.

She bolted from the car without saying a word,

wishing she could turn off her traitorous emotions. She read too much into every word he said and it would get her into trouble, big trouble. Thank goodness they'd be chaperoned for the next few days, otherwise there would be no telling what she'd be tempted to do.

'Looks like Ebony's arrived,' she called over her shoulder, looking forward to spending some time with her best friend. Though Dylan had initially been surprised at her friendship with a once-employer, he'd suggested she invite Ebony to stay as a chaperon; his old-fashioned values seemed overly-quaint, though she'd welcomed the opportunity. She'd missed their frank, girlie chats, though she'd have to stay on her toes not to let slip her burgeoning feelings where Dylan was concerned. Ebony was no fool and her best friend was renowned for putting two and two together and coming up with five.

'Great. It's been a couple of years since I've seen her,' he said, carrying their bags to the front door.

Before he could insert his key into the lock, the door flew open and Ebony raced onto the verandah and straight into Dylan's arms. 'Hey, stud. Long time no see.'

Sam struggled not to gape, a war of emotions

tearing through her, ranging from joy at seeing her best friend to stabbing jealousy at seeing Ebony draped over Dylan. And his reaction to her gorgeous friend didn't assuage her concern.

He pulled back a fraction and looked her up and down. 'Wow, look at you, *Bony*. You've filled out and then some.'

Ebony chuckled. 'Not so bony any more, huh?'

'Yeah, you can say that again.' He wolf-whistled as Ebony twirled, revealing long, tanned legs beneath a peasant skirt that screamed designer.

Sam stepped forward, wanting to deflect the attention away from Ebony and hating herself for it. 'Hi there, stranger. How are you?'

Ebony squealed and enveloped her in a bear hug. 'You're looking absolutely fab. Obviously, working for this tyrant can't be all that bad.'

Sam squeezed her back, wondering how the green-eyed monster could have raised its ugly head where her best friend was concerned. Why shouldn't Ebony greet Dylan with such enthusiasm? After all, they'd been family friends for years.

She pulled away and glanced across at the man in question, who looked surprisingly smug. He watched them both with an amused expression on his face, as if the thought of two women discussing him was a new experience, one he found exceedingly pleasant.

'Oh, you'd be surprised, Eb. Working for this guy can be hell at times.'

'Is that right?' Dylan winked at her and she nearly fell over. If she didn't know any better, she'd swear he was flirting with her and in front of Ebony, no less.

'We're going to have a great time,' Ebony said, wrapping her arms around their waists and dragging them towards the front door. 'And not too much work, you two. Time to live a little.'

Sam blushed. Funnily enough, she'd already taken Ebony's advice and look where it had got her. As much as she tried to deny it, she'd fallen for her boss and there wasn't one damn thing she could do about it.

CHAPTER SIX

SAM waited for the knock she knew would come. As if on cue, a loud rapping sounded at the door before it flew open and Ebony barged into her room.

Ebony threw herself face down on Sam's bed and rested her chin in her hands. 'Tell me *everything*. And don't leave out a single detail.'

Sam smiled and wondered how she'd survived the last few weeks without their chats. They'd shared every detail of their lives for as long as she could remember, yet how could she begin to describe the strange feelings her boss aroused within her? She could barely admit to them herself. She shrugged, aiming for nonchalant. 'Not much to tell.'

Ebony threw a pillow at her. 'Don't give me that! You're glowing and it can't be the smoggy Melbourne air that's caused it.'

Sam sat cross-legged on the floor next to the bed and stared up at her best friend. 'What can I say? I love my job.'

'You sure it's just the job you love?' Ebony wiggled her eyebrows suggestively and clutched at her heart.

'What else could it be?' Sam looked away quickly, tracing imaginary circles on the plush carpet.

'Oh-oh,' Ebony groaned. 'It's worse than I first thought. You've fallen for him, haven't you?'

'Don't be silly,' fibbed Sam. 'I'm just enjoying the challenge of working as a PA rather than sitting around and waiting for my crazy parents to marry me off to some decrepit old fool.'

'Speaking of which…' Ebony trailed off and Sam looked up. The expression on her friend's face didn't reassure her; far from it.

'What have they done this time?'

Ebony sighed and rolled her eyes. 'Well, that rat Quade told them you and Dylan are joined at the hip and should be announcing your engagement any day now.'

'So what's wrong with that? That was one of the major reasons I took this job, to get them off my case.'

Ebony held her hand up. 'Not so fast, Cinderella. Your folks are saying that if the announcement doesn't happen ASAP, they're going to ''send Max down to Melbourne to drag you back to Brisbane and up the aisle, no excuses this time'', end of quote.'

'What?' Sam leaped to her feet and started pacing the room. 'They can't seriously believe I'd consider marrying that old fogey? I've already told them how I feel.'

'You know your folks. They won't take no for an answer. They expect you to start acting like a princess, sooner rather than later.'

'How did you hear all this?' Sam stopped stomping around and stared at her friend.

Ebony blushed. 'Peter told me.'

'Don't tell me you still have a thing for my buffoon of a brother?'

Ebony shook her head as the rose colour staining her cheeks deepened. 'No, we're just friends. I happened to run into him at a charity dinner last week, that's all.'

Sam snorted. 'You're taste in men is deteriorating, as much as I'd love to have you as a sis-in-law.'

Ebony unfolded her long legs from the bed and stood. 'Hey, it's not my taste in men we're discussing here, it's yours.' She laid a hand on Sam's shoulder as her voice lowered to a conspiratorial level. 'Is it serious with Dylan?'

Sam paused before answering. If she told her

best friend the truth, would Ebony accidentally let something slip to Dylan? After all, they'd been friends for a long time and Ebony was renowned for her 'slip of the tongue' comments. Sam knew Dylan was probably toying with her—heck, he didn't have a reputation as one of Australia's most eligible bachelors for nothing. So what if he'd kissed her a few times and flirted like a pro? He probably did it every day of the week with the women in his sphere. She'd been the stupid one for reading more into it and she didn't need her best friend reinforcing it.

She swallowed and hoped her voice didn't quaver. 'Dylan's my boss. He's a nice guy and I enjoy working with him.' She hoped her evasive answer would satisfy her curious friend. After all, she hadn't lied—she just hadn't told the whole truth either.

Ebony tut-tutted. 'I know you, Sam. You're hiding something. And I could've sworn you wanted to tear my eyes out earlier when I threw myself at Dylan.' She chuckled. 'Why else do you think I did it? Nothing like testing the water.'

Sam grimaced, remembering her earlier jealousy. She hoped she wasn't that transparent; no wonder Dylan had looked so smug. 'Test all you like, *Bony*.'

Ebony's chuckles grew to raucous laughter. 'You *are* jealous. Though don't worry, I'm not interested in Dylan. I have other fish to fry and they're a whole lot more tastier than him.'

Sam seriously doubted that. She'd never met a man who compared to Dylan Harmon. It wasn't just his charm, his charisma or his looks, not to mention the fact he kissed like a dream. No, he exuded some indefinable quality that attracted her, against her better judgement. Now all she had to do was hide it for the next few months.

'So what are you going to do about your parents?'

Sam wrinkled her nose. 'Don't remind me. As long as they stay in Brisbane and keep that hound Max off my tail, I'm safe.' She paused for a moment, then clicked her fingers as an idea flashed into her head. 'That's where you come in.'

'Huh?'

Sam wrapped an arm around Ebony's shoulder. 'As my best friend, I see it as your duty to look after my interests.'

'What do you think I've been doing? Don't forget who got you this job in the first place.'

Sam nodded. 'I know, but I need your help. If you could feed back some vital info, like how close I am to Dylan, how an announcement isn't far off, how happy I am in Melbourne with him, then wouldn't that assuage their curiosity?'

Ebony's eyes narrowed. 'And how am I supposed to do this?'

Sam delivered her *coup de grâce*. 'Why, through your good *friend* Peter, of course. I'm sure you could arrange another *accidental* meeting.'

Once again, colour suffused her friend's cheeks. 'OK, smarty-pants. Maybe I have got a thing for your brother and our meeting wasn't so coincidental. But lying to him? Doesn't exactly help my cause, does it? What if he finds out? He won't look twice at me.'

'Please, Eb,' Sam cajoled. 'You don't want me married off to an ancient crony like Max and whisked away to Europe, do you?'

'As if that would happen,' Ebony snorted. 'Max is as Australian as you.'

'Who thinks like my father, a refugee of Russia's fifteenth century. So, what do you say? Will you do it?'

A mischievous gleam shone from Ebony's dark eyes. 'OK, I'll do it for you. On one condition.'

Doubt flickered through Sam. She desperately needed Ebony's co-operation if her plan was to succeed but she'd never been any good at paying a price. After all, wasn't that what had dragged her

into this mess in the first place? Her parents, thanks
to their old-fashioned European values, felt she
owed them and her heritage in some way. And,
according to them, the only way to do it was to
marry a fellow descendent of the Russian aristoc-
racy and produce a dozen royal heirs.

'What's the condition?'

'You put in a good word for me with Peter.'

Sam sighed in relief. Pointing out Ebony's good
points to her Neanderthal brother would be a small
price to pay for her friend's co-operation. 'Fine.
Though personally I think you need your head
read.'

'No accounting for taste, is there?'

Sam heard the uncertainty in her friend's voice
and remorse flooded her. Who was she to judge
where matters of the heart were concerned? Look
at the mess she'd made of her own love life.

She hugged Ebony. 'I'm glad you're here, Eb.
It'll be great catching up. I've missed you.'

'Ditto.' She squirmed out of Sam's arms.
'Enough of the mushy stuff. I'll leave you to un-
pack. See you at dinner.'

As Ebony left the room Sam wondered if she'd
seriously lost her mind. Here she was, working for
a man she grew to like more with each passing
day, lying to her family about the true relationship

they shared and hoping that the two would never meet. She must be nuts! *Or desperate*, she thought.

All she had to do was last a few more months; then she would tell her parents the truth, that she'd never really been involved with Dylan, that she'd been working for him and had proved that she could earn a living and eke out an existence without the protection of a man. Surely they would have to believe her then?

Turning to her overnight bag, she crossed her fingers behind her back.

Dylan sat on the veranda, enjoying the cool night air. Being at Budgeree never failed to invigorate him, every sound and scent wrapping him in a comforting familiarity. He'd grown up here, sticking close to his dad, learning the ins and outs of the business that his dad had valued more than life itself. Until he'd grown up, or so he'd thought at the time.

After all, what was so grown up about abandoning the family to spread his wings, traipsing around the world in search of the next best thing? Surprisingly, it'd been under his nose all along but he'd failed to recognise it. And his selfishness had killed his dad in the process.

'Feel like some company?'

He looked up at Sam and bit back his first retort of, Not really. Funnily enough, she fitted in around here, a fact that had surprised him. It wasn't her worn jeans, denim shirts or leather boots that gave him that impression; instead, it was just a feeling, an instinct that she genuinely belonged in this isolated countryside.

He gestured towards the rocking chair. 'Have a seat.'

She settled into the chair, the creaking wood reminding him of nights long ago when he used to perch on his mum's lap and she'd tell him wonderful stories about bunyips and wombats, while the night sounds of hooting owls and wheezing possums lulled him to sleep.

'You look like you're doing some serious thinking.'

'Just old memories.' He gazed out at the growing darkness, wishing it didn't feel so damn comfortable to be sitting here with her. He didn't want to feel this way where Sam was concerned. She'd be out of his life sooner rather than later and he'd had enough of losing people who mattered to him.

'Sure I'm not intruding?'

He heard the vulnerability in her voice and wished they had met in another time, another place. He wasn't ready for a relationship right now, no matter how wonderful the woman. Besides, he had enough responsibilities with the family and his dad's legacy and he would never shirk them again. Look what had happened the last time he'd done that.

He smiled. 'No, it's nice to have company out here. Usually I'm on my own.'

'Not that you seem bothered by that. I get the feeling you're a bit of a loner.'

'Psychoanalysing me again, Samantha?'

She chuckled, the light sound eliciting a response that was almost visceral. Who was he kidding? God, he had it bad. Though he'd done his best to keep their relationship strictly platonic since they'd been out here, he couldn't forget the few forbidden kisses they'd shared or the way she'd responded to him. Hell, wasn't that one of the reasons he'd invited Ebony out here, to act as some sort of Edwardian chaperon? Unfortunately, that little plan had backfired, as the wayward Ebony seemed to delight in taunting him and throwing the two of them together as much as possible. Though he'd known Sam had worked for the Larkins, he had had no idea the two girls were such firm friends. One woman ganging up on him at a time was more than enough.

'You're too complicated to figure out. Besides,

why should I bother?' Her smile lit up her eyes. She was one of the few people he knew who smiled like that, with her whole face and not just an upward movement of her lips.

'Aren't you up for the challenge?' A gradual warmth started in the vicinity of his chest and spread outward, making his insides do strange things as he contemplated the ways in which he would seriously like to challenge her. Starting with more eager responses from her luscious lips…

'I thrive on a challenge. Thought you'd have figured that out by now.' She fixed him with an indescribable stare from her cat-like eyes. 'After all, I work for you, don't I?'

He laughed, a genuine deep chuckle that echoed through the ghost gums. It felt good. In fact, it felt downright wonderful and he wondered how long it was since this place had heard any serious laughter. 'Touché, Miss Piper.'

A slight frown marred her perfect features as she looked away. 'Tell me about your life here.'

Surprised at her swift change of subject, he gave her the edited version. 'Budgeree's thousand acres was the first tract of land my dad bought here. Though he expanded the business over the years, this place held a special place in our hearts.' He paused, ignoring the stab of guilt that memories of his father and his love of the land always seemed to ignite within him. 'Still does.'

'Family means a lot to you, doesn't it?'

Her innocuous question unerringly honed in on his emotion whenever he sat in this very place and surveyed the property that would belong to the Harmons for generations to come. 'Family is everything.'

'But don't you ever feel stifled? Or need to run away?' He heard something in her voice that made him look up but when he studied her face the serene expression hadn't altered though she wouldn't meet his eyes.

'Never. Shirking responsibilities is for children. Or cowards.'

Sam's heart sank as Dylan's cold, curt words rang through her head. What would he think of her if he knew the truth, that she was one of those cowards that he'd just mentioned with such antipathy and loathing?

She responded more sharply than intended. 'Not everyone is cut out for shouldering the burdens of their family.'

He pinned her with a stare that took her breath away: intense, probing, willing her to listen. 'I wouldn't consider family expectations a burden. How about you?'

He had her there. She couldn't tell him yet another lie, not when she was living a lie every day.
'Everyone's family is different. Maybe I'm just not
ready to shoulder what my family expects me to.'

'Is that why you ran away?'

Ouch! He sure knew how to kick a girl when
she was down. She instilled as much calm into her
voice as she could muster before answering. 'I applied for a job working as your butler. How could
that be classed as running away?'

He shrugged, the simple action drawing her attention to the broad shoulders encased beneath a
cable knit and speeding up her pulse in the process.
'Call it a hunch. Even though you said you needed
the experience before branching into the business
world, I still don't understand why you'd want to
work for someone like me in such a role.'

'We're not all meant to be rulers in this world.'
She almost spat the words out, wishing she could
denounce her heritage as easily. For that was exactly what her family expected her to be, some rich
princess to sit upon a pretend throne and order
those around her to do her bidding. Hell would
freeze over before she succumbed to their wishes.

'Are you judging me for what I have and what
I do?' His dark eyes didn't waver as his stare bored
into her very soul.

She almost flinched at the icy contempt in his voice. If he only knew that she wasn't referring to the Harmons but her own illustrious Popov family, the masters of expectation.

She stood quickly, suddenly eager to escape before she said something she might regret. 'I'm not judging anybody. Goodnight, Dylan. See you in the morning.'

She walked away without looking back, missing the speculative gleam in Dylan's eyes as he admired her fluid movement.

Sam was hiding something, no doubt about it. She'd just reinforced the feeling he'd had when he'd first employed her and he would now make it his personal business to find out exactly what it was.

CHAPTER SEVEN

SAM knew she shouldn't do it. Every fibre of her being screamed that accompanying Dylan to this business dinner was the wrong thing to do, but what choice did she have when the man she fell for more and more each day had practically begged her?

She thought she'd been clever, pushing him away since they'd returned from Budgeree. However, her little plan had backfired and all she'd succeeded in doing was inflaming Dylan's curiosity further. Though their working relationship continued to flourish, he'd fired several probing questions at her when she'd least expected it, as if trying to discover her deepest secrets.

And now this.

Flying to Sydney with Dylan and attending some big function as his partner was *not* her idea of keeping her distance. Or her cool. She'd barely survived their week at Budgeree together and if Ebony hadn't been there she knew she would have done something stupid. Strangely enough, she'd felt a sense of peace, of belonging, at the isolated homestead that she'd yet to find elsewhere.

Initially, she'd put it down to the rugged beauty of the surroundings and the tranquillity that always seemed to pervade the outback. However, as the week passed in a flurry of business meetings, land surveillance and bookkeeping, she'd realised it was something more. Despite the giant chip of family responsibility that Dylan carried around on his broad shoulders, she'd grown to recognise that he thrived on it and, for a brief, irrational moment, she'd imagined what it would be like to share his dream, his vision, of making the barren tract of land flourish.

'You've been awfully quiet.'

She almost jumped as Dylan turned towards her, wishing the business class seats had more room between them. She'd been all too aware of his proximity since they'd first boarded the flight and even now, as he stared at her with those enigmatic dark eyes, had to resist from leaning into him.

'Just taking some time out. My boss is a slave-driver, you know. I barely have a minute to myself these days.' She rolled her eyes, enjoying the light-hearted expression that crossed his face whenever they exchanged this sort of banter. For a man his

age, Dylan Harmon was far too serious. Time for
him to lighten up—if that were possible.

'Your boss values your input, that's why he
drives you so hard.'

'Is that right?' She smiled, wondering how far
she could push him. 'So, is that why you invited
me along to this dinner? Because you value my
input?'

A flicker of appreciation shot through his eyes
as he stared at her lips. 'There are many reasons
why I invited you to this dinner.'

Her heart picked up tempo as he continued to
stare at her and she wondered what demon drove
her to flirt with him. She knew it was dangerous,
she knew it was wrong. Yet the gleam of desire in
his eyes was all the encouragement she needed.
'Why don't you tell me a few?'

He paused for a moment and she could've sworn
that he leaned even closer. 'You're smart, witty
and gorgeous, three attributes I value in a dinner
companion. How's that for starters?' His warm
breath caressed her cheek, sending a scattering of
goosebumps across her skin. She was playing with
fire and, if she wasn't careful, would get seriously
burned.

'Gorgeous, huh?'

'Come on, Samantha. Don't tell me I'm the first

man to ever tell you that.' He took hold of her chin and tilted her face upwards, scrutinizing it with the expertise of an art critic evaluating a priceless piece.

Sam could barely breathe, let alone respond, as his thumb gently brushed her bottom lip.

'You must have men falling at your feet, ready to whisk you up the aisle at a moment's encouragement.'

His words doused her like a bucket of cold water as an image of Max flashed across her mind. Though tall and distinguished for a man of fifty, there was something about the way he stared at her that made her skin crawl. Why would a man that age, who had everything that money could buy, want to get married to a girl he'd watched grow up? Several ideas crossed her mind, none of them pleasant.

She pulled away from Dylan, breaking his tenuous contact. 'I have no intention of traipsing up the aisle with any man.'

He raised an eyebrow at her sharp retort and she quickly softened it before his curiosity prompted him to ask any probing questions. 'I prefer to keep the hordes of men falling at my feet guessing.'

'Oh, really?'

She nodded, wishing he wouldn't stare at her

with those all-seeing, all-knowing eyes. 'Nothing like a bit of mystery to keep a man on his toes.'

'Is that why you won't tell me anything about yourself? Sticking to the old adage of "treat 'em mean, keep 'em keen"?'

'There's not much to tell.' She crossed her fingers, hoping God wouldn't strike her down for telling such a monstrous lie.

He smiled and her heart gave a treacherous lurch. 'You didn't ask if I was keen after the way you've treated me.'

The lurch gave way to pounding as her heart thundered in her chest. 'I treat you as a boss.'

'Yet I'm still keen.' He reached across and squeezed her hand, his touch sending her precarious sense of self-control spiralling downhill fast.

Hoping her voice wouldn't shake, she took a steadying breath before responding. 'I'll be leaving in a few weeks. Do you think it's worth starting something?'

'It's too late.' He interlaced his fingers with hers, drawing her hand to his lips. 'It's already started.'

His kiss burned into the back of her hand, leaving a scorching imprint like a brand. Suddenly, she realised it was true. They *had* started something, yet for the life of her she couldn't figure out what it was. Mutual attraction, deep friendship or a whole lot more?

As the plane descended into Sydney, Sam reclaimed her hand and fervently wished that, whatever she was feeling, it wasn't a 'whole lot more'. Falling in love with Dylan would be the stupidest thing she'd done in a long time—apart from running away from her family and agreeing to become his employee in the first place. But what if it was too late?

As Dylan slipped into his tux jacket and adjusted his bow-tie one last time he hoped that this evening wouldn't be too boring for Sam. He'd attended countless other dinners like this where rich land-owners mingled, talking 'shop' and not much else. Most of his fellow business associates were years older than he was and he had little in common with them, apart from a love of the land. In fact, he would have rather avoided this particular gathering altogether, if it wasn't for a small niggle deep in his gut telling him that if he could get Sam alone, away from work, she might open up to him.

So, he'd done it. Booked flights to Sydney, rooms in one of the city's top hotels and tickets to the conference and dinner, all in the hope that the woman who piqued his interest more with each passing day would come clean and divulge some small part of her life to him.

Despite many cunning attempts to drag any snippet of information from her, she'd held fast, not giving him one iota about herself. And the more she kept him guessing, the more intrigued he'd become, till he could hardly function these days without wondering what made Samantha Piper tick.

As for their physical attraction, he'd managed to keep his libido under control. Just. He'd grown used to cold showers at the end of a day's work, where he'd spent endless hours resisting the lure of her light, floral fragrance, the forbidden glimpse of cleavage as she reached across his desk or the tantalising sweep of her tongue as it moistened her lips while she concentrated on a particular task. Yes, it had been hell working with her these last few months and pretending he didn't feel anything for his luscious employee, but what else could he do?

He valued her astute opinions as a businesswoman and didn't want to risk losing her, despite his reluctance to hire her in the first place. Sure, he'd toyed with their attraction on a few occasions but, thankfully, she'd put him back in his place. At least one of them had some semblance of self-control; otherwise, he could see their whole arrangement going up in flames, in more ways than one.

Knocking briskly at Sam's door, he wondered if she'd make any reference to their interlude on the plane. She hadn't mentioned the other kisses they'd shared, though a small part of him wished she would.

However, as she opened the door, Dylan didn't have time to ponder Sam's reasoning. Instead, all he could do was gape at the exquisite vision before him. Her body was wrapped in a soft blue fabric that hugged in all the right places and brought out the matching flecks in her green eyes. She'd used subtle make-up to highlight her features and had pinned her curls back in some sort of elaborate arrangement. Her overall appearance screamed 'grab me' and he had to curb the sudden impulse to do exactly that.

'Right on time. I like a man who's punctual.' Sam smiled, taking Dylan's gob-smacked look as an indication of approval. She twirled, revelling in the unique feel of chiffon swishing around her ankles. 'You like?'

He nodded, an expression of wonder lighting up his face and she had her answer. 'You look incredible,' he murmured, surveying her from head to foot.

Her skin tingled under the intensity of his stare and she resisted the impulse to rub her bare arms. 'Good. I know this dinner is important to you and I wanted to make an impression.'

He whistled, long and low. 'Well, you've certainly done that.'

She picked up her evening bag and pretended to swat him with it. 'Not on you, on your colleagues.'

'Who?' He continued to stare at her and she wondered if he'd lost his mind.

'Your colleagues. You know, those people you do business with, the same ones we're going to have dinner with.'

He shook his head. 'Change of plans. Room service. Here. Now.'

She laughed and tucked her hand through the crook of his arm. 'Thanks for the compliment. Now let's go.'

When Sam had purchased the dress she had known it looked good on her: the strapless bodice had highlighted her delicate shoulders, the fitted line accentuating her slim figure. However, though she'd craved Dylan's approval, she'd been totally unprepared for the blatant desire that blazed from his eyes when he'd first seen her and for one dizzying moment she thought he might take her into his arms, back her into the room and kick the door shut.

'How do you expect me to concentrate on business tonight with you looking like that?'

'Like what?' She smiled, enjoying her power as a woman, one who could hold the interest of a man like Dylan.

He waited till the doors of the lift slid shut before answering. 'Like every man's fantasy come to life.'

The smile slipped from her face as he placed both hands on her shoulders and bent towards her, his lips brushing hers. She'd been unprepared for the kiss, though she didn't stop to analyse it as she responded with matching eagerness, wrapping her arms around him and moulding against the lean hardness of his body. He kissed her like a man starved, a deep, endless kiss that reached down to her very soul and it affected her more than she wanted to admit. She didn't need this complication in her life, this overwhelming, helpless feeling that she belonged to him.

He groaned as she pulled away and buried her face into the crook of his neck. However, rather than calming her, his aftershave infused her senses as she took a steadying breath and threatened to tear apart what was left of her self-control.

'Hey, no use in hiding,' he whispered in her ear, his lips raining a blazing trail of light kisses from her earlobe to the hollow above her collarbone.

'Dylan—'

He silenced her with a quick peck on the lips. 'Let's not talk about this right now.'

As she opened her mouth to respond, he placed a finger against it. 'Shh. Call it a momentary lapse on my part.'

Sam didn't have time to speak as the doors of the lift slid open and in walked the last man she had expected, or wanted, to see.

CHAPTER EIGHT

'HELLO, Samantha. What are you doing here?'

If Dylan's scintillating kiss hadn't already undermined Sam's confidence, the sight of Max Sherpov staring down his aristocratic nose at her would have.

She schooled her face into what she hoped was a mask of nonchalance while her insides churned with dread. 'Hi, Max. I'm here on business.'

'Oh?' Max raised an eyebrow and glanced at Dylan, at her dress and back again.

Resisting the urge to tug at her bodice, she squared her shoulders. 'Max, this is Dylan Harmon.' She had known the instant Max had entered the lift that her cover was about to be blown to kingdom come.

Dylan stuck out his hand. 'Pleased to meet you.' Though by the expression on his face Sam knew his words didn't ring true.

'Max is an old friend of the family,' she continued, wanting to fill the awkward silence that had descended on them.

As the doors slid open on the ground floor Max

shook his head, the supercilious smirk that she despised marring his haughty features. 'Come now, Samantha, I'm much more than that.'

Staring at Max with all the disdain she could muster, she said, 'If you'll excuse us, Max, our table is waiting. Nice seeing you again.' She slipped a hand into Dylan's and strolled from the lift, hoping her jelly-like legs would hold her upright, at least till they reached the ballroom.

Thankfully, Dylan seemed just as anxious to escape Max's overbearing presence and gave her hand a reassuring squeeze as they were led to their table. He didn't speak till they were seated, giving her valuable time to compose herself. Seeing Max had shaken her more than she cared to admit. Or was it the fact that she would now have to answer questions that may have far-reaching consequences to her future with the man still holding her hand?

'Nice company you keep.'

'Hey, I don't pick my parents' friends.'

'Is that all he is to you?'

Sam resisted the urge to stick her fingers down her throat and make vomiting sounds at the thought of Max being anything but a friend to her. 'What do you think?'

Dylan relinquished her hand, leaving her strangely bereft. 'I think that old guy is smitten with you.' She barely heard his, 'Not that I blame him.'

She shrugged, hating herself for having to perpetuate the lie she'd woven. 'He means nothing to me. My parents seem to like him, which is more than I can say for me.'

'He acted as if he owned you,' Dylan persisted, gnawing away at her waning resistance. 'Especially that wisecrack about meaning more to you.'

Sam couldn't hold out much longer. She needed to tell Dylan some snippet of truth, otherwise he wouldn't stop till he'd dragged the whole sordid story from her. She sighed, wishing she hadn't started down the disastrous road that her harebrained scheme had managed to steer her. 'My parents seem to think that Max would make good husband material.'

'*What?*' Dylan exploded. 'But he's old enough to be your father!'

'Try telling that to my folks.' She could hardly believe that after all the years her parents had lived in Australia they hadn't lost any of their European heritage, hanging on to archaic traditions with grim determination.

'But why?'

Sam had to tread carefully here if she didn't want her whole lie to unravel before her eyes.

'They have old-fashioned values, believing that every woman needs a man to take care of her, to provide for her. A woman's place should be in the home, not the boardroom.'

She watched the shock register in his eyes and hoped that his interrogation would end sooner rather than later. 'Then why let you attend university? Why the degree?'

Sam shrugged, remembering the fateful day when she'd enrolled in the course and plucked up the courage to tell her parents. 'Simple, really. I blackmailed them.'

His eyebrows shot up. 'Tell me more.'

'I told them that if they didn't let me attend university I'd elope with David Peters.'

Dylan shook his head. 'I'm almost afraid to ask.' A hint of a smile tugged at the corners of his mouth. 'Who is David Peters?'

'My high school sweetheart. Not that he knew anything about it.' She chuckled at the memory of freckly, brace-face David, wondering what she'd ever seen in her dorky lab partner. 'I just used the idea of him to frighten my parents into giving in to me.'

'You're amazing, you know that?' He reached over and twisted a stray curl around his fingertip, the tenderness in his gaze causing her heart to flip-flop. 'Let's make a deal. For tonight, there will be no more talk of David, Max or any other men you have hidden in your past. Tonight, there's just you and me.'

Her breath hitched as he leaned towards her and for one crazy moment she thought he would kiss her, just like he had in the lift. Instead, he whispered in her ear, 'Does that sound like a plan to you?'

Sam could only nod as he planted a soft kiss near her temple before he pulled away to acknowledge the first of the other table occupants to arrive. However, as the evening proceeded and she endured the endless small talk, the boring speeches and picked at the food on her plate, she was constantly aware of the man at her side and his overwhelming presence. And, furthermore, what would happen once he walked her back to her room?

Would she have the willpower to refuse him if he kissed her again? Did she really want to? Though her experience with men was limited, she knew that a man like Dylan wouldn't be satisfied with a few snatched kisses for long. In responding to his kisses she'd probably given him the wrong idea and what if he demanded more?

Sneaking a quick peek at the man in question, she knew her body would have little trouble in overruling her head if he wrapped her in his arms and kissed her senseless.

But what about her heart?

Unfortunately, she'd already lost that particular organ to Dylan Harmon and he held it right where she didn't want it—in the palm of his hand.

Dylan repeatedly punched and pummelled his pillow, hoping the simple action might help him fall asleep. It didn't. He'd tossed and turned for the last hour, his head filled with images of the woman in the room next door, taunting him to follow through with what he'd started earlier.

Damn, he'd been a fool, allowing her to slip through his fingers when, right now, he could be having the best sex of his life with a woman who fired his passion with a simple flick of her shoulder-length hair.

As expected, the evening had bored him to tears, yet he'd been aware of Sam for every second of it. Having her by his side had filled him with pride, though for the life of him he couldn't fathom why. She was his employee yet he'd treated her like a cherished partner, a fact that hadn't gone unnoticed by the bulk of his associates. He'd be the talk of Sydney in the morning—the sooner he escaped back to Melbourne with Sam, the better. Or, better yet, he could whisk her away to Budgeree and finish what they'd started.

Why hadn't he pushed her harder? He'd walked her back to her room, his hand in the small of her back doing little for his restraint. The feel of her hot skin through the thin, gauzy material of her dress had beckoned him, urging him to do something completely out of character, like tear it off her. Instead, he'd stood outside her door, staring at her with what he'd hoped was a clear message in his eyes, not saying much at all.

And what had she done? Planted an all-too-brief kiss on his cheek, thanked him for an 'interesting' evening and closed her door, leaving him gawking like a jilted teenager. So much for sweeping her off her feet and into his bed. All he'd succeeded in doing was gaining another sleepless night, though not for the reason he'd anticipated.

Rolling out of bed, he padded across the dark room and pulled back the curtains, taking in the glittering view of Sydney laid out like a sparkling fairyland many storeys below. He'd always had a soft spot for this city though his heart belonged on the vast tracts of land in northern Victoria, where he could ride for miles in solitude and gaze upon the Harmon acreage with pride. Sam had seemed to instinctively understand his love of Budgeree, even though she didn't share his love of family responsibility. Not that he blamed her, after hearing about her parents' archaic views on marriage.

He unwittingly clenched his fists at the thought of her tied to that ancient crone Max. Hell, he'd wanted to pummel the man to death for the lecherous way he'd looked at Sam, not to mention the pitying glance the old man had sent his way, as if he didn't stand a chance.

Do you want a chance?

Turning away from the million-dollar view, he rubbed his temples and headed back to bed. Damned if he knew.

Sam silently cursed as she walked along the concourse towards the boarding gate, seeing but not quite believing her eyes. She'd never believed in coincidence or bad karma, yet how could she explain running into Quade in Melbourne, Max last night and now this, the unexpected appearance of two other men in her life? It had to be fate's way of paying her back for all the lies she'd told over the last few months.

'Hey, Princess. Fancy seeing you here.' Nick, her youngest brother, enveloped her in a bear hug.

'Yeah, Sis. You're looking good. What are you doing in Sydney?' Peter, the second oldest, tweaked her nose just as he'd always done. 'And where's the man?'

Sam prayed that Dylan would not appear in the next few minutes. He'd wanted to buy some obscure farming magazine and she hoped that the newsagency had to go through a backlog of stock to find it.

'He's around,' she said, keeping her answer purposely vague. 'What are you two doing here?'

A faint blush stained Peter's cheeks. Unfortunately, he possessed the same fair Popov complexion she did. 'Uh, I was invited to some fancy party and Nicky wanted to accompany me, to scope out the ladies.'

'Whose party?' Sam hid a grin, knowing exactly whose event Peter had flown down to Sydney to attend. He must be keener than she had thought, because he usually hated leaving the Brisbane sunshine and he hated flying even more.

'Ebony's parents threw some fancy shindig to raise money for disadvantaged kids, so I thought I'd lend a helping hand.' Peter paused and looked away, cementing Sam's suspicions that her brother was more smitten than he'd like to believe. 'I'm surprised you weren't there, showing off your betrothed.'

'Her *what*?'

Sam jumped, unaware that Dylan had walked up

behind her. Before she could answer, Nick thrust out his hand. 'You must be Dylan. Pleased to meet you. I'm Nick and this is Pete, brothers to this crazy woman.'

She slowly exhaled, unaware that she'd been holding her breath. If Nick had mentioned their surname she would have really had some explaining to do. Not that she was off the hook entirely.

Something akin to relief flashed across Dylan's face. 'Yes, I'm Dylan, though you guys obviously know more about me than I know about you.'

Peter rolled his eyes. 'Yeah, that'd be right. Keeping you in the dark, is she? That's our sis.'

Sam intervened quickly, wishing she could drag Dylan away before things turned really ugly. 'Why would I talk about you two when we've got more important things to discuss?' She threaded her arm through Dylan's and stared up at him, hoping to convince her brothers about the authenticity of her make-believe betrothal yet not wanting to alert Dylan to the fact.

Nick guffawed. 'I just bet you do.' He grabbed Peter's arm. 'Come on. Let's leave the two love-birds alone. Later, Princess. Dylan.'

As her brothers walked away, chuckling at some joke, Sam wished the floor would open up and swallow her whole.

'Lovebirds? Betrothed?' Dylan said quietly, disengaging from her grip. 'Where did your brothers get that idea? And why does everyone you know call you princess?'

This was it. Sink or swim time. Once again, she opted for the partial truth rather than a full-blown lie.

'You don't know my brothers. The five of them are a pain in the butt. They've always teased me, especially about boyfriends and stuff like that. I told them you were my boss, so it's their warped sense of humour to tease me in front of you. And I've already explained the marriage thing. If I spend more than two seconds in the company of any man, they nearly send out the wedding invites! Sick, huh?' She swallowed, needing to ease the dryness of her parched throat. She'd never been any good at telling lies but, with this much practice, she would soon be an expert. 'As for the princess thing, same reason. My brothers and their friends have always called me that, just because I hate it.'

Dylan stared at her face, as if trying to read every telltale line. Thankfully, the final boarding call for their flight boomed from the loudspeakers and she bent to pick up her hand luggage, breaking his intense scrutiny.

'You certainly have an interesting family.'

She breathed a sigh of relief, knowing he'd bought her concocted story and hating every minute of it. 'You call them interesting. I prefer wacky.'

He laid a restraining hand on her arm as she turned away. 'Don't underestimate the value of family. They're the most important thing in the world.'

Sam stiffened but didn't respond. She didn't need a lecture on family values from a man who wouldn't understand what she'd been through growing up; it had been difficult enough being a teenager without the added pressure of some obsolete royal title being bestowed on her like a prize she should treasure yet didn't want. Let him spout a whole lot of platitudes about family—as far as she was concerned, nothing he could ever say would change how she felt.

'Let's get back to Melbourne,' she said, knowing that the further away she got from the far-reaching influence of the Popovs, the better.

If Dylan had thought that meeting Sam's brothers might encourage her to open up to him more, he was wrong. Despite his attempts to draw her into conversation regarding the rest of her family, her childhood or anything remotely personal, she'd thwarted him at every turn, leaving him with the distinct impression that she had some deep, dark secret. And now, as her three-month trial period drew to a close, he was no nearer to knowing anything about the woman who had sneaked under his carefully erected barriers against emotional involvement.

He wanted to make her position as his personal assistant permanent. It would be the perfect solution, providing him with a valuable asset to his business life and giving him an opportunity to explore the unfamiliar, burgeoning feelings that she'd aroused within him. For he couldn't deny it any longer; despite her attempts to keep him at arm's length since their return from Sydney, he knew that he wanted her. He genuinely liked her yet wouldn't go as far as to admit to the other 'L' word.

He still couldn't acknowledge that word or the helpless feelings it reinforced—he'd lost his father because he'd been too pig-headed to admit to that emotion, yet he'd be damned if he associated 'love' and 'Sam' in the same thought.

So, that left him with only one option. Offer her a permanent position as his PA and see what developed between them. Luckily, he knew just the way to convince her to accept his offer.

CHAPTER NINE

As soon as they entered the gates to Budgeree a strange sense of belonging enveloped Sam again. She stared out the window, wishing she didn't feel this way. It would be hard enough walking away from Dylan next week without the added complication of yearning for a lifestyle she could never have. Not that she'd harboured any desire to live on the land before now—in fact, she'd been a city girl her entire life, eagerly escaping her family's acres in northern Queensland to live the high life in Brisbane. Though that probably had more to do with leaving the shackles of the Popovs behind rather than any burning desire to live in the city.

'You like this place, don't you?' Dylan spoke softly, as if reluctant to break the spell that seemed to envelop them the moment he'd pulled up in front of the homestead and switched off the engine.

She nodded. 'There's just something about it that reaches out and grabs you.'

He smiled, his warmth infusing her with some indefinable emotion that she dare not analyse. 'I'm glad you feel that way. It makes things a lot easier.'

Sam looked away quickly before she drowned in the endless depths of his dark eyes, not willing to ask him what he meant by 'things'. Instead, she flung open the car door and climbed out, wondering what had possessed her to accompany him on this trip. Sure, he'd badgered her into it, saying her presence was vital in finalising a few business contracts, but she hadn't been fooled. She'd noticed a certain gleam in Dylan's eye since they'd returned from Sydney, as if he wouldn't take no for an answer the next time they were alone together.

And sure enough, he'd made it perfectly clear that there would be no 'chaperon' at Budgeree this time, a fact that had made her pulse race in a potent mixture of anticipation and trepidation.

She followed him into the house, admiring the long, confident strides that spoke volumes about the man. Nothing intimidated him and he walked as if he owned the world, allowing nobody to stand in his way. Even in faded jeans and a casual shirt, he exuded an aura of power, one that seemed to draw her in deeper with each passing day.

'You can sleep in here...if you want.' He deposited her bag in the spare room she'd inhabited last time, though his significant pause left her in little doubt as to where he hoped she'd be sleeping, or *not* sleeping, tonight.

'Thanks.' She strode across the room, pulled back the curtains and took in the stunning view, needing to focus on something, anything, other than Dylan. He seemed to dwarf everything in the room and the longer he stood there, staring at her with those enigmatic eyes, the harder it would be to maintain a platonic distance.

Hoping he'd take the hint that she wanted to be alone, Sam continued to stare out the window.

'Is everything all right?'

She jumped, wishing she hadn't turned her back on him. Rather than leaving the room, he'd sneaked up behind her, his voice a mere whisper away from her ear.

'I'm fine,' she said, moving away from the welcoming heat radiating off his body in waves.

'No, you're not.' He reached out and snagged her arm, stopping her in her tracks. 'Tell me what's wrong.'

She stared at his hand, wishing she could shake it off, pick up her bag and high tail it out of this house and out of his life. Who had she been kidding? She could no more resist this man than denounce her heritage—and the sooner she faced facts, the better.

'Maybe later.' She pulled away and, thankfully, he released her. She unzipped her bag and started fumbling with her clothes, furiously blinking away the tears that had inexplicably filled her eyes. She'd never been prone to tears, yet the way her emotions had been swinging lately, she'd been close to waterworks several times.

'I'm here for you, Samantha.' His low voice reached out and wrapped her in comforting warmth, beckoning her to turn around, bury her head against his chest and sob out her sorry tale.

Instead, she nodded, not trusting herself to speak as the tears trickled down her cheeks. Thankfully, he didn't touch her and only hesitated a moment longer before leaving the room. As soon as she heard the latch click, she sank on to the bed, buried her face in her hands and cried, though for the life of her she couldn't figure out if they were tears of regret for her soon-to-be departure, shame at her lies, or the fact that she was about to lose the man she'd been foolish enough to fall in love with.

Dylan had no idea why Sam had appeared so upset when they'd first arrived earlier that afternoon, though her strange behaviour had certainly put a dent in his plans. He'd had it all figured out—lay out a lavish dinner, ply her with fine wine, then offer her the job of a lifetime. And if anything else developed… Well, he'd managed to rein in his imagination before his libido took off at a gallop.

Now, he didn't know whether he should wait till tomorrow and try again or repack the four-wheel drive, throw in the towel and head back to Melbourne. Maybe he'd misread the signals and Sam wasn't interested in him after all? Perhaps she'd responded to his kisses out of some warped sense of duty for her boss rather than any real feeling? And maybe, just maybe, he'd been foolish enough to depend on this woman too much and couldn't bear the thought of losing her and that was why he was hell-bent on her accepting this job.

Dylan was no fool. He knew there would be other personal assistants just as competent as Sam, yet he was driven to make her accept his offer in the vain hope they could explore their developing feelings.

Correction. *His* developing feelings.

He grimaced, wondering when he'd become such a sucker. He'd managed to stay single and emotionally tangle-free for the last few years, just the way he liked it. Yet here he was, already pining for a pint-sized blonde dynamo who would probably walk out of his life in a week without a backward glance, taking her damn secrets with her.

'Women,' he muttered under his breath, slam-

ming the back door as he headed for the stables.
A fast and furious ride was in order, anything to
get the adrenaline flowing and to rid himself of this
emotional lethargy that seemed to be sapping him
of every ounce of common sense he possessed.

And if Sam wanted anything more from him
other than a pay cheque before the end of next
week, she would just have to show him.

Sam dug her heels into the mare's sides, urging
her to follow the distant streak across the horizon
at any pace faster than a slow trot. She'd ridden
Speedy last time, soon recognising that the plod-
ding mare had been named in the typical
Australian way of labelling opposite characteris-
tics: Bluey for redheads, Shorty for anyone over
six feet tall and Mouse for the powerful stallion
that Dylan now rode like a man possessed.

True to form, Speedy could barely raise a canter
as she followed her stable-mate and Sam resigned
herself to the fact that she'd eventually catch up
with Dylan and his mount—some time tomorrow!

She'd seen him tear out of the stable, driving his
horse like a madman with a million demons on his
tail. Strangely enough, she'd wanted to take a ride
this afternoon in the hope it might clear her head
and it seemed Dylan had the same idea. Though

she'd hardly call his hair-raising gallop a leisurely ride.

So she'd followed him, not wanting to lose her way on the vast plains of Budgeree and hoping that she'd know what to say the next time she saw him. Though the tears she'd shed earlier had been cathartic, she still had no idea how she could bear to leave Dylan next week. She had an inkling he might ask her to stay on in the position of PA but what would that achieve, apart from prolonging the agony?

Besides, her parents wouldn't wait too much longer to meet her 'betrothed' and she didn't want her elaborate lie falling down around her ears, with Dylan witnessing it. She'd had enough close calls as it was and couldn't believe that her luck had held out this far. No, she only had one choice and that was to leave next week as planned and return to her family, in the hope they would now accept the undeniable proof that she could make it on her own without the support of any man as her husband and chief protector. And, hopefully, Dylan would be none the wiser to his involvement in her plan or the fact that she'd lost her heart to him.

As if on cue, his vision rose before her, man and stallion standing still on a ridge, silhouetted against the vibrant ochre setting sun. Sam swallowed the lump of emotion that had risen in her throat, wishing she could imprint this moment on her mind for ever, a cherished memory she could resurrect at will during the lonely months ahead.

Dylan turned as if sensing her presence and guided Mouse down the hill towards her. She waited for him, suddenly overcome by a powerful desire that this could be a life she could get used to; riding out to meet the man of her dreams at the end of every day and accompanying him home, to their home, where they could stay wrapped in each other's arms all night and face whatever the next day would bring, together.

Sam resisted the urge to shake her head and dislodge the ridiculous fantasy that had popped into her mind. There would be no shared life at Budgeree, no welcoming homecomings, no man of her dreams. Instead, she would be left with nothing…apart from the chance to make the most of every second she had left with the man she loved. Once the idea insinuated its way into her head, she couldn't ignore it. What harm could it do, to make the most of their remaining time together? Treasured memories would be the only thing left to sustain her in the months ahead, when the full force of what she'd really lost would hit her.

Squaring her shoulders as he stopped beside her,

she smiled. 'Thought you might get lost out here on your own.'

His frown softened as he reached towards her and ran an index finger lightly down her cheek. 'You had a smudge of dirt there.' He straightened up quickly, depriving her of the chance to lean against his hand. 'You shouldn't have followed me out here. I don't have time to send out a search party if you'd got lost.'

Sam noted his rigid posture and the frown that hadn't quite disappeared yet. If she was going to make him want her tonight, she had her work cut out for her. 'I had no choice. When Speedy wants her man, she'll stop at nothing. I just sat along for the ride.'

His eyes darkened imperceptibly in the waning light and she resisted the urge to squirm in the saddle. 'Yeah, well, some females are like that.'

Silence stretched between them as she struggled to find something bright and witty to say. Thankfully, Mouse pawed the ground as if keen to get moving, breaking their deadlocked stare.

'Let's head back. I'm starving.' He wheeled around, not sending her a backward look.

So am I, Dylan.

Though Sam knew her hunger had nothing to do with food and everything to do with the man sitting proudly on his horse, surveying his land. She'd made a lightning-fast decision several minutes ago and she hoped she now had the guts to go through with it. If this was her last week with Dylan, she would make the most of it, no tears, no regrets. She wanted him, more than she'd ever wanted any man in her entire life and, for tonight, she would cast aside her inhibitions, her common sense and every self-preservation mechanism that screamed she was doing the wrong thing, and go after him. No holds barred.

She smiled as the homestead came into sight, knowing that Dylan wouldn't know what hit him when she pulled out all stops tonight. And prayed she'd have the strength to walk away when it was all over.

Dylan sat in the worn recliner that had been his dad's favourite and stretched his legs out towards the blazing fire.

'Here's your port. Cheers.' Sam touched the rim of her glass to his before raising it to her lips and taking a sip.

He gulped, wishing he could tear his gaze away from her mouth while simultaneously wishing for those lips to do a whole lot more.

'Cheers,' he murmured, knowing that for as long

as he lived he would never figure women out. Since their ride, Sam had done her best to appear cheerful and relaxed, the exact opposite of her demeanour when they'd arrived.

She'd made small talk over dinner and had appeared genuinely interested in his plans for this place, his pride and joy. He hadn't felt so comfortable in a woman's presence in a long time and knew that now was as good a time as any to broach the subject of her ongoing contract.

'Samantha, we need to talk.'

To his amazement, she laughed and reached for his glass. 'Are you ever going to lighten up and call me Sam?'

He could've sworn she sashayed across the room, setting their glasses on the mantelpiece before turning to face him, an inviting little smile playing across her lips. 'Well?'

He leaned back in the chair and placed his hands behind his head, admiring her silhouette with the fire at her back. In response, she stretched her arms back towards the heat and rubbed her hands together, the simple action pulling her shirt taut against her chest and outlining the curve of her breasts.

Heat surged through his body as he fought the impulse to drag her down to the sheepskin rug in front of the fire and tear open her shirt. 'So, you think I need to lighten up?'

'I know you do.' As if reading his mind, she sank on to the rug and he almost salivated as his fantasy took flight. He imagined peeling the clothes from her body, exposing the exquisite flesh beneath to his hands...

'Dylan?' Even the soft, breathy way she uttered his name had him focusing on all the wrong cues. If he didn't know any better, he could've sworn she wanted him as much as he wanted her.

He practically leaped from the chair and strode towards the door before he did something really dumb, like join her on that damn rug. 'I'm going to bed. See you in the morning.'

'Mind if I join you?'

Her whisper stopped him dead in his tracks.

'What did you just say?' He turned, knowing his fantasy must've turned into an auditory hallucination yet wishing against hope that he'd just heard correctly.

She didn't respond immediately and he knew he must be going mad. However, just as he was about to walk out the door, she held out her hand to him. 'Come here, Dylan.'

He crossed the room in an instant, sank to his

knees in front of the crackling fire and pulled her
into his arms.

'Well, don't just sit there. Aren't you going to
kiss me?'

Dylan didn't need further encouragement as he
bent his head and covered her mouth in a searing
kiss. She moaned and he lost all sense of control,
plundering her mouth with the abandon of a man
starved and pulling her flush against him, sealing
their bodies together, needing to feel her pressed
against him.

Rather than stopping him, which his dazed mind
half expected her to do, she melded into him, her
hands clamping around his neck and hanging on
for dear life. She stroked the nape of his neck, her
fingernails lightly grazing his skin while her mouth
nibbled hot kisses across his jaw. Sparks flew—
and not just from the sap of a log that suddenly
ignited in the hearth.

In a strangled voice he managed to ask, 'Are you
sure about this?'

'No more questions,' she whispered against the
side of his mouth. 'Tonight is about you and me.
Think you can handle it?'

Before he could answer, she pulled him towards
her for another kiss and they sank into the downy

softness of the rug. He claimed her lips, feasting on the sweetness of liquor and pure Sam.

'I want you, Sam,' he murmured, as he undid each button on her shirt before sliding his hand beneath the scrap of lace that encased her breasts, his fingers stroking the soft skin till he thought he'd lose his mind.

Sam arched towards Dylan as his thumb grazed her nipple, shards of electrifying fire shooting through her body. She'd lost control the minute he'd first touched her…and she was loving every minute of it.

'You pick a fine time to finally call me Sam,' she managed to gasp out as his fingers momentarily left her breast and splayed across her stomach before moving lower, creating an instant yearning that wouldn't be satisfied with anything less than his naked body joined with hers. The passion between them left her more than a little scared. In fact, right now, with his hands skating over her skin with skilled precision, she was downright terrified.

'Timing is everything, sweetheart.' He gathered her to him and cradled her, as if sensing her sudden panic.

She stared at the man she loved in the flickering firelight, wondering if the tenderness she glimpsed in his eyes was a figment of her overheated imagination.

'Trust me,' he whispered, brushing a wayward curl back from her face before tracing a slow, deliberate line from her temple to her lips, his finger skimming over her bottom lip repeatedly, firing her need with each gentle stroke.

She barely managed a nod as he rose, holding her in his arms and walked through the old homestead towards the master bedroom.

Sam woke to the raucous chuckles of a kookaburra and stretched, wondering what had happened to her cotton T-shirt during the night. She always wore the faded rugby shirt to bed yet it had miraculously disappeared. Suddenly, she sat bolt upright, clutched the sheet to her breasts and glanced around the room as memories of last night flooded back.

So, it hadn't been a dream.

She was in the master bedroom, with its antique Blackwood furniture and burgundy lined curtains, lying in the king-sized four-poster bed, wearing nothing but a smile. And the man who had put it there was nowhere in sight.

She'd been dreading this moment ever since she'd thrown caution to the wind yesterday and decided to make love with Dylan. How should she act afterwards? What should she say? After all, they weren't strangers who could walk away without a backward glance. She still had a job to do, even if it was only for another week. Yet how could she face him now, with the scorching memories of their lovemaking burned into her brain, and keep their relationship strictly platonic?

Determined not to make a fool of herself, she slid out of bed and winced, aching in muscles she didn't know existed. She needed a shower, fresh clothes and a steaming mug of coffee in that order. Then, and only then, could she entertain the thought of facing Dylan.

Picking up her discarded clothes from the floor, she crept across the hallway and scurried into her room, thankful that the man who had rocked her world last night was nowhere in sight. Maybe she'd figure out what to say during her shower? She should probably keep their initial conversation light, something like 'the overtime in this job is a killer.' Yeah, right, then he'd think she was a total loser.

She sighed with pleasure as she stepped into the steaming shower and let the hot water sluice down her body, wondering if he was avoiding her. Not that she could blame him—he probably thought she'd lost her marbles, coming on to him last night after practically falling apart earlier that afternoon.

No doubt about it. She would have a lot of explaining to do... If she ever plucked up enough courage to leave the shelter of her room.

Reaching for the soap, her hand stilled as a blast of cold air hit her back, closely followed by the enveloping warmth of a hard, male body. An *aroused*, male body, pressing firmly against her.

'Let me do that.' Dylan wrapped his arms around her from behind and she leaned back, her legs turning to jelly as he soaped the front of her body, circling her breasts in slow, concentric circles till she groaned aloud.

So much for figuring out what to say to him. There wasn't much need for talking as she lost herself in Dylan.

As her heart rate returned to a pace resembling normal, she sagged against him, not trusting herself to speak.

'See you in the kitchen. We've got work to do.' He planted a quick peck under her earlobe and stepped out of the shower, as if the last twenty-four hours had never happened.

And, just like that, Sam realised that the secret dream she'd been harbouring for the last few months, the one where Dylan would fall madly in love with her and really become her fiancé, had been just that, a fanciful dream.

Now, it was time to wake up.

CHAPTER TEN

SAM deserved an Oscar. In fact, she deserved a whole truckload of acting awards for the performance she'd put on today. She'd been the epitome of the efficient PA, just as her boss wanted. For that's how Dylan had behaved all day, like a tyrannical boss who demanded nothing less than perfection from an employee. There hadn't been a hint of the intimacies they'd shared last night, not to mention their steamy session in the shower this morning.

Instead, he'd pretended nothing had happened between them and she'd picked up on his cues and followed suit. After all, it was for the best. They had no future beyond next week and it was time she started to believe it.

'Could you pass me that document?' Dylan gestured towards the pile of papers to her left while studying the invoice in his hand.

'So much for the magical P word,' she muttered, resisting the urge to throw the paper at him.

'Don't be childish.' He glared at her as if she'd uttered some obscenity.

She quirked an eyebrow. 'Since when are manners considered childish?'

He ignored her and returned to studying the document, while her temper rose several notches. She'd tolerated his barked commands and surly attitude all day, knowing there was only so much she could take. Though he'd been demanding over the past few months, he'd never been rude and she wondered if his churlish display today was designed to push her away. If so, he was doing a fine job of it.

She took a calming breath and returned to adding the column of figures she'd been working on, wishing her own life was as easy to compute.

'By the way, we're leaving as soon as we've finished this pile.'

She looked up in time to find him staring at her with an odd expression on his face before he quickly returned to the paper in his hand.

'Thanks for the notice,' she said, wondering what had happened to the easy-going camaraderie they'd shared before last night. Rather than bringing them closer as she'd anticipated, their interlude had widened the gap between them to unbreachable proportions.

'I'm not in the mood, Samantha.'

That did it. She'd had enough of his condescending tone and all-round bad attitude for one day. Standing up, she slammed the completed spreadsheet on the table in front of him and walked towards the door, only pausing when she reached it. 'Pity you didn't say the same last night. Would've saved us your little performance today.'

Shock spread across his face though she didn't give him a chance to reply. 'I'll meet you out the front in fifteen minutes,' she said, hoping her voice wouldn't quaver. 'After all, our *business* here is finished.'

She walked away, head held high, while for the second time in as many days Sam fought a useless battle against tears as she silently cursed the man who had turned her world upside down.

On their return to Melbourne, Dylan stalked into his room and flung his bag on to the floor, wondering how he'd managed to make such a mess of things. Rather than a sojourn at Budgeree opening the door to a deeper relationship with Sam, the time they'd spent there had well and truly slammed it shut. He'd acted like a jerk today, saying the wrong things and behaving like an ass, when what he'd really felt like doing was dragging her back to his bed and making wild, passionate love to her all day long.

And what had he done about it? Pushed her
away in the coldest way possible, not daring to
believe that he'd been foolish enough to fall in love
with her. He didn't have room in his life for love.
It was a useless emotion that complicated simple
relationships and turned them into dependent affairs fraught with responsibilities. If anyone should
know, he should. Just look at what had happened
with his dad.

A knock interrupted his thoughts. 'Can I come
in, Son?'

'Sure, Mum.' He took a deep breath, hoping she
couldn't read the dejection on his face.

He should've known better. As soon as she entered the room, his mother honed in on his mood
immediately. 'Is everything all right, love?'

'Of course.' He avoided eye contact, knowing
he was a lousy liar when it came to the most important woman in his life. Pity he hadn't felt the
same about his mum's competition earlier that day;
after all, he'd had little trouble in hiding the truth
about his feelings from Sam.

She sat down on his bed and patted the spot next
to her. 'Come here and tell me all about it.'

He stiffened, not willing to admit the truth to his
mum. Hell, he was having a hard enough time admitting it to himself.

And then, with the unerring precision of a life-time spent reading her son, she honed in on the main problem. 'You're in love with her, aren't you?'

He schooled his face into an impassive mask, knowing it wouldn't fool his mum. 'You've been reading too many of those romance novels. Isn't it time you branched out into another genre, like crime?'

His mother shook her head, as if he'd disappointed her in some way. 'The only crime around here is the one occurring right in front of me. When are you going to learn that taking a chance on love isn't so bad?'

'Who said anything about love?'

She smiled, that same knowing smile she'd given him when he'd pulled out his first tooth and said that it had fallen out, when he'd fibbed about a stomach-ache to avoid an exam at school, when he'd said his first love bite was a result of a snooker cue accidentally hitting him in the neck. 'You don't have to say a thing. It's written all over your face.' She clasped her hands together as her grin broadened. 'A mother knows these things.'

'Leave it alone, Mum. I don't want to talk about it.' He paced the room, feeling like a circus lion about to be prodded into jumping through hoops.

'Well, if you don't want to talk to me, why don't you talk to the lady in question?'

An image of Sam's face as she'd flung that comment about his mood back at him before leaving Budgeree rose before his eyes; though she'd tried using sass to cover her hurt, he'd seen right through it, feeling like a real bastard in the process. And what had he done about it? Absolutely nothing.

'Sam and I need to sort out a few issues.' His mum's face brightened at his admission and he quickly held up a hand before she rushed out to start planning the wedding. 'They involve her on-going employment, not the state of her heart. Or mine, for that matter.'

'Oh.'

He wondered at his mother's disappointment and why she'd grown to like Sam so much. Sure, she wanted to see him married off; after all, she'd been not-so-subtle in shoving him in Monique Taylor's direction for years, but why push him towards Sam? His mum had always been a bit of a prude when it came to mixing business with pleasure, hinting on several occasions that it was improper for him to flirt with the hired help.

Yet here she was, almost forcing him to admit his love for Sam. Why?

'Fine. If you want to talk to your decrepit old mother, I'm here for you.' She stood up and straightened her skirt. 'Just remember, darling. Follow your heart.' She kissed him on the cheek, leaving him alone with a host of unwelcome thoughts, most of them centred around Sam and how he could possibly make up to her for his atrocious behaviour.

Sam didn't bother unpacking on her return to Melbourne. Why bother, when she'd have to repack in a week? Or less, if she had her way. After all, why prolong the agony? Dylan had made it more than clear that he couldn't tolerate her presence in his life any longer and, after the way he'd behaved today, the feeling was entirely mutual.

Ebony had been right—love was for suckers. Though, by the goofy look on her brother Pete's face when he had mentioned her friend at the airport in Sydney, Ebony could be heading for a big fall—if she hadn't fallen all ready.

Tears sprang to Sam's eyes as she thought about her friend. She really needed a shoulder to cry on at the moment and Ebony would be perfect. Wiping her eyes with an angry swipe of her hand and cursing her stupidity at shedding tears for a man who definitely wasn't worth it, she made her way

to the study, scanning the hall for the man she
didn't want to bump into. A quick phone call to
her friend would do wonders for her state of mind;
if anyone could talk sense into her, Ebony could.

She punched out the number with impatient jabs
of her index finger and held her breath while the
phone rang. Thankfully, Ebony picked up on the
fifth ring.

'Eb, it's me.'

'Hi, Sam. What's up? You sound awful.'

Sam sighed. 'That obvious, huh?'

'Oh-oh. What's he done?' Ebony always had the
unerring talent of honing right in on a problem. It
had annoyed Sam at times but, right now, she was
grateful for it.

And, just like that, Sam poured out the whole
sorry story to her best friend, leaving nothing out.

Ebony paused as Sam's tirade finished. 'Why
don't you tell him the truth?'

Sam laughed, a bitter sound far from happiness.
'And say what? "Hey, Dylan, even though I've
been your employee for the last three months, it's
all been a lie and what I really want is for us to
get married and live happily ever after." Yeah,
right. I'm sure he'd love that.'

'I meant tell him the truth about how you feel.
What have you got to lose?'

At that moment Sam heard a faint click behind her. She cupped a hand over the receiver and turned around, the sight of Dylan glowering at her sending her heart plummeting.

'We need to talk. Now.'

If she thought he'd been angry earlier, she'd underestimated him. The low, clipped tone he'd just used, along with the folded arms and fierce frown, indicated he'd surpassed anger and had entered the furious stage.

'I'll call you back later,' she said softly into the phone, swallowing to dislodge the lump of emotion that had risen in her throat.

'If that's who I think it is, go for it.' Another of Ebony's mottoes for life. Though, in this case, Sam knew it was way too late to follow her friend's advice. She'd already 'gone for it' and it had landed her in more trouble than it'd been worth.

'Bye.' As Sam replaced the receiver she wondered how much of her conversation Dylan had overheard. By the deepening frown and the way he stalked across the room towards her, he'd probably heard plenty.

'Sit down,' he snapped, pointing to the ergonomic chair she'd occupied almost every day over the last few months. 'And let's talk about your *employment*.'

'Don't make it sound so appealing,' she muttered, before quickly taking a seat. Though she didn't take kindly to being ordered around, she sensed that now was not the time to push the issue. Dylan looked mad as hell—and she'd been the one stupid enough to provoke him.

He clenched his fists and took several deep breaths before continuing. 'I actually came down here to offer you a permanent position as my PA. You've done a great job, better than I could've hoped for, and I thought it's time to cement our business arrangement.'

Sam didn't know what to say. She thought he'd overheard her conversation with Ebony and would subject her to an interrogation; instead, she almost sagged with relief as she realised he'd come down here to discuss her job. The angry mood was probably a carry-over from this morning—he hadn't spoken a word on their return trip to Melbourne, which had been fine with her. As she opened her mouth to respond, he held up a hand.

'Don't.'

He spat the word out and she knew in an instant that her relief had been short-lived.

'I don't want to hear another word out of your lying little mouth.' He stared at her, his eyes turning to molten chocolate as they smouldered with rage.

The little flicker of hope within Sam shrivelled and died as she realised he'd probably heard every damning word she'd just uttered on the phone. And she'd now have to come clean to the last man on earth she'd hoped would ever learn the truth.

'Let me explain—'

'I don't want to hear it,' he interrupted.

Sam sank further into the chair, wishing she could say something, anything, to allay the way he must be feeling right now. She hated being lied to, almost as much as she hated being pushed around by others, and she knew that Dylan wouldn't be satisfied with anything less than the truth.

However, before she could speak, he swung to face her again, neck muscles standing rigid against the collar of his shirt, an angry flush staining his tanned cheeks. 'I thought you were different, yet you're not. You're just like the rest. And I despise you for it.'

He'd startled her when he'd looked at her and her pulse had raced. Now, with icy contempt dripping from every word and his cold stare, the blood flowing in her veins froze.

'The rest?' She spoke quietly, hoping her tone would soothe him. It didn't.

'You lied to me, Samantha, just like the rest. I heard you admit it to whoever you were speaking to on the phone. You came here under the pretence of working for me, when all you really wanted was a ring on your finger and an easy way into the Harmon fortune. Well, forget it. Your little scheme hasn't worked. Now get out!'

Sam paled as Dylan fixed her with a stare that would have sent most of the men in his business world scuttling for cover. She didn't refute his accusations or offer any kind of explanation. Instead, she just sat there, clasping her hands together and shaking her head.

Pain, swift and raw, knifed his heart as he watched her, wishing she could have been different and knowing the wish was futile. He'd heard her say that her stint here had been a sham and what she'd hoped for was marriage.

So much for his instincts to read people. He'd been so careful in the past, not falling victim to the women who had entered his life with sweet, empty words designed to entice him. They hadn't loved him; instead, they'd all been out for one thing—an easy entry into the Harmon fortune. He'd managed to harden his heart and thwart them all. Until now.

However, all wasn't lost. He'd discovered Sam's

plan in time to save the family fortune, if not his heart.

He squared his shoulders and glared at her, instilling every ounce of hurt and betrayal into his voice. 'I said, get out!'

She stood and headed towards the door, not even casting a glance in his direction.

Dylan's heart shattered as he watched the woman he loved walk out of his life.

CHAPTER ELEVEN

'It's for the best…it's for the best…' Sam silently repeated the words over and over during the flight to Brisbane. However, as much as she tried to believe them, she couldn't ignore the image that seemed burned into her retinas, of Dylan's horrified expression as he'd flung accusations at her, hatred etched into every line of his face.

She should be angry. She should hate him for jumping to conclusions. Instead, she felt bereft, as if someone had reached into her chest and ripped her heart out. She'd never experienced such total and utter desolation and knew it would take a lifetime to recover from loving Dylan.

So what if her plan to prove her independence to her parents had succeeded? It would be a hollow victory, considering she'd lost her heart in the process.

Maybe she was just a tad mad at him for lumping her in with the rest of the bimbos who had tried to ensnare him, though she couldn't really blame him for adding two and two and coming up with five. He *had* overheard her say to Ebony she'd lied to him and, though she couldn't quite recall it, she'd mumbled something about marrying him too. Funnily enough, that little accusation hadn't been far from the truth. She would've married him in a second if he'd asked.

As the plane touched down and Sam disembarked, she scanned the crowd for her brother, Pete. Despite her protestations to Ebony that everything was all right when she'd called her from Melbourne airport, her friend had sensed trouble and insisted that she would notify Pete to pick her up when Sam arrived home. In no mood to argue at the time, Sam had reluctantly agreed. However, as Pete spotted her amongst the passengers and enveloped her in a bear hug, she wondered at her sanity. She was in no mood for lengthy interrogations or explanations, two things her brothers were experts at.

Stifling the urge to sob into Pete's shirt, Sam pulled away. 'Thanks for picking me up.'

'No problem.' Pete picked up her luggage and headed for the nearest exit, leaving Sam gaping.

'What? No questions? No prying?'

He stopped and turned around. 'Come on, Sis. It's me you're talking to.'

'That's what I'm afraid of. Since when did you become sensitive to my feelings?' Her brothers had taken it in turns to tease, berate and lecture her for most of her twenty-five years and she couldn't believe that Pete had turned over a new leaf now.

He shrugged, appearing strangely uncomfortable. 'I had a chat with Eb. She told me to lay off you, in no uncertain terms.'

Sam tried to smother a grin and failed. If she'd had any doubts about the blossoming relationship between Pete and her best friend, her brother had just laid them to rest. He must be head over heels to take advice from a woman, especially one as opinionated as Ebony.

'So, when's the wedding?' She couldn't resist teasing him, for it took the focus off her own problems for more than two seconds.

To her amazement, Pete blushed. 'She told you, didn't she?'

'Told me what?'

He shook his head. 'It's supposed to be a secret. Damn woman.'

Sam grabbed Pete's arm as a smidgeon of an idea took root and quickly grew to beanstalk proportions. '*You're* getting married?'

'Shh.' He glanced around as if she'd just announced it over the airport loudspeaker. 'Nobody knows and I'd like to keep it that way.'

'*You're* marrying *Ebony*?' Sam needed to find

the nearest chair—and fast—before she collapsed. 'You're kidding, right?'

Pete stared at her and she'd never seen her brother so serious. 'No, I'm not. We love each other, probably have for years, and it's time to make it official.'

'But why all the secrecy?'

'You of all people should know the answer to that one, Princess.'

And suddenly, with a blinding flash of clarity, Sam understood. While she'd been away, perhaps her brothers had borne some of her parents' pressure in 'holding up the Popov name' and 'marrying to fit their heritage'. At last, after all she'd had to endure over the last few years, she finally had an ally.

She leaned over and hugged Pete. 'I'm really happy for you. And, don't worry, your secret's safe with me. Though I'm going to kill Ebony. She didn't tell me a word.'

Pete squeezed her back. 'She didn't think it was the right time, what with your…um, situation…' He trailed off, as if he'd said too much.

Sam pasted a bright smile on her face, determined not to let her pain resurface in front of her brother. 'Hey, don't worry about me. I'll be fine.'

However, as he filled her in on the family news as they travelled home, Sam seriously wondered if she'd ever be fine again.

Dylan rarely drank, believing it impeded his judgement. However, as he downed a second straight whiskey in the space of an hour, he allowed himself the luxury of a wry smile. He hadn't needed alcohol to impede his judgement when it came to Sam—he'd done a damn good job of botching it all on his own.

Even now, after brooding on how foolish he'd been to fall for her little act, he couldn't believe that it was over. He dropped his head in his hands and rubbed his temples, wishing the hot blonde with the rapier mind and sharper wit had never entered his life three months ago. He'd been behaving out of character ever since and, despite her betrayal, a small part of him still wanted her more than he'd ever wanted any woman.

'Why did Sam leave?'

His head snapped up at the sound of his mother's voice. She must have sneaked into the study, just as he had several hours earlier, though what he'd overheard had changed his life for ever.

'She lied to me, Mum.'

His mother pulled up the nearest seat. 'So, she told you, huh?'

'You *knew* about this?' He shook his head, hearing but not quite believing his own mother would support such a scheme. She would obviously go to any lengths to see him married off and it sickened him, almost as much as Sam's betrayal.

His mother shrugged, as if supporting a gold-digger and her claims to lay a hand on the Harmon fortune was no big deal. 'Yes, I knew. I guessed the truth when I first saw her and we had a little chat that confirmed it.'

Dylan took a deep breath, struggling to get air into his constricting lungs. 'And you supported her?'

'Well, she explained things to me and I didn't see any harm in it.'

He leaped up from his chair, his temper flaring out of control for the second time that day. 'You didn't see the harm in that little schemer setting her sights on using me to get at our fortune?' His voice rose several octaves. 'What were you thinking, Mum?'

To his amazement, his mother laughed. Not just an intimidated titter or a smothered chuckle, but an all-out belly laugh. 'Where did you get the idea that Sam was after our fortune?'

He folded his arms and glared at the one woman in the world he thought he could trust. 'I overheard her on the phone to someone earlier. She said she'd lied to me all this time and that she wanted to marry me.'

'Oh, dear.' His mother wiped away the tears from the corners of her eyes. 'You've got it all wrong, dear.'

'Have I?'

His mother nodded and, by the grave expression on her face, he suddenly knew he wouldn't like what he was about to hear. 'Have you heard of the Popov family?'

'Of course. Who hasn't? They own most of Queensland.'

'Did you also know they are descendants of Russian royalty?'

Dylan couldn't fathom where all this was leading but he decided to give his mother the benefit of the doubt. She rarely minced words and was obviously leading somewhere with all this. 'Get to the point, Mum.'

She reached for a handkerchief and dabbed at her nose. 'I don't think Sam was after the Harmon fortune. She wouldn't need it. She's a princess, Dylan.'

'What?' He'd never thought that age had affected his mum but maybe senility had crept up on her overnight?

'Samantha is the only daughter of the Popov family. And a rich princess in her own right.' His mum had the grace to look away, not quite able to meet his eye.

He managed a laugh, a strange bitter sound that echoed in the large room. 'I don't understand. Why the ruse? Why change her surname, why work for me, why mention marriage?' He shook his head, trying to make sense of the barrage of questions that swirled around his brain.

'Why don't you ask *her*?' His mother stood up and laid a comforting hand on his shoulder. 'It's the only way, Son.'

He stared at his mother's retreating back before reaching for the phone.

Sam's reunion with her parents hadn't gone quite as expected. She'd anticipated an interrogation of mammoth proportions, mainly revolving around her absent fiancé. Instead, they'd welcomed her with open arms, lavishing her with more love than they had in her twenty-five years to date. Rather than plying her with questions, they'd smothered her with emotion, reinforcing how much they'd missed her.

She couldn't handle this drastic change in her strict, orthodox parents and the truth had spilled out before she could stop it. Well, most of the truth.

She told them about working for Dylan Harmon to prove her independence, about the liberated feeling of living away from her family, about how Max actually made her skin crawl and the thought of marrying him would drive her away permanently. She'd cried tears of relief when they embraced her and apologised for driving her to such lengths, admitting that they hadn't realised the pressure they'd been placing on her and the rest of their children. The experience had been a catalyst in changing her relationship with her parents and, if she'd known what her harebrained scheme would do, she would have done it a long time ago.

She'd told them almost everything—leaving out the part where she'd lost her heart to a man who now despised her.

However, she hadn't had time to dwell on that. Once Pete had seen his parents' change of attitude, he'd told them about marrying Ebony and the entire family had been coerced into making the wedding happen as soon as possible. It had barely been a week since she'd returned from Melbourne and today her best friend would become her sister-in-law.

Putting the finishing touches to her make-up, she

knocked on the interconnecting door of the hotel room that the girls had hired to get ready for the big day. 'Are you finished, Eb? It's almost time to go.'

The door swung open and, in typical flamboyant style, her friend struck a pose. 'What do you think? Do I look like a bride?'

Sam smiled and brushed away the tears that sprang to her eyes at the sight of her friend clad in an ivory sheath dotted with crystals, her usually flyaway hair smoothed into a sleek chignon and adorned with a sparkling tiara and sheer veil that dropped to the floor. 'You look incredible. Pete's going to pass out when he sees you.'

Ebony rolled her eyes. 'Let's hope not. It's taken too much effort to get him this far and I'll be damned if he backs out now.'

'Hey, there's no chance of that. My dorky brother's head-over-heels. Are you sure you want to become part of our crazy family?'

To her amazement, a sheen of tears glistened in Ebony's eyes. Her friend rarely cried; in fact, she could probably count the number of times that Ebony had let her emotions get the better of her. 'We're already family, Sis, and don't you forget it.'

Sam hugged her best friend and blinked back

her own tears, knowing that if she let them fall now, she'd never stop. Since her return from Melbourne and in the privacy of her room each night, she'd cried enough tears to fill the Pacific twice over and she'd be damned if she let her own heartbreak spoil Ebony and Pete's wedding day.

Ebony pulled away and bustled into her room. 'OK, time to get this show on the road. There's a chapel not far from here where Prince Charming is waiting.'

Sam chuckled, unable to associate the brother who had put frogs in her bed with Ebony's version of Prince Charming. 'If you say so. Though personally, I think that guy's a fable, ranking alongside Hansel and Gretel and that damned gingerbread house that I spent years searching our local rainforest for as a kid.'

'They're not all like Dylan, you know,' Ebony said, fixing her with a pointed stare.

Sam shrugged, wishing her friend hadn't brought up the subject of the man she'd been trying so desperately to forget. 'It's not his fault. I lied to him. It's natural he'd jump to conclusions about the rest of it.'

'If the man had half a brain in his head he would've followed you up here and given you a chance to explain. Don't you dare defend him!'

Sam squeezed Ebony's arm and led her to the door. 'Calm down. It isn't good for the bride to get this riled before the ceremony. Besides, Dylan Harmon is history. Let's focus on more important matters, like getting you married off.'

Thankfully, Ebony dropped the subject, leaving Sam to wonder how long it would take before she believed her own propaganda and relegated the memory of the one man she loved to past history.

After a week of endless business problems Dylan had finally managed to arrange a flight to Brisbane. He'd had to cancel the trip several times, leading him to believe that perhaps he wasn't destined to sort out the mess with Sam. However, he couldn't get her out of his mind and he knew he owed it to himself to find closure, one way or the other. He wanted answers to several unanswered questions and Sam was the only woman who could provide them.

Striding to the front door of the Popov mansion, he took in the sweeping river views, the manicured lawns and the impressive façade of the entrance, wondering for the hundredth time why a woman with this much wealth would want to marry him just for his money. There had to be more behind her scheme and he wouldn't leave Brisbane till he had all the answers.

He squared his shoulders and thumped on the door, slightly out of his depth for the first time in years and not relishing the feeling one bit.

As the door opened he fixed a smile on his face. However, the response he got wasn't quite what he'd expected.

'What the hell are you doing here?'

CHAPTER TWELVE

DYLAN held out his hand, hoping the other man wouldn't punch him on the nose, which was exactly what he looked as if he would do.

'Hi, Peter. I'm Dylan Harmon. We met at the airport in Sydney, when your sister was working for me?'

Peter stared at him as if he was pond scum and ignored his outstretched hand. 'I remember. Now answer my question. What are you doing here?'

He let his hand drop, wondering where the other man's animosity had sprung from. Surely he was the one who'd been wronged in this whole fiasco? Though with Sam's penchant for lying, who knew what story she'd given her family, which would certainly account for her brother's antagonistic behaviour now.

'I've come to see Sam. Is she here?'

To his surprise, Peter laughed. 'No, she isn't. She stayed at a hotel last night before heading to the chapel. Besides, haven't you left all this a bit late?'

Dylan's heart plummeted as the words penetrated his brain and he took in Peter's tuxedo. Surely Sam wasn't getting married?

Suddenly, the image of Sam and that old man they'd bumped into at the hotel in Sydney sprang to mind and it took all his willpower not to shake the truth out of her smug-looking brother. Dammit, she'd told him her parents had been trying to marry her off to that old fool. What if he'd been stupid enough to push her right into another man's arms?

'Where's the chapel?' He fixed Peter with a stony stare, hoping he'd get the message.

Peter shook his head. 'Oh no, you don't. There's no way you're going to disrupt this day. Just go away and leave my sister alone. She doesn't want to see you.'

Fury surged through Dylan's body, rooting him to the spot. He had to see Sam one last time, even if it was to tell her that she was making the biggest mistake of her life. Hell, she should be marrying him, not some sleazy old man and he'd be damned if he let this wedding go ahead.

He clenched and unclenched his fists, trying to calm down and knowing that what he said in the next few minutes could very well decide his fate. 'I love her,' he finally blurted out, the words scaring him more than he cared to admit.

To his amazement, Peter's expression changed

in an instant and he slapped him on the back. 'Why didn't you say so? Come on, you can ride to the chapel with me. Let's go.'

The limousine ride to the chapel was the longest in Dylan's entire life. He barely listened to Peter's small talk, his mind fixed on the image of Sam in a bridal dress being joined to old Max, whose name he'd finally remembered, in holy matrimony. The thought made him physically ill and he'd downed the several drinks Peter had handed him before he realised that he'd need a completely sober head if he was to convince Sam that she would be making the biggest mistake of her life if she married Max.

The car had barely pulled up when Dylan threw open the door and sprinted for the chapel.

'Hey, what's the hurry? There's plenty of time for you two to talk after the ceremony,' Peter yelled out, only serving to fuel Dylan's urgency.

Had the man lost his mind? After the ceremony would be too late and he'd be damned if he let the best thing that had happened to him slip through his fingers.

Guests stared at him as he ran through the grounds and burst into the chapel. Thankfully, Sam wasn't standing at the altar as he'd envisaged, though his relief was short-lived as a minister strolled down the aisle towards him.

'You're looking for the bride?'

Dylan nodded, swallowing the bitterness that arose at the thought of Sam shortly taking her place in front of that altar without him. 'Is she here?'

The minister pointed to a small room near the entrance. 'She's in there, looking absolutely radiant. I've seen a few brides in my time, but this one—'

'Thanks.' Dylan left the minister gaping as he ran towards the heavy mahogany door and pushed it open without knocking. His heart clenched at the sight of the woman in a beautiful wedding dress standing by the window, though the sunlight streaming through the stained glass window blinded him for a moment.

'Sam, we need to talk.' He strode into the room, determined to talk sense into her and stop this farcical wedding.

'Well, you won't find her here. She's taking a walk by the river.'

Dylan's jaw dropped as the woman by the window turned and walked towards him. 'Ebony? What the hell are you doing, all dressed up like that?'

Ebony rolled her eyes. 'I'm getting married, stupid. And this is what brides wear.'

'*You're* getting married?' Dylan stared at her as if she'd lost her mind. 'But what about Sam? And Max?'

'What about them?' The corners of Ebony's mouth twitched, leaving Dylan with the distinct urge to wipe the smirk off her face.

'Peter led me to believe that Sam was getting married today…' He trailed off, wondering if he'd jumped to conclusions yet again.

Ebony's smirk softened to a smile as she led him to the door and gave him a none-too-gentle shove. 'Why don't you go and find Sam? I think you two need to talk.'

He nodded, suddenly filled with a wild, unrestrained hope that maybe all wasn't lost. Following a winding path to the river, he spotted Sam sitting on a bench. His eyes drank in the sight of her like a thirst-starved man; she looked incredible, wearing a soft-flowing pink halter gown that accentuated her delicate blonde colouring, her curls loose around her shoulders and blowing gently in the breeze.

His reaction was instantaneous and purely visceral. He wanted this woman—no, he *needed* this woman—more than he'd ever needed anyone before. And he wouldn't leave here without her.

Sam glanced at her watch, knowing it was time to head back to the chapel yet reluctant to leave the tranquillity of the river. She took a deep breath, filled with a sense of calm that she rarely found anywhere else. The outback had a similar effect on her, though she quickly pushed that thought from her mind. It reminded her of Budgeree and dredged up a whole host of memories she could do without.

As she stood and brushed down her skirt a shadow fell across her.

'Hello, Sam.'

Her head snapped up at the sound of Dylan's voice and she resisted the urge to collapse back on to the bench. 'What are you doing here?'

'I came to see you.'

She stared at him in disbelief, hardly recognising the dishevelled man before her. What had happened to the suave, sophisticated Dylan Harmon she'd been stupid enough to fall in love with? This man bore little resemblance to him, with dark circles under his eyes indicating that sleep was a distant memory, his suit crumpled and the top button of his shirt undone with the tie awry. She'd never seen him like this and, for a brief moment, hoped he'd had as rough a time as she had over the last week.

She shook her head. 'You've wasted your time.'

'I don't think so. There's too much that needs to be said.'

She squinted up at him, suddenly wishing she hadn't left her sunglasses in the car. The last thing she needed was for him to read the hope, the yearning, in her eyes. 'I thought you'd said it all in Melbourne.' She folded her arms, remembering his accusations and the way he'd crushed her heart. 'Besides, aren't you nervous that I might be out to steal your precious fortune?'

He sat down and patted the seat next to him. 'Why didn't you tell me you were a princess?'

Her eyebrows shot up. 'Who told you that?' She perched on the edge of the bench, as far away from Dylan as possible. She could already smell his familiar cologne and her traitorous body had responded in ways it shouldn't have.

'Mum.' He paused for a moment, as if gathering his thoughts, and she resisted the urge to reach over and smooth away the frown that seemed permanently etched in his brow. 'Why didn't you tell me? And why the name change? Why work for me?' He shook his head. 'It just doesn't make any sense.'

Guilt filled her. She should never have involved him in her scheme to make her parents see sense. 'If I'd told you my history, I wouldn't have been hired. And I needed the job, desperately.'

'But why? You have all the money in the world.' He stared at her as if she'd lost her mind.

'It wasn't about the money.' She took a steadying breath, hoping he would understand. 'I've told you about my parents' expectations?' His slight nod encouraged her to continue. 'Well, it went deeper than that. They were so caught up in the traditions of their heritage that they made my life hell when I was growing up. I just had to buck the system and the only way I could think of was to prove to them that I could make it on my own in the world, without their influence or money.'

Despite her explanation, she caught the puzzled gleam in his eyes. 'Then why mention marriage to me?'

Sam swallowed, realising she'd have to be extremely careful in answering his question if she didn't want to reveal too much about her true feelings. 'What you overheard that day was a joke. Ebony is my best friend, she was in on the plan from the start, which is why she gave your mother a false reference. She also knew that I'd lied to my parents and told them that the reason I was going to Melbourne was to further a relationship with you. I was merely discussing that with her.'

An uncomfortable silence ensued and she wished he would say something, anything, to break the growing tension.

'What about the rest?'

'The rest?' She pretended not to understand the question, when in fact she knew exactly what Dylan referred to and the mere thought of it set her heart pounding.

'What happened at Budgeree. Was that just part of an act too?'

He'd given her the perfect opportunity to end it all, right here, right now. All she had to do was answer in the affirmative and she knew he'd walk out of her life for good. Sure, he'd accepted her explanation for lying to him about her work, but which man would tolerate a woman faking affection when it came to the bedroom?

She opened her mouth to say yes but couldn't do it. Despite everything that had happened and her week of self-indoctrination that she didn't love him, she couldn't lie to him about this.

'Sam?'

She heard the uncertainty in his voice and it undid the last of her fleeting resistance. Looking up, she stared him straight in the eye. 'No, that wasn't an act.'

His eyes burned with some indefinable emotion and darkened to almost black. 'Then what was it?'

No matter how much she loved him, she couldn't admit it. So what if he'd come up here? He still hadn't told her why and she'd be damned if she made a complete fool of herself by admitting her feelings.

Crossing her fingers in her lap and hoping she wouldn't get struck down for such a monstrous lie, she answered, 'I was attracted to you and assumed the feeling was mutual. We'd been flirting for a while, so it seemed natural to take it to the next level.'

'That's it?'

She schooled her features into a mask of indifference and shrugged. 'What else could it be?'

He paled slightly beneath his tan and she almost felt sorry for him. 'Uh…I thought you might have feelings for me.'

'Feelings?' She laughed, a bitter sound that did little to soothe the pain in her heart. Seeing Dylan again had resurrected her barely suppressed love for him, hearing him talk about feelings was proving to be too much. 'Come on, Dylan, we both know that would be disastrous.'

'Why?' He pinned her with a probing stare and she tried not to squirm.

'We're too different. I'm trying to escape the shackles of my family, you're so wound up in family responsibilities you can't see straight.'

His eyes widened a fraction, drawing her into their seductive depths. 'What's that supposed to mean?'

And suddenly she knew how to put an end to all this pain, all the heartache. 'From what I've heard, it doesn't take a genius to figure out you're carrying some huge chip on your shoulder because of your dad. Is that why you're so protective of the Harmon fortune?' There, she'd done it, hit him where he was most vulnerable. Surely he'd leave her alone now?

He stood up and thrust his hands in his pockets, anger radiating off him in waves, unable to meet her gaze. 'Sorry to have bothered you.'

'No bother. See you round.'

He didn't respond and she watched him walk away, her heart breaking all over again.

CHAPTER THIRTEEN

'YOU'RE crazy, no doubt about it.'

Sam stared at Ebony, surprised at her friend's vehement reaction. 'Thanks for the vote of confidence. You sure know how to kick a woman when she's down.'

The wedding and reception had gone off without a hitch, despite Sam's constant battle to hold back the waterworks. Now, as she helped her friend change into her 'going away' outfit, she'd finally told her what had happened with Dylan earlier. What she hadn't counted on was Ebony's reaction.

'Are you that thick? Can't you see the man's in love with you?'

Sam snorted. 'Yeah, right. That's why he went down on bended knee and professed his undying passion.' She turned away and busied herself with hanging Ebony's beautiful dress, wishing she could erase the dream of Dylan doing exactly that from her mind.

Ebony grabbed her arm. 'Did you give him a chance?'

Sam looked away, unable to meet her friend's

probing stare. 'What for? It's hopeless. We're too different.'

'See? What did I tell you? Crazy, with a capital C!'

Sam shook free of her grasp, blinking back tears for the hundredth time that day. 'Take it easy, Eb. I don't need this right now.'

Ebony shimmied into her skirt and zipped up, giving Sam time to compose herself. At least her friend hadn't turned into a heartless monster completely. However, her relief was short-lived.

'Look, I shouldn't be telling you this but you need to know. The worst thing you could've said to Dylan was accusing him of carrying around some baggage about his father.'

'Why?' By the sombre expression on her friend's face, Sam didn't want to know the answer.

'Because he *is* caught up on some weird guilt trip where his dad is concerned. His dad died while Dylan was overseas, kicking up his heels and shunning his family responsibilities.'

Just like her. The thought sprang to Sam's mind and she couldn't shake it. What if one of her parents had died while she'd been hiding in Melbourne? She would probably feel the same guilt Dylan did and would try to make up for it the best way she knew how. Was that what drove the man? It more than explained his ties to Budgeree and his distaste for her views on family that she'd expressed there.

Sam shook her head from side to side. 'I've made a huge mistake, haven't I?'

'Colossal!' Ebony guided her towards the door. 'Now, go after him.'

'To Melbourne?' Sam doubted she had the courage to fly down there and confront the man she'd hurt so much. Besides, what if her friend's assumptions were right and he did love her? Could that be possible? And, if so, what could she do about it to win him back?

Ebony grinned, the same cheeky smile Sam had grown to recognise meant 'trouble' over the years. 'No, silly. The man had enough class to come back to the chapel and wish me good luck after you'd broken his heart down by the river. And I managed to find out where he was staying tonight, just in case you'd botched things up, which his hangdog expression told me you had. So, go to the Marriott and start grovelling!'

Sam hugged her friend. 'What would I do without you?'

'Probably make a total hotchpotch of your life. Now go!' Ebony squeezed her back, before practically shoving her out the door.

*　　*　　*

Dylan turned off the taps and stepped from the shower, wishing the steamy blast of hot water had done more to soothe his aching body. He'd had a week of sleepless nights thanks to his obsession with Sam, tossing and turning till the wee hours. The flight to Brisbane hadn't helped. The only seat available had been economy and he wasn't used to folding his long legs into such cramped quarters.

To make matters worse, the entire trip had been a waste of time and he couldn't wait to return to Melbourne and put the whole sordid business behind him.

A tentative knock sounded at the door and he cursed whoever had the audacity to disrupt him tonight of all nights. He needed sleep, sleep and more sleep, which only the anonymity of a hotel room could provide.

Wrapping a towel around his waist, he padded across the plush carpet and wrenched open the door. 'Yes?'

Sam stood there, doing her utmost not to stare at his chest and failing miserably. It reminded him of the day they'd first met in his bedroom, when he'd seen the flicker of interest in her eyes despite her attempts to hide it. However, he wouldn't be so foolish this time—and he just had to hope that his body would respond accordingly.

'Can I come in?' Her voice came out in a whisper and for one insane moment, despite all that had happened and all that she'd said, he wanted to reach out and envelop her in his arms.

'I'm going to bed.' Unfortunately, his words conjured up visions of taking her with him and a certain part of his anatomy responded in predictable fashion.

'This won't take long.' She stared at him, her green eyes pleading. He'd never seen her like this and, despite his intentions to push her away, it shook him.

'Fine. But make it snappy.' He opened the door wider and gestured her in, trying to ignore the waft of floral perfume that enveloped him in a sensuous cloud as she came in. Rather than gaining control of his libido, his body flared with desire at the familiar scent and he mentally chastised himself for still wanting her.

She strolled to the window and looked at the view before squaring her shoulders and turning to face him. 'I came here to apologise.'

'Too late for that, isn't it?' No matter what she said now, it wouldn't make one iota of difference. He'd resolved to forget this woman and throw himself into what he knew best—making his family business flourish.

'I hope not.' She stood there, staring at him with those sad eyes, beseeching him to listen. 'I shouldn't have said those things about your father. I was way out of line and hope you'll forgive me.'

'Just forget it.' He waved away her apology as if it meant nothing. Words were useless at a time like this. Too much had happened for them to mean much.

'Please, let me finish.' She plucked at a loose thread on her gown and he suddenly wished the whole gossamer-thin thing would unravel before his eyes. Just another indication of how sleep-deprived he actually was. 'I know how you feel—'

'Give me a break!' His patience finally snapped. 'You have no idea how I feel. I was like you once, trying to shirk family responsibilities with every fibre of my being. And you know what happened? It killed my dad.' He stalked towards her, wishing she'd stop staring at him with pity in her eyes. 'I couldn't wait to escape, especially Budgeree. My dad would rave on for hours about how that piece of land would be the crowning jewel in the Harmon fortune and, all that time, I would listen and nod and plan my life away from it. So I did it. I left Dad, his pipe dreams and the whole damn lot behind me and didn't look back. And what happened? The pressure of running the business alone killed him. *I* killed him,' he shouted, willing her to listen. The sight of tears welling in her eyes did little to calm him.

He turned away from her, wishing she'd get the hell out of his life. He hadn't meant to tell her all that; it'd spilled out, leaving him strangely relieved. She'd been the first person he'd ever voiced those feelings to, though he knew his mum suspected how he felt.

'Don't you think he would've wanted you to live a little before taking on such a huge responsibility?'

'How would you know what he wanted? You weren't there. You didn't see the disappointment in his eyes the day I told him I was going away, with no idea of when I'd be back.' The pain of that memory had eaten away at Dylan for more years than he cared to remember, though he'd done his best to make up for it by shouldering the family responsibilities on his return.

'Your mum told me.'

'Told you what?'

'How your dad felt when you went away. We discussed it that first day when I told her my family secrets.'

Dylan turned around and stared at her, wanting to hear the truth yet wishing they'd never started this conversation. 'Tell me. Though why Mum would confide in you, the queen of deception, is beyond me.'

She ignored his barb, though he noted a downward turn of her lips. 'He loved you, more than you ever knew. He was so proud that you'd stayed around so long to learn the ropes from him and he hoped that you'd return one day to continue his dream. He never begrudged you that time away, nor did he kill himself trying to make up for your absence. Heart attacks happen for a lot of reasons and he died doing what he loved best, running the family business.' She paused to wipe away a lone tear that trickled down her cheek. 'Your mum said she's tried to tell you this several times but you always change the subject, so she decided to leave well enough alone. Though I think it's time you sat down with her and had a long chat about your dad, don't you?'

Rather than Sam's tears abating, as he'd expected once she'd finished her spiel, they now flowed unchecked, leaving him at a loss.

'Save the tears, Sam. I don't need your sympathy.' He turned his back on her and strolled towards the window, wishing she would leave him the hell alone. He needed to assimilate what she'd just told him, to sort out his feelings where his family was concerned.

'If you don't want my sympathy, what about my love?'

The whispered words slammed home, though it took him a good ten seconds to register their meaning.

'What did you say?' He jumped as she slid her arms around his waist and pressed her face against his back.

'I love you,' she said, squeezing him so tightly he could hardly breathe. Or was that the overwhelming sensation of disbelief that had him struggling for air?

He loosened her grip and turned to face her, searching for the right words and failing miserably.

Sam took a steadying breath and continued before she lost the last of her courage. 'I know you probably don't want to hear this, but I lied to you earlier. Again. What happened at Budgeree between us was proof of how I feel about you. I fell in love with you almost from the beginning but didn't want to admit it and when I thought our time together was drawing to a close, I wanted to take away some lasting memory of our time together.'

'So, you used me for sex?' To her delight, a

slow smile crept across his face, the same killer smile she'd grown to love and she knew in that moment that she had a chance to win him back.

'I wouldn't call it using.' She allowed her hands to play over his back, raking the bare skin lightly with her nails. 'Call it a mutually satisfying arrangement.'

He growled in response and pulled her close, his lips crushing hers in a scorching kiss. Her tongue snaked out to meet his, teasing, tasting, and she wanted him with a ferocity that was staggering. She'd thought that she would never have this chance again, so she'd thrown caution to the wind and admitted her true feelings. She loved Dylan Harmon and wanted to shout it to the world.

He leaned into her, the evidence of his arousal sending a sudden flood of pleasure rushing through her and with a slow, deliberate movement she ground her hips against his. He broke the kiss, staring at her with undisguised lust and more than a hint of confusion. 'You do know I love you too?'

As her body throbbed with powerful, soul-wrenching need, her mind managed to assimilate what he'd just said and she smiled, a seductive upturning of her lips designed to entice. 'Show me.'

EPILOGUE

SAM stared into the growing darkness and tried to ignore the faint niggle of apprehension in her gut. Dylan should have returned an hour ago and, despite his extensive knowledge of Budgeree and its surrounding lands, she couldn't help but worry. Even though they spent most of their time here, she knew the outback held a multitude of hidden dangers cleverly disguised by its raw, unadulterated beauty.

Turning away from the window, she busied herself with making a cup of tea, anything to take her mind off the absence of her husband.

Her husband.

Even after a year, the thought of Dylan Harmon being entirely hers still brought a smile to her face and a heated flush to her cheeks. They'd been married here at Budgeree, surrounded by family, in a quiet affair as they both had wanted. She still worked as his personal assistant, though some of the tasks in her job description seemed more *personal* than others—and she loved every minute of it.

She wandered out to the veranda and sat in her favourite rocking chair, cradling the mug of tea in her hands. Outback nights could plunge to subzero temperatures and tonight would prove to be no exception.

All the better to cuddle up with someone warm... Dylan's words popped into her mind and she took a sip of tea, wishing he'd appear.

She finished her tea and started rocking, the gentle motion soothing her.

'Wake up, Sleeping Beauty. Time to give your husband the welcome home he deserves.'

Sam jumped as Dylan brushed her lips with a feather-light kiss, not realising she'd managed to doze. She leaped from the chair and wrapped her arms around him, snuggling into the warmth of his body, breathing in the intoxicating mix of male sweat, horse and pure Dylan. 'Where have you been?'

He hugged her tight, stroking her hair away from her face. 'Working. You know, that thing I do for a living. Missed me, huh?'

'Come here, Wiseguy.' She pulled his head down and kissed him, her throat growing thick with the emotion she now recognised as true love.

'Now *that's* what I call a homecoming,' he murmured against the side of her mouth, his hands pulling her flush against him.

She pulled away slightly and quirked an eyebrow. 'Stick with me, honey, and you'll go places.'

'Is that so?' He twisted a curl around his finger and gently tugged on it, drawing her towards him again, his gaze firmly fixed on her lips.

She nodded, basking in the love they shared. 'So, think you can handle being married to royalty?' It was a question she often teased him with, knowing the answer before he opened his mouth to respond.

'With you by my side, Princess, I can handle anything.'

And he swept her into his arms and strode into the homestead to prove it.

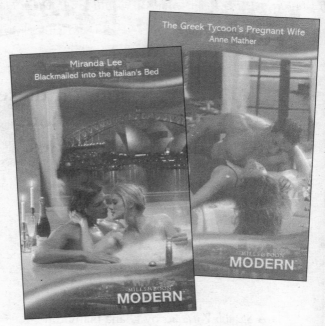

Celebrate 100 years of pure reading pleasure with Mills & Boon®

To mark our centenary, each month we're publishing a special 100th Birthday Edition. These celebratory editions are packed with extra features and include a FREE bonus story.

Now that's worth celebrating!

4th January 2008

The Vanishing Viscountess by Diane Gaston
With FREE story The Mysterious Miss M
This award-winning tale of the Regency Underworld launched Diane Gaston's writing career.

1st February 2008

Cattle Rancher, Secret Son by Margaret Way
With FREE story His Heiress Wife
Margaret Way excels at rugged Outback heroes...

15th February 2008

Raintree: Inferno by Linda Howard
With FREE story Loving Evangeline
A double dose of Linda Howard's heady mix of passion and adventure.

Don't miss out! From February you'll have the chance to enter our fabulous monthly prize draw. See special 100th Birthday Editions for details.

www.millsandboon.co.uk